THE DUKE

Silver Linings Mysteries Book 6

A Regency Romance

by Mary Kingswood

The Duke: Silver Linings Mysteries Book 6

Published by Sutors Publishing

Copyright © 2020 Mary Kingswood

ISBN: 978-1-912167-32-6 (paperback)

Cover design by: Shayne Rutherford of Darkmoon Graphics

All rights reserved. This is a work of fiction.

V5

Author's note:

this book is written using historic British terminology, so *saloon* instead of *salon*, *chaperon* instead of *chaperone* and so on. I follow Jane Austen's example and refer to a group of sisters as the Miss Wintertons.

The Duke: Silver Linings Mysteries Book 6

About this book: *The dramatic conclusion to the series!*

The sinking of the Brig Minerva results in many deaths, while for others, the future is suddenly brighter. But it's not always easy to leave the past behind…

Lord Randolph Litherholm has spent a year coming to terms with the death of his twin brother, Gervase, the 7th Duke of Falconbury. Now it's time to set aside his mourning and accept his role as the 8th Duke. It's not the management of the vast Litherholm wealth that bothers him, for he's been running the estate for years. No, his reluctance is all due to the marriage that was arranged for his brother, and the expectation that Ran will take on his brother's bride as well as his title.

Lady Ruth Grenaby's marriage was arranged when she was twelve. Now she's twenty-one and still waiting for her wedding day. Her intended husband is dead, but to her father, the younger brother will do just as well. He's a duke, after all, and his eldest daughter can't possibly marry a less exalted man. She's a dutiful daughter, so she'll do as her father says and marry Ran, even if he only sees her as another inherited obligation. But shattering events cause her to re-evaluate everything she's ever believed in, and she must decide between duty and love.

This is a complete story with a HEA. Book 6 of a 6 book series. A traditional Regency romance, drawing room rather than bedroom.

Isn't that what's-his-name? Regular readers will know that characters from previous books occasionally pop up. Lawyer Mr Willerton-Forbes, his flamboyant sidekick Captain Edgerton and the discreet Mr Neate have been helping my characters solve murders and other puzzles ever since *Lord Augustus*. The Duke of

The Duke: Silver Linings Mysteries Book 6

Camberley's heir, the Marquess of Ramsey, made a fleeting appearance in *The Earl of Deveron,* and became an improbable suitor in *The Betrothed.* The relations of Lord Randolph Litherholm, previously seen in *The Lacemaker,* include his uncle, Lord Arthur, his aunt, Lady Anne, and his sisters Lady Henrietta Redpath, Lady Alice Winne, Lady Elizabeth Litherholm, Lady Narfield (Georgiana). Lady Charlotte Litherholm and her timorous companion, Camilla, of Durran House, were last seen in *The Apothecary.* Mr Jonathan Ellsworthy, survivor of the *Brig Minerva,* and his particular friend, Miss Ginny Chandry, were previously seen in *The Clerk* and *The Orphan.* Ginny's brother, Mr Michael Chandry of Pendower, appeared in *The Clerk.* Lady Ruth Grenaby made a fleeting appearance in *The Orphan,* helping the distressed Violet Barantine.

About the Silver Linings Mysteries series: John Milton coined the phrase 'silver lining' in *Comus: A Mask Presented at Ludlow Castle,* 1634

> *Was I deceived, or did a sable cloud*
> *Turn forth her silver lining on the night?*
> *I did not err; there does a sable cloud*
> *Turn forth her silver lining on the night,*
> *And casts a gleam over this tufted grove.*

Ever since then, the term *'silver lining'* has become synonymous with the unexpected benefits arising from disaster. The sinking of the *Brig Minerva* results in many deaths, but for others, the future is suddenly brighter. But it's not always easy to leave the past behind...

Book 0: The Clerk: the sinking of the *Minerva* offers a young man a new life *(a novella, free to mailing list subscribers).*

Book 1: The Widow: the wife of the *Minerva's* captain is free from his cruelty, but can she learn to trust again?

Book 2: The Lacemaker: three sisters inherit a country cottage, but the locals are surprisingly interested in them.

Book 3: The Apothecary: a long-forgotten suitor returns, now a rich man, but is he all he seems?

Book 4: The Painter: two children are left to the care of a reclusive man.

Book 5: The Orphan: a wilful heiress is determined to choose a notorious rake as her guardian.

Book 6: The Duke: the heir to the dukedom is reluctant to step into his dead brother's shoes and accept his arranged marriage.

Want to be the first to hear about new releases? Sign up for my mailing list at http://marykingswood.co.uk.

Table of contents

The Litherholm Family

Hi-res version available at http://marykingswood.co.uk..

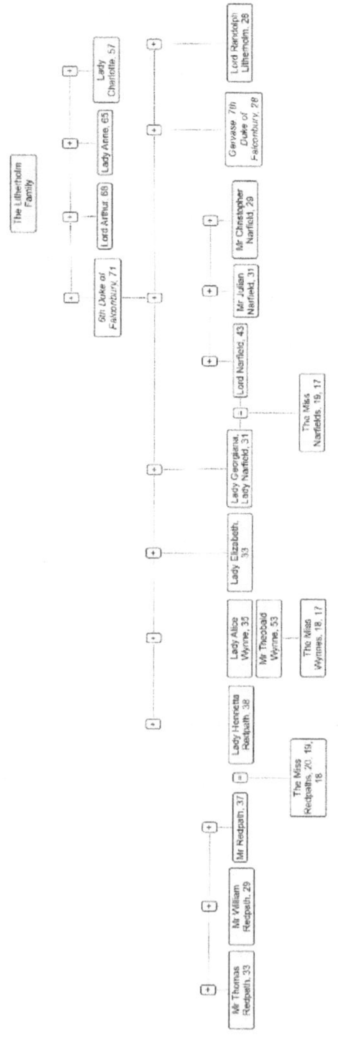

The Grenaby Family

Hi-res version available at http://marykingswood.co.uk..

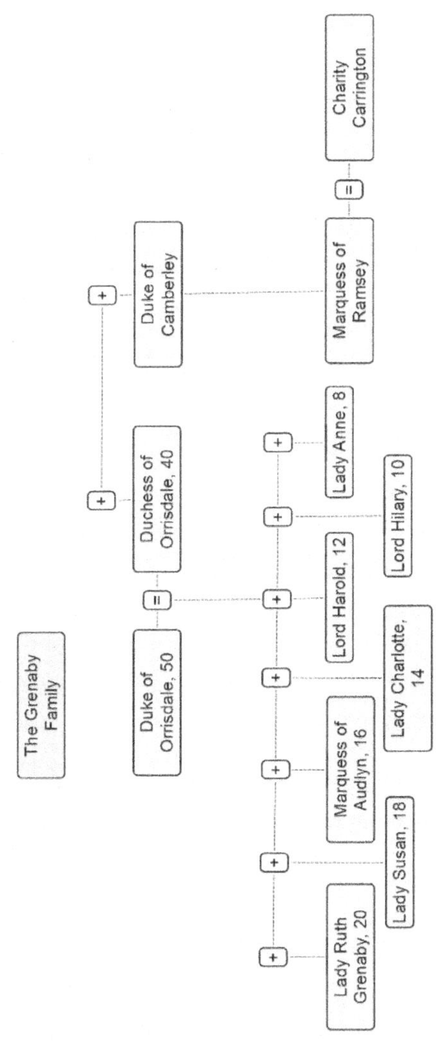

Prologue

SEVEN YEARS AGO

JULY

Valmont looked its best, the summer greenery not yet faded, the lodge gardens a blaze of colour as the carriage rolled onto the long drive. Lord Randolph Litherholm felt the customary bloom of pride when he looked at the avenue, the twin lines of trees in their mature splendour, each one a perfect specimen, marking the route to the house in satisfying symmetry. There was always a pleasure in coming home, no matter the circumstances. Beyond the Roman Arch, the avenue gave way to the formal gardens and Valmont itself, its imposing stone face shimmering with light from the myriad windows.

The carriage circled around the sparkling fountain to halt beneath the front doors.

"Lord Randolph! What an unexpected pleasure, my lord." Brent, the butler, trod lightly down the steps to greet the carriage. "Not bad news, I trust? Is Lord Marcus well?"

"A mild seizure, Brent. He will recover but I was very much in the way, so I thought it best to come home," Ran said, as he made his way up the steps. "How is my father?"

"His Grace is a little better, I fancy, my lord. His breathing is a little easier in this dry weather. He will be very happy to have you at home again, as will Lord Beckhampton, I make no doubt, although he is enjoying the company of the Lady Ruth Grenaby."

"Ah, the famous Lady Ruth. At last I shall meet her."

"A delightful young lady, if I may make so bold, my lord."

"So everyone says," Ran said, as they passed into the cavernous entrance hall. Valmont was built on a grand scale, as if it were a home for giants. Or kings, perhaps, since it was fashioned after the Palace of Versailles.

A drift of music emanated from the Grand Saloon on the far side of the hall, then, with a sudden clash of chords, a burst of laughter. Two voices, one familiar, the other high and girlish. With a smile, Ran waved away the hovering footmen and crossed the hall. The high doors to the Grand Saloon stood open, and there they were, the two of them, side by side on the stool before the pianoforte, giggling together. Gervase looked as he always did, slightly rumpled, the disorder about his hair owing more to carelessness than fashion. And Lady Ruth—

Ran's breath caught. He had mingled with the accredited beauties of the *ton*, but he had never in his life seen anyone to equal this girl. Everything about her was perfection, from the smoothness of her complexion to the hair that curled softly around her face, held in place with a simple ribbon. She looked up at him, and he gazed into her clear grey eyes and was lost. He could neither move nor speak.

Ger saw him too and jumped up. "Ran! You are back early — how famous!" He raced across to the door where Ran stood, and punched him on the shoulder. "This is wonderful, for you can meet Ruth at last. Ruth, come and meet my brother — the sensible one of us."

She rose and came smilingly towards them in a graceful motion. She would do everything gracefully, he realised. Even at fourteen, she was queenly and serene.

"Lord Randolph, what a pleasure to meet you at last. Ger has talked about you so much." They were on intimate terms already, then, if she called him Ger rather than Lord Beckhampton, without the least ceremony.

"Lady Ruth," he murmured, bowing over her hand. "Likewise. Are you enjoying your stay at Valmont?"

"Very much, as always." Her smile was gentle, but everything about her seemed to be gentle. "Ger is looking after me very well. Do you play the instrument, Lord Randolph?"

"Not at all. Ger is the one with the musical talent in this family. I am not even competent to turn the pages for him."

She laughed, a delicately musical sound, and he was enchanted. "Are you staying long, Lord Randolph? For you were not expected, I think. I am sure that Ger said you were engaged elsewhere for the full week of our visit."

"So I was, but Uncle Marcus suffered a mild seizure, nothing too serious, thank the Lord, but I thought it best to leave him to the leeches. But pray do not let me keep you from the instrument. I must go and pay my respects to your parents."

"They will be in the Royal Withdrawing Room with your father and uncle," she said, with another smile. "They enjoy these visits as much as I do, I believe."

Ran laughed. "Ah, the lure of the card table! I shall see you at dinner, my lady." And with a few words of greeting to the chaperon, sitting quietly with her needlework across the room, he made his exit.

Brent was lurking in the hall. "I have informed His Grace your father of your arrival, and he requests that you await him in the Ante-Chamber, my lord. Shall I bring you anything to eat?"

Ran handed his hat and gloves to a footman. "No, thank you, Brent."

He entered the Ante-Chamber and poured himself a glass of Canary, wondering a little at the order. His father was not usually so keen to see him, but perhaps he was concerned about Uncle Marcus. He picked up the London newspaper and settled down without impatience. The Duke of Falconbury was not a man to concern himself with keeping his second son waiting, and would arrive when it suited him and not a moment before.

In the event, it was no more than ten minutes before the door opened and the duke entered the room. Ran appraised his father carefully. The pallor of his skin, the slight puckering of the forehead, the dullness of the eyes that suggested pain were all much as he remembered from his Easter visit, the last time he had seen his father. No improvement to be seen there. But it was the stoop to the shoulders that made his heart ache, seeing the once strong and upright figure sliding into old age and illness. Not that he would admit to it, naturally.

"Good God, boy, what have you done to your hair?"

Ran laughed. "It is quite the fashion at Oxford, I assure you."

"I cannot say that I like it. Too short by half, and not a bit of powder. Not enamoured of that coat, either, but I am old-fashioned, I daresay. You young men have not a bit of style these days. Too drab altogether. But what is this about Marcus? Some kind of a seizure, Brent said."

"Not the first, seemingly. His physician believes he will make a full recovery, in time."

"Physicians? Bah! What do they know? Ignorant fools, the lot of them. Have you seen your brother yet?"

"Yes, sir. He was at the instrument with the Lady Ruth."

"Hmpf. So what do you think of her? Pretty little thing, eh?"

Pretty! Such a bland word for so much beauty, so much serene elegance. "Undoubtedly a diamond of the first water. She will do very well for Ger."

The duke's face softened. "She certainly will. It is all agreed with Orrisdale, thirty thousand, no less, and they will marry three years from now, when she is seventeen. Gervase will be four and twenty by then, a good age to be settled. Just as well you are back early, for I have Gurney harassing me about the Low Mead, and Camfield keeps bothering me about some investment or other. They do fuss so! Maybe you can look into that for me, eh? See what they want. And the London lawyers will be here next week and that will be hour after hour of dry legal business."

"I would be happy to take care of that for you, sir. I enjoy all that dry legal business, believe it or not."

"Good, and you can help Gervase with that side of things when I am gone, for he has no more sense than a rabbit, sometimes. Always at his music, or out on that ill-tempered beast of his. Good with the cards, though, I will say that for him. He has that from me, at least. I suppose the music came from his mother. I just wish he had a bit more address. Tongue-tied in company, and it won't do. He should exert himself more. He will be the Seventh Duke of Falconbury one day and he owes it to the family name to be a leader of men, not skulking in the shadows like the poor relation."

"Once he has more experience in society, he will learn how to put himself forward," Ran said, although he was not at all sure he believed it. "And when he marries, the Lady Ruth will help smooth his path."

"True, very true," the duke said, the lowering brows lifting a little. "She is a taking little thing, very demure and well-behaved, a good, dutiful daughter. She will make him an excellent duchess. Her parents have brought her up very well. Come and make your bows to them, eh, and then you can take yourself off, for they will not want you underfoot for the whole afternoon. Plenty of time for a few more rubbers of whist before the dressing bell."

Ran was allowed five minutes of polite conversation with the Duke and Duchess of Orrisdale before his father chased him out of the card room, and they settled down eagerly for more play. There were a dozen things he probably ought to be doing, but his footsteps drew him inexorably back towards the Grand Saloon, and the music drifting out of the open door.

She was singing, now, a melodic Italian tune, with Ger playing enthusiastically for her, and even the stolid chaperon had laid down her needle to listen, a smile on her face. Ran smiled, too, as he watched, entranced. Those grey eyes caught and held his, and he felt he could drown in that clear gaze. So much perfection in the shape of one girl… almost a woman. Ran had never imagined meeting anyone who was quite so perfect, but in a few years, the Lady Ruth Grenaby would embody every female grace in one person, the ideal of womanhood.

And then she would marry Ran's brother.

1: The Duke Of Falconbury

FEBRUARY

Ran picked up the nearest quill pen. As usual, there were precisely three laid out for his use, trimmed and prepared with meticulous care by one of his under-secretaries, but he always took the nearest to hand. He dipped the pen in the inkstand and wrote his name at the spot indicated by his attorney. The parchment was removed to be sanded by another of his under-secretaries, and a second parchment was placed before him. The pen was dipped a second time, his name inscribed, the parchment removed by yet another under-secretary.

In stately procession, the two parchments were carried around the mahogany desk, as large as many dining tables, and placed in front of the bluff, middle-aged farmer sitting on the opposite side, stiff in his Sunday best coat. He too chose a pen, dipped, signed, then dipped and signed again, laying his pen down with a sigh of obvious relief and a wide smile. Beside him, his country attorney, in a dazzlingly white neckcloth, no doubt bought new for the occasion, smiled also.

Then Max Lorrimer stepped forward with the sealing tray and the ducal seal for the final part of the ceremony. He himself, as the most senior secretary, undertook to melt the wax and apply a measure to each parchment, while Ran merely pressed the seal into the molten wax.

And then it was done. Another contract signed, another useful business added to the ducal estate, another very satisfactory day. Ran congratulated himself inwardly for his success. There were glasses of Madeira and dishes of sweetmeats and fifteen minutes of laboured conversation with the farmer and his attorney, every word no doubt to be remembered and carried back to their northern fastness, to be related to red-cheeked wives and daughters and wide-eyed neighbours, the glories of Valmont described in grandiose terms. Of the owner of so much splendour, less grandiose terms would be employed. Lord Randolph, the farmer would say, shaking his head sorrowfully, was nothing out of the way at all, and wore only a plain black coat, pale pantaloons and a triflingly simple neckcloth, such as a cheap attorney might wear, with not a bit of jewellery to be seen, apart from a paltry signet ring. Not at all like a duke.

When the visitors had been shown out, and the steward and various attorneys and secretaries dispersed to their usual tasks, Ran retreated to his own office, a much smaller and less imposing apartment one floor below.

"So… another wretched mine," Max said, his eyes brimming with laughter. "Your revered father would *not* have approved."

"Pooh! We have had the salt mine for ever, not to mention those tin mines in Cornwall. Coal is no different," Ran said, with a shrug. "And very profitable, which Father would most definitely have approved. Good management of the estate, that was his watchword."

"How many mines is that? Four? Five?"

"Six," Ran said. "What else do you have for me today, Max? Let us get down to business."

For more than an hour, they discussed estate matters — tenant houses, farming prospects, the shooting and fishing rights on a distant holding, some property in London that the lawyers were looking into. Secretaries and attorneys and footmen came and went, bearing letters to be signed, or notes of domestic matters, or occasionally whispering in Max's ear. Eventually, however, the stream of decisions to be made and letters to be signed and sales or purchases to be approved dwindled to a trickle, and the attorneys and under-secretaries disappeared. Only Max, Ran's oldest friend outside the family, remained.

"Come now, Max," Ran said at length. "Are we finished for the day? Pour me a glass of something, will you, and tell me what is in your mind, for you are unusually subdued."

Max obediently went to the sideboard where the decanters stood, and with the experience of many years' acquaintance, poured two glasses of Ran's favourite Canary.

"You are aware of the date, of course," he said, sliding the glass across the battered deal table that served as Ran's working desk. There was a large desk in a corner, as well as a cumbersome secretary and an elegant little escritoire, but Ran had always preferred the greater space of the table.

"Of course. A year since the *Brig Minerva* sank. A year since my brother died. How could I forget?"

"I beg your pardon. I did not mean to imply that you had forgotten. But Hammick is still in Boston, no doubt eating his head off at your expense, and awaiting further orders."

Ran sighed. "I am aware…"

"He has been to every single church on the east coast of America, and enquired of every family of consequence, and has found not the slightest indication that your brother married while he was there, nor fathered a legal heir. Not that anyone imagines that Gervase would have married without notifying you."

Another sigh. "No, you are quite right. There is no hope now of such a thing. Hammick may be relieved of his quest."

"There is another letter from Mr Willerton-Forbes, as well."

Ran groaned. "Does the fellow *never* give up? I neither want nor need the Benefactor's money."

Max laughed and shook his head. "He cannot give up! Do but consider his position, Ran. He has been charged by this mysterious Benefactor to transfer one thousand pounds to every survivor or next of kin of a victim of the *Brig Minerva*. He cannot complete his task without seeing every person so affected, and I daresay you are now the very last. How it must irk him! He must wish of all things to put the whole behind him, but he cannot, since you refuse to see him. Do you not want to meet him? I confess to some curiosity myself, after all the correspondence between you."

"Very well, very well! Make an appointment for him, if it must be so. And now, that must be all? I should like to go for a walk… get outside for a while. Ah… there is something else?"

"His Grace the Duke of Orrisdale arrived about two hours since."

Ran jumped to his feet. "And you only tell me now?"

"He gave strict instructions that you were not to be disturbed. Brent will have taken care of him, you know, and His Grace said that he would be happy to await your pleasure in the Porcelain Room."

Ran laughed. "Of course he would! But I shall not keep him waiting any longer."

The Porcelain Room was not one of the larger chambers at Valmont, being no more than an ante-room between two far more imposing apartments, but it was a charmingly elegant place, full of lightness and wintry sunshine. Here, amongst the delicate glass cabinets and multitude of pale oak shelves, stood the Duke of Orrisdale, a man of fifty, who was a looming figure half a head taller than Ran, and broad as well. He was not precisely fat, but he looked as if his tailor had been surreptitiously increasing the seams of his coats for some years now.

"I beg your pardon for not receiving you when you arrived," Ran said as he entered.

The duke did not glance up from the vase he held in his hands. "No need, no need," he said absently. "Your people have looked after me very well. This is a lovely piece, Litherholm! Not so fine as Sèvres, but almost so. Limoges, I think?"

"I cannot tell you," Ran said, smiling. "Mama was the expert. And Gervase, of course. Have you been given your usual room?"

"Oh yes, yes, no need for you to worry about that. Everything made ready within the twinkling of an eye, just as I like it, although I gave you not the least warning. But I could not let the day pass without notice, you know. Yet here you are, still in your black coat. It is a year now, Litherholm, a full year since your brother's tragic death. You might leave off the mourning garb now."

"True," Ran said colourlessly.

"Well, well, you must do as you think best, and I am not one of those thinking you should have stepped into Falconbury's place long since. It was very proper of you to wait and see if the lad might have fathered an heir while he was in foreign parts." He looked at Ran from beneath bushy eyebrows. "You have found none, I take it."

"No."

"Hmm. So you will claim your seat in the Lords now? I assure you there will not be the least difficulty there."

"When I go to town in the spring, I shall see about it," Ran said.

"Ah, excellent! That is what I wanted to hear." With a reluctant sigh, he set down the vase he had been holding and picked up a snuff box. "Now this is exquisite. Sèvres, of course."

"Is it?"

The duke chuckled. "You may have an excellent head for the management of your estates, Litherholm, but you are a philistine in matters of the decorative arts. Indeed it is Sèvres, and a finer example I never saw. Your mama had a wonderful eye for such things, and your brother too, but I daresay there will be no more added to the collection now that the dukedom is in *your* hands, eh? Shall you make many changes, once you assume the title?"

"Probably not. I like Valmont the way it is." He waited patiently, guessing that the duke was getting to the point in his roundabout way.

"How old are you now, Litherholm?"

"Eight and twenty, sir."

"The years fly by so. And my Ruthie is almost one and twenty."

Ran shivered. "And how is the Lady Ruth?" he said politely.

"Well enough, well enough, but... she has waited a long time, Litherholm."

"I am aware, Duke."

"Not that I will put any pressure on you, none at all, for that is not my way, and after all, the understanding was with your brother. They got on so well, right from the start, and although we never minded him jauntering about the world, for they were both very young then—" He stopped, twisting his lips thoughtfully.

Ran said nothing, for what after all was there to say?

"Well, we should like to know where we stand, that is all," the duke said bluntly. "There is Susan barely eighteen and already settled — not general knowledge yet, but I do not scruple to tell you — so you see, it would be as well if we could fire Ruthie off first. That is the proper way of it, the eldest daughter before the younger. The Duchess wants to hold a Grand Ball at Mallowfleet for Ruthie's birthday next month, and it would be the ideal time for an announcement... if there is to be an announcement. But it is for you to say, you know."

Taking a deep breath, Ran said, "You will not find me in the least unwilling, but..."

"But?"

"Ruth is such a beauty, and so accomplished... everything that any man could hope for in a wife. I understand why she would wait for Gervase, but I cannot imagine that she would be happy to accept me in his place. She must surely have a myriad of suitors... what about Claythorpe? His name has been mentioned."

"Pft, we were very taken in there! It is true that he was very attentive, and we did think... an earl, too, which would have been tolerable, and if she had liked the idea... but then it all went off, and he had the nerve to tell me later that he found her too cold and reserved. My Ruthie, as well-bred a daughter as ever lived! Aye, she has had suitors enough, but she has always been content to accept our choice for her. She is a good girl, and knows her duty to her mama and to me. She will certainly accept you if you make the offer."

"But I am so different from Gervase," Ran said. "Will she mind taking second best?"

"She will be taking the Duke of Falconbury, not some paltry younger son. It may not be precisely the husband she expected, but the position is the one she has been destined to occupy for years. You will not find her a troublesome wife."

"No, no! Indeed not, but I should like to talk to her before anything is irrevocably settled. To assure myself that she is happy with the arrangement. Will you bring her to stay here for a few days? So that we may get to know each other a little better? Then, if she wishes it, I shall come to Her Grace's Grand Ball and make my offer in form."

"That would be sensible," the duke said. "Next week, perhaps. Good, good, so that is all settled. You still keep your usual hours here? I shall have a lie down upstairs, then, before changing for dinner."

With obvious reluctance, he returned the Sèvres snuff box to its place. Impulsively, Ran picked it up and pressed it into his hand.

"Keep it, as… a token of my esteem and gratitude, and the connection between our two families."

"Well now… well now… how very kind! Your brother would not have given away a family heirloom so readily, you may be sure."

"I am not my brother," Ran said sadly.

After handing the duke over to the butler, Ran made his way to a small side door that gave onto the western gardens. Here he collected a weather-beaten felt hat and a greatcoat of an old-fashioned style, and set off along one of the wide gravel paths through the parterre. Just as the house was loosely based on the style of the Palace of Versailles, so Valmont's gardens, too, were laid out in a formal French manner, with an array of parterres and bosquets, pools and fountains, grottoes and a large labyrinth. Although there were shrubberies and even a so-called wilderness, these were artfully arranged and carefully managed. The more modern fashion for natural landscapes and deer parks had not yet overtaken the Litherholm family. Gervase, perhaps, would have swept away the formality and replaced it with something that looked just like any other garden, but Ran loved the straight lines and closely clipped hedges.

At the far end of the reflecting pool was a large, temple-like building in the Roman style, with lofty pillars topped by a pediment bearing the Litherholm coat of arms. The family mausoleum was not a cheerful place, but Ran did not regard the gloomy atmosphere. He strode up the steps and pushed open the great wooden door. High windows admitted enough light for him to make his way about halfway down one side. Here stood a black marble sarcophagus, very plain, engraved only with the words *'Gervase Septimus Litherholm, Seventh Duke of Falconbury'*.

"Well, you old rascal," Ran said, sitting cross-legged on the dusty floor. "A whole year, and now there is no escaping it. I am to have your title, whether I wish it or no, and I am to have your bride, too. You should have married Ruth before you left, you little idiot, and then I should be helping her to raise your son to be a true Litherholm, instead of trying to squeeze myself into a mould to which I am patently unfitted. Or maybe you would have stayed at home if you had had such a good reason. Whatever were you thinking, to go gadding about to the New World like that, and then getting yourself drowned? Perfectly imbecilic thing to do. And now I have to try to step into your shoes, and that is going to be so hard, Ger. So hard... I am a perfectly good steward, but there is more to being a duke than nurturing the estate for the next generation. And then there is Ruth... how can I make her happy, brother? What an idiot you are, to make her fall in love with you and then die. I shall do my best, God knows, but I shall always be second best. Always." He paused, the lump in his throat almost choking him. Resolutely, he got to his feet. "But I shall do my duty, as ever. Sleep well, you old rascal. Sleep well."

Slowly he made his way back across the gardens to the side door. Brent, the butler, was waiting inside for him, his face impassive. He was a solemn man of about sixty, who had served three Dukes of Falconbury, had seen everything and was the most imperturbable man Ran had ever known. Nothing ever rattled his poise.

"His Grace is resting on his bed, my lord," Brent said, deftly removing the greatcoat and accepting the elderly hat. "Monsieur has taken the liberty of preparing some sweetbreads for roasting, knowing as how His Grace is so fond of the dish, and Mrs Cromarty is to make a chestnut soup."

"That is very thoughtful," Ran said. "I can always depend on you all to rise to the occasion, even when His Grace arrives without notice. You have brought up some of the good claret from the cellar, I expect."

"Naturally, my lord, and the port His Grace the Sixth Duke laid down. Ah, there is a small tear in the pocket of this coat. I shall inform Mr Giggs."

Ran turned, looking the butler in the eye. "Do you know, Brent, my brother bought this coat when he first went up to Oxford, and as for the hat... I cannot tell you how ancient it is."

"I believe it was your father's, my lord."

"There you are, then. Tell Giggs he may dispose of them as he sees fit. He may leave my old olive driving coat here for my garden strolls. And pray tell him also that he may put away all my black coats. My year of mourning is over. For tonight, he may lay out my new blue coat, the Weston, and the cream waistcoat."

"Very good, my lord."

"And Brent... I shall be taking my seat in the Lords in the spring, so I suppose we had all better get used to the title, eh? Tell the other servants, will you."

The butler bowed deeply, and then his face creased into a most unaccustomed smile. "Yes, indeed I will... Your Grace."

2: To Valmont

Lady Ruth Grenaby was practising a complicated sonata on the pianoforte. At least, it was only the final movement, but there were some fine, uplifting passages that she liked rather well, so she chose to repeat the performance instead of trying to find another piece that she enjoyed. That was always the problem with music — one piece lifted one up, but the next was sure to cast one down, and she was not yet ready to be cast down.

In a corner, Aunt Maria and Cousin Patience sat quietly with their sewing. They were deeply respectful of Ruth's ability on the instrument, and never talked while she played. Perhaps, too, they enjoyed the respite from civil banalities.

Ruth was aware of the door opening quietly, followed by some whispering. Then the door closed again, and the only sound was the music. She had just begun her fourth passage through the movement when the door opened again, and this time she was aware that her mother stood waiting quietly for a pause in the music. Deftly, she ended with a flourish and turned towards the door, where her mother stood.

"How delightfully you play, Ruth, dear," she said, as she always did.

Ruth rose and curtsied. "Thank you, Mama. Did you wish to speak to me?"

"Your father is home," her mother said, an excited gleam in her eyes. "He wishes to see you."

"Of course," Ruth said evenly, but her stomach executed a painful somersault. He had returned from Valmont, so there would be… something to tell her. One way or the other.

As she made her way to the door, Aunt Maria smiled encouragingly at her. "It is good news, at last!" she whispered, as Ruth passed by. That caused another flip of her stomach. Good news could only be… but she must be calm. No use jumping to conclusions, and she would know soon enough.

The duke was in the tiny room he called his library. All the rooms at Mallowfleet were small and dark, hemmed in by wooden panels and latticed windows that admitted but little light. Even now, in the middle of the afternoon, there were candles lit in the sconces and the chandelier.

"Here she is," the duchess trilled, as Ruth curtsied to her father. "I have persuaded her to abandon the instrument for a while, for this is a momentous day, is it not?"

"Indeed, indeed," the duke said. "Well now, you are in looks, daughter, I am pleased to see."

"Ruth is always in looks," the duchess said complacently.

"So she is. I am just returned from Valmont, and all is settled, you will be pleased to hear. Litherholm — or Falconbury, I should say — will do his duty by you, daughter."

"He takes his title, then?" the duchess said excitedly. "At last! I cannot imagine why he should have waited so long."

"I cannot fault the boy for that," the duke said. "Very proper, I call it, to make every effort to ensure his brother left no heir. He has behaved just as he ought, but now he is to accept *all* his obligations. You will be a duchess by the summer, daughter. I congratulate you."

"Thank you, Papa."

"Before the summer, I trust," the duchess said quickly. "In May, during the season, so we may hold a ball to celebrate the occasion, and by special licence, to allow you to marry at Berkeley Square. One would not want to provide a spectacle for the masses by marrying in church. Then you may be presented at court this year."

"I have already been presented, Mama."

"As your father's daughter, but not as the Duchess of Falconbury. Such a satisfactory conclusion to all our anxiety! I thought he was going to cry off, truly I did. Keeping you waiting for such a time, the foolish boy."

"He has only just left off his black coats," her father said, frowning. "He lost his twin, Duchess, never forget that — he felt it exceedingly, and I think the better of him for showing some reluctance to step into his brother's shoes. But he knows what is expected of him. He will come to this ball of yours next month and the betrothal may be made there. They may marry as soon as the settlements have been drawn up, for I cannot think what need there is for further delay, now that all is decided."

"No need for anything as hasty as *that*," the duchess said, disparagingly. "We shall need to see about wedding clothes, but three months should be enough. Then we can settle Susan over the summer, although hers is nothing to yours, Ruth, dear. Only a barony. But there, as a younger daughter, what can she expect, and at least Crosby is a peer. I could not bear any of the girls to go to a *younger son*, you know. A mere Honourable, perhaps, or even a plain Mister!" She shuddered. "That would be a failure indeed. I shall write to my brother, I think. He will be pleased, I am sure. Should we invite him to stay for a while?"

"He may come to this ball next month if he pleases, and Ramsey too, but make no plans for the next week or two. We are to go to Valmont. Falconbury wants to spend some time with Ruth, you see — get to know each other better and so forth."

"Oh. I should have thought they already know each other perfectly well. Sufficient for marriage, at all events. He is not wavering, I trust?"

"Not at all, but it is his wish, and Ruthie will want to have a look about the place. See what changes she might make, that sort of thing."

"I should hardly do that yet, Papa," Ruth said quietly. "Besides, Valmont is so well managed, I cannot imagine any changes to be necessary."

"Indeed, I hope a daughter of mine would never be so vulgar as to *presume*," her mother said repressively. "She can hardly ask to inspect the silver safes, or anything of that nature."

"No, no, but... well, Falconbury will want to show her around, I am sure," her father said testily. "It is a great undertaking, to be mistress of Valmont."

"And one for which she has been trained all her life," the duchess said calmly. "Ruth, you will wish to inform Maria and Patience of the momentous news, and then you may return to your instrument."

"Yes, Mama."

~~~~~

Dinner was the ceremonial high point of every day in Mallowfleet, home for two centuries to the Grenaby family. Once a mere manor house, it had been extended in all directions in the Tudor period to create a substantial mansion. In recent generations, however, the family fortune had suffered depredations at the gaming tables. Although the present occupants were more circumspect, there had not been the funds for rebuilding in the modern style and so they tried to make a virtue of the antiquity of the ancestral pile. This meant uneven floors, awkward stairs, oddly-shaped rooms and draughty corridors. Ruth fortified herself with a cashmere shawl before venturing downstairs at the precise hour set by her mother's rules.

As the daughter of one duke and the wife of another, the duchess felt the honour of her position extremely. In her opinion, which was clearly the correct one, it was the duty of persons of high rank to set the example in society, imposing the rules of good breeding on everyone around her. Punctuality and dutiful obedience were the twin pillars of good conduct that she instilled into her daughters, together with reverence for the obligations of rank. These obligations seldom led her to do anything more than to entertain whenever she could. So it was that, apart from the ducal family, there were eight local worthies at the table that evening. Although the duchess grumbled at the necessity, so
~~~~~

many covers at table gave her an excuse to dine in the great hall, a setting that she felt more appropriate for the station of her husband than the rather paltry dining room.

The meal progressed as sedately as always, despite the news from Valmont. The duchess would have considered it unspeakably ill-bred to have revealed any hint of Ruth's impending change of circumstances to their guests, so the conversation ranged over the usual array of local matters, and no one outside the family, Ruth supposed, would for a moment suspect that her life had taken a decisive shift in direction.

Ruth herself was by far too well brought up to betray the least consciousness, but she had thought of little else as Pinnock had dressed her for the evening. During dinner, when there was no call for her to engage in conversation, she let her mind drift back to Valmont. To Ran. She had begun to wonder whether he would ever come up to scratch, and why should he, indeed? Ruth had been intended for Gervase from their first meeting, when she had been a wide-eyed girl of twelve and he had been a dashing figure of nineteen. Her parents had taken her to Valmont, and there Ger had been, with his shy smile, his careless style of dress and a heroic willingness to entertain her childish self. He had gone riding with her, driven her round the estate in his own curricle, played duets with her for hours and, one memorable wet afternoon, read the whole of *'A Midsummer Night's Dream'*, taking all the parts himself and infusing every character with dramatic life. Their two fathers had smiled and nodded and hatched their schemes. She had not even met Ran until two years later, and then he had been very much in his older brother's shadow, with none of Ger's cleverness or restless energy. Ran was the steady, serious foil to Ger's mercurial brilliance.

But Ger was dead, and Ran was alive, and she was to marry the duke and that was the end of it. Whether either of them wished it or not, they were to marry, because it had been arranged years ago and the death of the elder brother could not be allowed to interfere. The eldest daughter of the Duke of Orrisdale was to marry the Duke of Falconbury, and there was nothing more to be said. She would do her duty, and Ran, it seemed, would do his, and they would have one of those cool, distant marriages so often found amongst the nobility. Not for them the luxury of falling in love, as the common people did.

The ladies rose serenely from the table and made their way through the lamp-bright corridors to the winter saloon, where Charlotte and her governess joined them. Ruth played gentle music, not intrusive enough to overwhelm the conversation, for the ladies loved to talk. After a while, the gentlemen arrived, Charlotte went away and the tea things were brought in. After that, there was whist, which her father preferred, and vingt-et-un, her mother's favourite. Ruth played cribbage with Aunt Maria. At eleven o'clock precisely, there was a light supper and the guests mingled again for a short time before the carriages were brought round at midnight.

So it always was, for her mother loved everything to be orderly, everything done by rule. Ruth found herself wondering how it would be at Valmont when she was mistress. Would she and Ran fall into the same sort of pattern, everything predictable and familiar? She could not say. The late duke — the Sixth Duke, Ran's father — had kept to the old ways of dining early, with a hot supper at ten. Then the men and one or two of the ladies, too, had retreated to a room called the Pavilion, from the trompe l'oeil effect painted on the walls of drapery, like a tent. There the serious gaming had gone on, so that the following day often saw long faces from those who had dipped a little too deep. But whether such habits still prevailed she could not say. It was several years since she had stayed at Valmont as part of a large gathering. Once the old duke grew ill, the house had been quieter and her last visit, almost two years ago, had been very subdued, with everyone aware that his death was close at hand.

The departure of the guests drew Ruth out of her abstraction. When the last of them had been seen into their carriage, the family would have dispersed to their beds, but the duke said gruffly, "Come into the library, all of you. We should mark the occasion with a few words — a toast."

Clearly, he had planned the event, for there was a tray of glasses set out ready, and a decanter filled with wine. It was the good wine, laid down by Ruth's grandfather many years ago, for decent French wine was hard to come by at the present. Her father poured a little for everyone and they all stood silently, waiting for him to make whatever speech he had in mind.

"Well," he said gruffly, "you all know how it is. Falconbury will do what is rightful, and Ruthie will be a duchess at last. I know you will make us proud of you, daughter. You will behave just as you ought. Never given us a moment of worry, since the day you were born. You are a good girl, Ruth, and I congratulate you on your good fortune. You deserve it. Let us all drink to the future Duchess of Falconbury."

Ruth lowered her eyes demurely as they drank her health. The Duchess of Falconbury... but not the duke she had expected. How strange life was. How very strange.

"I must say," her father continued, "that I feel you have the better deal. Gervase was lively enough, but he had some odd humours now and then, very odd. Randolph is much steadier."

"So handsome, too!" Cousin Patience trilled. "A very well-looking man."

"That is hardly of consequence," the duchess said, giving her a reproving glance, "although his manner and bearing are always appropriate for his station, that I will grant you, whereas his brother— However, let us not say a word against the poor fellow, now that he is dead."

"No, indeed," the duke said. "Nothing wrong with Gervase, nothing at all, but Randolph will do very well by Ruthie, no doubt about it. He will behave towards you just as a gentleman should, you may be sure, and you will never have to tiptoe around him, daughter, or wonder where he has got to. He will always be just where one expects him to be. Very steady. No trouble from *him*."

He glanced at Susan momentarily, whose future husband was reputed to be anything but steady. She lifted her chin defiantly. "Better unsteady than dull, Papa."

The duchess put in quickly, "You have both made us proud, and secured husbands who will bring you consequence. I only hope Charlotte and Anne will be as successful, when their turns come."

Ruth sipped her wine and said nothing, hugging her thoughts to herself.

~~~~~

For the journey to Valmont, Ruth had been permitted to wear her newest pelisse and bonnet, bought for the season in London but
~~~~~

deemed suitable for the future duchess to wear when visiting her future home. The procession rolled ponderously through the tiny hamlet of Shallowford Green, no more than a collection of cottages and a duck pond, but the ducal crest on the carriages caused the few locals out and about to doff their caps or curtsy as they passed by. Then they were into a wooded lane and within a half mile had reached the northern lodge of Valmont, where the gates stood wide open in readiness for their arrival. A long, straight drive brought them after some time to the main entrance to the house. And such a house it was! Ruth had never been to Versailles and one could not tell merely from drawings, but Valmont was said to be built on the same palatial scale, a frontage hundreds of feet long and many stories high, constructed in a handsome grey stone. Used as she was to the great houses of the aristocracy, there was a majesty about Valmont that was unrivalled.

Ran was there to receive them. That did not surprise her. Ger had been unpredictable in that regard, just as likely to be out fishing for the day, but Ran was punctilious in the courtesies. He came down the steps to greet them, and when the footman opened the door and let down the steps, he was there with a few words of welcome, and his arm ready to assist the duchess to alight. Then Ruth, whose elevation in status caused her to share the forward-facing seat with her mother. Finally, Aunt Maria was handed down, setting the carriage rocking. There was a greeting for the duke, too, alighting last from the carriage with a sigh of relief.

"Do come inside," Ran said. "Your rooms are ready, if you wish to rest after the journey, or there are refreshments awaiting you, if you prefer."

"A glass of something," Ruth's father said. "Canary, Madeira, whatever you have."

Cousin Patience emerged from the second carriage, which she had shared with the two lady's maids and the valet. Ran assisted the duchess up the steps, then skipped lightly down again to offer his arm to Aunt Maria, but he threw Ruth a slight smile, as if to say that he would have preferred to escort her, but felt obliged to be polite to the older ladies in the party.

Ruth delicately lifted her skirts with one hand and made her way up the broad steps and into the entrance hall. Ah, Valmont! She sighed with pleasure as she gazed about her. Mallowfleet had antiquity and a certain faded charm, but Valmont had both grandeur and elegance, built as if for giants, with great pillars and ceilings high above. Ruth always felt like a queen, walking amongst such magnificence, everything larger than it needed to be. And to think she would be mistress of all this!

"Lady Ruth." Ran made her a respectful bow, both the welcome from a host to a guest, but also, she fancied, the acknowledgement of her future position here. "I am delighted to welcome you to Valmont once more."

Delighted? Even as she made her curtsy, she wondered at his choice of word. A mere politeness, surely, but then Ran had never lacked courtesy. What could she say in response? Dared she speak of her own delight? Probably not, for it might seem too forward. "It is always a pleasure to visit Valmont," she murmured.

There were refreshments laid out in one of the ante-rooms, which was built on a more intimate scale than most of the Valmont apartments. Not that she minded the vast size of the place, but for their small numbers she thought the ante-room an excellent choice. Apart from Ran himself, there was an uncle of his, Lord Arthur, and an aunt, Lady Anne, but no other relations. The elderly chaplain, Mr Ponsonby, was the only other present. It was a dreadfully large house for a single man like Ran to occupy, almost alone.

Ran served them himself, pouring wine and handing it round, and then offering biscuits and sweetbreads and hot pastries. Ruth sipped the sherry he gave her, refused the food and watched him surreptitiously as he moved here and there, always with ready words to set everyone at their ease. He looked, she thought, exactly as a duke ought to look. She had almost forgotten how handsome he was — better looking than Ger, whose appearance was so nondescript that he would have passed as a country attorney if one knew no better. But Ran looked every inch the aristocrat. His clothes were not ostentatious, but they were clearly fashioned by the very best tailors, his neckcloth was perfectly starched, his hair was carefully disordered and his bearing was noble. He was solemn-faced, but then he had always been the serious one of the two brothers. That was his nature, and she was not foolish enough to suppose that she could change him.

Once or twice she caught his eyes on her, but each time he quickly looked away again. Naturally he was inspecting her. He had seen her previously only as his brother's intended, but now... now she was *his* intended, and he was seeing her differently. Well, he would see nothing to disgust him. Her appearance, her deportment, her manners had been polished over the years and she knew them to be such as must please even the most fastidious. She was a nobleman's daughter, and had been destined from birth to be a nobleman's wife. She looked the part, of that there could be no doubt, and she would fulfil the rôle expected of her to perfection, just as he would fulfil his rôle, too. Both of them knew what was expected of them.

Was she unreasonable to want him to *like* her, too? *Please, please let him like her.*

3: A Courtship

Ran had hoped for a private conversation with Ruth to determine her feelings on the proposed match between them, but he found himself thwarted at every turn, for she was accompanied wherever she went by two watchful guards. Her parents created no difficulty, for the duke quickly got up a piquet club in the library with Uncle Arthur, or else read the newspapers, and the duchess was happy to sit with Aunt Anne, pretending to work on her tapestry but actually gossiping endlessly. But Lady Maria Grenaby and Miss Patience Bucknell were Ruth's designated chaperons, and they took their responsibilities very, very seriously. There was not a minute of the day when she was not attended by one or other of them, and usually both. Two determined spinsters were no match for a mere duke. Ran knew better than to ask formally for a private interview with Ruth, for only an offer of marriage could be the consequence of that.

He showed no frustration, naturally, for he was a gentleman and knew how to curb his tongue. Besides, the watchdogs permitted him to spend as much time as he liked in company with Ruth, so long as they were never alone, and so he had ample opportunity to improve his acquaintance with her. Not that he felt it necessary to do so, for although he had never been invited to Mallowfleet, she had visited Valmont several times and they had met often in town during the three seasons she had passed there. He knew her character well and had no doubt at all that she would make a wonderful duchess. Still, it was pleasant to be permitted to spend hours each day with her, for she was a gentle companion, never tongue-tied but not garrulous, either.

On the first day, the rain was too steady to permit any thought of venturing outdoors.

"What should you like to do this morning?" he said to Ruth, as they sat in the winter breakfast parlour.

"Shall we walk in the Long Gallery?" she said. "I like to take some exercise each day, and I may walk for miles there, you know. How long is it?"

"One hundred and fifty feet," he said, smiling suddenly. The Long Gallery! That would be fun indeed, for the family portraits were there and he could tell her some of the Litherholm history. She blinked at him as he spoke, some fleeting emotion crossing her face, but he could not interpret it. Perhaps she was merely surprised that he had such information at his fingertips.

Both Lady Maria and Miss Bucknell followed them at a few paces' distance as they walked, far enough for the illusion of privacy but close enough to hear every word that passed between two young people designated as a courting couple. He tried not to mind.

It turned out that Ruth had been to the Long Gallery several times before, and already had a good idea of the Litherholm ancestors.

"Ah, the Second Earl," she said knowledgeably. "He was the one who saved the day by arriving at the battlefield just when all was believed lost."

"He was the one who *got* lost," Ran said solemnly. "He took a wrong turning and led his men into a bog. Almost missed the battle altogether."

She raised her eyebrows, surprised. "This one is the Fifth Earl, who murdered his two older brothers in order to inherit. I am sure that *cannot* be so."

Ran laughed. "It was never proved, but they did die very conveniently. That may actually be true."

"Oh. Now this is the Third Marquess, who went mad and had to be kept locked up in the arch tower."

"Well… he was certainly not quite well." One could not mention the pox to a young lady. "He did live in the arch tower, because he suspected he was infectious."

"Oh. Now this handsome fellow is Lord Alfred Litherholm… who fled to the Continent because of gaming debts?"

"There may have been some, perhaps, because that generation gambled excessively, but I believe his journey was no more than the usual Grand Tour."

"Hmm. The Fourth Duke, who built Valmont. Correct?"

"Almost. The Third Duke bought the land and the original manor house, and commissioned the design, but he died before it was completed. His portrait hangs over the main staircase. The Fourth Duke is responsible for much of the interior, and he began the art collection."

"He had the eight lodges built to house all his mistresses… no? And secret passages and screens so he could spy on everyone."

"There is no knowing what his intention was. Everything about Valmont is so symmetrical that eight lodges, evenly spaced about the perimeter, align perfectly with the design, but he certainly used some of them to house his former mistresses, so that is partly true. As for the secret passages, there are a good number of concealed doors and service stairs, but that is normal in such houses to allow discreet access for servants. I take it Ger filled your head with so much nonsense?"

"You know what he was like," she said, lifting cool grey eyes to his. "Always making up stories. He was most entertaining when he was in a funning mood. I never took him entirely seriously. Oh… and there he is."

The last portrait in the gallery was the most recent, depicting the two sons of Valmont at the time of their majority. Ger, as befitted the elder, destined to be the duke, was shown raised on the second step outside the main entrance, one slender hand resting on a stone finial with the heir's ring prominent on the middle finger. Ran, the spare second son, stood on the drive below, looking up at his brother. The artist had captured them well, so well that Ran felt the same burst of grief whenever he looked at it. *Oh Ger, why did you have to die?*

Ruth stood quietly gazing at Ger, her face grave.

"Oh, such handsome young men!" Miss Bucknell cried, rummaging in her reticule for a handkerchief. "So *tragic!*"

"Too much sensibility, Patience," said Lady Maria crossly. "Do control yourself."

"I beg your pardon, Ran," Ruth said, her well-modulated voice a soothing contrast to the chaperons'. "This must be distressing for you. Shall we return to the Grand Saloon? I love to play the instrument there. It is such a magnificent Broadwood."

~~~~~

After three days of rain, there was finally an opportunity to escape from the house. Ruth was a fine horsewoman, he knew, but even so, his breath caught at the sight of her in her riding habit. Had ever a woman looked so lovely? He felt a surge of pure pleasure as he lifted her into the saddle, and watched her efficiently settle her skirts.

"Your horse awaits you, Your Grace," she said, with just the hint of a smile in those grey eyes.

"Oh… of course." Reluctantly he tore his eyes away from her, and hopped lightly onto his own mount.

Ran had hoped that this might be his opportunity to talk to Ruth, but still he was thwarted. The middle-aged Lady Maria had retired from the ranks, defeated, for she was no rider, but Miss Bucknell, being only a few years older than Ruth, was made of sterner stuff. She gamely appeared in the stables in a drab riding habit. She would not permit Ran or the groom to toss her into the saddle, preferring the mounting block, and arranging herself with a great deal of wriggling so that her voluminous habit afforded not a single glimpse even of her boot.

Ran led the ladies out of the stable yard, Ruth on a lively young mare, Miss Bucknell on a more placid mare and a stolid groom bringing up the rear. At first Ran maintained a slow pace, and Ruth rode alongside him, controlling her spirited mount without effort. She commented on some small changes since her
~~~~~

last visit two years earlier, and listened with seeming interest to his plans to renovate the grooms' quarters and the gardeners' cottages. But gradually he began to speed up, so that Miss Bucknell, no very confident rider, began to fall behind, with the groom watchfully bringing up the rear. Eventually, they came to an open stretch of ground, sloping down towards woodland some distance away.

"Shall we?" Ran said, with a quick smile at Ruth.

Almost before the words were spoken, she had urged her mount forward, faster and then faster still. Ran stayed slightly behind her. He told himself it was so that she could set her own pace, as she felt most comfortable, but it also gave him an admirable view of her as she flew over the smooth grass. Such a splendid rider! He thought he could watch her for ever.

All too soon they reached the woods, and here she pulled up, her horse tossing her head and Ruth herself flushed with the exhilaration of the ride. Ran could not take his eyes off her.

"That was such fun," she said, laughing, "but we had better wait for poor Cousin Patience to catch up."

Poor Cousin Patience was labouring at a steady trot across the greensward, as fast as her fat little mare would carry her, and would be with them in no more than a minute or two. Ran could not waste the opportunity. However odd it might seem to Ruth, still alight with the pleasure of the ride, he must speak now or there may never be another chance.

"Ruth…"

She turned to him, and he could see by her face that she understood, for instantly the polite mask she showed the world fell back into place.

"Ruth, forgive me, but I must say this. You have been put into a very awkward position by Ger's death, and to your father it must seem like the ideal solution for the understanding you had with him to transfer to me. I must ask you if... if you truly wish for this. I would not for the world have you pressed into a situation distasteful to you."

Her eyes slid to Miss Bucknell, growing nearer every second, but she answered calmly. "It is awkward for both of us, Ran. The same considerations apply to you, also."

To his ears, her voice sounded cold. What did she expect him to say? There was no time to consider his words, to craft the perfect response, but he was far more concerned with the risk of saying too much than too little. "Naturally I am very willing to—"

Was that a flash of anger in her eyes? "Then we are in accord," she said crisply, deftly turning her horse and urging her into the woods.

"Oh, Your Grace, such... a turn... of speed!" puffed Miss Bucknell as she reached them. "Must urge... more caution... What would dear Lady Ruth's parents say if—?"

"I beg your pardon for alarming you, Miss Bucknell," Ran said in flat tones. "Lady Ruth is a most accomplished rider, however. I do not believe there was any real danger."

But Ruth was gone, and heard nothing of the compliment.

That was the only private conversation Ran had with his future wife. For the rest of the visit, she was perfectly composed, the epitome of the gracious and charming guest, with not the slightest crack in the façade she presented to the world, and Ran could only suppose that it was as her father had said — that she accepted him in duty.

It was enough. It would have to be enough.

~~~~~

A few days after Ruth and her family had left, Ran and Max Lorrimer rode towards the eastern lodge. It was four in the afternoon, and already growing dusk. Ran dismounted to open the gate, and the two horsemen passed through. The eastern gate was one of several which had the usual carriage drive on the Valmont side, but no matching road on the other. There was, in fact, no need for drive or gate or lodge at all, but at Valmont, symmetry was all, so there the gate stood.

On the far side, a straight track led through old-established woodland of oak and beech, leafless still at this season, but dark and gloomy at this hour. The horses knew their way well, however, so the two men rode without haste for a mile or so, emerging by way of a wooden gate in a high brick wall into the clear signs of a gentleman's garden. Passing through the rather disordered shrubbery, they rode between scruffy lawns to a modest stable block, where an elderly groom with a lamp took charge of the horses. Across the yard, they entered the house through the kitchen door.

"There you are!" cried the young woman in a voluminous apron, as she manoeuvred a pot of something over the fire. "And Ran, too — how lovely! It is good to see you without your black coat, my dear. Visitors all gone?"
~~~~~

"All gone. How are you, Alice? It seems an age since I was here."

"Not since Twelfth Night, I think," she said. "What a stranger you have become lately. Peter will be pleased to see you."

Harebell Cottage was a modest house, not the largest in the village of St Peter's Cross, but home to some of Ran's dearest friends. Peter and Max, the two sons, had grown up alongside Ger and Ran, the four of them learning to ride and fish and shoot together, roaming the Valmont estates as a group and attending the same school and university. Although all were good friends, Peter and Ger had had an especial closeness, and Ran and Max likewise.

Their fathers had been wise enough not to interfere in this easy-going friendship, despite the very different destinies of their sons. Peter Lorrimer, the elder son, supplemented the modest competence he had inherited with attorney work. Max had become indispensable to Ran as his most trusted secretary. Their sister, Alice, kept house for her brothers. She was a lively, pretty girl, but had never married, despite numerous eligible offers, for why, she said, would she do so when she was already mistress of a perfectly good establishment?

Although he now lived at Valmont, once a week Max went home to eat his dinner with his family, and the Litherholm sons had always had an open invitation to avail themselves of the same hospitality. After the formality of a week with the Duke and Duchess of Orrisdale, Ran looked forward to a relaxing evening amongst friends.

They were too considerate to ask him directly about Ruth, but as soon as their dinner was laid out on the table and the manservant had withdrawn, Ran said, "I expect you have guessed it already, but I shall be going to Mallowfleet next month for Lady Ruth's birthday celebrations, and our betrothal will be announced there."

"Well now, how delightful it will be to have a duchess at Valmont again," Alice said, amidst the chorus of congratulations. "Is she as lovely as rumour makes her?"

"Lovelier," Ran said at once. "I never saw a more beautiful woman."

"Ah!" Alice said, laughing. "You like her, then, and you will make an ideal husband, Ran, with such an attitude."

"It is true," Max said. "She is a diamond of the first water, and wonderfully accomplished."

"All such ladies are wonderfully accomplished," Alice said, at once. "I set no store by *that*, but if Ran thinks her a beauty, that is an excellent foundation for marriage. And you are... content, Ran? She was destined for Ger, after all."

There was a sudden alert silence, like the dropping of a stone into a pond.

"I am content," he said without hesitation. "I was concerned that her father might be pushing her towards me, in place of Ger, but she... she is willing. We are... in accord." Her own words, and yet they made him shiver. What did they mean? Was she truly willing, as willing as he was, or was she simply accepting the duty laid upon her by her father?

"That is good," Alice said, calmly ignoring his hesitation. "And you are to take your seat in the House of Lords in the spring, or so Max tells us? So we must address you as *'Your Grace'* now."

"I trust that in private you will call me Ran, as always," he said, smiling. "There must be no formality between us, such good friends as we are."

After dinner, they played vingt-et-un for farthings, talking about the latest Royal scandals, the frailty of the Valmont chaplain, the new coal mine — anything and everything but Ran's forthcoming marriage. But as he and Max prepared to leave, Peter laid a hand on his arm.

"I wish you very happy, Ran, and Ger would have wished it too. He would have wanted you to go on with your life, and build a future. I hope Lady Ruth appreciates how lucky she is, and I say that as one of Ger's best friends in this world. He had many good qualities, and I loved him dearly, but I never thought that Lady Ruth was the right wife for him, or he the right husband for such a gently raised lady."

"Yet they were in love," Ran said. "Affection smooths a great many differences."

"I know nothing of that," Peter said. "Ger never spoke of her in such terms, so I cannot say what was in his heart, but you know what he was like, Ran. So volatile! Up in alt one minute, in despair the next, and I never knew anyone able to coax him out of his low spirits, not even you. Maybe Lady Ruth could have done it, I cannot say, but it always seemed to me that they were thrown together and the marriage expected, and a high-born lady like that— I wondered a great deal how it would work. But you are the most even-tempered man in Christendom, and the best mannered and most correct. Your wife will be a fortunate lady indeed, and Ger would have been the first to say so."

Ran could find nothing to say to such kindness, except to thank him and hope with all his heart that he might be right. There was nothing he wanted more in the world than to make Ruth happy. If only he could! But he was not Ger, was not the object of her affection and could never be so. He would always be second best. It was a dispiriting thought.

4: Identification

MARCH

The Benefactor's lawyer arrived on a cold, grey, windswept day, a last fling of winter before spring greenery burst forth everywhere. Mr Willerton-Forbes was attired in the very latest Bond Street style, and looked splendidly unlike a lawyer. He brought with him a Captain Edgerton, a small man flamboyantly dressed in the garish insignia of the Four-Horse Club and wearing a sword, and Mr Neate, a slender man dressed entirely in black and the only one of the three to look like a lawyer.

Ran saw them in his private office, with only Max in attendance. The business was mercifully brief, merely to confirm his identity, and that he was the next of kin of the late Seventh Duke of Falconbury, his brother.

"His Grace your brother left no wife, no child?" Willerton-Forbes said gently.

"None. I have spent a year fruitlessly searching for evidence of such a situation, but in vain," Ran said. "I must conclude that he never married."

"Then, Your Grace, I am pleased to inform you that I am empowered by the Benefactor to bestow upon you the sum of one thousand pounds," Willerton-Forbes said. "You may receive this benefice in any form that seems good to you, or, if you wish it to be invested or transferred to some other person, I shall, naturally, follow your instructions in the matter."

Ran had had a whole year to consider what he might do with this largesse. "I have no need of it, but there are five parishes within my gift," he said. "The sum of two hundred pounds apiece would alleviate a great deal of want amongst the parishioners. Mr Lorrimer will furnish you with a list."

"I shall be delighted to oblige you, Your Grace. That is most satisfactory, if I may say so. I am most relieved to have obtained an audience with you at last, for although we have corresponded on occasion, I cannot execute the Benefactor's instructions as I should wish without meeting each recipient in person. Your Grace, might I be permitted to ask a question, a matter that has been exercising me greatly and on which, perhaps, you may be able to set my mind at rest?" Ran nodded his acquiescence. "Are you the Benefactor?"

Ran could only laugh. "You do not know his identity? And whatever makes you think *I* might be responsible?"

"Your reluctance to receive me, Your Grace, and your wealth. There are few men in England who could afford the six and twenty thousand pounds the Benefactor has given."

"Plus expenses," Ran said, in amusement.

"Indeed," Willerton-Forbes said, eyes twinkling. "Plus *considerable* expenses. It would be an appropriate memorial to your brother, or so it seemed to me. And I note that you have not, in fact, answered the question, Your Grace."

Ran chuckled. "You must be formidable in court, Mr Willerton-Forbes. I did not want to see you, it is true, having no need of the Benefactor's charity. Perhaps it was discourteous of me, but I was sunk in grief and saw no one beyond the most minimal call of duty. But to answer your question, I am not the Benefactor, nor do I have the least idea who he may be."

"Ah. What a pity," Willerton-Forbes said. "It would have been such a neat solution to the question."

"Do you need to know who provides the money you so liberally bestow?" Ran said.

"No, but one so dislikes mysteries, Your Grace," Willerton-Forbes said. "My brief is, you may think, a simple one, yet I have been beset with mysteries. One wonders, for instance, why a sound ship, manned by a competent crew, and sailing in calm waters with good visibility, should drift onto rocks and founder. One wonders, for a further instance, why one of the passengers, travelling under the name of Louis Fields, should turn out to be a woman, and not a man at all. One wonders, for a third instance, why one particular passenger, a Mr Jonathan Ellsworthy, has no history and springs up out of nowhere on the *Brig Minerva*."

It was Max Lorrimer who cut in. "Must every man have a known history, Mr Willerton-Forbes?"

Captain Edgerton, who had been prowling restlessly about the room, stopped abruptly. "Every man has a history, sir. He may choose not to share it, but the history is there to be found, if only one knows where to look. But when a man says that he grew up in an orphanage in Carlisle, yet no such person is recorded in that fair city, one begins to wonder."

"Men change their names all the time," Max said in amused tones. "There is no crime in it. A man falls out with his family — or his orphanage, in this case — and wishes to begin his life anew, so he gives himself a new name. His given history — the orphanage in Carlisle — may still be true, even though the names do not match."

"There is much in what you say," Willerton-Forbes said, watching him steadily. "Mr Ellsworthy has exercised our minds for some time, for he is one of only three survivors of the foundering of the *Brig Minerva*, and therefore he is a person of some importance to us, concerned as we are with all those who boarded the ship that day in Dublin. He is a man of obvious respectability, with some education. A clerk, he said, who was bound for Southampton to obtain work with one of the ship owners there. He was on deck when the *Minerva* sank, and was washed ashore, half-dead, to be aided by a local family. And there he has stayed, becoming secretary to a local gentleman. His details, such as were known, were reported to the inquiry into the sinking, although Mr Ellsworthy himself was not called upon to speak, having no memory of the event."

"He was grievously injured, too," Captain Edgerton said.

"So he was, so he was," Willerton-Forbes said. "A badly broken leg, as I recall. Lucky to be alive, no doubt, and confined to his bed for some considerable time. It was three months before we ourselves were able to speak to him. But still, as we pursued our enquiries regarding the *Minerva*, Mr Ellsworthy was... an irritant, shall we say. A loose thread that could not be reconciled. Your brother regarded him as a friend, seemingly, and he stayed at the home of the Earl of Kilrannan in Dublin, just as His Grace did. And when the *Minerva* sailed, they were both aboard. Yet before those few days in Dublin, we could find no trace of Jonathan Ellsworthy, not in Ireland, nor in the New World, nor in Carlisle, where he claimed to have been raised. Mr Ellsworthy appeared, fully formed, in Dublin at the same time as your brother."

"I cannot see why it matters," Ran said restlessly. "A man may call himself whatever he wishes, if he has no foul purpose in mind."

"Precisely so," Willerton-Forbes said. "The possibility of a foul purpose is what bothered us, especially so when combined with the unexpected sinking of the ship and the presence on board of a duke. One begins to wonder..."

"You think the ship was sunk deliberately?" Ran said sharply. "Surely not!"

"It is a possibility that cannot be discounted," Willerton-Forbes said. "However, although many people benefited unexpectedly from the deaths aboard the *Minerva*, it is hard to see how it might have been accomplished, and the principal beneficiary of the late duke's death — yourself, Your Grace — has been so demonstrably reluctant to assume his mantle that the idea could not be sustained. Even so, Mr Ellsworthy was, as I mentioned, an irritant. I dislike mysteries, Your Grace, and Captain Edgerton is indefatigable in pursuing them. With the aid of Mr Neate, whose unassuming demeanour permits him access to a great deal of information of an unofficial nature, he pursued his enquiries in Carlisle, in Ireland and even in America. But we had a piece of good fortune. The generosity of the Benefactor had the not unexpected result of a great many letters written to us. Most, of course, claimed to have a relative aboard the *Minerva*, hoping for a share of the bounty being handed out, and most were obviously fraudulent. Because of that, we were, I fear, rather lax about investigating them. But when our attention was drawn to them, there was one of particular interest. A lady wrote to us from Carlisle — a place which immediately drew our notice, as you may suppose — of her brother, one Nigel Pike. He had grown up in an orphanage in Carlisle, from which place, after some pecuniary difficulties, he departed for America where he found employment as an actor with a travelling troop of players. This Mr Pike had written to his sister from Dublin to say that he would be aboard the *Minerva*. We could find no trace of Mr Pike in Ireland, or on the crossing from America, but our enquiries in America elicited the information that he had vanished from view some two… no, three years ago, now. And so it was that we found ourselves with a man, Nigel Pike, who grew up in Carlisle, went to America and then vanished, and another man, Jonathan Ellsworthy, who appeared from nowhere in Ireland. Do you see how satisfactory this is?"

Ran, who had long since lost interest in Pike and Ellsworthy and Willerton-Forbes' mysteries, made some non-committal noises.

"And so you will readily understand, Your Grace," Willerton-Forbes continued imperturbably, "why we are so curious about *your* little mystery."

"My mystery? There is nothing mysterious about me, or my circumstances."

Willerton-Forbes leaned back in his chair with a smug smile, steepling his fingers. "Permit me to disagree, Your Grace. It seems to me, as an outsider, that you took a great deal of time to come to terms with your brother's death and accept the dukedom that is now yours. Now, there may be nothing but caution in that, but one does wonder a little if there might have been something more to it."

"There was indeed caution, but necessarily so," Ran said. "My brother was in America for three years, and there was always the possibility that he married during that time and fathered a child. I had to be sure that was not so before claiming the title."

"Very true, very true. Even so, there might perhaps be some other concern in your mind? After all, with a sudden and unexpected death, a hasty identification under distressing circumstances... it might very well cross your mind that, despite everything, a mistake may have been made and—?"

"There was no mistake," Ran said hotly. "Mr Willerton-Forbes, I would give everything I have, even my very life, if there were the least chance that my brother were still alive. But there is none. I saw his body, remember, and I could not be mistaken in what I saw."

Willerton-Forbes coughed gently. "There was some... *disfigurement*, I understand? As a result of the way the ship was dragged into shallow water so that recovery might be made."

"Yes, his face was... was battered, it is true, but everything else was as it should be... his slight frame, the colour of his hair... and he wore my brother's linen embroidered with his crest, and carried his watch and seal. There was one other identifying feature, too, about which I could not be mistaken. Ger bore a small birthmark on the back of his neck, just above the hair line.

It was quite distinctive. I looked for that and found it, exactly where it should be."

"Ah," Willerton-Forbes said. "Then there is no possibility of doubt. I am glad of it."

"No, there is no doubt."

Ran got up and walked restlessly to the window. This room looked down into the courtyard between the two main wings of the building. The fountain was not playing today, for the river was low, and the flowerbeds were still a wintry brown, but in the summer these gardens were filled with colour, a mass of birds and butterflies and humming bees flitting about. It had been his mother's favourite place, and the only part of the gardens allowed to be full to bursting with flowers. Everywhere else was neat green hedges and topiary and carefully contrived regularity, but this spot was a joyous riot of colour.

He sighed, for his mother had been dead for many years now, and it was not like him to be maudlin. Still, there was a part of the past that must be told before it could be laid to rest.

"When we were boys," he said slowly, turning to face his visitors, "the future dukedom weighed heavily on my brother. He felt himself unsuited to the rôle and wished with all his heart that it should not be his. It is a strange thing to be a twin. Twenty minutes separated our births, such a trivial amount of time... that was the difference between us. He, the elder, was destined to inherit a great title and unimaginable wealth. I, the younger, had a noble lineage and a courtesy title but nothing else. Not a penny piece was mine, unless my father or my brother willed it. He would live his whole life in luxury while I would have to earn my bread, or live on charity. And all because of that twenty minutes.

Ger wished that it could be otherwise, that I could be the duke while he lived in relative obscurity, for I never feared it as he did. He thought I was better suited to high rank than he was, and although I disagreed with him, the notion never left him. If the law had permitted him to surrender all claim to the title, he would have done it without a second thought. *'The King may abdicate, if he will, so why should not I?'* he used to say. But since all legal avenues were closed to him, he considered all manner of other ways to achieve his aim. He would find a way to pretend to die, he said, so that I should inherit. His schemes were increasingly ingenious, for he realised that in order for a duke to be declared dead, there would have to be a body. A Mr Smith of Nowhere could vanish and be declared dead, in time, but the heir to a dukedom could not. There had to be a body, and the body would have to be identified as his. How was that to be done? And in time he came to see that it was impossible, for how else was he to find a body except to murder someone? And then *I* would have to identify that stranger's body as Ger. And so the idea was dropped."

"But when you heard that the *Minerva* was lost, you must have wondered?" Captain Edgerton said.

"I wondered, yes. Perhaps, somehow, Ger had succeeded in his crazy scheme. Perhaps, in some unfathomable way, he had contrived a body who was thought to be him. All I had to do was to identify the body as Ger, and he would be free! He could live his life as he wished, without the terrible weight of his inheritance dragging him down. So even as I travelled to Cornwall and waited there for the local fishermen to recover the bodies from the *Minerva*, some little gleam of hope at the back of my mind would not be repressed. I so badly wanted Ger to be free... to be *happy.*"

He paused, and there was silence in the room, apart from a slight shifting of the coals in the fireplace.

"But it was not so, gentlemen. I examined that body very carefully, and looked for the birthmark as the final proof. And there it was. No other could have had such a mark in such a place, and, together with the clothing and other articles, there can be no doubt. No doubt at all. None whatsoever."

Now the silence was even more profound.

It was Mr Neate who spoke, the first words he had uttered after entering the room. "And yet you *do* doubt. Don't you?"

Ran gave him a wintry smile. "What makes you think so, sir, when I have explained so very clearly why I do not?"

Neate looked him in the eye, unafraid. "I am not clever, like Mr Willerton-Forbes, or brave, like Captain Edgerton. But I am observant. My job is to sit in tap rooms and chop houses and listen. I talk to ostlers and valets and chambermaids, and try to work out who's telling the truth and who's telling part of the truth, and who's outright lying. So I'm very good at noticing faces and voices and the little habits people have that show when they're not telling the *whole* truth. Like rubbing the nose, as you've done several times now. And you've explained at great length why your brother must be dead — far greater length than we needed to hear. Almost as if you're trying to convince yourself, sir. Your Grace."

Ran studied him, trying to decide whether dislike or admiration was uppermost in his mind. Admiration, he decided. It was subtle, very subtle. He laughed, and went to a drawer in the desk. Opening it, he pulled out a ring.

"This was Ger's signet ring, the heir's ring. It has the word *'Beckhampton'* engraved on it, for that was Ger's courtesy title — the Marquess of Beckhampton. It was worn by all the heirs in adulthood, so it is a standard size. Most of them wore it on the little finger, as I wear my less exalted ring. But Ger had delicate hands with very slender fingers. He always wore this ring on the middle finger. When Ger's body was dragged from beneath the waves, he wore this ring — but not on the middle finger, where it ought to be. It was on the little finger. Such a tiny detail, yet it niggles at me. Why? Had his fingers swollen so much? Or is there the remotest possibility those were not Ger's fingers at all?"

"A tiny detail, indeed," Willerton-Forbes said in satisfaction. "So let us see if we can set your mind at rest. Amongst all our talks with survivors and relations of those who died aboard the *Minerva*, there were many references to the Duke of Falconbury on that last, fateful journey. Let us go back to London and gather all our notes for you, and we will see if we can find some other tiny details to set beside this one."

"Tiny details are the very best kind," Captain Edgerton said with satisfaction.

"And yet to imagine some meaning to this is nonsensical, Ran!" Max cried. "A drowned man's fingers swell, do they not?"

"I was assured that nothing at all had been touched, that Ger's body was just as it was found," Ran said. "Therefore that ring was on the wrong finger *before* he drowned."

"Then perhaps his fingers had grown swollen for some reason during his sojourn in America," Max said. "The different food, different habits… you refine upon nothing!"

"Perhaps nothing, or perhaps something," Captain Edgerton said, eyes gleaming. "It is intriguing, though, is it not?"

"No, it is not!" Max said with force. "Let the dead lie, Ran. It does no good to dig around in these stupid trivialities. Ger is gone, swollen fingers or not."

"I know," Ran said. "Truly, my friend, I know he is dead, for have I not seen his body? Have I not with my own eyes seen the proof of it, in that birthmark? I *know* that he lies in the Litherholm mausoleum, that he will never play the pianoforte again, will never race me across the Stony Field on that brute of a stallion of his, will never cuff me on the shoulder the way he used to. I *know* that. But the ring… however trivial it may be, it bothers me, and if Mr Willerton-Forbes and Captain Edgerton and Mr Neate can find an answer to that puzzle, I shall indeed be grateful to them."

5: A Betrothal

Ran took the smallest of the travelling carriages to Mallowfleet. It was only in Berkshire, the next county, a distance of under fifty miles on good roads, and he saw no need to take anyone but the coachman and groom, and his valet, Giggs. A single box contained adequate changes of clothing for the five days he was expected to stay. He had been instructed, in the politest possible terms, to present himself two days before the Grand Ball, and obediently he did so.

He beguiled the journey by considering how soon he would be able to make his offer to Ruth. Tomorrow, perhaps. Yes, that would be best. He might even have an opportunity to speak privately to the duke that evening, and could then request an interview with Ruth tomorrow. The offer itself had not much occupied his thoughts, for there was little enough to be said. No need to enumerate the advantages of the match, not to Ruth. But what should he say of his own feelings? That was more problematical. He could say, perhaps, that he held her in the highest esteem... no, that lwas too cold. The highest *regard*, perhaps. Then he would express his hope that he would be able to make her happy, as she deserved. Yes, as she deserved. He could never be the husband she had wanted and waited for, but he could be the second best. What did the marriage service say? *Wilt thou comfort her?* He hoped he could do that.

He arrived to find a much larger entourage already drawn up outside the mellow red brick façade of the manor house. Four carriages of various sizes were in the process of disgorging their occupants as outriders dismounted, grooms ran here and there, and a positive army of footmen unloaded boxes, bags and packages. Recognising the insignia of the Duke of Camberley ahead of him, and there being a steady drizzle falling, he settled down to wait his turn to drive under the porte-cochère.

The butler must have been on the watch for him, however, for he rushed out with an umbrella.

"Your Grace! Your Grace! Do enter at once, for His Grace is awaiting you in the library. Pray permit me to offer you my arm, Your Grace."

Ran refused the arm but was glad of the umbrella, reaching the porte-cochère almost completely dry. Stepping around the mountains of baggage deposited there, he allowed the butler to usher him into the house. Ahead of him, the great hall was filled with female chatter, and the swirl of fashionable coats.

"Do come this way, Your Grace," murmured the butler, lifting a velvet curtain to reveal a hidden door. "Let me take you at once to His Grace."

The door opened onto narrow stairs, not service stairs, for they were carpeted, with pictures hung at intervals. A private way to the family chambers, he guessed. On the first floor, a footman waited, who relieved Ran of his greatcoat, hat and gloves. He was to be taken at once to the Duke of Orrisdale, then.

He was too polite to object to such an arrangement, but he felt that it was a little abrupt. But perhaps the duke had some of his brothers with him, and merely wished to introduce Ran. It could not be a private interview, could it? Not so soon, when he had only just set foot in the house.

Ran was led along a dark passageway, past many doors. Mallowfleet was a venerable building, but the old-fashioned wood panels gave it a gloomy air. Throwing open a door identical to every other, the butler intoned portentously, "His Grace the Duke of Falconbury, Your Grace."

The duke was alone. "Ah, Falconbury, there you are! Been expecting you this last hour or more. What kept you?"

"I came by easy stages to save the horses," Ran said, bowing punctiliously.

"No need for that, you know. Could have sent teams ahead. Not short of the readies, are you?"

Ran laughed. "Not at all, but I have never been one for show, sir."

"True enough, true enough." The duke ran his eye over Ran's coat, which was fashionable without being ostentatious. "Different now, of course, given your rank, and once you are married... Not had second thoughts about that, then?"

That was very much to the point. Ran was not at all happy with such plain speaking, but he said only, "Not in the least, sir."

"Good, good. Well, no point waiting, is there? Shall we have Ruthie in and get the business over with?"

So that was how it was to be. Ran raised an eyebrow, but felt unable to cavil at it. This, after all, was what he was here for. "By all means."

The duke called for the butler, who had obviously been waiting outside the door, for he appeared instantly.

"Ask Her Grace and the Lady Ruth to step in," the duke said.

The ladies must have been in the very next room, for they too appeared almost at once, the duchess flushed and twittering happily, and Ruth becomingly demure, eyes lowered. The two women could not have been more different, and apart from a slight resemblance about the nose and chin, would not be taken as related at all. The duchess was short and rather stout, her gown elaborately over-trimmed and topped by a froth of a lace cap. Ruth was tall and willowy, her simple muslin falling in elegant folds about her feet. Her hair was a pale brown, almost blonde, arranged in a simple mound with just a few delicate curls about her cheeks and resting on her neck. She was enchanting, and Ran could hardly believe how lucky he was even to consider marrying such perfection.

"Come in, come in," the duke said in hearty tones. "Well, daughter, here is the Duke of Falconbury ready to marry you. What do you say, eh?"

Ran caught his breath. This was too fast, too public! There was no room here for the little speech he had envisaged, no opportunity to compose themselves and speak honestly, man to woman, about so momentous a decision as marriage.

Ruth raised cool, grey eyes to his, devoid of emotion. "His Grace is too obliging."

"I should be greatly honoured—" he began.

"The honour is all mine," she responded. So composed, so calm. Not like him, his heart thundering, his mind trying its best to keep up with the duke's manoeuvres.

He had to do *something*, some little thing to take control of the situation, to feel that he was steering his own ship and not merely swept along on the current of the duke's determination. He reached for Ruth's hand, lifted it in both of his, and gently raised it to his lips.

"We shall deal very well together, I am sure, and I will do my very best to make you happy, Ruth."

There was a glimpse of something in her eyes — surprise, perhaps — before she modestly lowered her gaze, and murmured, "Thank you."

Ran was clapped on the shoulder by the duke, the duchess exclaimed delightedly and then nothing would do but for them all to go to the State Saloon to announce the happy news to the assembled family. The room was full, eyes turning expectantly as they walked in, excited smiles on so many faces. They had gathered here in readiness, he realised, primed for the news. He was congratulated over and over, a score of people wished him joy, another score told him he was a lucky fellow and then there was champagne and trays of sweet things to eat and even the footmen and the butler smiling. The duke's heir, the Marquess of Audlyn, a sprig of but sixteen years, smirked knowingly at him, and hoped he would be invited to Valmont for the autumn shooting. Ruth's sisters, Lady Susan and Lady Charlotte, curtsied and professed the well-rehearsed wish that he would be very happy. Even the nursery party, Lord Harold, Lord Hilary and Lady

Anne were there to stare in wide-eyed awe at their soon-to-be brother-in-law. The Duke of Camberley's party was shown into the room in the midst of it all, and there was another round of announcements and congratulations and the well-wishes of people who were pleased but not surprised. No one was in the least surprised.

And all the while, Ruth's hand rested on his arm, her eyes cast down, her expression composed. Once or twice, when he laid his other hand over hers, he thought it cold, and perhaps there was a faint tremor there, but not once did she look at him. He had no idea what to make of that. And even as he smiled and told everyone how delighted and honoured he was, he wished more than he could express that he could have had even a few minutes alone with Ruth, to talk to her. To say just some of what was in his heart. To kiss her.

~~~~~

Ruth was giddy with relief. It had all gone off as planned, Ran had behaved exactly as he ought and she was betrothed. At last! After the years of waiting for Ger, with an understanding but no betrothal, finally it was done. And it was Ran, not Ger.

Of course, her father had rushed everything. He and Mama had planned it all, and everyone had known, but she had had to wait. How would he react? She had been terrified that he would baulk at the last minute, or say he needed more time. Or worse, perhaps, that he would choose to propose in his own good time and not be bounced into it, and then she would have been in a quiver of hope and anticipation for hours or days. Weeks, perhaps. But he had behaved so beautifully. Ran always did, of course. He never made a scene, never disappeared at the critical moment, never did anything to distress one. Then he had said he
~~~~~

would try to make her happy. She had not expected such courtesy. Honour and obligation, that she could understand, but to speak of happiness... did he know what was in her heart? No, how could he? Dear Ran, always so gentlemanly.

How hard it had been not to show her pleasure in the engagement! But Mama had drummed it into her, year after year — a lady displays no sensibility, ever, and certainly does not disgust her future husband with any vulgar show of emotion. No true gentleman could abide such behaviour. Serenity, that must be her watchword, always cool and serene, no matter the circumstances. Even as they had waited for Ran to arrive, her mother had lectured her on the subject, and Ruth thought she had managed it quite well, on the whole. Her hands had shaken rather, but her voice had been steady and so long as she had not looked at Ran, she found she could maintain her composure. It helped that he had been calm, for that had steadied her, and then she had only to hold tight to his arm and smile as they were congratulated.

After such an awkward start, he had clung to her side, as if he were truly glad about this betrothal. He had not left her for a moment all that first evening, and the following day he had waited for her in the breakfast room and stayed with her all day. There had been a little ceremony when he had presented her with a gift — a necklace of sapphires and pearls, with ear drops and a bracelet, very elegant, a family heirloom. "I shall buy you some *proper* jewellery when we get to town," he had said. Proper jewellery. As if she needed such things from him, but the gesture was sweet.

On the third day, she had been involved with preparations for the ball, but even so, he had often been with her, and twice, when she emerged from her mother's sitting room with more orders for the kitchen, he had been waiting there for her.

"Do you ever get time to rest?" he had said, and when her commission had been executed, insisted that she go to the State Saloon and sit down with a cup of tea. "I want you to have enough energy to dance with me tonight, for I give you fair warning that I plan to stand up with you for every dance. I am allowed to now, you know, since we are betrothed. No one will be the least censorious."

"Except my mother," she said, laughing. "She expects you to dance at least once with Susan and with Cousin Helen and with Lady Ruby Bucknell."

His face fell. "Must I? For I had far rather dance with you."

Who could be displeased by such words, whether he truly meant them or not? And when the evening came, he had led her out onto the floor in the great hall to open the ball with such a smile on his face as thrilled her to her very core. How she loved his smiles! He was so serious most of the time, but occasionally his whole face lit up in the most amazing smile. She could not help smiling in response, although his attention flustered her rather. She could feel herself blushing under his gaze, she who never blushed! But she supposed a newly betrothed woman might be expected to display a little sensibility, so she did not worry about it, and when Ran had returned her to her mother's side, she had smiled at her daughter and said, "Very good, dear. I am so proud of you." So that was all right.

Ran had done his duty by some of the other young ladies, but each time, as soon as he was free again, he returned to Ruth's side and asked for the next dance with her. Such seeming devotion was quite delightful, of course, but she had kept only the supper dance for him, because he had begged for it, and the final dance of the evening. She would have loved to dance the waltz with him, but her mama did not quite approve, even at a private ball, and so they were only country dances, but they were still wonderful, and she went to bed that night shivering with delight in her future husband.

He stayed for two more days, which were spent in a tedium of planning. The date of the wedding was fixed, the date of a ball to celebrate the marriage was fixed and, since her father, his face anxious, had taken Ran away to the library for a private discussion and emerged later wreathed in smiles, she assumed that the settlements were fixed, too.

"Should you like to make a honeymoon somewhere?" Ran asked her. "I have a small estate in Yorkshire where we might spend some time, if you were so minded, or if you wish to delay until the autumn, we could go to Italy."

"Oh, Ruth will not need a honeymoon," the duchess said firmly. "*You* will wish to be in London until Parliament ends, naturally, and *she* will want to go straight to Valmont after. There will be a great deal for her to take care of, for she will want to arrange everything there to her own liking."

"Should you like to visit in the next few weeks, to determine any immediate changes?" he said, addressing the question to Ruth.

Again her mother answered. "We shall be leaving for town in little more than a week... ten days, perhaps. You will be there yourself quite soon, Duke, I daresay?"

"I have not yet decided." Again he addressed himself to Ruth. "If you can visit, even for a day or two, you may decide which rooms you will like for your own, and I should like you to look at the carriages and—"

"Ruth will have a new carriage, naturally," the duchess said, in tones that brooked no argument. "As for rooms, no doubt the late duchess's apartments will be the most appropriate."

"Is that what you wish?" Ran said quietly to Ruth. "My mother's rooms?"

"Whatever you think best," she whispered.

"Very well. I will ensure they are in good order, but you can make a final decision when you are there. You must do whatever *you* prefer, you know. As for the carriages, there are seven in excellent order at Valmont and another three at Litherholm House. If you dislike all of them, then I shall order a new one for you."

Ruth kept her head lowered. There was no purpose to chafing her mother by argument. When she dared to lift her eyes to Ran's, she saw a gentle warmth there. He understood how she was situated, and would not press her. Once they were married, she would be mistress of Valmont in Hampshire and Litherholm House in London, and several other houses, too, and she could order them as she pleased. She would be free to ask for whatever she wanted and Ran, it appeared, was minded to grant her every wish.

Guilt, perhaps. For him, it was a marriage of convenience, an obligation imposed upon him by his brother's death. He had to step into Ger's shoes, as duke, as master of Valmont, as Ruth's husband. None of it was by his own choosing. Yet he gave every appearance of complaisance.

"I am very jealous," Susan said, bouncing into Ruth's bedroom as she was preparing for bed that night. "All the advantages of nobility and wealth, and he is young and handsome, too. A bit clinging, at present, but I daresay he feels that is expected of him. I am sure he will watch you less closely once you are married."

"I suppose so," Ruth said, her spirits drooping a little. That was very much as she had supposed, but it was disheartening to hear her sister say so explicitly. "Lord Crosby is less… *clinging* with you. I did not see him dance with you once."

Susan chuckled, sitting on the bed and drawing her knees up to her chin, as Pinnock collected discarded garments from around her. "Not he! Lord, I should be mortified if he hung about me all evening, and so I told him. He strolled about for a while and then disappeared into the card room, although I do not think he won for he was all frowns when he came out for supper."

"But you do like him?" Ruth asked gently.

"What does that have to say to anything?" Susan said robustly. "I shall like to be a baroness very well, and have plenty of pin money, although it will be nothing to yours, I daresay. Your duke must be one of the wealthiest men in England. Papa was very pleased with the dowry he offered to put up for you."

Ruth was sitting meekly while Pinnock brushed out her hair, but at these words she dismissed the maid. "Sister, you should not speak of such things before the servants. Pinnock is a dreadful gabster, and whatever you say will be all over the servants' hall. But what can you mean, that *Ran* is to put up a dowry for me? It is Papa who provides my dowry, surely?"

"Oh yes, but he has not enough, not with so many daughters to settle well and Audlyn having to maintain a certain style. Grandpapa was so profligate that there is not much of his fortune left, Mama says, and it is all she can do to keep up appearances. You are supposed to have thirty thousand, you know, as the eldest, but Papa has not near that amount, especially as he has agreed to give Crosby fifteen thousand to take me. So he told Falconbury that you would only have the seven thousand from Mama for certain, and Falconbury at once said that he had some holdings he had planned to consolidate anyway, to the sum of twenty thousand, and if Papa could come up with ten thousand, you should have your due amount after all. Which is very handsome of him, is it not?"

"It is, if it is true. Did Papa tell you this?"

"Lord, no! Audlyn got it out of him, for Papa had to settle a few small debts for him and for once he did not cut up stiff, as he usually did, and told Audlyn it was all on account of Falconbury being so generous. But Audlyn said he is as rich as a prince, and need not think twice about such paltry sums as twenty thousand. Heavens, Ruth, the jewels you will have! I am to have some of Crosby's mother's jewels but they are hideous things, so I shall have to get them remade before I can wear them, but I daresay Falconbury will buy you something new. I wish *I* could be a duchess! How lucky you are!"

Ruth could only agree with her, and wonder that Ran would even consider marrying her when he had to provide most of the settlement himself.

6: Visiting Lady Elizabeth

Ran returned to Valmont in an optimistic frame of mind. Ruth had no great affection for him, that he knew, but she would be a complaisant wife and it would be a joy to have her walking through life beside him. As soon as he had set aside his travelling clothes, he strode through the southern wing to the suite his mother had occupied. The instant he threw open the door he was filled with gloom. The rooms were a handsome size, it was true, but the furnishings were heavily ornate and old-fashioned, and everything dark and unwelcoming. And then there was the bedroom… he could not see the vast canopied bed without recalling his mother in it, at first a fretful invalid, and latterly a shrunken, grey-faced ghost waiting impatiently for her life to end. And finally, the still, small shape, shrouded in death. No, he could not bring his lovely bride here.

His first task was to write to the Duke and Duchess of Orrisdale to thank them for their hospitality, brief, carefully worded notes that he always wrote himself. But then he realised that he could now write to Ruth, if he wished. He did wish, he discovered. He wrote cautiously, for he suspected that the duchess would read it first.

The Duke: Silver Linings Mysteries Book 6

'Valmont, Beckhampton Cross, Hampshire. My dear Ruth, I trust you are not exhausted by the exertions of the last few days, and so much dancing. What an enjoyable evening it was, especially the three dances I shared with you. I have inspected my mother's apartments here and find that they will need a great deal of work to make them suitable for you. I will therefore arrange for my sister Elizabeth's rooms to be got ready for you just at first. She was the last of my sisters to leave Valmont and had excellent taste, so you will find everything very pretty and fresh, and decorated in almost the latest styles. Then you may refurbish my mother's rooms at your leisure, if you wish to use them. You may let me know, if you please, how well you liked Dawn Lady, the horse you rode here, for if you prefer something more spirited, I shall be able to look in at Tattersall's when I am in town. I shall not be there for two weeks at least, for I find I have much to do here beforehand. I shall let you know my intended dates of travel when I have settled my plans. Yours in affection, Randolph.'

Was that too strong? *'Yours in affection, Randolph.'* He was terrified of disgusting her by using too intimate a tone, for surely she would not expect or want it. Yet he could not be cold, not with her, and perhaps eventually she would learn to care for him just a little. Not *love*, but a certain fondness, perhaps, in the fullness of time.

The rest of the day he spent riding about the estate with Max and Gurney, the steward, inspecting the progress on the cottages and several of the lodges. When he returned to the stables, he found a fine pair of bays being tended with some respect by his head groom, and a stylish curricle sitting in the yard.

"What have we here, Cailey?"

"Markiss of Audalyn, Yer Grace. Arrived half an hour since. With luggage," he added disapprovingly.

Ran laughed. "He lives at Mallowfleet, so he is bound to stay overnight. Would you have me send him down to the Pig and Whistle?"

"Ah, Mallowfleet, is it?" the groom said knowingly. "Well, then. And I daresay you can squeeze him into a corner of the house somehow." He chuckled at his own wit. "Fine cattle."

Ran could only agree, his eye assessing the bays expertly. Fine cattle indeed, and expensive.

Inside the house, Brent directed him to the Bishop's Chamber, one of the grander apartments which Mrs Brack, the Mistress of the Chambers, had deemed suitable for the heir to a dukedom. Ran found Audlyn gazing in some awe around the regal appointments of his room. He was a well-built young man with fair hair arranged in the fashionably disordered style, his clothes expensive and ostentatiously stylish, but his smile held genuine warmth.

"Audlyn!" Ran said. "What a pleasant surprise! At least, I trust it is pleasant, and you are not the bearer of bad tidings?"

"No, nothing like that. Just bought those bays of mine, and fancied stretching their legs a little, and Mallowfleet was a trifle flat after all the excitement."

"You will find Valmont even flatter, I fear. A dead bore, in fact, for there is not a soul here apart from myself, an elderly aunt and uncle and an even more elderly chaplain, and I have a great deal of business to occupy me just now. However, you are welcome to try out whatever you can find of interest in the stables, and the gamekeeper will take you out for some rough shooting or fishing, whatever you want."

"You do not mind me descending on you unannounced? We are family now, after all. We shall be brothers very soon."

"Exactly so. Stay as long as you wish. I shall be glad of the company," he said politely, although he felt that the company of such a one as Audlyn, a schoolboy of just sixteen, could afford him little pleasure. In a large gathering the boy would have found plenty to do, but how Ran alone could keep him occupied was more than he could say. Still, he supposed that Audlyn would quickly tire of the staid society that Valmont afforded just now and disappear as abruptly as he had arrived.

However, that first evening it was clear that Audlyn was exerting himself to be an affable guest. He happily led Aunt Anne into dinner, and made easy conversation with everyone, even exchanging some thoughts on the relative merits of Horace and Virgil with Mr Ponsonby, the chaplain. After Aunt Anne had withdrawn to doze in the Grand Saloon, Audlyn asked some pertinent questions about the Valmont holdings and their management, and seemed genuinely interested in the answers.

"Father never says much about *our* estates," he said ingenuously, "for he thinks me too young, but I think I should learn, do you not agree, Duke?"

"It is for your father to determine what he wishes you to know," Ran said, although he softened the difference of opinion with a smile. "My own father was very happy for me, as the second son, to learn to manage the estate, but he felt that his heir should learn more about politics and society and the ways of power. You may find that your own father has some such scheme in mind."

"He certainly allows Harold and Hilary more freedom," Audlyn said with a sudden flash of bitterness. "They are allowed to do as they please, whereas everything I do comes under Father's eye."

"It is inevitable that a peer should take a closer interest in his heir than in the younger sons," Ran said, amused. "There are disadvantages to both states, in my opinion. And advantages, too. Those splendid bays you drove here today, for instance — it is a rare father who does not loosen the purse-strings a little for his eldest."

Audlyn's face lit up. "They are prime bits of blood, are they not? Better than my blacks, I swear — such sweet goers! You are quite right, sir, and I do not mean to complain about my father, not in the least. He cuts up rough if I exceed my allowance too far, but he always pays up. He is very good!"

"*Very* good, if he buys you horses like that," Max said. "May I pass you the port, Lord Audlyn?"

No one lingered in the saloon after the tea things had been brought in, for the older residents were ready for their beds. Ran took Audlyn and Max to the grandly-titled Royal Withdrawing Room, which was in fact a modestly-proportioned book room, as ornately decorated as every other part of Valmont, but somewhat cosier.

"What would you care to do, Audlyn?" he said. "We are too few for whist, but there is vingt-et-un or piquet or loo or cribbage, if you wish, or hazard, if you prefer dice. I can take you on at backgammon, or Max will give you a decent game of chess, if you prefer those. Or we can exchange scurrilous tales of our respective families, if that would amuse you."

Audlyn laughed a little self-consciously. "I like piquet, but I am not sure I should play against *you*, Falconbury. You are a capital player, by all accounts, and I am a dreadful one."

"You are thinking of my brother, not me," Ran said quietly, a pang of grief assailing him. "Ger was a brilliant player, whereas I am an indifferent one. Shall we play piquet, then? Max and I tend to play for shillings, but—"

There was relief on his face. "Shillings would be perfect. So it was your brother against whom I was warned, then? *'Never play against the Litherholms or Marfords'*, I was told."

"Good advice," Max said, setting up a card table. "Lord Humphrey Marford, in particular, but all the Marfords are to be treated with respect at the card table. But as for Ger... he famously beat Lord Humphrey."

Audlyn's face was alive with interest. "Did he so! Once? Many times?"

"They only played against each other once," Ran said. "We were all up at Oxford together, although Humphrey Marford was a year ahead of us, and moved in a very different crowd. He played deep, and although he mostly won, he lost some huge sums as well. Ger never played like that. He was happy to play high, but it had to be coins on the table. He would never accept or offer vowels, and naturally a lot of the serious players objected to that."

"An insult!" Audlyn said. "For a fellow not to accept another player's notes of hand—"

"Exactly so, but we had some family history," Ran said. "A great uncle, the heir in fact, who lost twenty thousand at a sitting, and was so ashamed of it that he blew his brains out. When Ger heard of it, he swore he would never play so deep, or encourage anyone else to, either. So, Ger and Marford never met at the tables, but their reputations were such that there was great interest in seeing them set against each other in a fair match. So it was agreed that each would bring three thousand in coins — no linen — to the table, and they would play one night until one or other of them won everything, or the dawn came. Naturally, there was a great deal of money changed hands amongst the onlookers, for both had their supporters, you know."

"What happened?" Audlyn said, his eyes shining.

"They sat down at about ten or so, and the luck — or skill, perhaps — went pretty evenly through the night. Marford had almost five thousand in his hand at one time, but at another time Ger had almost as much, before it went the other way again. But then the dawn came, everything was still in balance, and Marford said, *'One final hand, winner takes all.'* Ger agreed to it, and he won. But it could have gone either way, they both knew that. There was next to nothing to choose between them." Ran paused, his throat tight as he recalled his brother. "Ger said it was the best night's play he had ever had. The two of them shook hands over it, and there was never any bad feeling between them after."

"But they never played each other again," Audlyn said.

"No, they never did."

~~~~~
~~~~~

For three days, Lord Audlyn gamely followed Ran around the estate, riding from choice the ill-tempered mount of Ger's that no one else but one of the most experienced grooms could now handle. For the first few hours Wanderer gave him some trouble, but then he seemed to cede mastery to Audlyn and became, if not exactly tractable, at least less likely to attempt to unseat him every five minutes. Ran himself preferred a stolid beast, steady rather than fast or showy, and with Max and Gurney similarly mounted, Audlyn spent half his day galloping ahead then waiting for them to catch up.

One of the places they visited was Merrington House, a small property on the outskirts of Andover, where Ran's sister Elizabeth lived with an assortment of maternal relatives. It was one of many properties owned by the Valmont estate for the benefit of such kin, the obligation of the duke towards the indigent members of his family. Sometimes he was obliged to fund even the clothes they wore and the meat they ate, but Elizabeth had money of her own from her mother, and their uncle, Swithin Roswell, had an income, too, so the household was not a drain on his purse.

While Gurney and Max inspected the property, and Audlyn made himself agreeable to the aunts and uncles, Elizabeth took Ran for a stroll round the garden. This took the form of a brisk walk through the shrubbery to a small pavilion, surrounded by tubs of sweet-scented hyacinths in their gaudy colours. She lit a brazier and opened a cupboard to reveal bottles of Canary and glasses.

"So you have a little hideaway, I see," Ran said, amused.

She poured two generous measures of Canary, and plumped herself down on the cushioned bench beside him. "Dear Ran, what would you have me do? I live with seven other people, the youngest near twice my age. I love them all, but I need somewhere to escape sometimes, too. But did you get my letter? I wrote two pages of congratulations, I was so excited! I am so happy for you, Ran, I hardly know how to say it!"

"But you *did* know how, as you demonstrated over two whole pages, and the second page crossed as well, sister, dear."

He smiled affectionately at his sister. Elizabeth was three and thirty, a softly rounded woman who viewed life with amused detachment. She had been described as handsome in her youth, and retained much of her bloom, aided as she was by a comfortable income and a liking for flattering clothes, which hid the plumpness resulting from a fondness for sweet things. After some near-misses in earlier years, she had decided that matrimony was not for her and had retired from society, apart from a month at Valmont every summer, but she was an indefatigable letter writer, with correspondents in every great family in England.

"Oh, you received it, then. But how was Mallowfleet? There was no one from the Litherholm side invited, so Georgy said. She thought *they* might have been, Henry being a baron, but I daresay they felt if they invited the Narfields, they would have to invite everyone. Still, it seems a trifle rude, since it was your betrothal ball."

"Strictly speaking, it was Ruth's birthday ball, so naturally only the Grenaby side of the family was invited. The betrothal was merely an afterthought."

"An afterthought? I imagined the duchess to have been planning it so for an age past, and you were rushed into it, by all accounts. Swept out of your carriage and into a betrothal. Was I misinformed about that?"

"How do you get your information, sister?" But he shook his head ruefully. "I would not put it in those terms, although there is some truth in it. Still, I went there with the sole purpose of offering for Ruth, you know. The manner of it was—" He stopped, for he had begun to say *'unimportant'*, but that was not quite true. He would have liked to take charge of the business himself, without question, and although he had tried not to resent the cavalier way the Orrisdales had bounced him into it, he *did* resent it just a little. He had wanted to be alone with Ruth... still wanted that, if he were honest with himself. Everything felt... unfinished, somehow. A kiss... just one kiss would have made everything so much better.

"There was always something a little off about the Grenabys," his sister said, with the serene assurance of one whose line originated a hundred years earlier than theirs. "The duchess is not exactly ill-bred, for she puts herself on almost too high a form, very often, but it sounded not quite proper, to me. Mary — my particular friend, Mary Bucknell, you know — said that everyone knew why you were there, and they had all been gathered together to await the announcement. That is not very correct, in my view. But still, it is done, and I am so glad. This last year has been so unspeakably horrid, and now we can put it behind us, and there will be a future to look forward to — a wedding, and then babies, and soon you will begin to be yourself again."

"Have I not been myself?"

"Not in the least, although only those of us who know you well would be aware of it. Last summer... you were so cast down in spirits, almost as bad as Ger in his dark moods, but now you will go on better. Was Mallowfleet dreadful? Camberley and Ramsey were there, I heard. And Crosby," she added, her gaze dropping to where her hands were pleating her skirt. "He is betrothed to the next sister, is he not? An odd pairing, for he is five and forty now and she is barely eighteen. Did you speak to him?"

"Not much. I hardly know him. He has buried himself in the depths of Surrey for years."

"What is the sister like? Is she a beauty, like Ruth?"

"Lady Susan? I do not believe so." Ran frowned, trying to recall her and finding little trace of her in his memory, except that she was not the equal of his Ruth. "Prettyish. The usual accomplishments. Not as accomplished as Ruth, but few are."

"Is she a lively girl? Amiable, charming? Affectionate?" She looked up suddenly, and Ran was shocked at the pain in her eyes. "Tell me honestly, Ran, is he in love with her?"

"Ah, Lizzie, are you still wearing the willow for him?"

She sighed gustily. "Not exactly. Do not imagine me to be fading into spinsterhood on *his* account, I beg you! If a man of independent means had wanted me, a gentleman with a little estate in the country and capable of conversing sensibly and giving me a decent game of backgammon, I should have been very happy to marry, I assure you. Someone steady, which Luke was not, in those days. I did not blame Papa for scotching the affair, for I was too young and silly, and Luke was shockingly ineligible. The younger son of a younger son, and at the time there were five or six people between him and the title. And then he married that idiotic Swayle woman — men are so stupid sometimes! Well, he had a rotten time of it, and even though it was his own fault he did not deserve to be treated that way. Positively *flaunting* her lovers in Paris! Dreadful woman! When she finally died three years ago, I *did* wonder if— But there, after so many years, and such a bad experience, it would not have surprised me if he had lost faith in womankind altogether. But then to turn about as soon as he has the title and offer for a girl still in the schoolroom, not even out! I do not scruple to tell you, Ran, that I was insulted by that. Not that I would necessarily have accepted him, because we have both changed, I am sure, and one cannot recover the past, however much one might like to," she added, chuckling. "Still, I should have liked him to offer, or at the least to have sought me out and determined whether we might suit, since we were once so convinced of it. What *is* he like now? Do they seem a well-matched couple?"

"Do you know, I cannot recall that I ever saw them together," Ran said. "Not once. How odd."

"Well! That is strange. I suppose it is the old story — he wants an heir and she wants a title. Then they deserve each other," she said crisply. "Enough of Luke Crosby. If he does not care enough even to wonder about me, I am sure I care nothing for him either. Tell me what brings you here in all this state, for normally we only see Gurney if there is a broken window, or a chimney pot comes down, and I cannot remember the last time *you* came, except when I was ill that bad winter."

"I am looking at all my properties, to be sure that I am making the best use of them, and making sure everyone is content where they are. *Are* you content, Lizzie? You never complain, but this is not what you were born to, squeezed in here like cattle in the barn, and you only left Valmont because you fell out with Father. You could come back now, if you wish it."

"And get under Ruth's feet? I think not! Can there be anything worse for a new wife than an older sister-in-law helpfully telling her the way things have always been done, and half the servants saying after every order, *'I shall just ask Lady Elizabeth, Your Grace'*. No, indeed."

"No, that would be awkward. I was thinking of one of the lodges. You could be independent there, but still dine with us whenever you want."

"Oh!" She clapped her hands with glee. "Oh, *yes!* The south-western lodge would suit me perfectly — it is within walking distance of the village. Or the south-eastern. Oh, *Ran*, do you truly mean it? My own establishment? I should not need one of the uncles or aunts with me, just a friend — like Mary Bucknell, who is every bit as spinsterish as I am, but without a groat to her name and is treated abominably by her relatives, you know, just like a servant, it is wicked! Oh, may I truly? You are so *good* to me, brother!"

7: A Small Dinner

Two days later, Elizabeth arrived at Valmont in a battered old coach, accompanied by a surprisingly young and pretty French maid, to inspect the southwestern lodge. She found it full of men with ladders, saws and hammers, with painters in the bedrooms, carpenters attending to the shutters and a whole troop on the roof.

"Goodness, what a hive of activity!" she murmured, lifting her skirts delicately to step around a pile of fresh wood in the hall.

"I have not attempted anything in the public rooms," Ran said. "You may do what you please there, and send the bills to Max, naturally, but the bedrooms were very shabby, and if you dislike what has been done you may rework them at your leisure and send me the bill."

"How many bedrooms are there?"

"Four. Now, here is your drawing room, with a parlour or book room beside it, and the dining room across the hall. Then this room might be a breakfast parlour... or whatever you wish, of course."

"So big! Are all the lodges this size?"

"Identical. They were designed for just such a situation, you know — grown children of the family or ageing aunts, to be independent yet under the shelter of the head of the family. There is a kitchen garden and a chicken run at the back, but you may be supplied from the house, of course."

"Old Percy Coachman was here before, was he not? I know he died, but his wife and daughter—?"

"Have removed to the pensioners' cottages in the village," he said firmly. "Valmont was designed on very rational principles, Lizzie. Attics for the indoor servants, rooms above the stables for the grooms, cottages beyond the forcing houses for the gardeners, chambers over the dairy for the poultry and dairy maid, a row in the village for retired servants, three houses by the woods for the gamekeepers and the lodges for family or guests."

"Or mistresses," she said, eyes twinkling.

He smiled. "True enough, although not for some time, happily. Over the years it has all got muddled up, with people settling here and there, as they wanted, and the lodges full of gardeners while the cottages stood empty. This past year, I have been repairing all the cottages and the grooms' quarters, and now I have begun work on the lodges. I have three ready, but not this one. However, it does not need a great deal of work."

"How organised you are! And are you going to bring everyone here? I am happy to move back home, and Aunt Hetty may be amenable too, but Uncle Swithin likes the Andover house. He has a set of whist-playing friends that he would be loath to leave."

"I shall not force anyone to move, you may be sure, but there is a great deal of waste in the present arrangements. For instance, there is Durran House, which has twelve bedrooms and a staff of above twenty, occupied solely by Aunt Charlotte and that little mouse of a companion of hers. They neither entertain nor even leave the house, so far as I can determine, and that estate could be leased out to someone who would at least enjoy the fishing there, for what is the point of grounds that stretch down to the river when no one ever casts a line there?"

"Hmm… are we in the basket, Ran? Retrenching? Because a little bird told me that Orrisdale was not very forthcoming over the dowry, and—"

"How the devil does this stuff get about? But no, we are not in the basket, sister dear, far from it. I have been in sole charge of the management of the Litherholm estates for almost five years, since Father became too ill to concern himself with business matters, and I can assure you we are considerably better off now than we were then, Ruth's dowry notwithstanding. I am not concerned about the expenses of Durran House, if that is what you are inferring. It merely distresses me to have such a prime property occupied by two elderly ladies who make no use of it. If there were a family settled there, I should be perfectly content." He paused, frowning. "What happened to that old governess of yours?"

"Miss Draper? She went back to Romsey, I believe, to her sister's house. She must be eighty if she is a day, Ran. You will want someone younger for your own children."

He laughed and shook his head. "I wondered if she needed any help, that is all. Money, or a cottage here. With her sister, if she wishes. Will you write and ask her? And Hollingsworth, our last tutor. He was from somewhere near Birmingham. I will see if he needs anything, for his annuity is very small."

Elizabeth smiled at him. "What an excellent duke you are turning out to be, brother."

"I should like to be, one day. All these years I have been no more than a steward, continuing the rather haphazard policies Father began and all the time waiting — for Ger to take over and give me new policies. But now, I need wait no longer. I can do as I wish, and implement my own policies, more modern ideas, but systematically, rationally. Valmont is my responsibility now, and I like the feeling very well."

~~~~~

Before Audlyn and Elizabeth left Valmont, Ran arranged a small dinner for some of the local families. They sat down twenty four at table, which was a comfortable number for the smaller dining room, known as the Buttery. Ran took care to ensure there were three full courses, for his careful management of Valmont did not run to any economy towards guests.

With the exception of Audlyn, all those present knew each other well. The Lorrimers, the local squire, a baronet, the physician and some minor gentry made up the numbers, and amongst them was not the least ill-feeling towards Ran for not marrying the daughter of one or other of them, as might have been supposed. When the modest estate of a gentleman with a thousand or two a year abuts the vast holdings of a ducal estate like Valmont, the local residents tend to be grateful for any notice — some shooting in season, perhaps, and the occasional evening engagement, nothing more. Although they would have been glad indeed if the duke's eye had fallen on one of their daughters,
~~~~~

there were no expectations. Nobility must marry nobility, for that was the way of the world.

So there was genuine rejoicing at the news of Ran's betrothal, and a great curiosity to meet the brother of the future duchess.

"He will be a heart-breaker when he is a little older," Alice Lorrimer whispered to Ran, as they gathered in the Gold Saloon before dinner. "Very handsome. He will cause havoc amongst the ambitious mamas of the season. Or is he spoken for already, as Ger was?"

"Very likely. Orrisdale is most efficient in that way."

"Poor boy!"

"Because his father chooses a suitable bride for him?" Ran said, amused.

"Indeed! I feel myself very fortunate to have a completely free choice where to marry — or not to marry at all, if I please. I am very happy to keep house for my brothers. How lowering to be forced to marry someone who may not be compatible in the least, however suitable."

"No one can be *forced* to marry, you know. It is against the law."

She raised her eyebrows in disbelief. "Not forced at the point of a sword, perhaps, but there may be any amount of subtle pressure brought to bear — expectation, obligation, money. We are all of us raised to obey parental dictates, Ran, and matrimony is not excluded from that consideration, even, or one might say *especially,* amongst those of rank."

"You do not suppose that *I* was pressured, for—"

"No, no!"

"—I am very happy with my choice, I assure you."

"Doubtless, my friend, but what of Lady Ruth? She may feel obliged—"

Ran had no idea how to answer the point, for he could not in his heart be at all sure of Ruth's sentiments. He did not think she was being forced into marrying him, exactly, but he was not the man she would have chosen, that he knew. If Ger had not died, she would have gone gladly to the altar with him. Ran was very much her second choice, the expected choice. The suitable choice.

Fortunately, he was not required to formulate an answer, for the squire and his wife arrived just then, and Ran was drawn away to greet them, and smile politely as they congratulated him on his betrothal.

As the evening rolled on, Ran could not help thinking of Ger. He would have enjoyed the occasion, he knew, for he was amongst friends. There was nothing he had liked better than to spend an evening with a group of people who knew each other intimately. There was no pretence, he had always said, no need to stand on ceremony, no stupid formality. All was ease and pleasure.

In town, he had been nervous amongst such large crowds. *'They stare so, and only care about the title,'* he had said gloomily. *'I wish I were plain Mr Smith. An attorney, say, or… or a vintner, or some such. Or the proprietor of a gaming hell. I should do well at that, should I not?'* And Ran had reminded him that since he never accepted notes of hand, such a venture would be unlikely to thrive. But Father had insisted they both acquire some town bronze, so they had paraded themselves at Almack's and Carlton House and all the fashionable squeezes, and Ger had hated it more each year. As often as not, if there was an instrument to be found tucked away in a corner, there he would be hiding — anything to avoid dancing, or making insipid conversation. Poor Ger!

But this was just the sort of entertainment that had brought out the best in him, and Ran found it took all his powers of civility to play the host and move easily amongst his guests, when his mind's eye could see Ger lounging against the mantel with his mischievous grin, or engaged in a spirited debate with the squire about some horse or other, or sitting at the card table, an expression of amused benevolence on his face as the coins piled up in front of him.

It was foolish, he knew. Ger had left England four years ago, and had been lying in the mausoleum for a year. The initial shock had become disbelief, and that had gradually become grief, settling into a dull but steady ache that never left him. One day, perhaps, he would be free of it. But not yet.

~~~~~

APRIL

Mr Willerton-Forbes wrote that he had gathered together a number of references to Ger's time in America and his last days for Ran's perusal, and should His Grace wish to see them at once, or when he was up in town? Ran still had much to do at Valmont now that he had begun ordering matters in his own way, so he set a date for the lawyer to visit Valmont. He hoped, in that way, to set the final niggling concerns about Ger's death to rest before he travelled up to London to claim both his title and his bride.
~~~~~

He bethought him to reread Ger's letters, neatly collected in a box the estate carpenter had made for the purpose, the lid engraved *'Gervase in America'.* Ger had been an erratic correspondent, some letters being several sheets closely inscribed, and others, perhaps many weeks later, saying only *'Arrived in Boston. Hotel very bad.'* Ran took the box to the Long Gallery, and settled down on a sofa positioned directly opposite the portrait of the twins. It was the place he had gone to very often after Ger had gone to America, when their father was in his final decline and Ran had felt so alone. He never actually spoke out loud to Ger's image, as he did in the mausoleum, for one never knew when a footman might creep about and overhear one addressing a painting, and how peculiar that would look! But he had sat on the sofa and gazed at his brother's smiling countenance and remembered him in his high good humours.

Opening the box, he took out the first batch of letters and untied the ribbon that bound them. The earliest ones were all of the excitement of the adventure — the ship and the rough seas, and how exhilarating it was to be on deck at such times! And then landing in New York and the first taste of American society. But after two or three months, the tone had changed and excitement had given way to the familiar ennui. American hostesses, it appeared, were just as keen to entertain the Marquess of Beckhampton as English ones had been, and he had been fawned over and petted and grovelled to in much the same way. *'Thank God for Ruth,'* he had written, *'for at least I may truthfully say I am spoken for, and need not fear to raise expectations in their hopeful daughters.'*

But after a few months, there was a change of tone, as if he were somehow happier, or more settled. The grumbles ceased, and his reports of social events were more reasonably worded. He made no further complaint of the *'monstrous toad-eating'* he had encountered initially. Perhaps it was because his starchy valet had fallen ill and had to be left behind in New York, or perhaps it was that he had fallen in with a band of travelling actors, who treated him with a refreshing lack of deference, but he seemed to be enjoying himself, finally.

That lasted until word of Father's death reached him, several weeks after the event, the black-edged letter chasing him from town to town. *'Oh God, Ran, I am the duke now! How shall I bear it?'* he had written despairingly. Then there had been the sombre business of arranging passage back to England, and the long gap between letters as his ship traversed the Atlantic Ocean. And then nothing but brief announcements of his arrival in Ireland, his intention of travelling to Dublin to catch the Howth to Holyhead packet, and then one, final letter.

'Brother, A slight change to my plans, for there is a ship due in Dublin on Monday, the Brig Minerva, *which will bring me to Southampton, all being well, on Saturday. Is that not convenient? You will be able to meet me, and I shall be able to avoid the Holyhead road. Best of all, I shall have a surprise for you. I am very well entertained by Kilrannan and his three daughters until then. One of them even plays the harp tolerably. Gervase.'*

He would never now know what the surprise was.

~~~~~

Mr Willerton-Forbes and his companions, Captain Edgerton and Mr Neate, arrived promptly on the appointed day. Max had gone off to wrangle with the workmen at Elizabeth's lodge, so Ran saw the three alone. They brought several notebooks, the relevant
~~~~~

pages marked with neat strips of paper, wherein they had recorded the testimony of the numerous people they had interviewed in their endeavours.

The most interesting, in being the most descriptive, were those of the Earl of Kilrannan and his family and various guests. The earl occupied a mansion in Dublin and was most hospitable towards anyone of noble birth or wealth who passed through his town on the way to or from the English ports. There were several passages describing Ger, waxing lyrical about his style, his manners, his appearance and his open-handed nature, as would be expected of anyone of such rank. The observers were diplomatic about his faults, and Ran laughed at the circumspect way they spoke of *'His Grace's unequalled enthusiasm in the dance, which gave great pleasure to those privileged to watch it.'*

"Indeed, Ger was never the most elegant of dancers, for he paid no attention to the dancing masters Father employed, and hated balls so much that he never improved. But what does this mean? *'The duke also frequently graced the card tables, where his good humour, even under the worst runs of luck, won him many admirers."*

"It means that he lost large sums and made no fuss about it," Mr Neate said, with a smile.

"Lost large sums? He was an excellent card player."

"It is a courtesy in a wealthy guest to obligingly lose to the host's family," Mr Neate said.

"Hmm. That is possible, I suppose. Perhaps Ger had learnt the art of diplomacy at last."

"There was no mention in any of our original records of the ring His Grace wore," Mr Willerton-Forbes said. "I took the liberty of writing directly to Lord Kilrannan on the matter, and he confirms that it was worn on the little finger the whole time His Grace was at Kilrannan House, so you may set your mind at ease on that score, Your Grace. Nothing untoward happened with the ring during the voyage of the *Brig Minerva* or afterwards. Your Grace? You are still concerned on the matter?"

"The ring... I cannot say on that point, but it troubles me that he always lost at play. *'...the worst runs of luck...'*. Ger never had that kind of ill-luck. He played only games of skill, and he usually won. Furthermore, I have seen no mention of his playing of the pianoforte. He was a most accomplished player, yet no one ever mentions it, even in this lengthy description of a musical evening. He would certainly have performed on such an occasion."

For a long moment, all four men were sunk in thought. It was Mr Willerton-Forbes who broke the silence.

"If — and it is a most implausible notion, if I may say so but *if* this person was not, in fact, your brother, it raises a great many questions. Who was he, and why was he impersonating your brother, and, perhaps more to the point, where was your brother? Did he perhaps stay in America?"

"Impossible, for he wrote to me from Ireland, from Dublin, even, using the Beckhampton seal. He was *there* and he intended to take the *Brig Minerva*, so even if that person who wore his ring was not Ger, he was still on the ship and still drowned and it makes no difference. It is just... so strange."

"There is a way in which the matter might be set to rest," Willerton-Forbes said, steepling his hands. "If you have a painting or drawing of your brother, it could be sent to Lord Kilrannan to confirm once and for all whether the man claiming to be the Duke of Falconbury was your brother or not."

"Oh yes! A portrait! There is one, although it is full-size, and too big to be sent without difficulty."

"Mr Neate is a tolerable artist. He could take a likeness, I daresay."

"Let me show you, and then I shall find paper and pencils," Ran said eagerly.

He led them through corridors and up the back stairs to the Long Gallery, where the portrait of the two brothers stood. Captain Edgerton was distracted by a line of sabres mounted on the wall, but Willerton-Forbes and Neate drew near to the painting.

"Ah, an excellent likeness of you, Your Grace, and this must be—" Willerton-Forbes gave a strangled noise in his throat. "Michael! *Michael!*"

Captain Edgerton abandoned the sabres and wandered over. "What is it, Pettigrew? Oh, a fine piece of— *Good God!*"

"You know him?" Ran said, puzzled. Then, his voice suddenly hoarse, "You have *seen* him? *He is alive!*"

Willerton-Forbes only nodded, the power of speech having failed him, but Captain Edgerton said softly, "Oh yes. He is alive and living in Cornwall under the name of Jonathan Ellsworthy."

8: Trehannick Inn

"Are you quite certain?" Ran said. His voice sounded far away, as if under water. "There can be no mistake?"

"None," Captain Edgerton said. "Willerton-Forbes and I have met him three times now, and concluded from very good evidence that he was Nigel Pike from Carlisle. But although he calls himself Jonathan Ellsworthy, he is beyond doubt the man in that painting."

Joy bubbled up inside Ran. Ger was alive! He was not alone after all! "It is a miracle — the most wonderful news! You cannot imagine— But how? And *why?*"

Willerton-Forbes made some inarticulate noise in his throat, then, "Astonishing… I congratulate you, Your Grace."

Ran laughed. "I am not Your Grace any longer."

"Possibly," Edgerton said. "Best to say nothing until we have more information. Pettigrew, you are very pale."

"Such a shock!" Willerton-Forbes said. "How could we not have guessed? How could we be so wrong, Michael?"

"You are right, he is very pale," Ran said. "Do come downstairs, sir. Let me get you a brandy."

He took them to the Royal Withdrawing Room, brushing aside the curious butler and two footmen loitering in the hall. "Mr Willerton-Forbes felt a trifle faint. No, thank you, we shall not need you, Brent. A little brandy and a rest will do the trick."

"I believe Mr Vine is here to talk to you about the woodcock, Your Grace."

It was on the tip of Ran's tongue to blurt out that he was no longer a duke, that the real duke was alive and well, but he caught Edgerton's eye. "Please inform him that I shall not be able to see him today after all. I shall send word when I next have an opportunity. If Mr Lorrimer returns, pray tell him that I shall not need him for the rest of the day. The other secretaries, too."

"Very good, Your Grace. Shall I send for Mr Preston, Your Grace?"

"No, no. Mr Willerton-Forbes will be better directly. He does not need a physician."

The butler bowed with punctilious formality, rather put out to be summarily dismissed when there was clearly a crisis in the air, but Ran ushered his guests into the room and firmly shut the door.

"Edgerton, would you be so good as to light the fire? There, sir, sit down here and I shall find the brandy."

He poured three large measures, and was relieved to see that after a few sips, a little colour returned to Willerton-Forbes' face.

"Pray forgive my feebleness," he said, smiling wanly. "I cannot remember when I have sustained a greater shock, but one does greatly dislike being so sadly misled."

"I do not wonder at it, for my brother always had a great ability to play a part," Ran said, laughing. "He could have made a career on the stage, without a doubt. Lord, I can hardly believe this! Ger alive... but it is more than a year now. Why has he not contacted me?"

"It is possible," Willerton-Forbes said gently, "that he suffered some injury during the sinking that has caused him to forget his true identity. He was quite badly injured, I understand, and was unconscious for some time."

"Ah, yes. That is possible. How awkward *that* would be!" Ran said.

"Indeed. But... ah, such excellent brandy, thank you, my lord! I feel a great deal better already. But there is also the possibility that he simply prefers to be Mr Ellsworthy, a humble clerk. You said, I think, that he found his high rank a burden to him."

"Yes," Ran said, frowning. "I suppose... if he woke up one day, and everyone believed him to be Ellsworthy and the duke was dead — and I identified him, after all! — then he might choose to stay as Ellsworthy."

"And he might not wish to take up the mantle of high office again," the lawyer said quietly. "I believe you should prepare yourself for that, too, my lord."

"But either way — whether he has forgotten who he is, or is choosing to hide — it is all very awkward," Ran said. Some of his excitement began to drain away as he considered the difficulties.

"There is another, somewhat worse, possibility which we must consider," Edgerton said, moving away from the now-blazing fire. "You told us once, my lord, that your brother found the burden of his rank weighed so heavily on him that he considered ways to pretend to die in order to evade it. Is it conceivable that he intentionally ran the ship aground?"

"No!" cried Ran. "Ger would never do that! Just consider — if it were so, he must have driven the ship onto the rocks himself, and killed almost everyone aboard, in order to do so. It *must* have been an accident!"

"It would have been a great risk, and difficult to accomplish," Edgerton said thoughtfully. "He would have had to be on deck himself, then somehow taken control of the ship and steered it towards the shore. And then could he be sure that he would himself survive? He would have to jump overboard, avoiding the rocks, and swim a mile, perhaps two, in the dark in freezing water. Was your brother a good swimmer, my lord?"

"He was," Ran said, sitting down abruptly as his legs gave way. "But... I cannot believe such a thing of him! And he was injured... a broken leg, was it not? And unconscious. If he had walked out of the sea—"

"An excellent point," Willerton-Forbes said. "What do the notes say of his rescue, Michael?"

"Let me see... ah, here we are. He was washed up on the beach unmoving. One of the locals spotted his body and he was dragged from the water, half dead. In fact, he was thought to *be* dead. The Second Mate was fished out of the bay by a fellow in a boat, and the deck boy floated ashore on wreckage, more or less unscathed. I agree it seems implausible, but we should not discount any possibility until we have spoken to His Grace ourselves."

Ran jumped up at once. "I must go to him… find him…"

"And if he does not wish to be found, my lord?" Willerton-Forbes said gently. "What then?"

That brought Ran to an abrupt halt. "If that is so, then he must be left alone. He must do what makes him *happy*, for, God knows, he was never happy with the prospect of becoming a duke. If he has found a place for himself in the world where he can be completely content, then he may stay there for his whole life with my goodwill, and I will be the Duke of Falconbury in his stead."

"And how precisely would that work?" Willerton-Forbes said, his voice as soft as butter. "How can you be the Duke of Falconbury and take your seat in the Lords and marry and raise children, all the while knowing that the real duke is alive and well in Cornwall? Knowing that the deception could be uncovered at any moment and the inheritance, the title, *everything*, would be thrown into confusion?"

"I have no idea," Ran said bleakly. "I only know that it must be attempted, if that is what Ger needs to be happy."

~~~~~

Mr Willerton-Forbes arranged everything. Ger was living at the small fishing village of Pendower in Cornwall, but Ran could hardly turn up on the doorstep, unannounced, and give his
~~~~~

brother the shock of his life. Besides, if Ger intended to live out his life incognito, Ran could not go into Pendower at all, for he would be recognised. He had spent some time in the neighbourhood after the sinking of the *Brig Minerva* and during the inquests, so his face and identity were well known. There would have to be great secrecy in the meeting, to leave Ger the freedom to remain as Jonathan Ellsworthy, if he so wished.

The lawyer and his companions posted down to Cornwall, and found a busy coaching inn at the village of Trehannick about ten miles inland. It was away from the main London to Penzance route, where Ran might conceivably encounter acquaintances making their way up to London for the season, but the focus of enough well-used routes that a few extra travellers would occasion no comment. The story they had devised was that they were looking into the possibility of purchasing tin mines for a client. Willerton-Forbes and Captain Edgerton were so flamboyantly dressed that they would never be able to pass unnoticed anywhere, so they used their real names, but Ran was to be plain Mr Salterwood, a name taken from one of the family's minor titles. He could only hope that he was far enough from Pendower that no one would recognise him.

Willerton-Forbes sent a letter privately to Ran to inform him of the arrangements. This was not as easy to manage as might be supposed, for Ran had a veritable army of under-secretaries, whose job it was to open all his correspondence. Even a missive clearly marked *'Personal and Private'* might be opened by mistake, and that could not be risked. If a suspicion got out that Ran was not, in fact, the rightful duke, there would be no possibility of Ger hiding away. So a letter was sent to Peter Lorrimer, with the letter to Ran hidden inside.

When word came that all was ready, Ran ignored the shocked faces of his valet, coachman and grooms when he told them firmly that they were not needed, and took a post-chaise and four to Truro, with only a small portmanteau as luggage. From there, he hired a horse and rode on to Trehannick. He wore his oldest and plainest clothes, and although there was no hiding the quality of them, he was fairly certain that no one would immediately assume him to be of high rank.

The inn was noisy and crowded, but Willerton-Forbes had secured all the best bedchambers and a substantial private parlour. Nor was the dinner in any way lacking . It would not have pleased the most fastidious, but Ran was not of that ilk, and was besides in no mood to notice what he ate. Now that the moment of truth was upon him, he found his nerves to be lamentably shredded.

"I have written to Ellsworthy — to your brother," Willerton-Forbes said, "and he will attend us here tomorrow at noon. Here is his note of reply. You may verify that it is your brother's hand."

"It is," Ran said, his stomach churning painfully. It was true, then! There was not the smallest chance of error. Ger was alive and living in this remote part of the country under a false name. But *why?*

The evening passed with intolerable slowness. Neate was down in the tap room, mingling in his unobtrusive way with locals, but Willerton-Forbes and Edgerton stayed in the parlour with Ran after the table was cleared. Ran was minded neither for cards nor for reading, and after a while, guessing that his thoughts could not be drawn away from Ger, Edgerton said, "I am curious as to why your brother went to America in the first place.

It seems an odd turn for him. Do not most men go there to make their fortune?"

"Or to escape the law," Willerton-Forbes said.

Ran smiled. "It was neither of those, obviously. He had always wanted to visit, for he had some idea that his title would be of no account there. They talked so much, the Americans, of all men being equal, and such an idea was bound to appeal to Ger. He had met obsequiousness every day of his life, but the prospect of an entire country without it enchanted him. Of course, when he arrived, he found it was not at all like that and the Americans were as fascinated by his rank as anyone else. *'The world is nothing but disappointment,'* he said in one letter."

Ran sighed and fell silent, and the others respectfully forbore to press him. No doubt they understood the momentous precipice upon which he stood. What would tomorrow bring? A happy reunion, or anger and a breach? Or would Ger even recognise him? Unnerving thought. But perhaps it would help to talk about Ger, so after a while he spoke again.

"Ger and I were four and twenty, and Ruth —" Ruth! Oh God, what about Ruth? But there was no point in considering that yet until he knew Ger's mind. With an effort, he went on, "Lady Ruth Grenaby, whom Ger was expected to marry, was seventeen. She was about to be launched on society, and the marriage was finally resolved upon. They were not formally betrothed, but there was an understanding between them, and both families were happy with it. It was Ruth who hesitated. She felt too young, too unfamiliar with the world, she said. She would like to wait a year or two, to have some time in society and to gain a little experience of life before she was thrust into marriage and the running of Valmont.

"Father was very ill at that time, and not expected to survive for more than a year or two at most. He had already given me the authority to manage the estates in his stead, as I had been doing unofficially for some years, but now I had the legal power, too. He wanted… I think all he wanted was to be left in peace to die. And Ger was restless. He was often so, but the more Father declined, the more Ger fretted. He said that he felt the bars of the cage closing around him, and once he assumed his honours, he would never escape. So it was agreed that he should go to America, and get the fidgets out of him.

"Ger was only supposed to be away for a year or so, but Father lingered and there was no need to recall the heir, so there he stayed, seemingly enjoying himself, keeping himself busy. He was supposed to look at farms and land management and such like, but all he ever wrote about was social engagements. Balls, picnics, the theatre, card parties — a lot of card parties! I suspect he was financing himself with his winnings, for he never asked for more money. He moved around, but not as much as I would have expected. He seemed happy enough, until Father died and he had to return. That brought on the gloom again. I do believe, when I consider the matter, that if he had found himself unexpectedly living under a different name and his true self believed dead, he might well have imagined that Providence had blessed him, and stay silent."

"And if that is so, are you still minded to let him do so?" Willerton-Forbes said, quietly.

"Of course," Ran said. "I would not be so selfish as to drag him back against his will to a world where he was never comfortable. But the choice must be his."

Willerton-Forbes made no attempt to reiterate all the objections to such a scheme, but then he did not need to. Ran was all too aware of the impossible position in which he would be placed. He could never marry Ruth under such a deception. It was unthinkable.

~~~~~

Ran slept fitfully that night, and rose, unrefreshed, with the dawn. Then he had to wait until the boy brought up some barely tepid water for him to wash and shave before dressing. For a man who had had the expert services of a valet since he was ten years old, having to dress himself was more challenging than he might have supposed. Shaving and tying his cravat were matters he reserved to himself, but everything else would be handed to him at precisely the right moment, perfectly pressed, starched or polished. On his way down to Truro he had stayed at salubrious post houses where he was offered a man to help him, but here the inn was in a constant bustle and there was no one to spare. It was not until Neate knocked on the door and enquired if any assistance was required, for he had had some experience as a gentleman's gentleman, that he got on a little better, although most of his garments were sadly rumpled.

Then there was the wait until breakfast appeared. Captain Edgerton, quite unruffled, sat calmly reading a local newspaper, but Ran could only pace about, back and forth, like a beast in its cage at the menagerie. Willerton-Forbes, also assisted by Neate, was the last to appear, just as the dishes were being set out on the table. Neate again ate in the tap room, but Willerton-Forbes and Edgerton ate their way through everything provided for them, while Ran could manage no more than a slice of cold beef, and crumble bread in a fretful anxiety.
~~~~~

The morning hours crept by, and eleven o'clock was reached, and then the half hour. At about ten minutes to the hour, Neate poked his head round the door.

"Just arriving in the yard now."

"I will go down to meet him and bring him up here," Willerton-Forbes said.

Ran's heart was thundering. He took a deep breath, and then another.

"Courage!" Captain Edgerton said with a smile. "He is your brother, after all."

Ran smiled too, half-heartedly. Indeed, it must be Ger, everything proclaimed it, but would he be the Ger who had sailed away to America? Would he be angry with Ran for finding him? Would he even recognise him?

He was terrified.

There were steps on the stair, the sound of Willerton-Forbes' voice outside. "Pray go in before me, sir." The door was flung open.

And there he was. He had a slight limp, but otherwise he was Ger to the life, looking not a day older, gazing without interest around the parlour. Just an ordinary parlour at an ordinary inn.

Ran waited in dread.

Ger saw him. His lips parted in sudden shock. For an instant, they were both motionless, staring at each other. Then Ger's face broke into a huge grin.

"*Ran!*" he shrieked. "Good God, Ran, it *is* you! Oh, Ran!"

He hurled himself across the room and wrapped Ran in a tight embrace.

"I cannot tell you how glad I am to see you!" Ger whispered. "I have dreamt of this moment..."

Ran hugged him, and laughed, and then hugged him again. "You old rascal, Ger!"

Ger's smile faltered. "Oh brother, I have missed you so, so much. What an idiot I have been."

9: Questions Of Marriage

Ran discovered that the parlour was empty save for Ger and himself. The others had diplomatically withdrawn, once it was clear that the reunion was harmonious. With shaking hands, Ran poured the indifferent wine which was all the inn afforded, and the brothers sat down at one end of the table. Ran knew himself to be grinning inanely, but he was incapable of a more sober expression, and when he looked at Ger he saw the same exhilaration reflected there.

But he had to be serious for a while. "Ger, I want you to know that you need not return to Valmont if you dislike the idea, or do anything you do not want. If you are happy here, then I will not drag you away. No one knows of this except for Willerton-Forbes and his two colleagues. No one at Valmont knows, so if you want to—"

"No, no, no," Ger said, shaking his head emphatically. "I had already decided I have to return. The secrecy... pretending all the time... it eats at me inside. It was one thing to pretend to be nobody for a lark, but this—! I feel so guilty, and it was becoming dangerous. Cornwall is not the uncharted backwater you might suppose, brother, and I am not moving at such a low level of society as to avoid all possibility of meeting an acquaintance. My employer, Mr Pickering, even wishes me to go with him to London... London! Can you imagine? It would only take one person who knows me to expose everything. I cannot live my life in constant terror of recognition, and imagine if I am discovered in five or ten or twenty years' time — there would be the devil to pay. When I read in the London newspapers just two weeks since that you were to take your seat soon — Ran, I had assumed it done long since, but when I saw that, I knew I had to emerge from hiding, and at once. There is a letter on its way to you even now."

Ran exhaled slowly, as relief washed through him. Thank God! He would not have to pretend to be the duke after all. But there were still questions to be answered. "That is all very well, Ger, but who the deuce is lying in the family mausoleum?"

"His name is Joseph Meadows. Joe, I called him. An actor. I met him on the way to Boston, and he was so interested in all that I was doing, but not encroaching in the least. He wanted to see what Boston society was like, so when I got an invitation, I took him with me. Well, he has far more presence than I have, so when we were announced, everyone assumed *he* was the Marquess of Beckhampton! It was so funny, Ran, you would have laughed so much! But I could go and hide in a corner, you see, just as I always wished I could do, and Joe just loved the attention, so we agreed that he would be me, and I would be him. He changed his hair, he wore some of my London clothes that I never bothered with, and eventually I let him wear my signet ring and fob."

"He wore the ring on the wrong finger," Ran said.

"Ah… yes, his hands were different, but the hair… that was just like mine, do you not think? And when I told him about that stupid birthmark of mine, and showed him what it looked like, he went out and got it inked onto his head just the same, the way some sailors do. He insisted that if he were to be me, even temporarily, the thing must be done properly. I imagine that was why you thought he was me. That was hard to believe, and… well, I was so ill, just at first, that there was no strength in me to care what was happening. I was alive, and that was all that seemed to matter. I had been identified by the Second Mate as Jonathan Ellsworthy, so no suspicions were aroused, and I simply lay in bed and gradually mended. Joe's body was found, wearing my clothes — the ring and fob and my pocket watch, engraved with my name — but I assumed that you would take one look at him and deny him. I had planned, you know, to have him stay as me all the way to Southampton and give you a terrible shock when he stepped off the ship, everyone fawning around him, and then I would pop up and say, *'Surprise!'* It would have been such a good joke. Did I not write to tell you I had a surprise for you? But for you to identify his body as me — it must have been that wretched mark."

"It was. His face had been damaged, poor fellow, so although the clothes and the hair and so on were right, it was that birthmark that sealed it. And… and perhaps I did not look too hard. It is not an easy thing, I find, to gaze upon the dead form of a brother."

Ger reached across to clasp his hand. "Forgive me! Ran… are you angry with me?"

"Angry? Good God, no! I am only glad that you are alive, brother. It never felt right, taking your place. Believe me, I shall be heartily glad to relinquish it."

"You do not blame me? For not telling you I was alive? For a whole year you thought I was dead."

"And what would I have done if I had known? It would have put me in an impossible position. I could not have claimed your seat in the Lords, could never have married… no, if you chose to stay hidden, you could not have told me."

Ger swirled the wine in his glass, gazing down into it with sudden intensity. "You are betrothed to Ruth… that was in the Gazette, too."

Ran stilled, aware of the sudden tension crackling in the room, like a bolt of lightning. Ah yes, Ruth…

He took a sip of wine to steady himself. "I imagine Orrisdale will cut up rough about that, once you reappear. He wants her to be a duchess."

"What does she want for herself?" Ger said, his voice not quite level, still not looking at him.

"She has always had a fondness for you," Ran said. He tried to speak lightly, but his voice sounded oddly distant to his ears. "I imagine she will be glad to have you back."

"The trouble is… there is a complication." Ger rubbed his nose thoughtfully. "I have met someone, Ran."

"Oh." That was hopeful. If he no longer wished to marry Ruth…

"Her name is Ginny Chandry, and she is a wonderful person, Ran, just amazing." He looked up then, his face lit up with enthusiasm. "She is not a great beauty, and she has *no* accomplishments, but she is so good and sensible. I am calm when she is with me, not bouncing all over the place and not driven into despair. Ginny makes me feel as if *I* am a good person too, as if I am useful and worthy and life is worth living after all. She is the love of my life, brother, and I find it impossible to exist without her."

"I cannot wait to meet her!"

He laughed merrily. "You have already met her. She came to talk to you — about me, actually. Since I could not go myself, she attended a meeting at the Pendower Inn to report on what I remembered about the shipwreck."

Ran dredged through his memories, but could not remember a Ginny Chandry. "Hmm. There were a lot of people who came to talk to us, and I was... not myself. Everything was confused in my mind. I shall recognise her when I see her, no doubt, and if you love her, then she already has my regard, brother."

"I am sure you will like her. And..." He lowered his head shyly. "...there is a child coming... in the autumn."

"Then you are married!"

"No." A shadow crossed his face. "Not married."

"But you must marry at once, Ger. Or before the child is born, at least. What if it is a son — an *heir?* You *must* marry. Unless... Ger, is she dreadfully ineligible?"

"Well, *I* do not think so! I should never fall in love with a dairymaid, or anything of the sort. The Chandrys are perfectly respectable."

"Respectable?" That sounded suspiciously like lower gentry. Not at all suited to the peerage.

"They own half of Pendower, actually, and in Ginny's grandfather's day they were very well-to-do, but her father was something of a rogue. He scattered his affections liberally into every family in the district, and then when the inevitable by-blow happened, he let the family off paying their rents. Ginny and I have spent the past year trying to get the finances back into some sort of shape. So she is from a gentleman's family, but that is not it, Ran. The trouble is that she despises the nobility, root and branch, and when she finds out that I am a *duke*, I doubt she would even want to marry me."

Ran frowned over that. "So what will you do with her? Settle some money on her and leave her here, or—?"

"*No!* I promised her I would keep her with me, wherever I go, so she will come to Valmont with me. But after that... well, who knows, but first I must tell her all this. Lord, it will be a dreadful shock to her — that her humble clerk is actually a duke."

"Do you think... will she leave your protection?" Ran said, hesitantly. "After all, if she is so set against the nobility, she might want nothing more to do with you."

Ger drummed his fingers restlessly on the table. "I should not imagine so, but..." His voice tailed away, and the anxious look on his face reminded Ran of the times they had been summoned as boys to meet some great lord or other that their father was entertaining. Ran wanted to hug Ger and tell him, as he had so many times before, that it would be all right, everything would be fine, they would brush through it together.

Instead he said, "Do you want me to come back to Pendower with you today?"

He pondered that, frowning. "What do you think?"

"Better to bring her here. I might be recognised in Pendower, and that will raise all sorts of questions. You know how rumour flies about, and no one else must find out the truth before she does, because you might change your mind about returning to Valmont once you have talked to her."

"No," Ger said, his face sombre. "I have to do my duty, Ran, as you have always done. I thought for a while that I could evade it, but I cannot. I am my father's eldest son, if only by twenty minutes, and therefore I am the Duke of Falconbury now, whether I like it or not. Ginny will either accept that and come with me, or... or she will not," he ended bleakly.

"I hope, for your sake, that she will, but she has to be the first to know, and it needs to be done privately, Ger. Too late today, I daresay, but bring her here tomorrow. Then we can talk about this and see what is best to be done."

~~~~~

Willerton-Forbes and the captain forbore to question Ran, but over dinner that day, he told them everything. Concealment would be wrong, for the lawyer and his companions were responsible for the glorious discovery that Ger was still alive, and Ran must be forever grateful to them for that. Even if Ger had chosen to remain incognito, he would have known that his brother was still in the world and that would have been enough.
~~~~~

It might even have been simpler if he had done so. Now there were complications. Ruth was one such, and there was this Ginny Chandry for another.

So he concealed nothing from the lawyer and his friends. Surprisingly, it was Neate who had most to say.

"While we were waiting for you to arrive, my lord, I took the liberty of wandering over to Pendower, and putting up at the White Horse inn for a couple of nights. Your brother the duke is well established in the village, and no one in the least suspicious. Said to be quiet, keeps himself to himself, but good with money and happy to help out when needed. He acts as secretary to a ship owner. The Chandry family…" He laughed, and tugged his ear, pulling a rueful face. "Bit wild! The father died a couple of years back, having married three times. The first wife was from the local landowner's family. One son, who married one of the Thorneywell girls, Earl of Furneish's line. Miss Chandry is from the second wife. She has a brother who's a bit of a rogue like his father, although no harm in him. Then three younger children from the third marriage. Eldest girl married to the landowner's son. Step-mother married the landowner — Lord Carsham, and he lives in the house with them. Expect you know him?"

"A little. I stayed with him last year, after—"

"So you did, so you did. Anyway, Miss Chandry is five and twenty, pretty, lively, and very well liked, although she has a reputation for eccentricity and for speaking her mind. Never married, although she's had plenty of offers. Was thought to be entirely lacking in susceptibility to persons of the male variety until His Grace happened along. Everyone is very pleased with the way matters have worked out, what with a personable young man washing up practically at her feet and the romantic way she nursed him back to health. A marriage is widely expected."

There was a long silence.

"She seems very well connected," Captain Edgerton said cautiously. "Lord Carsham, the Earl of Furneish…"

"But not a suitable duchess," Ran said, and no one contradicted him.

Another long silence.

"She is with child," Ran said baldly, and an uneasy sigh escaped from the captain.

"*That* makes things awkward, but such problems are not insuperable. A cottage somewhere, an annuity…"

Neate tugged at his ear again. "From what I hear, the lodges at Valmont have been used for such purposes in the past."

"That might be too close for his duchess," Willerton-Forbes said, adding gently, "He will have to marry, of course."

There was a long, sympathetic silence.

"He was supposed to marry the Lady Ruth Grenaby," Ran said bleakly. "Who is presently betrothed to me."

~~~~~

Ginny Chandry was taller than Ran had expected, a softly rounded woman who entered the parlour at Trehannick without a trace of anxiety, her clear blue eyes gazing at him with undisguised curiosity. Her hair would have been a dull brown without the hint of red that gave it the look of burnished wood. A sprinkle of freckles across her nose was the only defect to an
~~~~~

otherwise pretty face. An unadorned, practical gown, plain straw bonnet and a dark green pelisse that might have been fashionable five years ago made her look exactly as she was — a provincial spinster of little wealth and no elegance. But her smile was warm and open, and the shine in Ger's eyes as he looked at her ensured that Ran would find no fault with her.

"Ginny, you will remember Lord Randolph Litherholm. Miss Virginia Chandry."

She curtsied, he bowed. "Of course I remember you, my lord."

A long pause as Ger chewed his lip and looked anxious. It was clear that he had not yet revealed his secret.

"Ginny… I need to explain that…" A long pause, as Ger took a nervous gulp. "Ran is my brother."

Ran held his breath, but the blue eyes showed no shock. Instead, her smile widened. "Oh, I know. You are the duke that was thought to be drowned. I have known that for a long time."

Ger's look of astonishment was so great that Ran burst out laughing. "Well, you said she was an amazing person, Ger, and so she is. I did not expect *that*, and neither did you, it seems."

"Oh, you call him Ger!" she cried. "Gervase, of course. Ger and Ran. Ran and Ger. I like that." Her accent was good, he noted with relief, although there was just a hint of Cornish lilt to it.

"I am glad to discover there is something you did not know about us, ma'am," Ran said, bowing. "Please sit, have some wine and pray explain how you know who Ger is."

"I should like a little wine, thank you," she said, taking the chair he held out for her, "but it would please me if you were to call me Ginny, as Jon — I mean, Gervase — does. You are brothers, after all, and ma'am sounds so horridly grand."

"You mean that I am being condescending," he said ruefully. "I beg your pardon! I meant only to be polite."

"Oh yes, I know, and if we were strangers— Of course, we *are* strangers, but I hope that will not be so for long."

Her expression was so guileless that he could not be offended, but he wondered if she fully appreciated the enormity of the step that Ger was taking. Did she think this was just a passing visit, and Ran might drop by from time to time? Or did she understand that Ger was about to leave Cornwall altogether? His heart misgave him. However cleverly she had deduced the truth, she could not possibly appreciate the world that the Duke of Falconbury inhabited.

But he could not express such fears, so he poured wine for them, and produced a plate of cakes wheedled from the kitchen by the persuasive tongue of Captain Edgerton, and sat down to listen.

"When Jon was first brought to Pendower House, he was nine parts dead — a broken leg, and battered about everywhere, so he lay unconscious in his bed, and I was set to watch him for a while, as I was sewing. For a moment, he came half to his senses and cried out, *'Ran! Ran!'* Nothing else. Well, naturally I assumed he was talking about the ship — that he ran away from a big wave, or some such. Or perhaps he'd run away from some past life. But he never said it again, and I never asked him what he meant. If a man has secrets, it is not for me to coax them out of him. Quite a while later, Mr Willerton-Forbes came to give Jon his thousand pounds from the Benefactor and he mentioned your name — Lord Randolph Litherholm. And Jon jumped. Oh, he recovered very quickly, but he started because the name meant something to him, and that puzzled me. That night, when I was just dropping off to sleep, I realised — *Ran!* How odd it is when that happens, that something pops into one's mind at the most unexpected moment. And then everything made sense, because it was obvious that Jon was very… very cultured, I suppose. Understanding Latin and playing the pianoforte, and he knows about faro banks and the government and the old wars — things that most ordinary people know nothing about. And it was also obvious that he'd had a different life in the past, and he was not used to being a mere secretary. He talked about horses to my brother, many horses, and he has never been a groom, so it was not hard to work out."

"How did you account for the fact that the duke had seemingly been identified and buried?" Ran said.

"Oh, I just assumed you'd made a mistake, my lord," she said, with a smile. "Easily done, under the circumstances."

There was an assurance about her that unsettled him, for he liked a woman who was gentle and graceful, like Ruth, rather than this confidence that bordered on pertness, but when she smiled, her whole face softened and her eyes twinkled in such a charming manner, that he could entirely understand her fascination for his brother.

And yet… she was hardly eligible to be a duchess.

"Ginny," he said cautiously, "Ger is set upon taking up the reins of his old life… becoming the Duke of Falconbury again."

"I guessed as much," she said, quite composed.

"Where do you feel you would fit into that life? Or would you prefer not to?"

For the first time, there was a flicker of uncertainty. She threw an anxious glance at Ger. "You won't leave me behind?"

"Never," he said. "You have my word on it, and if you want us to marry—"

Her face relaxed. "Not marriage, no. I shall fit into your life exactly as I do now — as your mistress."

Ger frowned. "Is that truly what you want?"

"Of course it is," she said, her composure absolute. "Why do you think I've never pressed you to marry me? Why do you think I came to your bed without a wedding ring? You are a *duke*, Jon, and you have to marry someone from that world — a grand lady who knows how to behave. Not Ginny Chandry from Pendower. If you had stayed as Jonathan Ellsworthy of Pendower, well, we would have shared a little cottage somewhere and no one would have cared about it, except the parson, maybe. But if you are to go back to being a duke, then, if you marry at all, you have to marry your grand lady and I have to be your mistress, and that is an end to it."

"Then I shall not marry at all," he said defiantly. "We shall live in unwedded bliss, my love, and Ran will marry and produce the heirs to continue the line."

Ran laughed, relief warming him. "That suits me very well."

10: Of Dandies And Valets

Once Ger had made his decision to return to Valmont, he was all for leaving at once.

"What is the point of lingering?" he said with a shrug. "Let us get the business over with. Besides, I can barely wait to show Ginny the Long Gallery and the Porcelain Room and the State Banqueting Room and the Roman Grotto."

"Ginny has lived in the same house for her entire life," Ran said, amused. "She can hardly throw a nightgown and a couple of spare handkerchiefs in a valise and leave on the instant. Let the village give her a proper farewell."

But Ginny, he discovered, was made of sterner stuff. "Since I own precisely five day gowns and two evening, two pelisses, one cloak and three bonnets, including my Sunday best, it should not take me more than an hour to pack. Jon — I mean, Gervase — owns even fewer clothes than I do. We can tell everyone this evening, pack tomorrow and then leave the day after."

"We shall need a carriage for Ginny," Ger said. "You and I can ride."

"What about a maid? Or a valet?" Ran said, but they just laughed.

After they had gone back to Pendower, Ran spent the rest of the day writing letters. It had been agreed that, in order to avoid awkward questions, they would simply say that Ger had lost his memory when his head was hit during the shipwreck. And it was true enough, after all, for he *had* lost his memory.

Ran had thought to bring his address book with him, but before he had finished the first sheet, he devoutly wished he had brought his secretary as well. He was not used to so much quill work. There was one person he missed even more than his secretary, however, so his first, heartfelt, letter was to his valet.

'Trehannick Inn, Cornwall. Giggs, For the love of all that is Holy, get yourself and some decent clothes for me to the Half Moon Hotel in Exeter as fast as you can fly and await me there. Take the big travelling coach and a team of four. Spare no expense! I depend upon you so do not fail me. Randolph Litherholm'

He wrote then to Max, to warn him of the impending upheaval, and to ask him to alert the servants when he felt the time was right. Then to his four sisters, to his uncles and aunts, to a number of cousins, and to one surviving great-aunt. Lawyers, bankers, agents, managers. Family friends who would expect to be informed. The King and the Prime Minister. And finally, to the Duke of Orrisdale, a difficult letter, but he felt rather pleased with the wording.

'Trehannick Inn, Cornwall. My Lord Duke, I write to inform you that my brother Gervase was not drowned aboard the Brig Minerva *as supposed. He survived, although suffering from loss of*

memory, and has now been discovered alive in Cornwall. We leave for Valmont almost at once. I leave it to you to convey the news of my change in status to the Lady Ruth as you think best. This will delay my arrival in town, but I shall come to see you as soon as I am able. Randolph Litherholm.'

He sealed them with the ducal seal, for he had no other with him, although he remembered not to frank them, took them all to the mail office on the inn's ground floor and left them to catch the night mail coach.

The next morning, after again receiving assistance in dressing from Mr Neate, he rode with Captain Edgerton for company across the furze-spattered downs to Pendower. It was a nondescript fishing village, one of scores such along the southern Cornish coast, with a single road winding down into the bay where the bulk of the cottages huddled around the inn, and a few better dwellings on higher land. Pendower House, Ran was surprised to see, was the largest of them, three stories built of mellow stone with sizable gardens about it, and a ring of trees sheltering it from storms. A groom came to take his horse, and the door was opened to him by a liveried manservant. Clearly he was expected, for he was shown directly into a book room. The manservant offered him refreshments, and when he refused, left him alone in the room.

He was not alone for long. One by one the other inhabitants of the house came in, greeting him with friendly openness. "Are you really Jon's brother?" one of the children said, wide-eyed. "Tell us about the great big house he owns," said another. The adults asked with interest about travel arrangements and the House of Lords and whether Ger would be in trouble for hiding away for so long.

And most of all they asked about Ginny Chandry. Would she have servants to wait on her? Would she have her own carriage? Would she go to London and meet the Queen? They were not questions Ran felt he could answer. Lord Carsham, with whom Ran had stayed the previous year, understood the difficulty and turned all such questions aside.

Ginny's older brother, Michael, who had a roguish eye and a great deal of charm, said, "Is it true there are sixty horses at Valmont, my lord? So Jon said, and all of them prime blood. I should dearly like to see that!"

"That was a few years ago, when my sisters were still at home and some of the cousins, too, and the stables were full of hunters. I should be surprised if we have much above thirty beasts now."

"Thirty…" he said, his eyes round with desire. "And stabling enough for a hundred! How many grooms?"

"Currently eleven, as well as the coachmen and the smith and his boy, but we are sadly understaffed at the moment."

"A smith… you have your own smithy!"

"We have everything — brewery, dairy, bakery, apiary, poultry-yard, butchery, stew ponds, laundry, ice-house, mill. The home farm, of course. We are sufficient to ourselves in all our food needs, apart from what the sea provides."

"How many servants?"

"Altogether? Indoor and outdoor, one hundred and two at present, including the gamekeepers and land managers, but excluding the farm."

"But you are sadly understaffed, of course," Michael said, eyes crinkling with laughter.

"Dreadfully so," Ran said, chuckling. "How we contrive, I cannot imagine."

He was half afraid that the fellow would want to accompany them to Valmont, if only to see the fabled stables, but when he tentatively suggested such a thing, Ginny said robustly, "Not this time, Michael. When we are settled, perhaps Jon — I mean Gervase will invite you to visit, but there will be much for him to do just at first. He will not have the leisure to show you around when he will have a great many duties to attend to."

"But he's a duke!" Michael said, in wide-eyed innocence. "He can do whatever he likes!"

Ginny laughed at him.

One matter had been exercising Ran's mind rather. It was all very well for Ginny to talk glibly of being Ger's mistress, but travelling with two men not related to her without a maid or the least sign of a chaperon was still not something he liked. And then there was Valmont. Ger would not hear of installing her in one of the lodges — she was to stay in the house itself, and be treated with all the courtesy due to a guest of the duke's.

"You will set everyone by the ears!" Ran protested, as he watched his brother packing a small box in his room. "A little discretion never goes amiss, Ger."

"I will not have her hidden away, as if I am ashamed of her," Ger said.

"No, but to flaunt your mistress—"

"*Flaunt!*"

Ginny came in just then with a couple of gowns, and began to fold them into the box.

Ran bit his lip, then began again. "To keep your mistress at Valmont is just not done, Ger."

"Well, it is now. Ginny may not hold high rank, but she is a gentleman's daughter, not some lightskirt picked up in Covent Garden."

"Then you should not allow her to travel without a chaperon."

Ginny gave a throaty laugh. "Are you worried about my reputation? That horse has bolted already, my lord. Several months ago, to be precise."

"But there is no reason to advertise the fact," Ran said patiently. "You need a chaperon for the journey, and none of this packing everything into a single box. You will need separate boxes to go to your separate bedrooms at the post houses."

They both laughed at that. But fortunately there was one person in the house on Ran's side. Molly was the former nurse to Michael and Ginny, who had evolved into a mainstay of the household as the general factotum who nagged everyone into compliance, servants and family alike, took charge in every crisis and was universally loved and looked up to.

"You'll not go nowhere without female company, Miss Ginny, and if your mama can spare me, I'll go myself, just to make sure you're looked after, for if there's one thing that can't never be depended on, it's gentlemen looking after a lady properly."

Ger and Ginny could argue indefinitely with Ran, but no one could hold out against Molly. So it was that when the post-chaise drew up outside Pendower House, two separate boxes were strapped to the roof, and two ladies were handed into it. Ger and Ran were to ride alongside, and as Captain Edgerton and Michael were to ride with them as far as Truro to set them on their way, and the entire village had turned out to see them off, their departure was impressive indeed.

Ran watched his brother carefully as he made his farewells. This had been his family for a year now, a family who had rescued him from the sea, mended him, accepted him without question and given him a home and affection. And love, he realised. Every time Ger looked at Ginny there was an unmistakable glow in his eyes, and likewise in hers. Clearly they would never be happy to be parted, but of the rest of the family, Ger seemed unaffected. He shook hands with them all, hugged one or two, ruffled the hair of the youngest boy and then smiled as he left them behind. He was not, then, having any doubts about the wisdom of his re-emergence from seclusion.

Nor did the Chandry family seem hostile towards him, which was somewhat forbearing of them, under the circumstances. Ger was the man who had accepted their hospitality, lied to them repeatedly, seduced their daughter and then told them he was not who they thought he was. Now he was taking Ginny away to an unknown future, where he would be a great man, moving freely in the highest circles and she would be forever excluded from all good society, although perhaps they were not yet aware of that. Maybe her condition was not yet general knowledge, or they expected Ger to marry her, in time.

Whatever the cause, there was no sign of resentment towards Ger. When Ginny's step-mother hugged him and whispered, "Take care of her," he responded instantly, "Of course

I will." And she smiled through her tears and nodded, reassured. She trusted Ger. After a year of living with him under a fake name and an invented history, she could see the true man beneath the falsity, who would look after Ginny come what may.

They got under way. The village urchins ran alongside the post-chaise, waving and yelling encouragement to the postilions as the horses slowly trotted down into the village and across the bridge beside the inn, where a large contingent of the fishermen had apparently deemed the occasion worthy of a holiday, and were already well refreshed. Then they laboured up the other side of the little valley until the flatter ground was reached and, after a twist or two, the road turned inland. Here the horses picked up speed and the urchins were left behind.

Ran was glad to stretch his horse's legs a little, and although his hired hack was not the equal of the other mounts, it was not a total slug at this early stage of the day. Later, perhaps, it would fade, but for now, with the Cornish air fresh and clear, the breeze gentle and the sun warming, he was content. As he cantered along, he counted up the distances in his head. Almost twenty miles to Truro, where he had acquired his horse. He might be able to pick up a better mount there, but this one would serve if not. Then on to St Columb, where they would rest for a while, and take up fresh horses for the post-chaise. Another thirty miles to Launceston, where they would put up at the Kings' Arms. No great distance for a day's driving, but the Cornish roads were rough, and the women would be ready to stop for the night by then. After that, if there were no mishaps — please let there be no mishaps! — there were only forty miles or so to Exeter and the Half Moon Hotel and Giggs, bearing the miracle of freshly laundered shirts and immaculate breeches and, he very much hoped, his favourite soap, which he had forgotten to pack. Then he could abandon this indifferent horse for the comfort of the travelling coach and his own coachmen. Ger's coachmen now, he supposed. The Litherholm coachmen, he told himself sternly, to which he had just as much right as his brother.

Edgerton and Michael Chandry, having better horses or more energy, rode ahead of the chaise, but Ger dropped back to ride beside Ran.

"This is fun, do you not think?" he said, his face alight with enthusiasm. "The English countryside is glorious at this time of year, and I have not been so far afield for a while. I missed all this when I was in America. There are parts that are almost the same, but not precisely so, and nothing is quite so *green* as the English spring." He laughed suddenly. "It is nothing to you, brother, for you have seen it every year, but to go away and then return to all this, and to be myself again, with no pretending... it is wonderful!"

Such good humour could not fail to lift Ran's spirits, too, and his worries about the journey receded somewhat. His mind being still on clean linen, however, he said, "How do you contrive without a valet? I feel horribly rumpled without mine, and grubby, too. I am missing Giggs abominably."

"What a dandy you are!" Ger said, laughing merrily. "Most of the world manages perfectly without valets, brother. There is always someone to do a little laundry, or press anything that needs pressing, or put in a stitch here and there, and I can clean my own boots, I hope."

"Really?"

"It is not terribly hard. Some patent boot blacking and a decent pair of brushes is all that is required. I have never been much interested in my appearance, you know, and when that snooping valet that Father foisted on me took to his bed in New York, I was never so glad of anything in my life. He used to sneak off to tell Father everything I did, and when we were in America he wrote long letters to him, no doubt reporting on everyone I met and everywhere I went."

"He did. Max opened one of them once, by mistake, and was quite shocked. After that, we burnt every letter from him."

"Did you indeed?" Ger said, the scowl that had momentarily marred his features lifting again. "Ha! I wish I had known that. He is still in New York, you know. He found an American fellow who liked the idea of an English valet, who is welcome to him, frankly. I suppose I shall have to have a valet, for Heaven forfend that the Duke of Falconbury present a rumpled appearance to the world, but I shall choose my own this time. Lord, this road goes up and down a great deal. Ginny will be quite seasick. I shall just ride forward and see how she does."

~~~~~

No mishaps occurred, and Launceston was reached without difficulty, and the only small change of plan was that Captain Edgerton and Michael Chandry chose to continue with the travellers as far as Exeter. Since they had brought changes of clothing in their saddle bags, this was clearly by design.

"I am acting under orders from Mr Willerton-Forbes," the captain said apologetically. "I am not to leave you unattended on the road until you are reunited with your own people, just in case of any misunderstandings with the locals."
~~~~~

"You think we might be held up?" Ran said.

"These remote parts are not necessarily safe, and with a private chaise and two obviously well-breeched riders, you might look vulnerable to a desperate man. Whereas my sword is visible, my greatcoat has pockets large enough to conceal a dozen pistols and young Chandry looks like a handy man in a mill. Once you get to Exeter, however, and I am satisfied that you have enough protection, we shall disappear, I assure you."

"And if we say you are not wanted, you will just follow anyway, I daresay," Ran said, grinning.

"It is a public highway," Edgerton said, innocently. "Anyone may freely use the road, after all."

"You are right, of course, and it would be a shocking thing to find the missing duke after all this time, only to have him fall victim to a highwayman. I should have thought of it myself, only I am not used to travelling so informally."

The chaise rolled into the Half Moon Hotel's yard in the middle of the afternoon, and the first person Ran saw was the Valmont deputy coachman, industriously polishing the ducal coat of arms on the door of the Litherholm coach.

"Tennant! How good to see you," Ran cried, as he dismounted rather gingerly, his muscles protesting at the change in posture. "You got here safe and sound then."

"No trouble, Your Grace."

"Not Your Grace any more, Tennant," Ran said easily.

"Not... not Your Grace?" Tennant said, bewildered. "I don't understand."

"Oh." Ran gave a rueful chuckle. "Oh dear, you must have left Valmont in a great hurry."

"Within an hour of Mr Giggs receiving your letter, Your—What am I to call you, then?"

Just at that moment, Ger emerged from the far side of the post-chaise, leading his horse. Tennant, who had grown up at Valmont, recognised him instantly and gave a great shout. "Milord! Your Grace! *Mr Vane!* Come and see!"

The head coachman's face peered out from one of the stable doors. "What's afoot, lad?"

"Come and see! It's His Grace!"

Vane laughed, seeing only Ran and therefore not understanding the flap, but he willingly moved out into the yard. Only when he rounded the coach and had full sight of Ger's grin did he stop, mouth agape. "My *God!* Is it really you, milord?" And then the grizzled old retainer, who had maintained his phlegmatic composure through fifty years of Litherholm family trials, burst into tears.

"Giggs," Ran murmured distractedly. "I must tell Giggs myself."

"More fun if it is a surprise, surely?" Ger said, shaking Vane's hand and clapping him briskly on the shoulder.

"And have him leave in high dudgeon, so that I have to find myself another valet? I thank you, but no!"

Ger laughed, and shook his head. "Such craven dependence on a man whose sole talent is in polishing boots."

"Sole talent!" Ran said, shocked. "I should not employ him for five minutes if it were so. His way with a wine stain on a silk waistcoat is nothing short of miraculous, I assure you. Take care of things here, will you, brother, while I inform Giggs that he is no longer valet to a duke."

"Maybe I shall steal him from you, then," Ger said easily.

Ran was momentarily horrified, before he recognised the mischievous twinkle in his brother's eye. Ger was a dreadful tease, and knew just how to get under his skin, the wretch.

He left Ger to soothe the coachmen while Captain Edgerton and Michael Chandry assisted the ladies, and went to find his valet before his dignity, too, was stretched beyond endurance by the shock of Ger's return from the dead. Giggs bore with noble fortitude the unexpected reduction in his master's, and therefore his own, rank, and declared himself in flat tones to be overcome with joy on the occasion.

"His Grace has been doing for himself for some time, Giggs, as you will no doubt be able to tell as soon as you see him," Ran said.

That softened the valet's stiff expression slightly. "Ah, but that was always his way, Your— milord. His Grace was never so particular about his appearance as your lordship is. Always a credit to yourself, you've been, milord."

"The credit is entirely yours, Giggs, as you well know. But His Grace will need a valet in the future, and I depend upon you to advise on the choice and to help bring the fellow up to the mark, for we cannot expect to find another such as you, can we? That would be too much to hope for."

Giggs bowed at these compliments, taking them entirely as his due, and Ran felt he had done enough to assuage the terrifying prospect of losing his highly-valued and expert valet to his brother, who cared nothing for his appearance.

11: Return To Valmont

The Half Moon Hotel took with aplomb the discovery that the Duke of Falconbury was travelling with the unexpected addition of five extra persons, nor were they thrown by the duke turning out to be a different person. A duke had been expected and a duke had arrived, and it was likely that any inconvenience was far outweighed by the wonder of being in the middle of such a tale.

Ran was a little surprised to hear that Neate had also followed them east, and was presently sitting in the common room.

"What is going on, Edgerton?" Ran said in sharp tones. "Why are your people following us?"

They were in the private parlour that had been engaged for them, the finest in the building with a splendid view over the street outside, the view of which was currently occupying Ger, Ginny and Molly. With a slight tilt of his head to indicate that Ran should follow, Edgerton made for the door. He walked down the corridor opening doors, attracting annoyed exclamations, until he found an empty room.

"You are very secretive, Captain," Ran said, amused despite himself. "I take it this is all part of Mr Willerton-Forbes' instructions?"

"He feels in some way responsible for all that has occurred, and that we should have discovered His Grace much earlier. This has put you all in a very awkward position."

"That is our problem, not yours," Ran said firmly. "Besides, no one could blame you in the slightest for not realising who the mysterious Mr Ellsworthy was."

"We blame ourselves, but that is water under the bridge," Edgerton said. "We all feel a responsibility to ensure that the duke reaches Valmont in safety, and at Pendower... forgive me, my lord, but you were there quite alone, without so much as a groom, planning a journey with a man who is no longer used to the ceremony of his rank and a woman who despises it. Nor do I consider Miss Chandry's former nurse a particularly effective bodyguard. Mr Willerton-Forbes had no hesitation in asking me to keep an eye on you, and Mr Chandry was easily recruited — he is game as a pebble, that one! Neate's talents are not in swaggering round with a sword, as I am wont to do, but in sitting quietly in tap rooms and chop houses, and listening. Between the three of us, we have kept you safe."

"But we have encountered no difficulties," Ran protested.

"Indeed you have not. There were enough of us to deter the two men who habitually watch the road south of Bodmin, for instance, and there is a well-known shortcut near Truro that your postilions would have taken by arrangement, where a spurious toll gate would have relieved you of a pound or two, and perhaps more if they had considered it worthwhile. Neate informed me of both of those dangers. And who knows how many men eyed your post-chaise and decided against it. But if you assure me that you will engage three or four armed outriders, and I am sure your coachmen are armed, I shall consider that you have sufficient protection."

"And will follow anyway, I daresay," Ran said resignedly.

"At a discreet distance, naturally," Edgerton said, his grin revealing even white teeth. "You would not deprive us of our fun, surely, my lord?"

"I certainly would, for I plan to make you work for it. I hereby appoint you the duke's personal protection officer. As I am His Grace's closest adviser and man of business, you have my authority to satisfy yourself on the provisions made for His Grace's journey, and to engage such additional persons as needed."

Edgerton's face lit up. "Are you serious? And may I keep Chandry with me?"

"If you must. Neate will do as he pleases, as always, I daresay. And you may tell Mr Willerton-Forbes from me that he is a devious scoundrel, and he has my sincere thanks."

~~~~~

Ruth was sitting in the drawing room of the Berkeley Square house, receiving morning callers with her mother, her sister and Aunt Maria. Their visitors were four rather stuffy matrons, the daughters of two of them, and the sons of the other two. The Dowager Lady Crosby was also there, making stilted conversation with her future daughter-in-law, Susan, who was far more
~~~~~

interested in catching the eye of the handsome young viscount across the room.

It was Susan's first season, so perhaps she could be excused some exuberance at encountering so many charming, rich and well-connected young men all at once. The season had long since lost its novelty for Ruth, being her fourth, and had become no more than a pleasant way to meet friends. She had missed last year's season, for Ger had just died and Ruth was in no mood for the frivolities of the *ton.* She could not go into mourning since there had been no official betrothal, but her parents approved of her desire to stay secluded for a while. Papa had to make his speeches in the House, and Mama had gone with him, but Ruth had stayed quietly at Mallowfleet, apart from brief shopping forays. The days had passed slowly, even though every hour had some task for her to do — working on her embroidery and watercolours, reading an improving work, practising at the instrument and riding — while she waited.

She had waited for Ran to come. Sooner or later, she felt sure, he would recognise the obligation and come for her. Dear Ran! Always so correct... she had known it would happen. If Ger had not died, she would have been married last year. Perhaps there would already be a child, or very soon. An heir. Another duty accomplished. But Ger was dead, and Ran had come and she permitted herself a little glow inside whenever she thought of him. She knew he had offered from obligation, it was understood, and he need never know about the little glow. Her mother had taught her that persons of her rank did not fall in love, were not suited to it, and certainly her husband would not want her hanging about his neck or making an unseemly show of affection.

That was understood, too. She knew her duty, she hoped. But the little glow was there, all the same. It was Ruth's little secret.

Lady Crosby's frown was deepening, so when a shift in the company offered an opportunity, Ruth moved to sit next to her. Susan immediately made some excuse and escaped from her future mother-in-law.

"She is very young," Lady Crosby said, watching her go.

"True, but she will settle down once she is married," Ruth said, although she hoped rather than believed it to be true.

"I cannot see why he had to choose someone so *young*," Lady Crosby said waspishly. "Or why he has to marry in such haste at all. He had only had the title for a few months, and off he goes to Dallerton, with no thought in his head but a gay time to liven his spirits, and he comes home betrothed! And he seemed just as shocked by it as I was. Tell me, Lady Ruth, why do men become so foolish in the presence of pretty girls?"

Ruth laughed. "I am hardly qualified to answer your question, ma'am. Men are a mystery to me. My father, my brothers... my own future husband. Impossible to say with good conscience that I understand any of them very well. I was not at Dallerton last summer, so I cannot give you any inkling of what happened, except to say that I believe my parents were startled by it, too."

"Perhaps that does not matter, for such matches do happen," the dowager said. "My own was all settled in under a month, from first meeting to betrothal, so it is not that. But... she is so *young*." She gazed helplessly across the room, to where Susan was openly flirting with the viscount, while carefully avoiding any visible impropriety that might incur the censure of her mother. "Is she a proper wife for a sober man of five and forty? Will she make him happy? For his first choice was—"

She stopped abruptly, perhaps realising to whom she was speaking, but Ruth said quickly, "Susan is young enough to be excited by her first season, and to enjoy testing her attractiveness to men. Many girls of her age are a little giddy just at first."

"You were never so, I wager." Then, without waiting for an answer she went on, "He should be here, of course. Foolish man, *he* should be the one flirting with her, but he sits at home pretending that he has so much work to do on the estate. Well, if he will not come to her, she shall go to him. When I return to Crosby Manor, I shall take Lady Susan with me. She will not flirt with all these frivolous young men when she is with Luke."

Ruth thought she might flirt even more openly if she once escaped her mother's eye, but she decided not to say so. The duchess was a vigilant mother, insisting on the perfect behaviour to be expected of the daughters of a duke, and ruthless in enforcing her dictates. Ruth had long since surrendered to her mother's will, finding life smoother if she suppressed any hint of resistance. Susan, however, had taken a different route, her outward compliance hiding a great deal of covert rebellion, but the duchess's presence kept her worst excesses in check. Ruth could not feel with any confidence that a stay at Crosby Manor would improve her flirtatious tendencies. Nor would she like to be torn away from town to rusticate just when the season was getting under way.

She was just beginning, rather tentatively, to express this point of view, and to urge her ladyship to persuade Lord Crosby to come to town instead, when the house was rent by a great howl of anguish. The drawing room fell into instant silence. No further sound came.

Ruth rose. "I shall go and see what has happened," she said calmly.

"Oh yes, dear, do," her mother said. "I daresay one of the footmen dropped something on his—"

Another howl, louder, and this time it was clear that it was not a footman. "That is Papa!" Susan cried.

There was a rush to the door, but Ruth was already halfway there and so reached the landing a little before the others. Looking down the stairs, her father stood in the hall below, his coat off, a letter in his hand. His face was whiter than Ruth had ever seen it.

"Ruth," he said, then, seeing the duchess emerging, "Alicia... both of you, come down here. At once!"

Heart in mouth, Ruth sped down the stairs and into her father's book room. The duchess rushed too, and was panting when she finally gained the book room. The duke looked back up the stairs at the astonished faces gazing down at him. "Oh... go away and drink your tea, all of you!" Then he ushered them into the book room and slammed the door.

"Whatever is it, John," the duchess cried, frantically twisting a handkerchief. "Tell me the worst! Is it Audlyn? Camberley? Ramsey? Who is dead?"

"He is *not* dead! Falconbury is *not* dead!"

Ruth could not make head or tail of it. Ran was not dead? But he had never been thought to be dead, so how was it possible that— "Gervase," she whispered. "Gervase is alive."

"That is what I said," her father snapped. "He is not dead! This is beyond anything! How *dare* he!"

The duchess made a little mewing sound of distress.

"But this is good news," Ruth said, puzzled by her father's anger.

"Good news? *Good* news? It is the most awkward thing in the world, with your betrothal puffed off everywhere barely a month ago, and now *this.* Oh, you silly girl, do you not see?"

"I see that I shall not be a duchess after all, and if that disappoints you, I am sorry for it, but—"

"*If that disappoints you?* Is that all you can say? It is impossible, of course. You cannot marry a *second* son. I absolutely forbid it."

"No!" An icy chill ran through Ruth, but she lifted her chin and looked her father straight in the eye. "I am betrothed to Lord Randolph, Papa. It is agreed, the marriage date is set, my wedding clothes are being made, it is settled."

"You are betrothed to the Duke of Falconbury," he said coldly. "It matters not one whit which brother it is. You will cry off, on the grounds that you have been grossly misled, and then you will marry Falconbury."

"You wrong him! Ran did not mislead me, Papa! This must be as great a shock to him as to us. There was no deceit, he truly believed that Gervase was dead and so the betrothal must stand."

"My consent is withdrawn," her father said, eyes narrowed.

"I am of age, so your consent is not needed," she cried.

"Oh, you would defy me, would you? Think you know better than your father, do you? I never expected to see such conceit, such wilfulness in a daughter of mine. You will obey me, do you hear? You will not marry against my wishes, and it is my wish that you marry the Duke of Falconbury."

"He might already be married," Ruth said desperately.

Her father frowned, for that was a thought that had not occurred to him. The duchess gave a little moan, and sat down abruptly in a chair. "Whatever are we to do?" she whimpered.

Ruth rushed to kneel at her feet, chafing her hands. "Poor Mama! This is a terrible shock to all of us. Do you have smelling salts in your reticule? Would you like some brandy? Shall I send for Grimson?"

But she could only moan, "What are we to do?" over and over.

"I shall tell you what we are to do, Duchess," the duke said, in a voice that permitted no contradiction. "We shall go to Valmont, and confront the duke and *insist* he makes everything right with Ruthie. She was promised a duke, so a duke is what she must have."

This brought the prostrate duchess upright again. "Leave town, at the beginning of the season? Impossible, John! What of Susan? We have so much planned for her."

"She has her baron secured, so what does it matter?"

"But we cannot leave her here alone!" the duchess said, outraged. "Maria is very good, but she is *not* a suitable chaperon for Susan, not in town in the season, you must see that. A duke's daughter must be brought out by her mother, John."

"Then she can go back to Mallowfleet until this is sorted out."

"If I might suggest," Ruth said timidly, "Lady Crosby mentioned that she would like to take Susan on a visit to Crosby Manor. If she were to do so, then—"

"There you are, you see, Alicia," the duke said. "The girl has a good head on her shoulders, when she sets her mind into the proper channels. Susan may go to Crosby Manor with Maria to keep an eye on her, and you and Ruth and I will go to Valmont to see how things stand there. But I warn you, Ruthie, you had better do what your parents think best for you. That is your filial duty and what I expect of you, and if you do not, then you are no daughter of mine and I shall cast you off utterly."

Ruth said nothing, for what was there to say? She lowered her head and breathed slowly as the little glow inside her flickered, almost but not quite extinguished. Hope was not yet entirely lost.

<p style="text-align:center">~~~~~</p>

The Litherholm travelling coach was large enough to seat six persons inside in great comfort, so Ran and Ger decided to sit with Ginny, Molly and Giggs. Outside, Edgerton's precautions had provided two bulky footmen to sit behind, and no fewer than six outriders. Vane, the coachman, declared it quite took him back to the young days of the Sixth Duke.

"Always had *style,* His Late Grace, that's what I say, and so attentive to Her Grace's consequence even above his own. Mind you, he'd have thought only one carriage pretty shabby, and the maid and valet riding with the family — that would never have done."

"It does perfectly well for me, however," Ger said, amused.

Ran was pleased that Ger's good humour was holding fast, but then the novelty of the ever-changing scenery, the regular appearance of picturesque villages or charming towns, and of simply going somewhere kept his spirits high. He spent his days sitting beside Ginny on the forward-facing seat in the coach, pointing out features of interest and telling her what he remembered about them. Ran had forgotten how knowledgeable his brother was, for he was never at a loss for a battle or famous resident or historical disaster, wherever they went. On farms and crops and the varieties of cattle, he knew nothing, but during their overnight stay at Sherborne, he regaled them with the full history of both abbey and castle, holding them riveted over dinner and for some time afterwards.

Late in the afternoon of their fourth day of travel, they entered the village of Beckhampton Cross, at the southern end of the principal Valmont pleasure grounds. They discovered that the entire village was awaiting their arrival. There were flags draped or waved everywhere, an impromptu group of musicians was playing, and as they rattled over the cobbles of the main square every man and woman bowed or curtsied. Then they were through the gates and the noise died away behind them.

"Welcome to Valmont," Ger said to Ginny, with a warm smile.

She peered through the window at the lodge as they past by. "It's not as big as I'd expected."

Ger laughed. "That is only the Beckhampton Lodge. There are seven more like that, but Valmont itself is... quite a bit bigger."

The avenue was long and straight, and the trees and the lowness of the ground hid the house from view, but about half way along there was a great commemorative arch, and beyond it the first view of the house. Ger stopped the carriage there for the benefit of those seeing it for the first time. The footmen let down the steps and everyone climbed out of the coach.

Ginny gazed down impassively at the vast frontage of Valmont, some four hundred and fifty feet from end to end, and the acres of formal gardens surrounding it.

"All this is yours?" she said to Ger.

"Everything you can see from this point is Valmont land. Mine."

"Doesn't your brother get anything at all?"

"I have no idea. Ran, did Father leave you anything in his will? Not everything is entailed, after all."

"He left me three estates — Durran House, where Aunt Charlotte lives, Merrington House, presently occupied by Uncle Swithin and assorted relations of Mama's, and Whinmore."

"Whinmore? The hunting lodge?" Ger gave a bark of laughter. "You, who have never hunted, to own a hunting lodge? That is rich! I suppose I shall have to pay you for the privilege of using it, will I?"

"None of us can use it before next Lady Day, since it is leased out, although I get a good rent for it. Nothing from the others, but unless you plan to throw me out of Valmont, I hardly need them or the income from them."

"Your home is here for as long as you wish it," Ger said fiercely. "We shall talk about this later, but let us get the business of arriving over with, shall we? If the village is anything to go by, we shall have a reception at the house."

"All the servants will be lined up." Ran hesitated, feeling oddly awkward. "Ger, have you thought how you want to introduce Ginny into the house? She might find it overwhelming to have a hundred servants gawking at her. She could stay in the carriage and go in through the stable door."

"No," Ger said quietly. "Ginny walks in through the front door with me."

Ran nodded, knowing better than to attempt argument. He well knew that mulish set to Ger's mouth. Silently, they drove the remaining half mile to the house, the avenue of trees giving way to rows of neatly clipped balls of greenery and low-edged beds of herbs. The fountain had been brought into operation, he saw, and there at the great doors, twenty feet high, long lines of servants were filing out, and gardeners and grooms appearing from the side of the house. He sighed, and could only hope that Ginny's assurance would not desert her at this critical moment.

They stopped, the footmen jumped down to open the door and let down the steps. Ger jumped down first, and then turned with a wide smile to hand Ginny out. Then Ran descended. Molly and Giggs would stay inside and be driven round to the stables.

"No lingering," Ran whispered to Ger. "Let us get inside as quick as may be."

He nodded and, with a quick smile and a wave to the assembled servants, he ushered Ginny up the steps, with Ran following. He only caught glimpses of Ginny's face, but she seemed composed, even happy. She was smiling at the senior staff on the upper steps. Then they were through the door and into the entrance hall, where Ran drew up in horror. The hall was built on an imposing scale, but even so it was filled to capacity. As if the servants were not enough, now they had to face the assembled ranks of the Litherholm family. Every relation with the slightest claim had come to welcome home the lost Duke of Falconbury.

Ger stopped dead, his face aghast. To one side of the hall, the indoor servants were now filing back to form a long line, all watching with avid interest. On the other side, some sixty or more aunts, uncles, cousins and assorted in-laws beamed in delight, their voices rising in a chorus of welcome.

"No," Ger whispered. "Not now. Get rid of them, Ran! Get them out of this house, *now!*"

And with that he gripped Ginny firmly by the hand, marched straight past the assembled masses and up the stairs.

12: The State Banqueting Room

The outraged voices rose to a cacophony. "Well, that was most uncivil, when we have come all this way to greet him!" said one aunt.

"Who is that woman?" another said pointedly. "Is he *married?*"

With a slight jerk of his head, Ran dismissed the servants, who scuttled away to the nether parts of the house. The relations were more difficult to shift. The gentlemen included at least seven peers of the realm and none of them, of either sex, were likely to leave merely because he asked them to. Many of them had grown up at Valmont, and they were all accustomed to spend several weeks each summer at the family seat, with shooting in the autumn for those who wished it. They were family, and it was inconceivable to any of them that Ger would not be thrilled by their presence.

Whatever was to be done with them, it was certain that nothing could be achieved so late in the day. Ran smiled benignly.

"Let us go back to— where were you sitting? The Queen's Room? Then let us go there and I shall tell you all."

Since this was what they most wished for, there was no resistance to the idea. They drifted through the Grand Saloon and past the Winter Court into the Queen's Room, which overlooked the gardens. Tea things and trays of cakes and pastries were already laid out, and every surface laden with discarded plates, cups of tea and half-drunk glasses of Madeira. Brent and two footmen were already hard at work replenishing supplies. The explanations had to wait until the servants withdrew, Ran closed the door firmly and turned to his expectant audience.

"I beg your pardon, everyone, but you will appreciate that Ger has had a difficult journey to make. He was badly injured in the wreck of the *Brig Minerva* and his memory was affected. It has not been easy for him to accept that he must return here."

"Yes, yes, but who is the young woman with him? He has not married someone unsuitable, I trust?"

That was Aunt Anne's voice, but he saw the same anxious looks all around him.

"Ger is not married." A little sigh of relief ran round the room. "The lady is Miss Chandry, daughter of Mr Patrick Chandry of Pendower House in Cornwall. The Chandrys are the principal family of Pendower." Not that that was saying a great deal, but the assembly would not know that. "Miss Chandry was the person who rescued Ger from the sea and nursed him back to health. We all owe her a great debt. She is here as Ger's guest."

There! He had told the story they had agreed upon, and they could make of it what they would. He did not suppose they would be satisfied, and he was right. They peppered him with questions and interrupted his answers and talked across each other until his head was spinning. His throat burned from repeating the same trite words a hundred times. But eventually the dressing bell sounded and there was a general movement towards the stairs.

Ran took the opportunity to slip away to find Max. He located him in the butler's pantry, in harassed conference with Mrs Newall, the housekeeper. After a rapid discussion in lowered voices, she rushed away.

Max laughed and poured him a large brandy. "Here. Brent keeps a secret supply, and you look as if you need it."

"Have some yourself. I imagine you need it, too, with so many of the family arriving unexpectedly." Ran sat on a battered leather wing chair.

"I dare not," Max said, flopping into a matching chair. "Have to keep a clear head. I know they mean well, but good Lord, it has been a nightmare. We sat down sixty three to dinner last night. We had to open the State Banqueting Room for the purpose, and you cannot conceive of the inconvenience."

"Why did they come?" Ran said, sipping the brandy appreciatively. "My letters made it very clear that they should not expect to see Ger until the summer. Well, I suppose it is a wonderful thing that he is safe after all, and they mean it for the best. You have borne the brunt of it all and coped splendidly, I make no doubt."

"I cannot quite agree there. Mrs Newall and I have been horribly flustered, I assure you. Fortunately, Monsieur Duvalle and Mrs Cromarty were enlivened by the challenge, so there were no problems in the kitchen, and it is impossible to conceive how we should have contrived without Mrs Brack."

"Really? I have often wondered why we needed a Mistress of the Chambers at all, and why Mrs Newall could not see to all that, so it is reassuring to know that she has a useful function after all."

"Useful function? She has been magnificent, Ran. All these carriages kept arriving, disgorging Lord This and Lady That, not to mention maids and valets and footmen and grooms and so on and so forth, and no warning whatsoever, and she recognised everyone on sight and assigned them to their favourite rooms without the slightest hesitation, remembering fresh flowers for this lady and a certain kind of soap for another. Lady Jane will only use jonquil-scented soap, did you know that?"

"I did not even know that such a thing existed," Ran said laughing.

"Nor I, but it does, and Mrs Brack keeps a supply on hand especially for her ladyship. And so calm, never the least bit agitated. She has even found accommodation for all the hangers on. Wonderful woman. So we have... not coped splendidly, precisely, but we survived. How long will they stay, do you suppose?"

"If Ger has his way, they will be gone tomorrow," Ran said.

"What! You will never get them all out just like that!"

"Ger wants them gone, so go they must," Ran said, with a shrug. "He is duke now, so his wishes must prevail, although how it is to be done I cannot immediately determine. If they set their minds to it, they are perfectly capable of staying for a month."

"Heaven forbid! We shall see about that. But how is he, Ran? I was tucked away behind the footmen, so I did not get a good look at him, but he looked well to me. A slight limp, I thought."

"Yes, from the broken leg he suffered in the shipwreck." Ran sighed and sipped his brandy. A footman ran in and had some hurried words with Max before dashing off again.

Max sat down and heaved a sigh. "He is bound to have changed, I suppose. Three years in America, then surviving the shipwreck followed by a year of living under a false name, pretending to be a clerk... he is bound to be a little different. He still dislikes huge gatherings, though." He chuckled. "Although I must confess, the massed ranks of the Litherholms and assorted connections is an appalling sight. I do not blame him for running away. Will he come down to dinner, do you think?"

"Who can say? He is a little unpredictable just at the moment. Sixty three at table? He will not like that! I daresay he will stay in his rooms until everyone has gone."

"They will not do so until they have seen him, Ran. That is what they came for, after all. If he cannot face dinner, see if you can persuade him to appear after the tea has been brought in. He can show them that he is safe and well, and tell them to remove their unwanted selves from the hallowed grounds of Valmont. Or some such. I am sure you can devise something conciliatory. But *you* will dine with us, I hope?"

"Certainly, and I had better go and change. Giggs will have unpacked for me by now. Is there any major news I should know about?"

"Oh… a fire at the mill, but quickly put out, thank God. Very little damage. Peckham's eldest had a nasty fall, trying to trim a damaged oak up by Shallowford Woods. Leg very badly broken. The surgeon thought it might have to come off, but it looks like it will hold. Not sure what a farmer's son will do if he can barely walk."

"We will find him work somewhere on the estate."

"I knew you would say so, and ventured to offer that reassurance to Peckham. Oh, and Lady Elizabeth moved into her lodge three days ago. So she is one who will not be leaving."

"Excellent. At least she is of an age to offer some companionship to Miss Chandry. I should not like Aunt Anne to be the only other female in the house."

"I am not sure that Lady Elizabeth and Miss Chandry have much in common," Max said in a cool voice. "What exactly is her position here, might one enquire?"

Ran was rather taken aback by such obvious disdain of Ginny, about whom Max knew nothing. "She is Ger's guest."

Max gave a derisory snort. "That story will not fly! Is he planning to wed her, or is she his *chère-amie?*"

"Must those be the only choices?"

"Come now, Ran, I was not born yesterday!"

Ran reached for the brandy decanter, then thought better of it, for there was a whole long, difficult evening to be got through and he would survive it all the better for not being foxed. Well, not yet, at all events.

"It is the devil of a coil, Max. She is happy to call herself his mistress, and there is no doubt of it, for she is with child, but he wants her treated with respect, and to live here as a guest. Did you get my letter? About preparing the Violet Room?"

He nodded briefly. "Lord, that will set all the old aunts by the ears — the duke's mistress living right here in the house. And in the family wing? They will never wear it, you know. There will be the most almighty fuss."

"He is the duke," Ran said again. "He can do what he likes in his own house."

"We shall just have to get rid of her. No, stop laughing, I am serious. If he is so lost to all that is due to his name, you must make him understand it."

Ran drained the brandy glass and set it down on a table with a sharp click. "Let us have one thing very clear between us, Max. It is not my rôle in life to impose my own precepts onto my brother. God has seen fit to make *him* the duke and not me, and Ger must make his own decisions and set his own standard of conduct. My only rôle is to support him in everything he does — unswervingly. And yours too, I trust. Understood?"

"Perfectly."

"Good. Then I shall see you at dinner."

Ran made his way up a minor stairway known as the Stable Stair, since it connected the door nearest to the stables with the family's private quarters. Here on the second floor was the apartment that Ger and Ran had shared since they were ten years old, and had graduated from the nursery wing to the adult world of valets and dressing rooms and full-sized beds. Their rooms occupied the entire end of the wing, with a bedroom and dressing room each, and in between them, a vast sitting room equipped with a dining table as well as comfortable chairs, bookcases, writing desks and a pianoforte.

The corridor, however, bore the surprising sight of Captain Edgerton, conspicuously wearing his sword and holding a pistol. Beside him, Michael Chandry carried a second pistol.

"Are we expecting trouble?" Ran said, not sure whether to be concerned or diverted.

"Just a gentle deterrent, my lord," Edgerton said smoothly. "His Grace's relations, it seems, were very keen to convey their good wishes to him in person. His Grace, it transpired, was less enthusiastic about receiving such good wishes, at least in such large quantities."

"He told us to get rid of them if any more came, and if they wouldn't go, to shoot them," Chandry said with a grin. "And when the captain said, *'What, even your Aunt Agatha?'*, he said, *'Especially Aunt Agatha.'* He's a right one, ain't he, for all he's a duke?"

"If you mean he is rude and curmudgeonly, I can only agree," Ran said ruefully. "Are you going to shoot me, too?"

"Only if you offer His Grace good wishes," Edgerton said. "He is in that room there."

Ran was about to open the designated door when he turned back to Edgerton. "Have you been provided with somewhere to sleep? We are a bit overrun with visiting servants just now but—"

"Mr Neate has engaged rooms for us at the Pig and Whistle, in Beckhampton."

"Naturally he has. I would expect nothing less of him, especially when he was last seen in Exeter. How does he contrive to travel round the country so quickly? Hires a hack mount and labours along in our dust, I suppose, for I never once saw him."

"He takes the stage," Edgerton said, grinning. "The mail, if a route offers itself, but otherwise the common stage. He invariably arrives before we do, and you would not notice him if you were to observe him, my lord. He is very unobtrusive — it is his special skill. He will be here later. The three of us have a rota worked out, so you need not worry that His Grace will be left unprotected."

"You are very efficient, Captain," Ran said, laughing. "I thank you, but please try not to shoot anyone, not even Aunt Agatha."

Ran opened the door and entered the sitting room. At the far end, the dining table was set for three persons, but only Ger and Ginny sat there, calmly eating from the array of dishes laid out there.

"There you are, Ran! Could you not escape them sooner? We started without you, for we were famished."

"You are not planning to dine with the family, then?" Ran said, frowning.

"Are they still here?"

"Of course they are still here! It would be unconscionable to toss sixty relations out to fend for themselves at this hour. I will see what I can do to get rid of them in the morning, but they will dine here tonight, in the State Banqueting Room, if you please!"

"Oh, I should like to see that!" Ginny said. "Jon has told me so much about the different rooms here, but that is one of the most splendid, isn't it? What a pity we have already had our dinner."

Ger looked so horrified that Ran laughed. "You are a remarkable woman, Miss Chandry, but you will never persuade Ger that eating with sixty or more relations is an enjoyable occasion."

"I have no objection to them in small numbers," Ger said. "In the summer, they come and go, so we never have more than a dozen or two here at a time. But sixty! What are they about, coming here like carrion crows to poke and pry? It is the outside of enough."

"They want to see you," Ran said gently, "and I am afraid they will not leave until they have done so. I cannot make them, you know, and nor can you, if they refuse to leave. Much better to show yourself once or twice, and then they will be satisfied and go away."

"I cannot, Ran, you know that. I hate all such crowds, where everyone is pointing at me. If I can slip away into a corner, such gatherings are tolerable — amusing, even, sometimes. But to be the centre of attention — no, it is too difficult."

"Do you think you could manage to put in an appearance after tea... just drop in, say a few words here and there? For a few minutes, perhaps?"

But he shook his head decisively, and Ran gave it up, and went to his own room to change. He had to scramble into his evening clothes, which he hated doing, but it was already past the dinner hour, and when he reached the State Boudoir, he found everyone assembled awaiting his arrival in varying degrees of impatience, all in their evening finery. Considering that it was no more than a family gathering, there was so much silk and gold and jewellery on display that Ran felt quite nauseous. He signed to Brent to announce dinner almost immediately.

The State Banqueting Room had probably not been used for ten years or more, not since the Sixth Duke had last been well enough to entertain on his traditional lavish scale. It was reputed to hold one hundred diners in tolerable comfort, but even the four and sixty gathered that evening made the room look full. Like all the state rooms on the first floor, the Banqueting Room boasted high, arching ceilings, with massive chandeliers and mirrors everywhere, so the room was as dazzlingly bright as a summer's day. There was still the odd cobweb here and there if one looked closely, but the housemaids had done a good job of preparing the room at such short notice. Far above them, the diners' appetites were encouraged by Biblical feast scenes painted onto the ceiling. Around the walls, the finest of Valmont's collection of paintings — Titians and Van Dycks, two Canalettos and a Rubens, and others Ran could not remember. Ger would know what they all were, and their histories, but he did not.

Ran sat in the middle of one side, for the two end chairs, as massively ornate as thrones, were kept for the duke and duchess only. No one else was permitted to sit there. Ran wondered idly if, when Ger entertained here, he would seat Ginny in the duchess's chair. Probably he would, for he had enough effrontery even for that. But no, for Ger himself would never entertain here. It would be far too large a gathering for him.

The first course was already set out before them, and Ran could only applaud the ingenuity of the kitchens in providing so lavish a feast at such short notice. The guests ate and talked and drank and talked, and Ran smiled until he felt his cheeks stiffen. So much civility was exhausting. A second course was set out, then some desserts. The ladies withdrew, and the gentlemen gathered around Ran to ask more probing questions about *'that pretty little filly of Gervase's'*, questions which Ran could not answer to his own satisfaction, let alone theirs. Eventually, he felt that duty had been done and returned to the State Boudoir, fervently hoping the tea had arrived.

It had not, but all thought of it was swept away by the sight of Ger hesitantly entering the room from the opposite door — and with Ginny on his arm. Ran almost groaned at the sight, for this was exactly the sort of flaunting he had feared. It was too brazen... in fact, it was outrageous to introduce his mistress to the respectable matrons and spinsters of the family. But there was nothing to be done except to smile yet again and pretend that all was well, for any attempt to intervene would cause exactly the kind of uproar he hoped to avoid.

The two had not donned evening wear, but Ger had put on a different coat and Ginny a fresh gown, with a delicate shawl draped over her arms. She had one hand tucked into Ger's arm, and she was smiling with unmistakable warmth, a vivid contrast to Ger's uncertainty. She, at least, was happy to meet the family, even sixty at a time. Slowly they moved around the room, and it was Ginny who did the talking, Ran observed, Ginny who responded with faultless accent and unwavering grace to the endless questions, Ginny who patted Ger's arm gently whenever he showed signs of panic. And it was Ginny who drew the attention of all eyes.

As the gentlemen drifted into the room, Ger showed signs of being ready to bolt, but they had progressed to the far side of the room and it was not easy to escape. They were close to the pianoforte, however, and Ginny turned to Ger and said, "Would you like to play something? I am sure everyone would care for a little music."

His eyes met hers. "Would *you* care for it?"

"Very much."

Without another word, he sat down at the instrument and began to play. He needed no light, no music, no one to turn the pages. His fingers knew their way, and within moments he was lost in the music, his audience entirely forgotten. Ginny continued moving round the room, talking to whoever wished to speak to her, sitting beside formidable Aunt Jane when she patted the sofa imperiously, blushing prettily when Uncle Arthur patted her cheek, and moving politely away when Cousin James tried to flirt with her. And all the while, she watched Ger carefully for the least sign of distress.

Ran could only applaud, and for now, it would do well enough. But when all these relations came back in the summer and Ginny's condition was obvious — what then? How on earth was he to get her discreetly tucked away out of sight, as any mistress must be? Or was Max's solution the only option — to get rid of her altogether? He could not see a way forward that would appease Ger's notions of what was due to Ginny, and also avoid scandal. At all costs, the proprieties must be observed, for anything else was too distressing for words.

13: Early Awakening

Ran dropped into an exhausted sleep the instant he lay down, but he woke early, refreshed and invigorated. He liked to sleep with the shutters open, so golden morning light poured into the room, warming the air. He stretched languorously, then let out a laugh of pure pleasure. This was a good day to be alive! He was home at Valmont, and Ger was there with him again. They were together, just as they should be, he in his bed and Ger in his. It was still early, he saw from the clock on the mantle. Too early for Ger, perhaps.

He threw back the covers and pulled on a banyan, padding on bare feet through the small antechamber to the sitting room. The fire had been re-laid but not yet lit, the chairs straightened and all evidence of the evening tidied away. He smiled, imagining the chamber maid finding Captain Edgerton on guard duty and pleading to be let in to do her work. Had he stood over her to be sure she did not wander off to oppress Ger with unwanted good wishes? He shook his head ruefully. The good captain was a little over zealous, perhaps, but his good offices had saved them from inconvenience or worse on the journey, and were now ensuring that Ger had the quietude his soul craved.

Ger was not in the sitting room, so he must still be abed. Ran's smile broadened. It was time he was awake, the slug-a-bed! Quietly he crept out of the sitting room and through Ger's antechamber, then, opening the door inch by inch to forestall squeaks, he slipped inside Ger's room. It was still dark, the shutters closed, the curtains still drawn round the bed. Ran tiptoed across the room, then with one swift tug, parted the curtains.

"Good morning, you lazy—"

The round face of Ginny Chandry peeped up at him with a mischievous expression. The covers were pulled up to her shoulders but even with her abundant hair tumbling loose, he could see that she wore no nightgown. Ger lay fast asleep with his bare back towards Ran, his face buried in Ginny's hair and one arm resting casually across her.

"Oh!" Ran flicked the curtains closed again, mortified. "I beg your pardon."

Ginny giggled, and Ger's sleepy voice murmured, "Ran? What o'clock is it?"

"Six. Just after six."

Then he turned and fled, Ginny's giggles following him all the way. *Damnation!* He was not sure whether he was most annoyed with Ger for taking his lightskirt into his own bed, right here in Valmont, or with himself for not guessing that it was just the sort of stupid thing that he would do. And beyond that was another, stronger feeling — was it jealousy? How glorious it must be to wake up beside the woman of one's heart in that way, and one day, perhaps— But he dared not think of it. Everything was too uncertain. Devil take Ger for such foolishness!

In the sitting room, he rang the bell violently, and then, three seconds later, rang it again, even harder. Then, realising that Giggs must be in the dressing room already, he stormed away to find him and send him for coffee.

When he returned to the sitting room, Ger was just emerging, yawning, from his own room, more decorously attired in a nightgown and robe.

"What is *she* doing in there?" Ran burst out.

Ger raised his eyebrows. "Where else should she be but in my bed? She is my lover, Ran. My mistress. I *want* her with me, all night and every night."

"Not in *that* bed! Not in *that* room!"

"Why ever not?"

"Because—" Ran stopped, realising that if Ger did not instinctively understand the issue, there was no conceivable way of explaining it to him. "Never mind."

"No, tell me," Ger said. "Ah, is that coffee, Giggs? Excellent fellow. Put it over here, will you."

Ran prowled about the room while Giggs fussed about with the coffee tray, but eventually he was gone. Ger poured at the small table where they had customarily eaten their breakfast, or drunk brandy into the small hours, or played backgammon, one of few games where Ran could compete with Ger.

"Sit down and drink your coffee, brother," Ger said equably. "Or at least drink while you pace about, but it would be better for you to sit. Watching you prowling about is making me tired."

Ran chuckled. When Ger was in humour, he could charm the roses into bloom, and he could certainly soothe Ran's ruffles. He sat down and picked up his coffee cup.

Ger said gently, "You have never been in love, have you, brother? If you had, you would understand how it is to want to be with someone and never be apart. I cannot bear to be separated from Ginny, even for an hour, and the journey here was torture. Now she is back with me all the time, and it is *wonderful!* She makes me so happy."

"Then that makes me happy, too," Ran said. "But— No, it does not matter."

"Indeed it does!" Ger cried. "You must tell me what is in your heart, for we have never had secrets from each other, have we? You always knew my sentiments on any subject, and I yours. We are not alike, in fact I swear no two brothers were ever less alike in temperament or ways, excepting only the closeness we share and will always share. So tell me honestly why you dislike Ginny."

Ran gazed at him in astonishment. "Is that what you believe? You could not be further from the truth, I assure you. I like her very well, and every day increases my admiration for her. That she has won your affections would be enough to recommend her to me, but I have seen the calm way she has endured this upheaval in her life. There is not a woman in a thousand who could have accepted this change with such equanimity, and yet she is not devoid of sensibility. Look at the way she handled the aunts land uncles last night, diverting their attention away from you, and all the while offering you constant reassurance. It was very well done."

"Oh," Ger said, surprised. "Then what troubles you?"

"It is not Ginny herself, it is the situation," Ran said firmly. "She is your *mistress*, Ger, and you cannot have her living here at Valmont, not permanently."

Ger's expression darkened. "She is my guest, Ran, and I will not have her—"

"—disrespected, I know. But people *will* disrespect her, because you have dishonoured her and reduced her from respectability to degradation. Yes, degradation, for make no mistake, brother, she may be a duke's mistress, but she is still a *mistress* and therefore outside all good society. No, no, hear me out!" he cried, as Ger jumped to his feet in anger. "You must see what you are doing, both to her and to Valmont. You may do what you wish here, of course, for the house is yours, but what happens if you marry?"

"I shall never marry!"

"But I shall, and I cannot bring my wife to a house that contains your mistress. Half your relations would shun you. Your neighbours would decline your invitations. Your own sisters could not visit you, for they have their own and their daughters' reputations to consider. Can you not understand that?"

Ger's face for the first time registered chagrin. "Would it truly be as bad as that?"

"You know it would."

"Then what is to be done?" he whispered.

"Nothing hasty. Ginny's condition is not obvious as yet, so for now everyone is taking you at your word that she is your guest. But in a few weeks..."

Ger's face was bleak. "I cannot send her away, Ran. I *will* not! I swore an oath that I would keep her with me no matter where I should go, and I cannot break my word."

"No, no! Of course you cannot. You have a duty of responsibility towards her and her child, naturally, and a mistress is not at all unusual in our level of society, so long as she is kept out of public view. Discretion is vital. But we may be able to find a way to keep her close to you without her being precisely in Valmont itself. She could live in one of the lodges, perhaps, or the Old Manor. Or a house in Beckhampton, although that would be rather public."

Ger pulled a face. "And every time I want to see her, I have to go out in the rain or the wind or some icy blast. Or perhaps I should call the carriage out every time? As for Ginny, she would be there alone while I am away being the duke. Can you not understand that Ginny is not some cheap woman of pleasure, to be picked up and dropped on a whim? I *love* her, Ran! She is everything to me, and I will not throw her out of my home just because society might disapprove."

"I understand, but—"

"No, I cannot think that you do! She has to be by my side, not exiled to some inconvenient little house somewhere, where the neighbours all pretend to respect her but secretly look down their arrogant noses at her."

"No one respects a mistress!" Ran said in annoyance. "You are asking for the moon!"

"They will respect *my* mistress, because I will not countenance anything less."

"And they will appear to do it, just as long as you are there, but it will all be a lie, Ger. Can you not see that?"

Instantly the fight went out of him. "Because I dishonoured her," he said, rubbing one hand tiredly across his face. "What am I to do, brother?"

"There is one obvious solution," Ran said slowly. "It would set the tabbies frothing for a while, but they would accept it in the end."

"What is that?"

"You could marry her."

A sound made him pause. The door from Ger's room had been left open and Ginny stood there, in her nightgown, but wrapped in a voluminous shawl. The hair — her lovely, red-tinged hair — was now caught up in a simple knot.

"No," she said quietly. "No marriage. I want nothing to do with being a duchess. Sorry if I interrupt you, but you were yelling at each other, and I would not have you quarrel on my account."

Ger jumped to his feet, his face softening instantly at the sight of her. "Not quarrelling, my love."

"Arguing then," she said, her quick smile. "Disputing, fighting, squabbling, bickering, falling out—"

He laughed but shook his head. "Ran and I never fall out, I assure you. We may have differences of opinion but—"

"Loud ones!"

"—we shall never be other than the best of friends."

"We do fight, though," Ran put in. "With swords. I usually win."

"That is only because you have a longer reach than I do," Ger said. "You are taller than me, and fatter."

"My skill is greater, that is all," Ran said grinning. "And I am not fat — that is all muscle, Mr Weakling. But if I *am* larger than you, that just gives you an easier mark to hit."

"Now, now, children!" Ginny said, laughing at them. "This is not convincing evidence that you never fall out, so stop it at once. Pour me some coffee, my love, and Lord Randolph may tell me what you were *not* quarrelling about."

"Since we are all in our night attire still, I believe we may dispense with the formalities, Ginny. Call me Ran, if you please."

She nodded her acquiescence, seeming pleased, and while Ger rummaged in a cupboard for a spare cup and poured coffee, Ran repeated all that he had said to Ger.

Ginny sipped thoughtfully, listening without interruption, and shushing Ger whenever he tried to speak. When Ran had finished, she said, "What is usual, in your world? How would a nobleman establish a mistress?"

"Is that truly what you want?" Ran said. "To be Ger's mistress rather than his wife? Your children will be illegitimate, with all the difficulties that brings, and you will never be accepted by society. You would prefer that?"

She looked at him consideringly. "I would," she said quietly. "We all have our place in the world, and it upsets the balance if we step outside our natural sphere. Gervase was destined to live his life high in the social order, and I am destined to be far below him. I shall be very content as his mistress, making a refuge for him from the hurly-burly of his public life. So tell me, what is the usual way for a great lord to deal with a mistress?"

"He would buy her a house somewhere, furnish it and provide the necessities — a carriage, horses, servants," Ran said. "In an inconspicuous part of London, perhaps, or else in a quiet little town in the shires. She would receive an allowance. There is often a contract drawn up to specify what happens when they part, the arrangements for children, that sort of thing. Not legally enforceable, but the man is honour-bound to conform to the terms agreed upon."

"You know a great deal about such matters," Ger said, eyes twinkling. He had one arm curled around Ginny's back as they sat close together on the sofa, and all his good humour had returned in force. "Can it be that you have a little lady of your own tucked away somewhere?"

Ran laughed and disclaimed any personal knowledge. "I have had to go through Father's papers since his death, so naturally I have seen how he managed his affairs."

"Father had a mistress?" Ger cried, eyes round. "Truly?"

"Lord, yes! And Grandfather, too. His papers are still there. There is a locked box for private family documents of that type, which no one but me has read. Grandfather kept his current mistress in the Old Manor, for convenience, and then settled them in the north. One went to Harrogate, I recall. Scarborough for another. Father had a place in town for a mistress when he was young and was not so much at Valmont, but once he married and settled here, and it became tedious haring back and forth to town all the time, he bought Merrington House, up at Andover."

"What, Uncle Swithin's place? Good grief! Why not the Old Manor? Or one of the lodges?"

"I can only guess that he wanted the lady kept well out of sight," Ran said. "Father was always very conscious of Mother's consequence, and would never allow the least thing to disturb her tranquillity."

"Well!" Ger said. "It was certainly out of *my* sight. I never suspected it for a moment, imagining him to be a faithful and affectionate husband."

"The affection was real, I believe, but he was never faithful, and maintained a mistress all his adult life, until illness caught up with him."

"You can hardly be shocked by it," Ginny said, taking hold of Ger's hand and gently stroking it. "Men are lamentably fond of distributing their affections far and wide, and such a tendency is hardly a great secret. My own father produced any number of bastards, and it looks like I shall follow where he led." She chuckled, not at all discomfited by the idea. "As for the nobs like you, I thought they all had mistresses."

"Many do, it is true," Ger said. "When a man is obliged to marry for duty, he looks for affection elsewhere, and when one is heir to a great title, one is very much expected to marry for duty. In fact, a likely bride is selected at an early age."

"An arranged marriage?" Ginny said. "How quaint! Who was to be your bride?"

"The Lady Ruth Grenaby, eldest daughter of the Duke of Orrisdale. The two fathers hatched the plan between them. So *suitable*, you see. Duke's son, duke's daughter."

"Oh, yes, just like Hannah Packer from the Pendower inn marrying William Gardiner from the Carsham Arms at Yarlford. Innkeeper's son, innkeeper's daughter."

Ran spluttered into his coffee. "Ginny, you are the most complete hand!"

"Well, it *is* the same, isn't it, although I expect the dowry was a bit different. Hannah had a hundred pounds and two barrels of the good ale. I imagine a duke's daughter has a slightly higher price."

"Just slightly. Ruth has thirty thousand," Ran said, still laughing.

"A tidy sum indeed," Ginny said. "You ought to snaffle her at once, Jon."

"If you will not have me, dearest, then I shall not marry anyone," Ger said lightly.

"Poor Lady Ruth! Will she have to settle for a mere marquess now?"

"It is even worse than that," Ran said. "She will be obliged to settle for the mere second son of a duke."

There was a momentary pause, then she worked it out. "You?"

"We were betrothed last month. It was in all the newspapers."

Ginny stared at him, her face troubled. "I never read the newspapers. But then... she thought you were the duke. You thought Ger was dead and you were the duke, so you took on the bride that should have been Jon's and she agreed to it. An arranged marriage."

That shot straight to the heart of the matter. Ginny was too perceptive by half.

"It does not necessarily follow that an arranged marriage must be unwelcome," Ran said, warily. Even to his brother, he hesitated to say too much.

"No, but… she was supposed to marry a duke and now she gets you instead, and she might be upset not to be a duchess after all. Or she might not like you as well as Jon… Gervase."

"We are betrothed," Ran said again. "That is a promise almost as binding as marriage. We are to be married in three weeks. Ruth will not cry off."

He spoke the words with assurance, but underneath he quailed. He could not honourably withdraw, but Ruth certainly could, and the change in his rank would be all the explanation the world would need. All he could do was to cling to the hope that Ruth's sense of honour was as great as his own.

14: The Ways Of Nobles

It took five days for all the aunts, uncles and cousins to be persuaded that they would be better entertained elsewhere. They were provided with every comfort, and a splendid dinner each night, but the only amusement was such as they could contrive for themselves, since Ger and the interesting Miss Chandry stayed resolutely out of sight.

Ran recruited his sisters to the Herculean task of ridding Valmont of its unwanted guests. Henrietta, Alice, Elizabeth and Georgiana were perfectly willing to oblige him, and with the aid of the London newspapers and letters from friends, gradually convinced the lingerers of the delights of the season that were passing them by. At first, the party atmosphere prevailed, but it was not long before the lack of sport began to bear down on the gentlemen, the flow of family news dwindled amongst the ladies and the long-standing feud between two regal dowagers, usually maintained by icily polite insults, flared into open warfare. By the third day, the State Banqueting Room had been closed up in favour of the Dining Room, holding a mere forty covers, and finally to the Buttery, with its limit of four and twenty. Eventually the day came when the last carriage was waved off. Only Elizabeth remained, as well as Uncle Arthur and Aunt Anne.

"Will Ger and Miss Chandry dine with us tonight, Ran?" Elizabeth said, as the great entrance doors, two storeys high, closed for the last time. "That would make eight covers only, so long as you do not object to my presence, but my cook does not arrive until next week and Mary Bucknell not until the week after. However, I shall eat cold boiled mutton and cheese in my own house, if you prefer it."

Ran laughed. "You are welcome to eat your mutton with us — hot, I hope! — every day, if you wish it, and Mary too."

"Oh no, I shall not inflict myself on you more than once or twice a week. Sunday would suit me, so that my cook may have an easier day, and perhaps Wednesdays, but otherwise I shall not trouble you, for I do not mean to be a charge upon Valmont. I am very grateful for my little lodge house, but I shall keep my own cook and stable my own horses and carriage."

They had reached the Royal Withdrawing Room, and she seemed to want to talk, so he ushered her inside. "You are never a trouble, sister. As to your first question, I cannot answer for Ger or Ginny."

"I hope they will emerge from hiding soon, for I have a great wish to get to know Miss Chandry better. I take it she is not just a passing visitor?"

"No, she will make her home here... or nearby, at any event."

"Ah," Elizabeth said pensively. "That is as I thought. What sort of man was her father?"

"A gentleman, although he also acted as estate manager for a shipowner. From what I have gleaned, the family is not so well off as it once was, but they are well-regarded in the county."

"Respectable?"

Ran thought of the bastards supposedly set at Patrick Chandry's door, and hesitated momentarily. He had taken care of his by-blows, however, so even if he had been a libertine, he was not dishonourable. "A bit ramshackle," he said eventually, "but respectable, yes."

"Could she conceivably be moulded into a duchess?"

"She has no wish to be a duchess," Ran said.

"I wonder why. Most women would jump at it. And I note that you only speak of *her* wish. Ger is perfectly capable of deciding to marry such a woman on a whim."

"It would not be a whim."

"Perhaps not, but I wonder sometimes if Ger truly knows what is due to the honour of this family. He has always shied away from his obligations, Ran. He *says* he will do it, like agreeing to marry Lady Ruth, but when it came to the sticking point, he jibbed at it and fled to America."

"That was not—"

"Oh, I know. Not the only reason. But then he stayed away, even when it was obvious... Ah well, at least he is here now, but I am still not clear on whether he will fulfil his obligations. Will he take his seat this session?"

"I believe not."

"There you are, then. *You* would have done so. *You* understand your duty, and have behaved just as you ought. But Ger cannot be depended on in the least, and now this Miss Chandry complicates matters considerably. If he will not marry her, then we shall just have to make sure that he appreciates what he must do and will resume his betrothal to Lady Ruth as soon as may be. Her father will be compliant, I am sure. He will prefer his daughter to be the Duchess of Falconbury rather than Lady Randolph. I am sorry for it for *your* sake, for it would have been a good match for you, but I imagine you will not have much choice in the matter. You will need to look a little lower for a wife now, but you will not have the slightest difficulty there. You are not as lively as Ger can be, but a steady man makes a better husband. Well, I shall go and tell Mrs Newall that we may be eight for dinner."

She bustled out, leaving Ran quivering with fear. He could almost feel Ruth drifting slowly but inexorably away from him.

~~~~~

Ran was up early the following morning to write some brief personal letters. There were always personal letters to be written. He had a great many friends, and many of them had heard of Ger's return, and had sent congratulations or anxious enquiries, according to their temperaments. Two or three also asked in roundabout ways whether his engagement was now at an end. No one was crass enough to say it directly, merely asking vaguely whether the wedding would be affected and how had his betrothed taken the news and wondering what Ger thought of his engagement. His reply was always the same. *'I have no additional news of my own wedding plans.'*
~~~~~

As always when he thought of Ruth, a ripple of anxiety ran through him. It had been so wonderful — too wonderful, of course. How could he ever aspire to marry a woman as perfect as Ruth? No, not perfect, for no one was perfect. What were her faults? He considered for some time before he could find one, for her virtues were many. She was so composed, so ladylike. Her manners were flawless, and she moved in any company with well-bred ease, yet without condescension. There was no undue pride or hauteur, indeed she was modest in demeanour. Her clothes were elegant without ostentation. She was accomplished beyond the common meaning of that word — her music, her painting, her embroidery! Her mind was improved. She rode well and danced well. Her temper was even, with a charming sweetness. And she was beautiful! Those lovely grey eyes, and her hair — not quite golden, but pale brown like sun-bleached wood.

He could not suppress a smile as he thought of her. But a fault? He decided in the end that she had little sensibility. Not that she was unfeeling, for she was considerate. Once when she had visited — she must have been about fifteen or so — one of the horses grew lame, and she gave up her own so that a cousin might ride instead. And later, when a different horse fell and broke a leg, she had cried and cried, sobbing her heart out. Ger had hugged her until the tears stopped, and then let her win five times at cribbage.

It seemed churlish to praise her composure and modesty, and yet also to wish that she could be a little more communicative, but so it was. If she had feelings or opinions on a subject, it would not be improper for her to express them, and yet she never did. When he had sat beside her at the Mallowfleet dining table and asked which dish she would like him to serve her, she invariably chose the nearest. When he had taken her into the Valmont stables and enquired which horse she would like to ride, she had asked him to choose one for her. And when he had asked if she were being pressured to marry him, she had turned the question back at him. Even now, he had no idea what was in her mind… or her heart.

Pointless to wonder about it, he supposed. When he went to London, he would talk to her father and learn his mind. Perhaps they could still come to some accommodation. The engagement had been puffed off in all the newspapers, everyone had been informed, the date had been set. The duke's sense of honour might overcome his ambition, and he had three other daughters, after all. And then… Ran would either marry Ruth or he would not, and that was all there was to it. In another week or ten days, he would make the journey to town and then he would know his fate.

He finished his letters in sombre mood, then dressed and sat down in the shared sitting room to eat an early breakfast. There was no sign of Ger, but before too long the connecting door opened and Ginny's face peered round it.

"May I come in? Please do not be polite, for if you had sooner be alone, I shall not mind a bit. Jon is always cross in the mornings, just until he wakes up properly, so I quite understand."

"Do come in, and have some breakfast with me. I am never cross in the mornings, but then I wilt if the evening goes on too long. Ger and I are opposites in that, as in much else."

She slipped into the room, shutting the door quietly. Her round gown of plain cotton was unassuming and she wore her hair in a simple knot, but there was a certain dignity to her bearing that Ran rather liked. On their journey from Cornwall, he had thought her a provincial nobody, but she had not been overwhelmed by the grandeur of Valmont, or the combined majesty of the Litherholm family in all its fashionable, expensive glory. She had, by some feminine art, persuaded Ger to show himself on that first night, and if he had been as nervous as a girl, Ginny had displayed a becoming decorum. Whatever her origins, she was not out of place at Valmont.

And yet, her position was quite untenable.

"Is Ger still sleeping?"

She laughed. "Oh yes! He kept me up half the night, talking. He enjoyed himself eventually last night, I think." She sat down opposite him, quite unselfconscious, and began helping herself from the various dishes as he poured her coffee. "He took five hundred pounds off your uncle at piquet, in the end. I think you had gone to bed before Lord Arthur finally admitted defeat. And then he played whist with Captain Edgerton, Mr Lorrimer and my brother. He won two hundred pounds there. He was as merry as a grig, I can tell you."

"He has always been at his best in intimate gatherings, where everyone is well-known to him. The addition of Captain Edgerton and your brother was well done, I think. They are both lively, entertaining company."

"That is what I thought — useful to take the attention away from Jon. I mean Gervase. I shall have to get used to his real name, I suppose."

"So it was your idea to include them? Then you have my thanks. You have a deft hand with these situations, and you have learnt quickly what he can cope with comfortably and what will be a trial to him."

"Well, he talks to me, you see," she said simply. "He tells me everything that is in his heart and so I can suggest ways to make him easier. It does surprise me that he is so averse to large crowds. I never noticed it at home... although he tended to sit in a corner, avoiding attention. That is what he dislikes so, being stared at."

"I think that was Father's fault. Ger was the heir, so he was produced for inspection, as it were, whenever Father entertained, even as a boy."

"And you were not?"

"Not until I was older. But you can imagine the effect on a shy boy of six or seven to be brought into a room full of men of power, and all of them looking at him, asking him questions he could not answer, judging him. Even when I was permitted to accompany him, no one ever took any notice of me. It was all Ger. As he grew up, he became adept at finding ways to avoid such encounters. The fewer people he has to deal with, the better he gets on."

"Poor little boys!" she said, unexpectedly. "The one overwhelmed with attention and the other ignored. I am not sure which is worse."

"I cannot say," he said. "Ginny... may I speak frankly to you? Your position here is... awkward, to make no bones about it. When I first met you, I thought you would find the adjustment to the Valmont way of life difficult — perhaps impossible. But it is not so. You are not rattled by anything, are you? It seems to me that, even though you have not been brought up to it, you would make an excellent duchess."

She chortled merrily. "Oh no, no, no! Don't you start! I'm not going to marry him, not for anything. I could never be comfortable with a fancy title."

"You would grow accustomed."

She looked at him sorrowfully. "You don't understand. It is not just that I wouldn't fit in to your world, I don't *want* to fit in. To me, the peerage is an abomination. What purpose does it serve?"

"Someone has to rule, to make the laws and ensure that they are obeyed, or there would be chaos. Someone has to collect the taxes to maintain our army and navy, and protect us from the French. The few are needed to guide the country so that the many may grow their crops and make their goods and raise their families in peace and plenty."

"And how is it right for those few people to claim the right to rule over everyone else, to have vast wealth, to do nothing useful with their lives, to be so pampered they can't even dress themselves — and all because they were born to one family rather than another? The many work from dawn to dusk so that the few may sit about as idle parasites."

"You think we do no work, is that it?"

"Unless you count inspecting the stables and changing your clothes five times a day as work," she said, laughing merrily.

"Then finish your coffee, and let me show you what this particular idle parasite does with his useless, pampered life."

"Jon — Gervase — will wonder where I am."

"Ah, let me show you our secret message board." He crossed the room to where a nondescript mirror hung by a chain from a single nail. Flipping it over, it became a chalk board. He rummaged in a drawer for chalks. *'Taken Ginny to see the offices. R.'*

"Clever," she said, setting down her coffee cup and rising from her chair. "Lead on, Ran."

He took her down one floor to his formal office, all mirrors, polished wood, painted ceilings and gilded majesty. The massive desk dominated the room. "This is where I sign contracts and legal documents. On Lady Day, the tenants come here to pay their rent. They come in through the front door, up the Grand Staircase, through the State Apartments to here, where I greet them affably, take their money and offer them a small glass of sherry and a ratafia biscuit. They seem to like it. But this is not where the real work is done."

He led her down again to the mezzanine floor. "The offices. The domestic offices are on the ground floor, but this is where the estate is managed."

He threw open the door to the under-secretaries' room, where four faces looked up, four men jumped to their feet. Ran introduced each one to Ginny, and they bowed politely. Then it was on to the steward's office, with Gurney and his assistant, the Comptroller's office, with its two large safes, and finally the attorneys' office. As they left, Ginny pointed to the brass name-plates on the door.

"So many Honourables. What does that mean?"

"An Honourable is the son of a nobleman."

Ginny frowned. "Are there not men of lower rank just as fitted to be secretaries and attorneys?"

"Younger sons are obliged to make their own way in the world," Ran said with a rueful smile, "or make themselves useful in other ways. But also, the sons of the nobility are less likely to stutter and stumble if they should happen to meet a marquess or two roaming the corridors."

"And these people are all here to manage Valmont?"

"And its many holdings — land and other property, principally, but there are businesses, too. Mines, manufactories, mills and so on. We have managers for those, and bailiffs and gamekeepers for the land. The offices here are just a small part of it. Oh, and we have some very grand London lawyers who draw up all the significant estate papers — wills, marriage settlements, that sort of thing. Markham, Willerton-Forbes and Browning."

"Is that *the* Mr Willerton-Forbes?"

"No, Sir Rathbone Willerton-Forbes is the family lawyer. Mr Pettigrew Willerton-Forbes is his nephew, and was not known to me before he became entangled with the Benefactor."

She chuckled suddenly. "Oh, that explains something that puzzled me greatly at the time. When Mr Willerton-Forbes first came to Pendower, Jon was terrified at the very name, but of course he thought the family lawyers had found him out. And then he discovered that he was to receive a thousand pounds from the Benefactor instead, and he was so relieved. How funny!"

They had come to the final room, somewhat larger than the rest. Here two identical deal tables sat facing each other, and

Max Lorrimer was hard at work at one of them, head bent over a sheet of paper, writing swiftly. He looked up with a smile, which slipped a little when he saw Ginny, but he rose politely, and bowed to her.

"Max, I am trying to prove to Miss Chandry that I am not the idle good-for-nothing she believes me to be. Would you be so good as to tell her of my schedule for the day?"

"Of course, my lord," he said politely, but without warmth. "Letters first, six personal and three and twenty related to estate business. Mr Vine will be here at ten to discuss the woodcock problems, then Mr Downer about the drainage in the Upper Shallowford fields. At eleven, Mr Morrell wishes you to review the new leases for Brackbury. If you have time, Sir Henry would like you to look over the accounts, but you must be down at the stables by noon sharp to ride out to Claverley Mill. The insurance man will meet you there. I told Mr Peckham that you might call in on your way home, but that you might not have time without making yourself late for dinner."

"And all of these people, and many more besides, have employment and live in comfort because of it," Ran said.

"Enough! You have convinced me you are not totally without purpose," Ginny said, but distractedly, for her eye had been drawn to a series of maps pinned to the wall. "This is Valmont, isn't it?"

"Yes. The main house, the eight lodges, the three adjoining villages, stables, estate cottages, ice house up here, Old Manor in the trees here. This one is the larger Valmont estate, showing the outer fields and woods, and the other map over there is of England and Wales, showing all the Valmont holdings elsewhere."

She peered more closely at the Valmont map. "What is this oddly drawn path that seems to have trees growing out of it?"

Ran laughed. "That marks the tunnel that connects the Old Manor to the main house. The Third Duke lived in the Old Manor while Valmont was being built, and after one dreadful winter with snow piled up everywhere, he ordered the tunnel built. It is used for storage now, but it is still sound."

"What is the Old Manor like?" she said, turning clear blue eyes on him.

"Rambling, dark, dismal and possibly haunted. Very old-fashioned. Six bedrooms. We use it occasionally when we get a newly-married pair here, but most of the family dislike it."

"But it might suit me very well, do you not think?" she said. "Then I can stay out of sight of all your grand relations, and no one will be shocked by me."

"It might, with a bit of work," he said, in pleased surprise. She was a sensible and practical young lady, he was realising. "Ger will not like it, though. I believe he wants to shock them."

She gave a low, throaty laugh. "Leave me to manage Ger."

Ran smiled his approval, but Max merely glowered silently at her.

15: Meetings

MAY

Ruth's father was all for leaving town immediately, but for once the duchess stood her ground. Susan could not be abandoned, she told her husband firmly. He must wait until she had worked upon Lady Crosby and persuaded that lady that her plan for Susan to visit Crosby Manor must be very soon. The dowager grumbled and fussed and protested that she had too many engagements to leave town just now, but in the end she was brought to appreciate the urgency, and all was set in motion. Even then it took her several days to prepare herself for the journey. All the while Ruth's father fretted and brooded, and it was only when Ruth helped him to calculate just how many days it would be before Ran and Ger reached Valmont that his grumbles abated.

It was fortunate for Ruth that they could not leave at once, for never had her thoughts and emotions been so turbulent. Ger alive! It was almost too much to take in. How was it possible? Where had he been for the past year — more than a year? What had he been doing? It was too puzzling for words. She had asked her father if she might read the letter bringing the tidings, and he had thrust it into her hands.

"There! See if you can make out that the fellow understands what is due to us, for I am sure I do not see it. Seems to think everything will go on just as it was. He is as foolish as you, Ruthie."

But the letter had provided little explanation.

'Trehannick Inn, Cornwall. My Lord Duke, I write to inform you that my brother Gervase was not drowned aboard the Brig Minerva *as supposed. He survived, although suffering from loss of memory, and has now been discovered alive in Cornwall. We leave for Valmont almost at once. I leave it to you to convey the news of my change in status to the Lady Ruth as you think best. This will delay my arrival in town, but I shall come to see you as soon as I am able. Randolph Litherholm.'*

Cornwall! That was where the ship had been wrecked, so he had found his way ashore, with no notion of who he was, and perhaps been cared for by the local people. Now his memory had returned. But there was nothing to tell her how Ger was — badly injured, perhaps, or with lingering effects from the head injuries that caused him to lose his memory. And what did Ran mean when he talked of coming to see them in town? To marry her or to jilt her? Did it make a difference to him? He had offered to marry her from duty because he was the duke and it was a long-standing obligation, but now, perhaps, he could honourably withdraw. He was not a duke after all, and any obligation sat with Ger. Although... *'convey the news of my change in status'*. That seemed as though he expected the marriage to proceed despite events. How confusing it was! She would not know what he intended until she could see him again.

Of her own feelings, Ruth was no more clear. The little glow that had warmed her ever since her betrothal was now dimmed. For two days she wrestled with the problem whenever she had a quiet moment during the day, and for long, long hours at night, as she lay wakeful beside Susan's slumbering form.

Her certainty of the rightness of her course had been swept away, she decided. When Ran was thought to be the duke, her parents' wishes, her sense of duty and her own preference had been in alignment. Now she was facing a terrible dilemma. If she were to insist on marrying Ran, and he were willing, then she would be putting herself against her father, and that would be a terrible thing. A rift with her own family would make her desperately unhappy. Could marriage to Ran be enough to compensate her for the breach? She would have no dowry, and perhaps he could not even afford to marry her without it, now that he had not the wealth of a dukedom to call upon.

Yet if she did not, could she marry Ger after all? Her father would be pleased, but Ger had been away for four years. He might have changed beyond recognition, even supposing he remained unmarried. She could barely remember him. It was Ran whose face rose most readily to her mind. And if she married neither of them, what would become of her? She was one and twenty, entering her fourth season, and the prospect of abandoning the Litherholms and beginning her search for a husband elsewhere was daunting.

She had reached no conclusions by the time the day of departure arrived. Susan, in sulky mood, had been carried away in Lady Crosby's vast travelling coach the day before, with Aunt Maria in attendance. Now the usual three coaches drew up outside the Berkeley Square house — the luxurious travelling coach, the considerably less luxurious second coach, bearing Papa's valet and the two lady's maids, and the lumbering baggage coach. Such a drama, with footmen rushing about with boxes and valises and band boxes and oddly-shaped packages, and why the need for three parasols apiece, anyway? And then there were horses stamping, coachmen shouting instructions and outriders milling about. A small crowd of passers-by had stopped to watch the performance, and three small boys were dodging about almost under the horses' hooves and making a thorough nuisance of themselves. Ruth felt a headache coming on.

Eventually, they were away, and Ruth's miserable confusion of mind now bore the added burden of many hours in the confinement of her parents' company. Her mother, normally too dignified to admit of any discomfort, felt at liberty in the privacy of her own carriage to complain of every lurch and jolt. She fancied herself a poor traveller, and required much sympathy and application of a vinaigrette to sustain her spirits on the journey, a task which the duke left to Ruth by the simple expedient of ignoring his wife. He, for his part, was still angry with Ran, although it was hardly his fault that he was not a duke. Ruth knew better than to offer any comment more challenging than "Yes, Papa," or "No, Papa," at regular intervals. There was no point in provoking him. Soon, very soon, she would see Ran again, and then she would know what her fate was to be.

They stayed overnight at Basingstoke, and early in the afternoon of the second day they turned in through the gates of Valmont.

"At what hour are we expected?" the duchess said. "I trust we are not too early. There is nothing so inconvenient as arriving exhausted to find nothing in readiness."

"Oh, well… I have not exactly advised them of our coming at all," the duke said, running a finger inside his high collar. "No need, you know… always very hospitable to unexpected arrivals… never at a loss. The rooms will be ready in a twinkling, I assure you."

The duchess moaned, but Ruth could not refrain from saying incredulously, "You have not *told* him we are coming? Have you replied to his letter at all?"

"No need, no need. Reply not expected, you know. Litherholm will be perfectly happy to see us."

Ruth fervently hoped he was right.

The Valmont servants had spotted the train of carriages arriving, and were awaiting them on the entrance steps. Ruth helped her mother out of the carriage and up the steps to the entrance hall, where she made a miraculous recovery from her indisposition, arranging herself elegantly on a wooden bench carved in the Egyptian style, with her maid and a footman in solicitous attendance. The duke was engaged in supervising the unloading of the luggage. It was left to Ruth to smile ruefully at the butler.

"Good day, Brent. What a troublesome family we are, to be sure, descending upon you unannounced in this ramshackle way."

"My lady's presence at Valmont could never be anything less than a pleasure, and your rooms will be prepared in a trice."

"You are very good. Ah, there you are, Pinnock." She allowed the maid to help her out of bonnet, pelisse and gloves. "Is Lord Randolph at home, Brent?"

"I regret to say that his lordship is out with the steward at present, and not expected back for two or three hours." He hesitated. "His Grace is at home, however. Shall I inform him of your ladyship's arrival? Or Lord Arthur may be in the Queen's Room."

"Lord Arthur will be enjoying his little snooze, and His Grace is at the instrument, I think. That music I hear can only be by his hand. Do not disturb them, if you please. Is the fire lit in the Ante-Chamber? We shall await Lord Randolph there. My father would be glad of something to revive his spirits, and some tea for my mother."

"I shall attend to it at once, my lady."

The butler bowed, and moved away, leaving Ruth alone in the middle of the entrance hall. In the distance, music drifted out from the Grand Saloon and she was irresistibly drawn in that direction, step by slow step. Nearer and nearer until she stood outside the gilded doors, listening in enchantment. She could not help herself... she gently turned the doorknob and pushed open the door a little way.

There he was, seated at the Broadwood looking just as he had always done. His hair was a little longer than was fashionable, but he wore his clothes in the same careless way, as if he had merely shrugged himself into whatever came to hand. His neckcloth looked as if he had tied it all by guess, without the benefit of a mirror. But he was the same Ger, throwing himself intensely into the performance, lost in his music.

He came to the end of the piece, and for a moment he sat motionless, the glow still upon his face. Then he somehow divined her presence, turned, smiled.

"Dussek," she said.

"Yes!" he cried, the smile breaking into a wide beam. "You know this sonata?"

"I learnt it last year. A lovely piece."

"Come, play it for me!" He jumped up and waved her to the stool. "Nothing is equal to the pleasure of hearing a piece played by another hand, especially yours. I shall turn for you."

Laughing, she did as she was bid, for the instrument was so fine that any invitation to play it was to be welcomed. For some minutes she played, but then her fingers ceased to move.

"What is it?" he said. "You were doing well."

"But not as well as you. You draw out something deeper, more moving that I cannot grasp."

"That is only because I have played nothing else for three days," he said. "See, this part here…"

He sat down beside her on the stool to demonstrate, and to Ruth, the years rolled away. She was twelve again, meeting Ger for the first time and discovering a fellow musician who talked to her, not as teacher to pupil, but as one performer to another. Such delight in having a friend with whom to discuss the nuances of this piece or that, the best way to play each one, the emotions that underlie a simple arrangement of notes. Until that moment, she had understood music only as an accomplishment to impress a potential husband. Ger had taught her that it was a pleasure to be enjoyed for its own self, for the joy it gave the performer, whether anyone else listened or not.

How long they sat there she could not say. There was laughter and teasing and threads of serious discourse, and she felt exactly as she had when they had first known each other, and she had realised that she had found a friend, and possibly a husband. It was only later, when she met Ran, and discovered that the lively, open-hearted Ger was sometimes replaced by a darkly moody stranger, that she had wondered how comfortable marriage to Ger might be. When he had seemingly died, therefore, it had not been hard to see in Ran a pleasingly acceptable substitute. Yet now, the delightful Ger was back, and if her father were to get his way and betroth her to Ger instead, she could not at that moment be displeased with the idea.

The door opened a little wider, accompanied by a delicate tapping and the simpering face of the duchess. "May I come in? But I have no wish to disturb such a charming picture as you present."

"Mama," Ruth said, rising to curtsy. "I beg your pardon, I have been neglecting you shamefully."

"Not at all. I have been very well attended, I assure you. There is tea, if you want some. How are you, Duke? Are you quite recovered from your dreadful ordeal? But such a miracle that you have been spared after all, and are returned to us again! I cannot tell you how thrilled we are to have you restored to us."

He bowed and murmured something civil, but there was a wariness in his eyes that surprised Ruth. They followed the duchess to the Ante-Chamber, where the duke pumped Ger's hand hard enough to make him wince, and they were plied with tea and sherry and macaroons and sugared cherries.

"You must forgive the rest of the family for not coming to greet you," Ger said. "My brother is out just now, my uncle and aunt are resting, and even the chaplain… where is Mr Ponsonby, Brent?"

"Visiting old Mrs Brown, Your Grace. Word has been sent to Lady Elizabeth, Your Grace, although I believe she has gone to Andover."

"Have you sent word also to Miss Chandry? She is at the Old Manor."

There was just the slightest hesitation before the butler said, "I shall see to that at once, Your Grace." He bowed and withdrew.

"Well, I must just entertain you single-handed until reinforcements arrive," Ger said cheerfully. "Ah, I see you admiring the Mennecy vase, sir. One of my favourites."

They fell immediately into a discussion of porcelain, and before two minutes had passed, Ruth's father had persuaded Ger to explain some finer point of a piece in the Porcelain Room and they had gone. Ruth and her mother were left alone with their tea on a sofa beside the fire.

"Well, this is very satisfactory," the duchess said. "I had thought things might be a trifle sticky just at first, until your papa had explained what he expects of Falconbury, but when I saw you sitting at the instrument together, it became clear that there will be no difficulty at all."

Ruth could foresee any number of possible difficulties, but she said nothing. Contradicting her mother served no purpose other than to make her cross, and nothing that was said changed the situation one whit. She was engaged to Ran, and it was at present uncertain whether he would be willing to release her, or that Ger would wish to marry her instead. Until such questions were answered it was best not to speculate.

Her mother, however, could not be kept from doing so. "How clever of your father to contrive an excuse to get Falconbury alone. He will have an excellent opportunity to talk to him, as one man to another. I daresay by the time they return, they will have settled it all between them. *Most* satisfactory."

When the two men returned twenty minutes later, Ruth could not tell whether anything was settled or not. They both smiled and seemed on good terms, but the wariness in Ger's expression was even more pronounced. Her father picked up his sherry glass and sat down on the sofa opposite Ruth and her mother. Ger accepted a cup of tea and took a chair nearby. For several minutes, the four laboured diligently to make stilted conversation. All Ger's animation at the instrument or when discussing his beloved porcelain had dropped away, and he seemed nervous and uneasy.

The door opened and a head peeped round. "Ah, here you are! I thought Brent meant the other Ante-Chamber."

Ruth guessed instantly that this was the Miss Chandry about whom the butler had misgivings. She was not young — Ruth guessed perhaps five and twenty — but tall, with a well-formed figure and a pretty face. Her clothes identified her instantly as lower gentry, but she had a graceful self-assurance that showed she had moved in society somewhat.

At once, Ger's face lit up and he leapt to his feet. "Come in, come in and meet everyone. This is Her Grace the Duchess of Orrisdale. The Lady Ruth Orrisdale. His Grace the Duke of Orrisdale. This is Miss Chandry of Pendower in Cornwall, who rescued me from the English Channel one dark night last year, and then nursed me back to health. She is my very good friend."

There were slight bows from Ruth and her parents, and deep curtsies from the girl. Then, before anyone else could speak, she tucked her arm proprietorially into Ger's, looked Ruth straight in the eye and said, "I'm his mistress, and I'm with child. Best you should know it straight away."

"Ginny!" Ger cried, turning reproachful eyes on her.

The silence was so profound one might drown in it. Ruth could not, for the moment, feel anything except outrage. How dared the girl make such a shameless confession in her presence! And how dared Ger introduce such a person to her! It was an unforgivable discourtesy. She was too shocked to move or to speak.

The duchess, however, was equal to the occasion. With commendable steadiness of hand, she set her tea cup and saucer on a table beside her. Then she rose.

"Come, Ruth," she said calmly. "Let us leave now."

Head high, she walked majestically past the girl without looking at her, and made for the door. Ruth followed her, casting the girl a puzzled glance as she went by. She still held Ger's arm, calm, unafraid, very sure of herself. Ger was looking rueful, and a little embarrassed.

In the entrance hall, the housekeeper waited. "Your Grace? My lady? Your rooms are prepared for you."

They followed her up the stairs, but when they reached Ruth's room, the duchess followed her in, and chased out the maid, pressing Ruth into one of the two chairs beside the fire. She herself took the other.

"Now, listen carefully, Ruth, for you are a good girl, and I know you will not be missish about this. All men of our rank have mistresses, although not usually quite such brazen hussies as this one. Your papa has had several, and as for Uncle James— Well, the less said about that the better. It means nothing to them. Men are... different from women. They have baser instincts and enjoy horrid sports involving fighting or killing things, and they enjoy women in the same low way. So they have mistresses."

"I know, Mama."

"It does not — or *should* not — affect their wives in any way. A considerate man will ensure that his wife knows nothing of that side of his life. A sensible wife will ignore it if it should happen to come to her notice, and you are a very sensible girl, Ruth. Indeed, I do not often say such things, for one would not wish you to become too puffed up in your own conceit, but you are the very best of my daughters. Susan has such an unbecoming forwardness, and Charlotte has far too much sensibility — her nature is romantical, I fear. And as for Anne! Such a hoyden that I do not know what is to become of her, truly I do not. But you have always made me proud of you, a good, obedient girl with no foolish romantic notions in your head. Whatever happens to the others, however sadly they lack beauty or temper or accomplishments, none of them matter, because *you* are everything I could ever have hoped for. Now you are going to make me prouder than I have ever been, for you are going to follow in my footsteps and become a duchess. Falconbury will give you the title and position in society that you deserve. You will be a great lady, you will be respected and honoured by everyone, and it will be your privilege to continue the Litherholm line. What more could any woman want?"

"What about love?" Ruth hazarded.

"People of our level of society do not need love," her mother said disdainfully. "If, when you have done your duty by your husband, you feel the need for... something more, then, provided you are discreet, you may do as you wish, but expecting to be loved is to set oneself up for disappointment, believe me. So my mother taught me, and she was perfectly right. I had... hopes of your father when we first married, and when those hopes were not fulfilled I was quite miserable for a while. But I soon came to accept the folly of such girlish dreams. As soon as I stopped expecting love, I became perfectly contented with my lot. Take your satisfaction from your children and from knowing you are a good wife and a good duchess. You will have all the fulfilment you desire if you do your duty, daughter, as you have been taught, take it from me."

16: Considerations

The duchess summoned the maid back into the room, instructed her to find the blue muslin with the fluted sleeves and told Ruth to change, before sweeping regally out of the room. Obediently, Ruth changed, and allowed Pinnock to dress her hair a little more elaborately. Then, too agitated to stay in her room, she made her way to the head of the stairs.

She was alone. This was the first day in her life when she had been quite alone, with neither nurse, nor maid, nor chaperon with her. It had not occurred to her when she had sat at the instrument with Ger, and although they had been unchaperoned, the door had been open with all the bustle of arrival going on in the entrance hall just beyond. But now, no one was watching her. Her mother was in her own room. Aunt Maria was watching over Susan at Crosby Hall. Cousin Patience had gone off to play the poor relation with a different branch of the family, for a change. Pinnock was busy in the dressing room. Ruth was utterly alone.

Before her mother or her maid should realise, she set off with quick steps down the corridor, but when she came to the Grand Staircase, where a footman stood immobile, waiting for a summons, she turned into the Long Gallery. She had no plan except to find a quiet corner where she could hide away, but when she came to the end of the Gallery, she saw the portrait of Ran and Ger. There she stopped, sitting on the sofa conveniently placed directly opposite and gazing at the two familiar faces, the one to whom she was still betrothed, and the one she was expected to marry.

It was peaceful there. Occasionally voices drifted up from below, or footsteps sounded on bare boards somewhere. Once a footman walked past without noticing her, but mostly there was nothing to disturb her thoughts. She could not settle her swirling mind. To marry Ger would be the culmination of many years of gentle contrivance, and would please her parents. Yet he had a mistress… Could she cope with that? And if she did *not* marry him, what was to become of her?

There was no making sense of any of it, so she sat and looked at the two brothers and wallowed in the pleasure of solitude. At some point, slow footsteps brought Brent to stand before her.

"Is there anything I may bring you, my lady?"

"No, thank you. I am… just resting."

"Her Grace is taking tea in the Queen's Room, my lady. When Her Grace enquired for you, I suggested that you might have gone out for a walk in the gardens, the weather being so balmy."

She looked at him in surprise, unsure whether he truly thought she had gone out or was defending her against her mother, but his expression was inscrutable. "Thank you, Brent. I shall join her in a while. When I have rested."

"Very good, my lady."

He walked off again, his measured footsteps fading away down the Gallery. Not long after, she heard quicker steps approaching. Ran, his face creased in anxiety. Always so serious! But at the sight of his dear face, her heart gave a little leap. So handsome, and even coming to her straight from the stables, as the mud on his boots proclaimed, he was the epitome of the gentleman of quiet distinction.

"Ruth! I am so sorry I — Are you all right?"

"Yes... I am well. Thank you."

"Hmm." He frowned, and sat down beside her. "Have you seen Ger?"

"Oh yes. He is just the same, is he not? I thought he might be... changed but..." She stumbled to an uncertain halt. Was he unchanged? He had a mistress now, and yet, when they had sat at the instrument side by side, he had been the same old Ger she remembered.

"Just the same wild, reckless Ger," Ran said. Was that a note of bitterness? "He never does anything by halves, and to reappear just at this time... it is awkward, very awkward. Another two weeks and we should have been married. I had already made arrangements for the special licence, and the lawyers were working on the settlements. Well, I have put a stop to that now that my circumstances have changed." A hesitation, and then he took her hand in his. Such intimacy, for a man to hold her ungloved hand! His head was lowered, not looking her in the eye. "Ruth, your father wishes to break our engagement so that you may marry Ger, as originally planned, but there is... a complication."

"Miss Chandry," she said. "His mistress." Ran's head flew up, shocked. "She told me so," Ruth said quietly. "She said it was better for me to know, and about the child, too."

"She said *that?* Good God! That is outrageous! To subject you to such insult! I cannot believe—! But Ger encourages such behaviour by housing her within the family wing, allowing her to dine with the family—"

"Does she so? Mama will not sit at table with her, nor allow me to do so."

"No, of course not, but Ger wants her treated with *respect*. He does not seem to understand... but you and Her Grace must not be subjected to such unpardonable incivility. Ruth..." He stroked her hand almost absently, watching her with a serious expression. "You see how difficult it all is. I understand your father's concern that you should marry according to your rank, but there are many other considerations and... I would urge you to make no irrevocable decisions until we have all thought carefully on the matter. There is so much to take into account beyond obligation and eligibility and duty. Marriage is for life, and I would not have you made unhappy by a wrong choice. If our engagement stands and I am so fortunate as to become your husband, I will do everything in my power to make you happy, but you must follow your heart above all. Do not choose merely in obedience to your father or because you feel that honour dictates it. Choose rather what will bring you the greatest happiness in your life, for nothing would grieve me more than to see you made miserable."

Dear Ran! Such generous thoughts almost overwhelmed her. She could feel tears prickling — she, who never cried! But the concern in his eyes, the gentle touch of his hand on hers, the kindly words he spoke brought home to her something that she had never allowed herself to admit before — that little glow inside was something more than gratitude or mere liking. She *loved* Ran, in a way that she had never felt for any other man. Not Ger, certainly. When he was in affable mood, he was the best of men, but she had seen his darker moods, too, and the recklessness that Ran had mentioned. She was fond of Ger, as of any friend of long-standing, but it was Ran she loved.

Love could not blind her, however, to the meaning beneath his words. He would try to make her happy if he married her, he had said. Such a cool declaration! No word of affection, no mention of *his* heart… no sign of love. At Mallowfleet he had seemed to display a pleasing warmth, but there was no hint of it now, only conventional politeness. *'…if I am so fortunate as to become your husband…'* Just a form of words, for if he truly wanted her as his wife, would he not fight for her? Would he tamely surrender her to his brother? Would he not passionately declare himself?

But there was no passion in him. He was restrained, courteous, cool. He did not love her.

"Thank you, Ran. I shall consider most carefully what to do. Now perhaps I had better go to Mama. She must be wondering what has become of me."

"Pray give her my apologies and tell her that I shall attend her as soon as I have changed out of my riding clothes."

He rose, bowed and took two steps away before turning with a puzzled expression. "How did you contrive to escape your watchdogs?"

She interpreted this to mean her chaperons. Laughing, she said, "Aunt Maria and Cousin Patience were required elsewhere. There is only Mama to watch over me now."

"Are you in the Lilac Room? I asked Mrs Brack to put you in there if you should visit again."

An odd thing to do, for she had made no complaint about the Bluebell Room, and the two rooms seemed identical, but she replied politely, "Yes, indeed. Thank you for—"

"If you need to escape, there is a secret door behind the escritoire in the corner. Just pull on the sconce."

With a quick nod, he strode away without a backward glance. Ruth gave a little gasp that was half laughter and half sob. To be thinking of that at such a time! And yet, it was typical of his consideration. He had seen how hemmed about she was, and tried to help her. *'If you need to escape…'* Oh, if only she could! If only she could go back to London. If only Ger had not come back, or at least had waited a little longer. Another month and she would have been safely married. But what then would have been Ran's feelings? To be forced into an unwanted marriage—

She stopped, shocked at her own thoughts, for was that not exactly what she herself was contemplating, to marry Ger when she loved Ran? *'Follow your heart'* he had told her, but she could hardly do so. To insist upon marrying Ran would make her parents very unhappy and cause an irrevocable breach. Ger would be deprived of the duchess he had expected. And Ran… poor Ran would gallantly smile and pretend he was fortunate. Everyone would be unhappy, and that would make her unhappy too.

Yet if she married Ger… that would make her unhappy, too. To live here at Valmont and see Ran every day, to watch him marry some other lucky woman, would be hideous. No, for then *he* would be happy and—

It was too difficult. All her life she had been told what to do, by her nurse, her governess, her mother, her aunts and cousins and the mothers of her friends. Trying to work things out for herself was too complicated, and she could see no solution that would please everyone.

Ruth sat for a few moments longer, trying to stamp out the little flames of anguish that were springing up inside her. Then she rose and resolutely shook out her skirts. Head high, she went to find her mother.

~~~~~

Ran strode along narrow corridors and up the service stairs to reach his room, where Giggs, alerted by the stables, had already laid out his clothes. Ran was helped out of his coat and boots, then tore off neckcloth, waistcoat and breeches, finally the shirt and a quick wash in cold water, for there was no time to wait for hot. His dressing had progressed to a fresh shirt and pantaloons, when he heard music and laughter drifting from the sitting room. With a tut of annoyance, he marched through the ante-room and flung open the door. Ger was seated at the pianoforte, with Ginny hanging over him, whispering in his ear, both of them laughing like a pair of silly girls.

With all that had happened, with all that was about to happen and the difficulties they were in, how could Ger sit there enjoying himself, when he should be doing the pretty to the duke and duchess, and Ruth?
~~~~~

"What the *devil* are you doing here?" Ran said.

"Ran! You are back! You have missed a great deal of drama. Ginny—"

"I know what Ginny did. What are you doing, skulking away up here?"

"Hiding from the Grenabys," Ger said with a rueful grin. "They ran away when Ginny said… well, you seem to know what she said. Ran, Orrisdale wants me to marry Ruth. That is what he is here for, to persuade me that I have an obligation because we were as good as betrothed before, and I am bound in honour to marry her. What shall I do?"

"What do you want to do?" Ran said.

Ger's face creased into worried lines. "I cannot tell you! I like her, of course, but… *marriage!* I assumed the betrothal would hold and you would still marry her, but Orrisdale said that there was no conceivable way he would agree to let Ruth marry you, not when you are only a younger son. What is to be done, Ran?"

Well. There it was, openly expressed, exactly the outcome he had dreaded. Ruth was lost to him. Damnation! Frustration made him terse. "Nothing immediately. We must all have time to reflect on this, for it is no easy matter to resolve. The first priority is for you to entertain your guests and for Ginny to stay out of sight. She cannot come down to dinner tonight."

"Now wait—" Ger began.

"No, listen to me," Ran said brusquely. "The story about her being your guest may have worked with the family, because even though most of them guessed the truth, they cared enough for you to pretend that they did not. But now that Ginny has blurted out the whole to the Grenabys, there is no possibility of pretence. You may say all you like that everyone must respect Ginny, but you know what happened as soon as they were faced with the truth. The duchess will not stand to be in the same room as her, let alone sit down at table with her, nor will Ruth, and why should they? The Royal Princes may flaunt their mistresses with impunity, and any number of married women have lovers and still move in society, but Ginny is not married, and has rubbed our guests' high-bred noses in her status and her pregnancy. She cannot come down to dinner while they are here."

"Then I shall not go either," Ger said mulishly.

"For God's sake! Is Ginny so important to you that you cannot even put up with a few days of inconvenience?"

"Yes! Ginny is more important to me than anything!"

"Is she so?" Ran said acidly. "I thought you wanted to do what was right, Ger, to be the duke, as you were born to be. I thought you had finally accepted your destiny, but here you are, still skirting around it. This is not one of your stupid *games*, where you get to play duke when it suits you and run away when it all gets difficult. This is your *life*, Ger, as it has been mine for ten years or more, waiting for you to grow up. But if Ginny means more to you than your duty or the family or the country you are supposed to help lead, then maybe you should just take her back to Cornwall and stay there, for you are of no use to anyone here!"

There was a stunned silence. Ger and Ginny stared at him, aghast.

Ran rubbed his face tiredly. "Oh God, Ger, I am so sorry! I did not mean a word of it, I hope you—"

Ger launched himself across the room and wrapped his arms around him. "Forgive me," he whispered. "I have been unpardonably selfish all my life, and *you* have borne the brunt of it. Never could a man have a better brother! You are quite right — I am determined to fulfil my rôle as you expect of me... as *everyone* expects of me." He stepped away, and turned to Ginny. "You see, we never fall out. We may yell at each other, but that is all."

His words awoke no smile from her. "This is my fault," she said in a low voice. "What I said to them — that's what brought this on. I thought it would help. Well, I thought Lady Ruth had a right to know everything before she took a step she couldn't back away from, and it seemed if I made a song and dance about it, they would be so shocked they would go away and not bother us again, and then Ran could marry Ruth. Because you want to, don't you? You said, *'It does not necessarily follow that an arranged marriage must be unwelcome'*."

Helplessly, he nodded. "I do want to, but whatever happens, I never will, not now."

"Why ever not?" she said, puzzled. "Why can you not marry the woman you love?"

He winced at her plain speaking. "Because her father is determined that she marry a man of high rank, and a younger son, even the younger son of a duke, is not good enough."

"But to break off an engagement so close to the wedding," she said. "Even in my far less exalted world, that is a very bad thing to do. Only two weeks away, Ran! Her father cannot prevent it, not if she is set upon it."

"No, for we are both of age, and the announcement has been made publicly, so in any normal situation there would be nothing to prevent it. But this is not a normal situation. Our betrothal was based on the mistaken idea that I was the duke, which I am not."

"But you are the same man!" she cried. "What difference does it make?"

He gave a wry smile. "All the difference in the world. Amongst the nobility, marriage is a business arrangement. Both sides lay out their assets. For the man, an estate, an income of so much per year, his position in society, which becomes hers upon marriage. For the woman, her dowry, her beauty and temperament, her ability to manage his house, raise his children, bring credit upon him socially. Her position in society matters, too, for the connections it brings, but less than his. As a duke, with vast holdings and an income of thirty thousand pounds a year, I was very eligible. As a younger son, with a small estate, two houses without land and an allowance from my brother, I have less than one thousand pounds a year. It is not enough! Even if by some miracle Ruth were to hold to the betrothal, her father will not settle so much as a farthing on her, and I cannot afford to."

"People marry without settlements all the time," she said gently. "If she loves you—"

"But she does not, and even if she did, I cannot ask the daughter of a duke to bind herself to me for a thousand a year and no protection at all if I should die. It is useless to think of it. Forgive me, but I must go and dance attendance on our unwelcome guests."

17: Games Of Cards

The evening was got through somehow. They sat down eleven to dinner, and Ran thanked providence for the presence of Captain Edgerton, who flirted gently with the ladies, told slightly warm stories to the gentlemen and was agreeable to all. Michael Chandry had been intercepted on arrival and dispatched to bear his sister company, by which means the company was relieved of the name of Chandry altogether. That did not stop Uncle Arthur plaintively enquiring after him, and protesting that the chaplain was not an adequate substitute at the whist table.

Ran could see that Ger was not in spirits. He put a brave face on it, but his conversation was languid and he seemed relieved whenever something occurred to distract attention from him. When the gentlemen were alone, he became altogether silent.

"Are you minded for cards?" Ran whispered to him as they made their way to join the ladies. Ger shook his head, and immediately went to sit by Ruth, who was at the instrument. She was playing a charming, lilting piece, perhaps Irish, and when she looked up at Ger and he smiled, she smiled back. Even though the sight was like a knife twisted in his stomach, Ran could see the value in keeping the two of them apart from the company, engrossed in their music.

Since Lady Anne was already asleep, and he wanted to make up two card tables, he was obliged to join one of them himself, although he was an indifferent player at best, and tonight he was certainly not at his best. Even Elizabeth, the most relaxed of his sisters, berated him soundly.

"Really, Ran, what are you about to be throwing away a trump like that? Where have your wits gone a-begging?"

"I beg your pardon," he said for the twentieth time.

Eventually, his group of card players yawned, stretched and declared themselves tired of the game. Ran had lost eighty pounds, and cared not one whit. Even the chaplain had taken money off him, for once. On the other table, the brandy was flowing freely and Uncle Arthur, the duke, Captain Edgerton and Max were settling in for the night.

Ruth was sitting on her own, absorbed in her stitchery. It was an opportunity he could not resist. He no longer wished to have any private talk with her, for what was the point, now? Still, her serenity drew him and perhaps her gentle company would soothe his jangled nerves, so he crossed the room and sat down beside her. They had exchanged not two sentences, and rather innocuous ones, when the duchess materialised and sat down beside her daughter.

"I declare, travelling is the most tiring thing in the world, is it not, Lord Randolph?"

"Indeed it is, Duchess," he said politely.

"I find myself quite exhausted, and you are looking a little tired, daughter, too. You are suffering from too much jolting in the carriage and not enough rest, I daresay. Junketing about all over the garden in the afternoon sun is never a good idea, and quite alone, too, with no one to advise you not to overexert yourself. You must not do so again."

"No, Mama," she said colourlessly.

"We shall go to bed now."

"Yes, Mama." Ruth tucked her needlework away into a work bag.

"Allow me to escort you to your rooms," Ran said, as they all rose.

"I would not for the world take you from your guests," the duchess said coldly. "We can find our way very easily."

"Then I shall bid you both a good night, and may you enjoy your repose."

As Ruth followed her mother from the room, she half turned and mouthed, "Thank you," to Ran, although for what, he could not say.

Apart from the avid card players, the rest of the company drifted away too. Elizabeth departed for her little lodge and Ponsonby for his rooms near the chapel. Aunt Anne and Ger had disappeared long since. Ran felt it safe to leave, too. He was tired and unhappy, and a whole evening of pretending otherwise had taxed his resources to the utmost. He would have a brandy before bed, and then, he supposed, lie awake wondering what torments the next day would bring.

Giggs was waiting for him in his room.

"Help me out of my coat, will you, and then you may go. I shall not need you again tonight. Off you go, then."

"Very good, milord. I shall hold myself in readiness in case your lordship should require anything further."

"No need for that. I can pull a nightshirt over my head unaided, you know. I am not entirely helpless."

"And yet I fancy you were very glad to see me in Exeter, milord."

Ran smiled at him. "So I was, Giggs. You are a very good fellow, but I shall do well enough now. Go to bed."

When the valet had gone, Ran went through to the sitting room, to find it lit as bright as day. Ger and Chandry were huddled over the card table, with three candelabra beside them. In a corner, Ginny and Molly were stitching with the aid of working candles.

"Ran!" Ger cried, with a pleased smile. "Have they all gone to bed? Are you cross with me for abandoning you?"

"No and no," Ran said. "Chandry, why are you letting him fleece you? Oh — buttons! Well, at least you have the good sense not to play for money."

"Lord, no, I'm not such a fool," Chandry said. "I know he's going to beat me into a cocked hat, but that's how you learn, by playing against the best."

"And what does he get out of it?"

"Buttons!" Chandry said, pointing to the great mound of them in front of Ger. "And the delights of my charming company."

Ger smiled. "He cheers me up, Ran, so please do not be cross with me. I know I should not have left you but—"

"I have already said that I am not cross. You lasted as long as supper and no one noticed you leave so I am not minded to censure you, even if it were my place to do so. Have you drunk all the brandy?"

"We're not drinking," Chandry said. "Have to keep a clear head for this."

Ran poured his brandy and went to sit with the women. "How are you, Molly? Have you been well looked after below stairs?"

"Now, isn't that just like you to ask so kindly after me, but then everyone here is so pleasant and friendly. I'm very well, milord, and most comfortably situated in an attic room just at the top of the servants' stairs. Lovely room, and spacious and done up so pretty, for all there's no flying babies on the ceiling."

"Only the State Apartments have... erm, flying babies on the ceiling," Ran said solemnly. "Should you like some? I can arrange it."

"Dear me, no! Faces looking down at me as I lie in my bed, or..." She went slightly pink. "...when I'm dressing and what not? No, no! I couldn't."

"I have not seen you since we arrived. Have you been avoiding me?" Ran said lightly.

Molly pursed her lips primly, but Ger laughed. "It is not you whom Molly has been avoiding, Ran. She disapproves mightily of me."

"Well, I do, and I make no bones about it," the nurse answered. "Thought he was such a gentleman, I did, when he first arrived at Pendower, and so quiet and well behaved and all the time he was talking sweet to Miss Ginny and making her forget the respectable way she was brought up. It's wicked, it is."

"You have forgotten the less-than-respectable example Papa set," Ginny said, laughing.

"I don't forget, but he kept himself to married women, as a rule, unless a maid threw herself at his head. Which they did, sometimes. Powerful attractive to the women, your pa was, and he has some of that, too," she added, nodding at Michael Chandry. "Although to be fair, he's not as free with himself as his pa was. But him!" Her eye fell on Ger. "A real gentleman with such pretty manners and so polite, he shouldn't be taking respectable maids, not without marrying them."

"She will not have me," Ger said, with a little laugh. "Not for all my grand titles and great estates will she be my wife."

"It is *because* of the titles and estates that I can never marry you," Ginny said, laying down her sewing. "I cannot possibly marry the Duke of Falconbury."

Ger gazed at her, bemused. "Would you have married Jonathan Ellsworthy?"

"Yes."

He cried out in anguish, his cards tossed aside. "Yet you never said... I had no idea..."

"Of course not. Didn't you realise? I thought you might have worked it out by now. I knew almost from the start that you were not a humble clerk, that you were the duke who was supposed to be drowned, but you said nothing. You were content to be Jonathan Ellsworthy, clerk. You told me once that life weighed hard on you, but what you meant was that being the duke weighed hard. And then one day you woke up and found that you were not that person any more. You had escaped, and could live a different life. But I was never sure whether you would be content to stay free for ever or whether there would come a time when you would want to go back to your life of wealth and power and be a nobleman instead of a clerk. So... I decided to test you. I came to your bed and seduced you, and for all Molly's tutting, it was I who did the seducing, not you. If you were ready to spend the rest of your life as Jonathan Ellsworthy, I knew you would ask me to marry you, but if you were not... Well, I had my answer, and I am content. We are together, whether I have a wedding ring or not, and that is all that matters to me. I have never cared much about the conventional proprieties, no matter how much the parson preaches. My father's blood, I'm afraid."

Ger was too distressed to speak, but Ran said, "I do not see why you cannot marry Ger even now, even knowing him to be the duke. He can marry where he chooses, you know. There is no bar."

"No, no, no!" she cried. "He must marry his own kind! Ran, do you remember when you were at the Pendower inn with all those great men? Lord This and Sir Something, every last one of them. You all treated me with so much courtesy, just as if I were a real lady, but I am not and never will be. Gervase moves in a different world from the likes of me, and even though you have convinced me that nobles are not all entirely useless, still I can't ever be one. It is impossible."

"You did well with the relatives that first night," Ran said. "No society lady could have done better."

"Oh, I have been in society a little. I know the essentials. But when I saw Lady Ruth… she is so far above me in every way! I am like a donkey to her thoroughbred mare. She has been trained from birth to marry a man of high rank, and I have not been trained for anything. I have always known that Gervase would marry someone like that, someone who was his equal. I am only fit to be his mistress."

Ger made an inarticulate sound of distress.

"No, it is true, love. I shall live in the Old Manor and keep out of the way and be there whenever you need me, and you will marry someone who will support you in your public life. I am resolved on this, and nothing you say will change my mind, so finish your game, my love, for it is growing late, and tomorrow you must decide your future course."

"Do you think I should marry Ruth?" Ger said.

Ginny threw a quick look at Ran, then said carefully, "If that is the best answer for everyone."

Molly sniffed. "He should marry *you*, Miss Ginny, and that's the truth. What's to become of you without a husband?"

"Gervase will look after me."

After a while the women left but Ran sat on in the corner, watching the card players. Both played quickly and decisively, with no dithering. Chandry maintained a steady patter of inconsequential nonsense, perhaps to distract his opponent. Ger said nothing not pertaining to the game. He looked calm, but there was an excitement in his eyes as he made his plays. In the

Grand Saloon or at dinner, he had looked uneasy and uncomfortably out of place, but here he was in his element. He was alive, his fears submerged, in a way he was not when he was required to be formal, and be the duke. His music was another means for him to lose himself. Ran and Ginny would have to find a way to protect him from too many public duties. Ran had been taking that rôle for some years now, and it would not hurt to continue.

"Another *partie*?" Chandry said optimistically, pushing buttons across the table as Ger scooped up the cards.

Ger shook his head. "It is late, and Ginny is right, as usual — tomorrow I must decide what to do. What do you think, Michael? Should I marry Ruth?"

Chandry looked at him thoughtfully. "Ginny's right about most things, but she doesn't know your world, and nor do I. Ask your brother."

"He only asks me what *I* want to do."

"Well then, do that. You're a duke, you can do whatever you want, so marry or not, as you please. No one can tell you what to do, except the King or the Prince of Wales, I suppose, but myself, I'd hesitate to keep two women under the same roof. Asking for trouble, that is."

"Ginny will be living at the Old Manor," Ger said.

"Which is what, a quarter of a mile away? Rather you than me! Thank you for taking all my buttons. Good night to you both."

After he had gone, Ger sat unmoving for some time, his hands restlessly shuffling the cards, passing them back and forth from one hand to the other.

"Brandy?" Ran said eventually.

"Ah! Good idea." Then, hesitantly, he went on, "I wish you *would* tell me what to do, Ran. I want to do the right thing for everyone, but I have not the least notion what that may be."

Ran handed him a glass, and then took Chandry's seat opposite him. "Ger, when I want to decide whether to do something to do with the estate — take an interest in a mine, for instance, or sell a piece of land — I try to work out what the benefit will be, but also the risks, so let us try that here. If you marry Ruth, the benefit is that you obtain a perfect wife who will do everything expected of a duchess. She will always behave impeccably, no matter the occasion, and she will raise your heirs in the traditional manner. Society will approve your choice. She will not be disturbed by the fact that you have a mistress, so long as you keep the two apart, and even if they meet occasionally, they are both sensible."

"You do not agree with Michael's qualms, then?"

"No. So long as you do nothing outrageous, such as expecting them to dine together, there will be no trouble. It is only when you house Ginny within Valmont itself, and talk about society respecting her that I take issue with you. Your wife will be respected by the *beau monde,* your mistress never will be. I do not foresee difficulties if you marry Ruth, so long as you conform somewhat to society's strictures. If you do *not* marry Ruth, however—"

He stopped, aware that each breath was harder to take now. How difficult to talk calmly about such matters! To play the disinterested adviser when he was anything but disinterested. But it had to be done. He would support his brother in all things, and that meant giving him the very best, the most objective advice within his power.

"If you do not marry Ruth, her father might well consider that you have broken faith with him. He could, if he were to be vindictive, abuse your good name all over town, and you may be sure that Ginny's name would be mentioned, too. And Ruth would be left unwed and unpromised at the age of one and twenty. She chose to wait for you, Ger, even though she had several very eligible offers, to my certain knowledge. If you reject her now, she will be obliged to look elsewhere for a husband."

"But not far, surely? You are very willing to have her."

"More than willing, but it is impossible. Even if she would have me, I cannot afford to take her."

"Not even if Orrisdale could be persuaded to pay up the full thirty thousand?" Ger said.

Ran shook his head. "He is all to pieces, Ger. He can only manage ten thousand. I was obliged to put in twenty thousand myself, which I no longer have."

"He promised me thirty," Ger said, eyes narrowing. "He is calling on me to honour a bargain which he himself repudiates. Am I constrained in honour to this, brother, or do I have a free choice?"

"No one is constrained in honour except for myself," Ran said wryly. "I am still betrothed to Ruth, since neither she nor her father has told me otherwise. Orrisdale has talked to you, but has said not a word on the subject to me."

"That is unpardonably rude, to be trying to arrange a new betrothal when the original is still in existence," Ger said, indignantly. "Shall I tell him I want no part of it? That would give him back his own! And if he can spread tales all over town, so can I. It would be amusing, would it not?"

"No, it would not! For God's sake, Ger, this is about *Ruth*, not her father, nor about me, either. Let us not get distracted. I cannot marry her, despite the betrothal, so it is up to you. Do you like her well enough to marry her?"

"I *do* like her," Ger said softly. "I have always held her in great affection, and when I saw her today and we sat down at the instrument together — I like her very well. She appeals to something in me that I can never share with Ginny. She is such a wonderful musician, so passionate and eager! She *feels* it, just as I do."

"Passionate?" Ran said, bemused, trying to reconcile the word with the cool, composed Ruth he knew. "Is she?"

"Oh, yes! You have probably only heard her restrained public performances, but when she plays for herself, she is very different, I assure you."

"I did not know," Ran said wonderingly. "Well, offer for her then if you think it will answer, but Ger, promise me this — you must make it absolutely clear that she must answer according to her own wishes, and not simply do as her father bids her. You must both of you enter into marriage with willing hearts. If I cannot have her myself, then at least let me know that she chose her own path. You will take the greatest care of her, will you not?"

"I promise you I will be the best husband I can possibly be."

It was not quite the reassurance Ran had hoped for.

18: Morning Prayers

When Ruth reached her dressing room, she found that a bed had been made up there.

"I'm to sleep in here now," Pinnock said, a hint of defiance in her tone. "The door from your bedroom to the corridor is to be kept locked at night, too. Her Grace's orders, milady."

"Am I a prisoner?" Ruth said, in her mildest tones, although she seethed below the surface.

Pinnock reddened. "Her Grace was very worried about you this afternoon, when you went wandering about the gardens all alone, and no one could find you. There were footmen combing the grounds looking for you. Her Grace doesn't want any... mishaps, not at this stage."

Mishaps! No damage to her oh-so-valuable reputation, she meant. It was hard to see to what harm she could possibly have come, when the only single gentlemen in the house were Ran and Ger. And Uncle Arthur, she supposed, but the thought made her laugh.

"It isn't funny!" Pinnock said.

Ruth raised her eyebrows at the maid. "You forget yourself, Pinnock. Why have you not unfastened my necklace yet?"

After that, the business of undressing was accomplished in silence. Pinnock would have followed her through to the bedroom to draw the curtains around the bed, but Ruth said, "Thank you, but I shall read for a while."

"What book is it? Her Grace will want to know."

"The Bible, Pinnock," Ruth said gently. "Or my Prayer Book, for I have no other books here."

The maid's lips clamped shut. She looked as if she was sure there was some deception, but she did not quite have the brazenness to insist upon seeing the Bible for herself.

Ruth bade her a good night, entered her bedroom and firmly closed the door. She had no particular wish to read her Bible, but nor did she wish to be caught in a lie if Pinnock or, even worse, the duchess should come to check on her. Accordingly, she lit some reading candles, arranged them around the chair beside the unlit fire, and settled the Bible upon her knees, opened at a random page. She memorised the first three verses, just in case. Then she closed her eyes and allowed her anger to wash over her. To be locked into her room, as if she were a naughty child or a madwoman! It was insulting.

And yet, even at one and twenty years of age, she was still dependent on her parents for her home, for her clothes, even the food she ate. She could not do as she pleased, even in such trivial matters as walking alone around a house where she was a guest. She must wear the clothes her mother deemed suitable, go where they sent her, behave as they wished. And all of this would continue until she married.

But then... ah, then she would be free indeed! She would be the mistress of her own house, she would order the meals, manage the servants, entertain visitors if she wished or spend the evening alone if she wished. No... not alone. There would be her husband's wishes to consider, but her own wishes would also be of importance. She would not be stifled, as she currently was. Marriage would set her free as she was not now.

Or perhaps she was. There was the secret door. Picking up a candelabrum, she crossed the room to the corner where the escritoire stood. The flickering light of the candles showed no obvious sign of a door, only a succession of papered panels. But there! Yes, the faintest crack showed where the door would open, and the sconce, just within reach, which would release it.

Dear Ran! He had noticed how hedged about she was, and after she had left he had gone to the Mistress of the Chambers and told her to put Ruth in this room, if ever she came again as a visitor. And the Mistress of the Chambers would have gone to her visitors' book and found Ruth's name and scratched out the words *'Bluebell Room'* next to it and substituted *'Lilac Room'*. Ran had thought of it, and so it had been done.

And now she had a secret door. She withdrew to her chair and picked up the Bible again. She had no wish to walk the corridors of Valmont at night, creeping about in her nightgown like a ghost, but still, it was curiously comforting to know that she could, if she wished. But would she ever dare to do it? If her mama could retaliate by locking her in after she had been alone for no more than an hour, what might she do if she discovered that Ruth had crept away through a secret passage? She could be locked up for weeks... months! She shivered.

Fear of her mother's disapprobation had kept her docile and well-behaved for years now. Ruth had never had Susan's rebellious tendencies, or her willingness to lie brazenly. The smallest deception reduced Ruth to quivering torment, in perpetual terror of discovery, and so she had striven to be the dutiful, well-behaved daughter her mother expected. Any diversion from instant obedience brought her too much distress to contemplate. It was cowardice, she accepted that, but she preferred the clear conscience of compliance to the wretchedness of guilt.

She closed the Bible, blew out the candles, and went to bed.

~~~~~

Ruth had not expected to sleep well, and so was not disappointed when, after a restless night, she woke at an early hour. Her Bible still sat where she had left it the night before, reproaching her for her modest subterfuge the night before. If she dressed at once, she would be in time for Morning Prayers in the chapel. She could assuage her guilty conscience in a proper manner.

Pinnock was not pleased to be summoned so early, but she was mercifully silent as she helped Ruth to dress. Taking her Prayer Book, Ruth made her way downstairs to the chapel. The maid, unsurprisingly, followed her. The duchess's orders, no doubt. When her mother was not able to watch Ruth herself, Pinnock was to creep about behind her like a little brown shadow, watching and noting everything Ruth did, so that she could report it all to the duchess. Ruth chose to make no comment, but it was humiliating that she could not even pray without her mother knowing it.
~~~~~

Unlike the rest of Valmont, the chapel was a starkly plain room, the arched roof embellished with the branching tops of the pilasters along the walls, but with no other decoration apart from a rather beautiful fresco of the Holy Family behind the altar. No one sat in the ornate family pews at the front, but the servants' rather plainer ones held a few maids and footmen, and two of the gardeners. At the far end of one such pew sat Ran, head low, his expression disconsolate. What was he thinking? Impossible to tell. He had not noticed her, and she could hardly squeeze past the footmen to sit beside him so she passed by and entered a pew near the front.

She had hoped the service would soothe her restlessness. Instead, she found herself watching Mr Ponsonby, and wondering why chaplains were always tall and spare and solemn, as he was. They were never fat and jolly, entertaining the table at dinner, nor young and handsome, riding energetically to hounds and marrying a daughter of the house. Why was that? Perhaps being chaplain to a great family was a situation which drew a certain type of man, unsuited to the rigours of parish life, or perhaps the great families themselves preferred such men. It was puzzling, although not as puzzling as the question of why she should wonder about such matters at all. Her mind was so frayed that she could not even concentrate on the words of the service.

After the dismissal, she rose and turned to leave, just as Ran slipped out of the door, head down. He must have seen her there, yet he had no wish to speak to her, not even to exchange a courteous greeting. That cut like a knife! He had hardly spoken a word to her since their meeting in the Long Gallery. He had been serious then, too, but he had spoken to her kindly, wishing her to be happy, to make the right choice. Even last night, he had tried to speak to her. He had not avoided her as he was doing now, nor had he seemed so lost and forlorn. How she wished she could offer him some comfort for whatever trouble he was suffering, but she knew not how. Comfort was not routinely offered in the Grenaby family. If one was upset, one would be told briskly to pull oneself together.

Another face attracted her attention — the mistress! Miss Chandry was sitting several rows back, in the final line of ornate pews before the servants' seats. She knew her place, then. Her eyes were fixed on Ruth, and she divined some intensity in them, as if she would speak but dared not.

Ruth had taken only a few steps, but now she stopped. Pinnock, she saw, was waiting for her, so she waved the maid towards her.

"I shall stay a while to pray before I begin my practice at the instrument. Take my Prayer Book back to my room, if you please." Pinnock looked sceptical, so Ruth added, "I shall not stir from the chapel, I promise you."

She turned back and resumed her seat, bowing her head, the picture of pious womanhood, she hoped. Behind her, the shufflings of the attendees diminished. The doors closed with a thunk. Mr Ponsonby, now without his vestments, passed her, the door opened, closed again.

Almost at once the pew door opened and the woman sat down beside her. "They watch you closely, don't they?" she said, with a low ripple of laughter. "I should hate to be so caged."

"I hate it too," Ruth said, surprising even herself. It was impossible to dislike Miss Chandry, with her open countenance and guileless eyes. Nor did she want to, she realised. She liked such refreshing honesty. "My maid will be back very soon, so if you wish to talk to me—"

"I only wish to say that I won't cause you any grief when you are married to Ger. *If* you marry him, of course. You don't have to. We all have the choice, after all. But if you do, I won't get in your way or cause trouble. I am the one who wants him to marry someone like you, after all."

"Are you?" That was a surprise.

"Well, can you see me in charge of a place like this?" she said, grimacing. "Raising the next duke, meeting the Queen, mingling with the peers? That's not me! But you can do all that as easy as pie. I must go before Miss Poker-Face returns, but if ever you can escape from your gaolers, I'm at the Old Manor most mornings."

She slipped away, and Ruth heard the door open and close again. She was, for a brief moment, alone.

~~~~~

Ruth breakfasted with her father in the Buttery, her mother following her usual custom of breakfasting in her room. Ran had already been and gone, and of Ger there was no sign. Lady Elizabeth came in while they were still at table.

"Good morning, Duke! Good morning, Lady Ruth!" she said cheerfully. "I have decided to bear you company today, knowing that my brothers could not be depended upon to do so. Ah, good morning, Brent. Chocolate, if you please. Well, the other reason I came is to enjoy Mrs Cromarty's delicious chocolate, for my own cook has not the way of it as yet, and there is nothing better to start the day, I find. Mmm, Bath buns, my favourites. Should you
~~~~~

care for one, Lady Ruth? I can recommend them as a very nourishing treat, and how better to enjoy them but with Valmont's own apricot preserve. We have wonderful apricots here, the trees are most productive and give a good crop every year."

She chattered away in this artless fashion for some minutes, requiring very little in the way of response from Ruth, and none at all from the duke, whose eyebrows drew steadily lower and lower in annoyance.

Eventually, he got to his feet. "I shall take a turn about the gardens. The exercise will do me good."

He stomped out of the room, and Lady Elizabeth heaved a noisy sigh. "I knew I should drive him away sooner or later. If you have eaten your fill, let us go somewhere quiet and have a comfortable coze."

The two made their way out of the Buttery, practically tripping over Pinnock who was lurking in the passageway.

"Oh! Who are you?" Lady Elizabeth cried. "Lady Ruth's maid, I suppose. Do you have a message for your mistress?"

"I'm to stay with her, milady," Pinnock said. "Her Grace's orders. I'm not to leave her alone."

"A chaperon! How proper. But you see, it is quite all right, for your mistress is with me now, and I shall be her chaperon. Tell Her Grace that Lady Ruth is in the Spinsters' Parlour with Lady Elizabeth. Perfectly unobjectionable. Off you go now."

And Pinnock went. Suspicious and unconvinced, but she went.

Ruth laughed. "I wish I could get rid of her so easily."

"I am autocratic by nature, so I never have the least difficulty, not with lady's maids, in any event. Dowager duchesses are more of a challenge."

"Are we really going to the Spinsters' Parlour? I have never heard of it."

"Ah, a little known secret. It is not restricted to spinsters these days, but it makes a pleasantly cosy morning room for the ladies of the household. This way."

The Spinsters' Parlour was set on a mezzanine floor above a low-ceilinged passageway, and was indeed a cosy room, by Valmont standards, being no more than thirty feet from end to end, and half that in width. It was furnished with an assortment of well-used sofas, chairs and work-tables, with one wall given over to bookshelves and another providing a splendid view towards the stables, a miniature version of the house.

"Now then, tell me about yourself, for we have not had a chance to talk yet, and if you are to marry Ger—"

"Am I?"

"Are you not? I thought— Oh. I suppose it is not quite decided yet. Yes, Brent, what is it?"

"Begging your pardon for intruding, my lady, but the letters have been collected from Andover, and this one is addressed to His Grace the Duke of Orrisdale. However, His Grace is convinced it is instead for Her Grace, and begs that the Lady Ruth be so good as to give it to her when Her Grace arises from her repose."

"How strange!" Ruth said, taking the letter. "The direction is written very ill, so it could be *'His Grace'* or *'Her Grace'*, but this word is very clearly *'Duke'*, so why would he—? Oh, I see, it is from Aunt Maria, and she only ever writes to Mama. Thank you, Brent. I shall see that Her Grace receives this. Poor Aunt Maria! She never writes anything worth hearing, but she insists on writing every Monday, if we happen to be—" She paused, realising. "Monday… this is not one of her routine letters. Oh dear! Something is amiss."

"Take it to your father without delay," Lady Elizabeth said.

Ruth had no sooner resolved upon this course, when the duke burst into the room, an opened letter in one hand, holding out his other hand imperiously. "Maria's letter! Quick, quick!"

He tore open the seal and unfolded two sheets, his eyes racing from line to line so fast that Ruth could not believe he understood what he read.

"Papa, what is it? What has happened?"

"Audlyn, the little fool! And Susan! My God, was ever a father cursed with so silly a daughter?"

"Papa, tell me at once, I beg you! Are they injured? Not *dead?*"

"Oh… as to that… not as bad as that, no. Audlyn's letter was so garbled I could make nothing of it, but Maria is more sensible and makes it sound not so hopeless. Audlyn has been rusticated from school for some prank or other of which he does not even dare to tell me the details. Well, young men will have their little outbreaks of mischief, I daresay. I shall have to pay off a few people by the sound of it, and for the damage caused, whatever it is, but that is not the worst of it. Your sister, Ruthie, has quarrelled with Crosby, if you please, and been obliged to leave Crosby Manor under a cloud."

"Oh, poor Susan!" Ruth cried.

"Poor Crosby is more to the point. For a man of his position to be swept this way and that by a chit barely out of the schoolroom — it is unforgivable. Ah, but Maria thinks the match may still be saved. The engagement is not yet broken off, and he cannot cry off, you know. He will not, anyway. Man of honour, Crosby. And so long as Susan can be persuaded not to end it herself, we shall do well enough. Lord, these children of mine. And there is one line that makes me want to whip the lot of them. *'Charlotte has been crying all night'*, if you please! What has *she* to cry about, I should like to know? Susan holds her head high, and shows not a drop of remorse, and *Charlotte* is the one who cries over it. On days like this, I thank the Good Lord for my one sensible child, who has never given me a moment's worry. You are a good girl, Ruthie, a very good girl. It is the greatest comfort to know that at least one of my children will never grieve her father and mother."

Ruth bowed her head in acknowledgement of the compliment, but it was not so welcome as her father might suppose. To be the good, obedient one of the family made her also the cowardly, timorous one. Her brothers and sisters might be naughty sometimes, but they were also courageous and spirited, following their own way. Too much of that would make them wayward, and Susan, perhaps, was already far along that path, but sometimes Ruth wished she had but a tenth of Susan's boldness.

Then perhaps she could follow Ran's advice. *'You must follow your heart above all. Do not choose merely in obedience to your father or because you feel that honour dictates it. Choose rather what will bring you the greatest happiness in your life.'*

But she did not dare. Defiance was not in her nature.

19: Making A Choice

The duke and duchess were closeted away in an upstairs room for some time, but Lady Elizabeth stayed with Ruth and protected her from Pinnock's doggedly determined attendance. There were great heaps of London journals in the Spinsters' Parlour, so they browsed through those and discussed the fashions and read out interesting paragraphs. Ruth felt that she had made a friend or perhaps an older sister. Lady Elizabeth was the only one of the Litherholm sisters of whom she had previously no knowledge beyond hearsay. She was more than ten years Ruth's senior and stayed away from London, so their paths had never crossed before. All Ruth knew of her was that she had had a rather scandalous past, with rumours of elopements and jiltings. Whatever the truth of it, she had never married and seemed unconcerned by that. She was not in the least starchy, exuding a relaxed and open confidence that Ruth very much envied. She tried herself to project a similar ease, but whereas her own manner was assumed and felt false, Elizabeth's felt entirely genuine.

Eventually, Ruth was summoned to her parents. To her surprise, she found them smiling.

"We are agreed, daughter," the duchess said, "that there will be no lasting damage to the family name by either Audlyn or Susan. Besides, all such considerations fade to nothing when compared with the glorious future we have arranged for you. We are to meet with Falconbury in an hour and your father will insist that he behaves honourably towards you. He will, I am certain of it, despite this — this *creature* that he has imposed upon our notice. After all, there has long been an understanding between you, there can be no denying it. Everyone knew of it, and the marriage was expected. He knows what is due to you."

Yet she twisted her lips anxiously. Despite the confident words, she sounded uncertain. Would Ger agree to it, or would he choose to walk away from the match? And if he did, what would become of Ruth, deprived of both possible husbands at once?

They met in the Ante-Chamber, the duke and duchess, Ruth, Ran and Ger. The duke looked belligerent. The duchess looked worried. Ger looked oddly mischievous, but then his moods were never predictable. Ran — he was as inscrutable as ever, his expression serious. When he smiled, he could make Ruth's heart somersault, but he seldom did so, and not at all lately. She thought again with yearning of those few days at Mallowfleet, when he had followed her everywhere, and there had been a glow in his eyes that had given her hope. But all that was gone. It had been merely a game to him, perhaps, or part of his gentlemanly code to flatter his future bride, and she was that no longer.

The duke began at once. He spoke of honour and obligation, of understandings and agreements. He told Ger exactly what he expected him to do, without prevarication. He strode back and forth across the rug in front of the hearth, occasionally stabbing the air to make a point. Ruth and her mother sat, straight-backed, on a sofa. Ger, who looked as if he were trying not to laugh, sat opposite them. Ran seemed half-detached from the proceedings, for he stood leaning against the wall across the room, arms folded across his chest, his eyes fixed with unblinking intensity on Ruth. She tried not to look at him, for the sight of him unnerved her.

As for Ruth, she was terrified. Nothing in her life had prepared her for the turmoil of mind in which she now found herself. Loving Ran as she did, yet she might leave that room betrothed to his brother, and she could not interpret her tangled feelings about that. She had thought her life was settled, that she would marry Ran and be a duchess, her life unfolding exactly as she had always expected, except for the tiny detail that her duke would be Ran and not Ger. But this… this was outside her realm of experience, and she quaked inside. How would it end? When she walked out of this room, her life would be irrevocably changed. She stood on the edge of the cliff, knowing she had to jump and without the strength or the will to turn and walk away. Her parents would push her over the edge, and she was powerless to resist. So she sat, her hands folded neatly in her lap, and waited for fate to engulf her.

"So there it is, Falconbury," the duke said eventually. "You know what I want, and I expect you to keep to your word."

Before Ger could speak, Ran shifted restlessly. "You have told us a great deal about what *you* want, Orrisdale. What about what Ruth wants?"

"She will do what I tell her," he blustered. "It is not for her to make such momentous decisions by herself. Her parents are best placed to choose her husband."

"She is of age," Ran said. "She can marry where she pleases."

"Not while she lives under my roof and expects a dowry from me," the duke shot back. "Why are you interfering, Litherholm? What is it to do with you anyway?"

That raised the glimmer of a smile from Ran. "Your memory is failing you, Duke. Have you forgotten that I am betrothed to Ruth?"

"Nonsense! That ended the moment Falconbury was found. You did not think... how could you imagine... naturally that is all done with. Is it not obvious? My daughter marry a *younger son?* It is unthinkable! The betrothal is at an end."

"Not so," Ran said, his calm tone a striking contrast to the duke's loud hectoring. "A betrothal is an agreement between two people, and only those two may end it. Since I am a gentleman and shall never do so, it is for the lady to put a stop to it... if she so wishes."

"Brother..." Ger said, jumping to his feet, and crossing the room to stand beside Ran. "I thought—"

Ran waved him to silence. During the entire exchange, he had not for a moment taken his eyes off Ruth. She felt as if a great weight were pressing down on her. Must she speak? She could not!

"Tell him, daughter," her father said abruptly. "Put an end to this nonsense once and for all, because I tell you here and now, if you marry a worthless younger son like Litherholm, you will be no daughter of mine. There will be no dowry, no parental blessing on your nuptials, no notice of you. You will never return to Mallowfleet, and none of the family will ever acknowledge you in public. Your own brothers and sisters will give you the cut direct. I will see to it, you have my word on that."

"Then you would be very wrong!" Ger cried, but Ran laid a hand on his arm.

"Let Ruth speak," he said quietly. "Let her say what she must."

All eyes turned to Ruth.

"Speak, daughter," her father said impatiently. "Tell him it is ended."

There was no avoiding it. Her father expected it, and Ran, too, seemed resigned to it. He was right, of course, to want to hear his dismissal from her own lips, but oh, how she dreaded it! Yet it must be done, and done graciously.

She rose, crossing the room to stand before him. Ran, the man she loved, the man she wanted to spend her life with, the man who gazed at her impassively as she drew on all her courage to end their betrothal. And that, finally, gave her the spurt of anger she needed. How dared he let her go without a fight! How dared he simply accept his dismissal so passively! And her anger gave her, if not eloquence, at least the strength to say what had to be said.

"Ran, I am very honoured that you wished to marry me, but I find it impossible to be your wife. I am very sorry."

For an instant his eyes flashed with some strong emotion, but he mastered himself almost at once. "I am sorry, too," he said simply. Then he lifted her hand to his lips. Oh God, the touch of his lips on her bare hand! And this was not the gentlemanly pretend kiss without touching, but a shockingly warm pressure that lasted for several heartbeats. Or would have done, if her heart had not seemingly stopped beating altogether.

Then he released her hand, and for the first time his eyes left hers. "Your daughter is now free again, Duke," he said. Did she imagine it or was there a slight tremor in his voice?

Her father moved closer to her. "There now, daughter, there now. Well done." Taking her hand, still trembling from the feel of Ran's lips upon it, he would have passed it directly to Ger, but Ruth whisked out of his grasp.

"You will not mind if I sit down, Papa?" So saying, she moved directly back to the sofa to sit beside her mother.

The duchess patted her hand. So many people touching her... hemming her in... closing in around her... her breathing was heavy and ragged. She looked at Ran, but he was staring at his boots, as if he were bored. She turned her own gaze downwards. If only this could be over!

"Falconbury," her father said. "Now it is your turn."

And then Ger was there before her. She saw his Hessians, badly polished, and his pantaloons, not clinging enough for fashion. And then, because she would not, could not look up, she saw his face as he knelt before her. There was concern there, genuine concern, and she lifted her head a little to look him in the eye.

"Ruth," he began, "your father wants me to offer for you, and I am very happy to do so. How could I not be, for who could possibly be a more perfect wife than you, so lovely and so accomplished as you are? So many young ladies are said to be accomplished, but you truly are. I would be very happy to have you for my wife, but I want you to understand that you have more than one choice. You can marry me, if that is your wish, and be the Duchess of Falconbury and mistress of Valmont and mother of my heirs, with all that entails. That would make me very proud and pleased. Or you could still marry Ran, if you prefer. You would—"

"Now wait a moment!" the duke said.

"Hush!" Ger said sharply. "You have made your speech, now it is my turn. You said so yourself." Turning back to her, he went on, "Ruth, if you wish to marry Ran and your father withholds your dowry, then I shall myself settle on you the full amount that is your due. And since I have no wish to look elsewhere for a wife, I shall stay single, and you will therefore still be mistress of Valmont and raise the next duke, since Ran is my heir."

"Ridiculous nonsense!" the duke cried. "Take no notice, daughter."

"Silence!" Ger said. "I can also assure you that you will suffer no social disgrace by marrying Ran, I shall see to that. The Litherholm family does have some influence, I would suggest. Or there is yet another choice — you could marry neither of us. You could go back to town and look about you for a man who suits you better than either of us. You are free to do as you wish. This is the nineteenth century, after all, and no one is forced to marry any more. Your father may offer you his counsel, but the choice should be your own, Ruth. Your life is yours to live in whatever manner makes you happiest."

She could hardly take it in. Her father was ranting about traitors and wickedness, but it was just a rumble of noise in the background. Her mother was screeching in her ear, but she could not make sense of that, either. Ger was still kneeling, looking up at her with such a gentle smile on his face and that calmed her a little.

But then her eyes fell on Ran and he looked so shocked that her breath caught. All his insouciance had fled now, and he was showing real emotion for the first time. He had not known what Ger would say, she could see, and now he was horrified at the prospect of being drawn back into an engagement that he had only just escaped. An engagement that was distasteful to him, that much was clear.

Could she marry him for her own selfish reasons, knowing that her love would never be returned, knowing that he had been manipulated into it? He would be unhappy, her parents would be angry, Ger would be left without a duchess and what of herself? She could hardly be happy if Ran were not. There could only be heartbreak in a marriage based on unrequited love. She shrank from the idea.

For all Ger's fine words, her options were limited. She could not marry Ran, and she dreaded the prospect of walking out of Valmont unbetrothed. Could she… should she marry Ger? Her parents wished it… no, they depended on it, and with the rest of the family in turmoil, she was their brightest hope of a great match. They had always wanted her to be a duchess, not solely from ambition but because she had the temperament and, she hoped, the ability to bring honour to the position. And Ger himself liked her and they got on well. Even the mistress would not be a problem, it seemed. And she herself would be free at last, which was by no means the least of it.

There was a rightness to it, she decided. It was as they had agreed long ago, and Ger had been happy with the plan then and his softly smiling face suggested he was happy with it now. It would delight her parents, and that was no small consideration. For twenty years she had schooled herself into unquestioning obedience, and the prospect of displeasing them brought her to quivering terror. She could not defy them! To do what was expected and to obey was like prayer, it soothed her and made her happy. Ran had told her to listen to her heart and her heart told her to obey her parents.

She cleared her throat and gazed into Ger's eyes.

"Thank you, Ger. I accept your most obliging offer."

Her mother sighed gustily, and her father said, "Thank God! Now we can put all this unfortunate business behind us."

Ger's smile did not falter, but he said, "And this is your own choice, Ruth? Yours, not just your father's?"

She dropped her gaze. "My choice, but I am content to follow my father's counsel in such an important decision."

"Then you have made me very happy," Ger said.

She could not tell whether he meant it or not.

~~~~~

Ran slipped out of the room unnoticed and strode across the entrance hall, where the butler and a footman jumped to attention.
~~~~~

"Brent, tell the stables to have Thunderbolt ready for me in the yard in ten minutes," he said without breaking stride. "Send Giggs up to me at once."

"Very good, my lord," he said to Ran's retreating back.

Ran paused, frowned, spun round. "Also… I shall not be in for dinner. I shall dine at the Lorrimers'"

Did Brent's eyebrows rise a fraction. "Yes, my lord."

Ran resumed his progress to the stairs, and had set his foot upon the bottom step when Elizabeth materialised from behind a plinth bearing a Roman bust.

"Ran! What happened? Has she—? Oh Ran!" Her face changed abruptly. "Oh brother, I am so sorry! I had not realised you were so—"

"Not now, Lizzie. Just leave me alone."

Without another word, he took the stairs two at a time, his long legs striding through the State Apartments and into the family wing. He reached his dressing room just as Giggs flew up the service stairs, panting for breath.

"Beg pardon, milord. I'll have your riding outfit ready in no time."

While Giggs, catching the urgency, frantically pulled garments from closets and drawers, Ran ripped clothing from his back, scattering items about the room. The valet hustled him into the new outfit and had him out of the door in record time. Even then it was not fast enough for Ran. He needed to be gone *now!*

Thunderbolt was just being led out as Ran arrived, almost at a run, in the stable yard. He vaulted straight into the saddle, and was in motion instantly, the beast reaching a gallop before the stables had been well left behind.

And then he was free, flying over the close-cropped turf, head low over his mount's neck, the wind on his face, his muscles working and his mind, mercifully, too occupied to think any more. But he was not too occupied to feel, and all the roiling emotions of the last month rose up unchecked to drown him. He rode hard across the park, and through the Stony Field, but when he reached the edge of the woods he could go no further.

He pulled the horse to a halt and leapt from his back. Then, overwhelmed and desperately unhappy, he leaned his head against the nearest tree and wept.

20: Friends And Advice

By the time Ran returned to the house, it was obvious that the entire household was aware that he had been thrown over, that Ruth was to marry Ger and that he himself had stormed out in a tantrum. The grooms avoided his eyes, and Giggs helped him dress for the evening with such an oily solicitude that Ran wanted to throttle him.

The Lorrimers were more considerate. Max beguiled the ride to Harebell Cottage, taken at a far more sedate pace than Ran's mad afternoon gallop, with all the trivial dealings in the offices that day. The rest of the family greeted Ran with their usual quiet pleasure, and the talk was all of local matters — a bull escaping, a scything mishap, an unexpected death, a new baby in the village. Ger was mentioned, for the return of the lost Duke of Falconbury could not pass unremarked, but the questions were easy ones — was he well? Would he take his seat this year? Would he go to London at all? Had he any plans to entertain? No one mentioned Ginny or Ruth.

Ran imagined that he was taking his share of the conversation, and perhaps at first he had done so, but gradually he grew quieter and quieter. Sometimes there would be an odd little silence, and he became guiltily aware that his mind had drifted away and someone had addressed a question to him, unheard. But then Max would answer for him, and gratefully Ran would drift off again. It was peaceful, being surrounded by such undemanding friends.

It was Ran himself who brought the difficult subjects into the open. At the end of dinner, when Alice rose to leave the gentlemen, Ran said, "Stay a moment, Alice. You have all been very kind, and undoubtedly you know this already but I must get used to talking about it. Ger is to marry Ruth."

"Ah, we did know it, of course," Alice said. "The servants know so everybody knows. Is Ger happy with it?"

"Who can say with Ger?" Ran said, too despondent to care what he said. "He says he is, and I know he likes Ruth well enough, but it is not Ger who worries me. He is capable of making up his own mind, but Ruth—! She has done exactly what I most hoped to prevent — she is marrying him because her father wishes it. She said as much."

"She may also wish it herself, and makes a virtue of her own inclinations," Alice suggested gently.

"Perhaps it is so, but—" He stopped, reluctant to expose his own selfish emotions, but then went on, "No, I will tell you this, no matter how much it hurts. Ger told Ruth that if she wanted to marry *me*, he would ensure she lost nothing by it. He would provide her dowry if her father would not, and he would not marry elsewhere so she would still be mistress of Valmont and mother to a future duke. She could accept either one of us, and there would be virtually nothing to choose between us. Yet she chose *him*. And that means either that she wants to be a duchess above any other consideration, which would be a dreadful thing for me to believe of her, or—"

He could not even say the words.

It was Alice who finished the sentence. "Or she prefers him to you."

"Yes. That hurts so much, you cannot imagine. It should not, I know, but—"

"It is natural," she said quickly, covering his hand with her own. "Of course you wanted her to like you better. But if she *does* truly like him, and he likes her, then even without love their marriage will prosper, Ran. It is a good start."

"So long as nothing comes between them," said Max, frowning.

"You mean so long as *no one* comes between them," Ran said. "Such as Ginny Chandry, I suppose. She is sensible, Max. She knows her place."

"But Ger does not!" he growled. "I am sorry to say it of your brother, Ran, but the fellow is an idiot sometimes. He must be aware of how you feel about Lady Ruth, yet he takes her away from you anyway, so now he has two women within shouting distance of each other, and nothing he has done so far convinces me that he can manage even one woman with discretion. Lady Ruth will have a miserable time of it, if you ask me. Which you have not, of course," he added wryly, catching Alice's look of irritation.

"Not helpful," she said crisply. "I daresay the affair with the mistress will come to the usual end, in time. She will move on, or return to Cornwall, perhaps."

"But she can cause no end of trouble before then," Max said. "From all I have seen and heard of her, she is sufficiently high in her own self-esteem to consider herself fit to move in society at some level, yet has not enough wisdom to do so without disgracing Ger and the family name. She is a bad influence on him, Ran, and will do him nothing but harm."

"She seems sensible enough to me, and she deals well with Ger's uneven temperament," Ran said. "What in the world makes you take her in such dislike?"

Max sighed and ran a hand through his hair. "Well, I shall show you." He got up, leaving the room momentarily and returning with an opened letter. It read in its entirety, *'Kill the fatted calf, the Prodigal Duke is coming home. Tell Ran, will you.'*

Ran laughed. It was so like Ger to get into one of his mischievous moods and write light-heartedly about such a major decision in his life. Naturally he would joke about it, it was his way of dealing with awkward communications. But... he frowned. There was something wrong with it. It was *too* short, too uncommunicative.

"You *would* think it is funny," Max said crossly. "You were always too lenient with him. Of course, by the time we received this letter, you had already gone haring off to Cornwall, and we had no need to tell you anything, but really, what a letter to be sending on such an occasion! I was so cross with him! It is so frivolous and it is all that woman's fault. She is a bad influence on him, Ran, and... What is it?"

"You were *cross* with him? A man you believed to be dead for a year writes to you out of the blue, and you were cross? Not astonished, Max? Not disbelieving? Not shocked speechless?"

The silence around the table was suddenly uncomfortable. Ran could scarce believe it, but their faces gave it away.

"You knew," Ran said tersely. "You knew he was alive, yet you said nothing. How long have you known?"

It was Peter Lorrimer who answered. "Almost from the beginning... within a month of the shipwreck. He wrote to me here, and I went to see him in—"

"To see him!"

"—Cornwall. There were money matters... legal matters he wanted arranged. He swore us all to the utmost secrecy, Ran, and no one could possibly be more pleased than we are that his survival is now known to the world at large, and we no longer have this terrible secret burdening us."

"But... if I had taken the seat in the Lords... married Ruth... you would have stood by and said nothing?" He could not even be angry with them, for it was too shocking for anger.

"That was his wish. He said you would make a better duke than he ever could, and a better husband for Ruth. He *wanted* you to have it all, Ran! He said—"

"Never mind what he *said* or what he *wanted!* How *dared* you keep such information from me! You of all people know how I grieved for him, how reluctant I was to step into his honours. You should have told me, at least."

"You were the very last person we could tell," Peter said sharply. "Think, Ran! What would you have done? What *could* you have done? You would have been frozen, unable to accept the title, unable to marry openly knowing you were not the duke. No one could know."

That was true, and Ran was honest enough to admit it, despite his anger. "Then why even tell you? What were these money matters and legal matters?"

Peter sighed and the Lorrimers exchanged glances.

"I think we may tell a little of it without breaking confidence," Peter said. "Ran, your brother always had money that was separate from the estate. There were a couple of small bequests from relations when he was a boy, and he had a huge allowance that he rarely spent. Later there were his winnings from cards. He had secret accounts set up so that, if ever he should manage to pretend to be dead, as he used to joke about, he would have money to live upon. He had long since given up hope of ever achieving such an outcome, of course, because of the difficulties of arranging it. But when he found himself, most unexpectedly, in exactly such a position, he contacted me to release those funds. Later, he wanted to draw up a will to the benefit of Miss Chandry, and most recently, he added a clause to benefit any children of hers as well. I met him in February for that purpose, and he was very agitated about the child, Ran. He had not intended any such thing since marriage was... problematic, under the circumstances, but she had..." He glanced at Alice, and fell silent.

"I am not twelve, Peter," she said. "Besides, Max told me the whole of it. Ran, Miss Chandry simply slipped into Ger's bed one night. My imperfect understanding of such matters is that no normal man would be able to resist such temptation."

"But you may appreciate now," Max said, "why I disapprove so thoroughly of Miss Chandry. She has put Ger in an intolerable position. She wanted to force him into marriage, of course, and many a young woman has used just such a strategy on a reluctant swain, but she could not have known how impossible that was for him, in his peculiar situation."

"No," Ran said thoughtfully. "You wrong her, Max. Her intentions were good. She knew almost from the start who he was, but she wanted to make him choose. Knowing him well, his propensity to dither and postpone difficult decisions was familiar to her. So she forced the issue. If he were fully committed to staying as Jonathan Ellsworthy, he would have married her and that would have been an end to it. But he did not, and so she knew he would, one day, return to his true identity. Even then, he dithered. It must be three months or so since she played her little trick, but it was only when he realised that I had not yet been summoned to the Lords that he acted."

"Ah. Interesting," Max said. "But still, I cannot approve her actions. She is not a virtuous woman."

"I fear that as a family we are a tad more strait-laced than the nobility," Peter said, with a rueful smile. "For myself, I cannot approve Ger's actions, either."

"Keeping a mistress is a sensible approach to a marriage without affection," Ran said. "A nobleman must marry suitably for his position."

"*You* would not take a mistress, I think, Ran."

"I would not, but that is easy to say when one has never been tempted," he said, with a slight lift of one shoulder. With a fresh burst of grief, he thought of Ruth and how little temptation he would have to seek comfort elsewhere if she were his wife.

Ran and Max rode back to Valmont in unusual silence, and it did not feel like a comfortable state. A lifetime's friendship could not be undamaged by the revelation of such a momentous secret, but Ran was not one to let a grievance fester. He pulled his horse to a halt, and Max stopped as well, although it was too dark to read his expression.

"Max, we are friends of too many years' standing to fall out over this, but I cannot like it. I can see that your hands were tied, and of the others I have no censure, but you! For a full year you have been my secretary and adviser in all matters, yet aware of information that, had I known it, would have affected every decision I made. You cannot have been unaware of the deceit of your position."

"I was all too aware of it," Max said quietly. "In fact, I wanted to resign at once, but Peter and Alice persuaded me to stay. I could give you no reason for leaving that would be credible, and we were all agreed that we must do nothing at all to make you suspicious."

"It would have been better if you had known nothing of it."

"Perhaps. But when Ger wrote, he used the old code we used for childhood secret messages — addressing it to William Titmuss. The accident had damaged his hands and affected his handwriting, and he had no seal, so it was the only way he could think of to convince us that it was truly him. Naturally, Alice thought it was from you so she gave it to me. We decided it was for the best for at least I would know if you had any suspicions that Ger was not dead."

"You were to keep watch on me, I suppose," Ran said acidly.

"With the most benevolent motives," Max said. "As to advising you, when have you ever listened to my advice? I have spoken against these mines and cotton mills a hundred times, yet you buy them anyway."

Ran gave a bark of laughter. "True! They are very profitable, you must admit it."

"Indeed, and you have installed enough managers and directors to lift you a notch or two above trade, so I suppose it will do. But as far as your personal affairs are concerned — the title or your marriage — if ever you asked me what you should do, I answered that you could do this thing or that thing or this other thing, and you replied that you will do the other thing, which was precisely what you wanted to do anyway. I have never, ever steered you in one direction or another. My conscience is clear on that score."

Ran merely grunted, not entirely mollified.

Max went on, "Not withstanding all that, I am not just your secretary, I am also your friend, and I hope, a true and honest one. On that basis, I am going to give you some advice now. This situation you have got into with Ger and his mistress and Lady Ruth is untenable. It can only end in disaster."

"Ger understands the position, and can handle it, Max."

"I am not interested in Ger. He must make his own decisions and live with the consequences. I am concerned for *you*, Ran."

"What has it to do with me?" he said, with only the merest hint of bitterness.

"You know the answer to that. You are in love with Lady Ruth, and Ger is in love with this woman of his, and you know what Ger is like. Sooner or later, he will do something to distress

Lady Ruth and there you will be, a conveniently placed source of comfort."

"You cannot imagine that I would behave as you imply!" Ran cried. "A fine opinion of me you have!"

"And yet you said yourself that you have never been tempted. If she were to ask it of you—"

"Ruth would never do such a thing!"

"You cannot predict what anyone will do in a desperate situation, and the risk is too great, Ran. My advice to you is to leave Valmont at once."

"Leave? Impossible! I manage all the estates."

"Other managers may be found," Max said. "If you truly love Lady Ruth, then you should remove yourself and your affection for her to a safe distance, if only for her sake. You will still be obliged to meet sometimes, but not every day, not in a situation where you will become a natural confidante and eventually something more. That is my advice, honestly given, with nothing but your welfare in mind. You may take it or leave it, as always."

So saying, he urged his horse into motion again. Ran followed and they entered the stables and handed the horses to the yawning grooms in silence. It was only when they had entered the house, mounted the Stable Stair and reached the point of separation that Ran turned to his friend.

"I will consider all you have said," he said quietly. "Thank you for your honesty."

Max smiled and they parted in silence.

Ran found Molly sewing all alone in the sitting room.

"Has Ger gone to bed already?" he said.

Molly shook her head. "Taking money off your Uncle Arthur, I expect."

"He needs no help with that, but if he has become trapped by a chatty duchess, he may need reinforcements."

He made his way downstairs to the Grand Saloon, but found only Uncle Arthur, the duke and duchess and Captain Edgerton engrossed in whist, and the rest of the room in darkness. Puzzled, he tried the Queen's Room and then the Royal Withdrawing Room, but encountered only emptiness. The door porter in the entrance hall confirmed that Ger had not passed that way since just after dinner. Defeated on the ground floor, he climbed the Grand Staircase where the footman stationed there pointed him towards the Long Gallery, and soon he saw the flickering light of candles and heard voices. No, some kind of music… humming, perhaps. And then giggling, a low voice and more humming.

A romantic assignation. He stopped uncertainly, but a gleam of something shimmering caught his eye. A lady's evening gown, the spangles on her train catching the light even though she herself was in darkness. But he knew her. Even though he could distinguish only the pale outline of her form, it could only be Ruth. She stood in the shadow of a draped curtain, silent and motionless, peering down the Long Gallery, watching.

Ran took a cautious step forward, but he already knew what he would see. Ger and Ginny stood side by side, dancing the waltz. Ger was humming the tune, while she practised the steps, and if that had been all, it might not, perhaps, have been so terrible. But they were gazing into each other's eyes with such fiery intensity that his breath caught in his throat. So much joy was written on their faces... so much desire... so much love. He dared not intrude, and yet he was mesmerised, quite unable to look away.

Clearly Ruth had the same difficulty. She was oblivious of Ran's presence, blind to all but the ecstatic pair before her, and they were too engrossed in each other to know that they were observed.

Ruth gave a little sob. Then, turning, she fled, not towards the brightly lit Grand Staircase but along the darker passage that led to the chapel. Ran could not bear to see her so distressed. He followed, thankful for the deep carpeting on this floor that muffled the sound of his boots as he ran. Ruth came to the door to the chapel gallery. Owing to the tradition of burning candles constantly in the chapel, a dim light illuminated the gallery and Ruth slipped inside. Again Ran followed.

She sat on the cushioned bench against the wall, head down, sobbing piteously. Without the least hesitation, he sat down beside her and took her in his arms, and she turned to him at once, weeping into his shoulder.

"Hush now," he murmured. "It will be all right. Hush, hush."

She lifted her head. "He will never love me that way, never!" she whispered.

He stroked her cheek. "But he *will* love you. How could he not? In time, he will grow to love you just as much as—" He caught himself in time. "—as any man who knows you must. It will be all right."

And as she looked trustingly into his eyes, her cheeks washed with tears, he bent his head and kissed her.

21: Two Galleries

Surprisingly, she allowed herself to be kissed. Ran had expected her to push him away as soon as his lips had touched hers, but instead she leaned against him and relaxed in his arms. All the tension seemed to drop out of her as she closed her eyes and surrendered to his kisses.

Ran was shocked by his own actions. How could he possibly be so weak and foolish? But he could not withdraw, for she seemed to need the comfort. All he could do was to suppress the passion that boiled up inside him. It was the chastest kiss imaginable, gentle and light and delicate, but if a kiss could help her to cope with the wildness of her emotions, then a kiss she should have. It was wrong and he dared not imagine the consequences, but he could deny her nothing she wanted.

Eventually, with the utmost reluctance, he drew back and she sighed, leaning her head against his shoulder, her face buried in his coat. For a long, long time they stayed thus, as his heart gradually slowed its frantic beating, and his ragged breathing steadied a little.

Eventually, she lifted her face a little, although her eyes were still lowered. "Thank you, Ran," she murmured, her voice calm. "You are such a good friend to me."

It was like a stab through the heart. He had anticipated emotion — anger, perhaps, or dismay, but not this placid understanding. She made no move to escape from his embrace, so he held her fast in his arms, quite unable to form any sensible words. She might be calm, but he was a maelstrom of raging emotions.

"It was the realisation, you see," she went on. "Knowing that I will always be second best."

"You will be his *wife!*" Ran said fiercely, stung into speech. "You will have his name, you will bear the children who will continue the family line, you will preside at his table, you will be his *equal.* She will only ever be his mistress. *She* will be second best, not you."

"To the world it may be so, but you and I will know differently. He will never love me as he loves her."

"As he loves her now, perhaps," Ran said. "Mistresses come and go but a wife is for ever. He will always hold you in respect and affection."

"Will he?" she said, sitting a little more upright.

"Of course he will. It will be all right."

"Will it?" she said, moving away from him slightly, and again his throat was too tight to answer her. She rose to her feet, wiping the tears from her face with her hands. "Thank you for... for comforting me, but I must get to my room before I am missed."

"That is one benefit you will gain by marriage," he said with some heat. "You will be free from this perpetual guarding."

"Oh yes, I will be free," she said, but he thought there was sadness in her voice.

To avoid the eyes of the footmen, he led her by little-used passages and echoing stone stairways to a place close to her bedroom door, then bade her a whispered goodnight, before making his way to his own room. Giggs was astute enough to attend him silently, although with all the tender solicitude of a nurse assisting a sick charge to bed. He clearly expected to follow the prescribed routine of settling his master into bed and drawing the curtains, and Ran had no energy to withstand him. But when Giggs had withdrawn, he sat upright and pondered all that the last two days had brought him.

Two days! Was it only yesterday that Ruth and her parents had arrived and torn his life into tiny shreds? It seemed like weeks… months. Yesterday he had, on the whole, behaved properly, but today! Today had been a disaster. He had allowed anger and dark despair to overwhelm him in the afternoon, storming out of the house and riding like a madman, and now he had kissed her. Of all the impossibly disastrous things he could have done, it was hard to conceive of anything worse.

There was only one bright spot in the entire sorry episode, and that was that she had seen it as no more than a friendly gesture, an offering of comfort in her distress. If she had been shocked or angry, it would have been a thousand times worse. He had not yet broken her trust in him. But that was small consolation.

Max, devil take him, had been in the right. At the first temptation, Ran had fallen into wickedness, and it must never be allowed to happen again, on that he was resolved. He must follow Max's advice, and leave Valmont. But where could he go? And how could he contrive to leave his brother without the world suspecting a rift or, worse, the truth?

Worst of all, how could he leave Ruth behind? Yet he must, beyond all doubt he must. His future could not be bleaker.

~~~~~

Ruth found Pinnock waiting for her, smiling for once.

"There you are, milady. I was beginning to wonder what had happened to you, until I remembered that you would be with His Grace, of course. Your future husband," she gushed. "Such a fine young man, and so polite and charming."

The maid had gushed just as irritatingly when Ruth had been betrothed to Ran. All the upper servants had been allowed onto the gallery overlooking the Mallowfleet ballroom to watch Ran lead her out onto the floor to open the ball, and there had been bowls of punch sent down to the servants' hall for them to celebrate. Now it was Ger, and there was no thought of Ran at all. Dear Ran, who had held her and consoled her.

"How happy you will be, milady! Everything is just as it should be again."

Ruth said nothing. How could she speak, after what had happened? Ran had kissed her! He had held her in his arms and kissed her and it had broken her utterly. She had simply melted into his arms as if she had every right to be there, and for those few minutes everything in her world had been in harmony. If only
~~~~~

she could have stayed in his embrace! One word from him and she could never have let him go. Everything she felt would have poured out of her in an unstoppable torrent. One word...

But there was no word, and twist it as she might, she could not interpret his kiss as a sign of love. Affection, yes, as a man might show to his brother's wife, but was there anything more to it than that? Ran was always so perfectly correct that he could not mean anything by it. He had seen her unhappiness, and offered her some gentle comfort. That was all it was, surely, for if he felt anything for her beyond that, if he *loved* her, he could not have stood by that day and calmly handed her to Ger.

That was what broke her inside, the certainty that her love was not, could never be, returned. Even though he held her, soothed her, *kissed* her, he did not love her. He was being friendly, that was all, for never was there a better or more amiable man. Dearest Ran. The man she loved. The brother of her future husband. He must never know how she had crumbled inside! After that kiss, it had taken her such a long time to compose herself. She had had to call upon a lifetime of self-control to speak to him with any semblance of calmness.

"Shall you keep to the same wedding date, milady?" Pinnock said brightly from behind her back as she unfastened endless buttons.

"No!" she said, without thinking. If only Pinnock would go away and leave her in peace! How could she think or settle her wildly disordered emotions when the woman talked and talked?

Pinnock's hands stilled in surprise. "No, milady? Your clothes are made, and he could get a special licence, I daresay, being a duke and all. Mr Brent said the Archbishop would most likely agree to it."

"I am sure he would, Pinnock," she said, using all her willpower to speak calmly, "but His Grace has only just returned home and it might be inconvenient for him to rush into marriage at a moment's notice. There is no need for undue haste."

"No, milady." She sounded disappointed.

When Pinnock had left her, Ruth lay for some time in bed, trying to make sense of all that had happened. Only that afternoon, she had been quite certain that she was making the correct choice, but almost as soon as she had accepted Ger's offer, small doubts had assailed her. When she had turned round to look for Ran, he had gone, slipping away without a word. Then he had not come down to dinner, and although she tried to tell herself that he was delicately allowing Ger to celebrate his betrothal without the distracting presence of the former betrothed, she wondered if perhaps they had quarrelled, or if perhaps Ran was upset with *her*. Had she offended him, somehow? Yet when she had met him later in the chapel gallery, he had been all solicitude, so that did not seem likely.

It was unsettling, all the same. And then there was Ger. He had been all gentle courtesy during the evening and they had played duets together after dinner, but then at some point he had disappeared. She had not intended to spy on him, but when she was making her way up to bed, alone for once, she had thought to sit in the Long Gallery for a few minutes.

What she had seen there had shaken all her confidence to nothing. Such an intimate moment she had witnessed as they danced! The expressions of their faces, their eyes aflame with love… they needed nothing else. She understood for the first time why Miss Chandry was content with her situation. What need had she for wealth or rank, when she had a man who loved her so passionately, so completely? Ger had no need to look elsewhere for love, for he had that in abundance from her.

And what of Ruth? She would be respected as the Duchess of Falconbury, certainly. She would even be admired, perhaps. She would be a leader of society. Men would strive for her favours, and women would copy her styles of bonnet or sleeve, but she would never be *loved*, and the realisation was bitter. Oh, Ger would hold her in some affection, undoubtedly, but theirs would be more of a friendship than a marriage. They would smile and play the perfect hosts for their guests, and then he would disappear to be with his true love. In town, he would chafe to be back at Valmont, in his mistress's arms. Perhaps he would want her with him even there. He would love her children more than his heirs, because they had her sparkling eyes or freckled complexion or warm smile. *She* would know only happiness in the years to come.

For Ruth, there was no such knowledge. Such a long, bleak future stretched ahead of her. She could endure it, she thought, because she must. It would be no more than she had anticipated, this cool marriage of convenience, and a mild degree of fondness was all she expected from it. But she could not help thinking of Ran and his kiss — so warm yet so gentle. She shivered, remembering again the feel of his arms holding her against him, and how much his strength had soothed her troubled heart. He was not in love with her, but he could offer her the comfort of his kiss in her distress. He *cared* about her.

Ger had never held her, never kissed her, never even touched her except for her gloved hand. And yet he must. It was an essential part of the bargain, and surely he *must* kiss her? What would his kisses be like — warm and reassuring, like Ran's, or constrained, cool? Whatever they were like, they had to be enough for her. She would never be loved, but she absolutely needed some affection in her marriage, for it would be unbearable to spend her whole married life alone.

She slept fitfully, troubled by strange, vivid dreams where she stood in the chapel beside Ger reciting her vows, and it was the mistress wearing the clerical robes and holding the Prayer Book, as Ger gazed adoringly at her. Or else Ruth was seated at one end of the long table in the State Banqueting Room, Ger at the other, and the mistress sat beside Ger, as he laughed and teased her and rested his hand on hers.

Ruth woke, heavy-eyed and miserable. No matter how many times she told herself that she was doing the right thing, that there was satisfaction in obediently doing her duty and making a marriage that pleased her parents, still her heart was heavy with foreboding. How could this end well when Ger was so much in love with another woman? He could not possibly have any affection to spare for his wife. Yet what could she do about it? She would not even know how it would be until after she had bound herself for life to Ger, and then it would be too late.

Pulling aside the curtains, she silently crossed the room and opened the window a fraction more. Cool morning air flowed over her, refreshing her. Below her, a mass of colourful flowers surrounded the fountain, its cascades catching the morning light and turning to a thousand tiny diamonds, sparkling as they fell. It was beautiful, and the sight would always be hers to enjoy, for

Valmont was her home now, or very soon would be. All these splendid rooms in the house, all the parterres and grottoes and pools in the grounds, even the Broadwood instrument in the Grand Saloon — they were hers. That was some consolation, surely, so why was her heart so heavy?

She would be free, and that was another consolation, as Ran had pointed out to her. As a married woman she would escape the constant chaperonage, free from her mother's perpetual agonising over propriety and her father's ambition. She would be free to go where and when she pleased. Except that she would not. Her parents had taught her well — had taught her to be this timorous, cowardly creature who *dared* not break free from their constraints. Would she ever be able to do so?

The hidden door in the wall drew her eye. Now that she knew it was there, it was obvious, yet she was sure that Pinnock had not noticed it. She took a step nearer to it, and then another and another. She ran her hand along the almost-invisible crack. Then, in great trepidation, she reached for the sconce. And pulled...

Instantly, the door opened, as silently as if the hinges had been greased, and perhaps they had. It was just the sort of detail that Ran would think of. Light flooded out from a narrow window, lighting a small, square staircase with polished wooden steps leading down. Lord, how tempted she was, but she could hardly go wandering about in her nightgown, and what if her mother should find out?

She took a deep breath. She was one and twenty years old, about to be married, to be a duchess, for Heaven's sake! It was time to stop being afraid of her mother's disapprobation. Crossing the room with quick steps, she listened at the dressing room door. The faint rumble of snores reassured her, but she drew the curtains round the bed once more, just in case the maid should check. Then she pulled on a wrap and entered the secret stair.

Down and down she went, past one window, and then another, before reaching a lower door. This, too, opened at a touch, and she found herself in an unfamiliar corridor, half hidden behind a vase taller than she was. After a moment she got her bearings. Further down, she could see the entrance to the chapel gallery where she and Ran had sat the previous night. Opposite her was another gallery entrance, one which had been concealed in darkness last night. The library, she guessed, remembering the layout of rooms. With a quick, nervous check to ensure there was no one about, she sped across the corridor, lifted the latch and entered the gallery.

Unlike the chapel, whose gallery was only at one end of the room, the library gallery ran all the way round the room, wide enough for comfortable chairs to be grouped around low tables. Here and there were globes, small tables embedded with chess or backgammon boards, and an orrery. Down below were the bookcases, interspersed with statuary on plinths and framed maps hung on the walls. One long table filled the central space, and here a man sat, books spread all around him. Her heart lurched, for it was Ran, dressed in nightgown and robe, just as she was, his hair tousled. He had a pen in his hand, and was furiously scratching away with his right hand, making notes on a paper, while his left forefinger rested on a book, picking out the words he was copying. He stopped, threw down the pen, pulled another book towards him and started frantically leafing through pages. A large atlas lay open to one side. What on earth was he doing?

But she could not ask, nor did she wish to intrude on whatever project impelled him with such urgency. If he chose to work on some secret matter at this ungodly hour of the day, it was in the expectation of privacy, so he must certainly have it.

She crept out of the library and, the corridor being still empty, she walked with fast steps to the chapel gallery. There she sat for some time, trying to pray and instead thinking only of gentle words and strong arms and warm kisses. But in such thoughts lay only madness and grief. Ran could never be more to her than a friend, and her husband's brother.

Giving it up, she crept on silent feet back to the hidden stair and returned to her room, heart pounding. At the top of the steps, she paused, listening. Would she open the door to find her mother or Pinnock waiting to berate her? But all was silent. She pushed open the door, slipped into her still-deserted room, and smiled in pure triumph. She had done it! For a little while, she had done what she wanted. She had been free. Such a small success, but it gave her hope.

22: Reconsiderations

Ran was in his office early, arriving even before Max was at his desk. He began reading through the piles of letters to be dealt with, but he could not summon any enthusiasm for the task. What was the point of discussing land acquisitions or repairs to tenant's houses when he would not be here to see the outcome? He must be gone, and soon, and now that the decision had been made, he chafed at the bit, anxious to be away from Valmont and the temptation of proximity to Ruth.

As soon as Max arrived, Ran burst out, "You are quite correct, Max. I have to leave here at once. I have been thinking that I might offer myself as a secretary of sorts to... well, I am not sure to whom. I have been looking up the Peerage to see who might suit. What about Dunmorton? He lives up in some God-forsaken place in the far north — Northumberland or some such. He might want an extra secretary. Or Carrbridge — he is in Yorkshire. That would be far enough. He has that clever Merton fellow looking after his affairs, but now that he is taking more interest in politics and will be in town more often, he might want someone to keep an eye on the Yorkshire holdings. Or there is—"

"Wait, wait!" Max said, holding up a hand. "Last night you told me you would consider it. Now you are on fire to leave this very minute. What on earth has happened to bring about this change?"

A long hesitation. "Do not ask me," Ran said in a low voice. "Suffice it to say that leave I must."

"Ah. Very well. But I did not mean that you should pack up and leave instantly, nor that you should take paid employment. If you do anything of the sort, there will be no end of rumours, and you would not want that. You will have to be at the wedding, naturally, to show by your smiling face that you are not in the least bit dismayed by the loss of your betrothed. You will be able to display a smiling face, I take it?"

"I... probably," Ran said, grimacing.

"You are very good at hiding what you feel, so I am sure you will pull it off splendidly," Max said. "It would be unexceptional to give the newly-married couple some privacy, so you might take a few weeks inspecting all these wretched mills in Lancashire. By the summer, it will be safe to return because Valmont will be full of relations and you will be well protected. In the autumn, Ger will be off hunting on someone else's patch, and that will get you through to Christmas. Make sure you invite a few people to stay. Then another round of inspecting far-flung estates. That is all I had in mind. Do you see?" Ran nodded, uncertainly. "Shall we begin the letters? Oh, there was a special package for you. One of the lawyers came all the way from town to deliver it by hand, and ensure that it was given to you personally. I had to swear on the Bible to do so before the fellow would entrust it to me. Let me fetch it."

He unlocked the safe, and drew forth a neatly wrapped package tied up with string and then sealed.

"I cannot imagine what is so important that it needs such pomp," Ran said, his fingers carefully unwrapping it. "It will be a title of some sort. Oh, perhaps it is about that new farm in Yorkshire that Spark and Morrell went up to sign for. Or it might be—"

He stopped with a strangled cry.

"Whatever is it?" Max said.

Ran's voice was hollow. "It is a special licence for a marriage between Lord Randolph Litherholm and Lady Ruth Grenaby. You see, it is even in my correct name. I asked the lawyers to arrange it for me weeks ago, since I thought I might not have enough time myself. When Ger was found, I advised them of my reversion to the old name and to stop work on the settlements, but I said nothing about the special licence. The covering letter explains quite proudly that they made sure the licence reflects the new name. Oh God! I have a licence for a wedding that will never take place."

"Do you want me to burn it?" Max said.

Ran considered it, gazing at the elegant script and the Archbishop's seal. "No. I shall keep it as a reminder of a happier time, and of the foolishness of false hopes."

"It was hardly that," Max said. "You were betrothed, after all. You had every expectation of a long and happy marriage. You are entitled to feel... disgruntled, at the least."

"If I could be merely disgruntled, that would content me," Ran said bleakly. "My future is so dark and empty that it is impossible to imagine how I am to get through it."

"Yet you will," Max said. "You will look back on this time from a happier place. After all, you were in just such despair when news came of the wreck of the *Brig Minerva*, and look how that ended."

Ran smiled and nodded, but he could no longer view the return of his brother with such unalloyed gladness. It was Ger, after all, who had destroyed all Ran's hopes.

~~~~~

Ruth allowed Pinnock to arrange her hair in a more elaborate style than usual. She cared nothing for such matters, not when her entire future was in such a state of upheaval, but it delayed the moment of truth.

She had reached a decision. Ran's kiss had brought her to acknowledge an unsuspected element of her character — that although she could be cool and restrained in public and present a composed façade to the world, in private she needed something more. It was impossible to live her whole life without tenderness. It did not need to be love, but her husband needed to be gentle and caring, if nothing more, and if Ran could manage to offer her the sweet affection of friendship, as he had so generously proved, she could expect nothing less from Ger.

When she was dressed, she went downstairs and found the butler. Pinnock followed her, of course, but she cared nothing for that.

"Is His Grace of Falconbury up and about yet, Brent?"
~~~~~

"Not yet, my lady, but his washing water went up about half an hour ago."

"When he comes down, would you tell him, if you please, that I wish to speak to him on a matter of importance. May I await him in the Ante-Chamber?"

"Certainly, my lady. Should you like some tea sent in?"

"No, thank you."

She entered the Ante-Chamber, Pinnock at her heels. Then she calmly took a seat.

"You ought to have Her Grace with you if you're going to talk to His Grace," Pinnock said. "It's not proper."

"When I want your advice, Pinnock, I shall ask for it, but I may as well tell you at once that I shall never require your advice on any matter of propriety."

"But Her Grace would say—"

"Thank you, Pinnock. You may remain silent."

The maid pursed her lips disapprovingly, but she could not disobey a direct order, so she lurked suspiciously near the door. It was only a few minutes before the door opened, and Ger came in with his ready smile. He looked, as always, slightly dishevelled, like a small boy who could not quite keep himself tidy. His appearance never failed to make her smile, whereas Ran drew her admiration for his impeccable style. So elegant, so— But she must not think of Ran.

"Ruth! Did you wish to see me? I am entirely at your disposal." Ger bowed with a flourish.

She rose and crossed the room. "Thank you! You are very good. I do wish to see you, yes. Pinnock, you may leave us now."

"Can't do that, milady," the maid said smugly. "Her Grace's orders."

"I wish to discuss a matter with my betrothed. It is perfectly acceptable to do so alone."

"Her Grace told me never to let you out of my sight, unless she was with you, milady."

Ruth went to the door and opened it. "You may walk out, Pinnock, or I shall ask the footmen to carry you out. The choice is yours."

For a long moment, the maid weighed the duchess's orders against her dignity. Eventually, two spots of colour on her cheeks, dignity won and she stalked out of the room. Ruth quietly closed the door behind her.

"How may I be of service to you?" Ger said.

"I should like you to kiss me," Ruth said.

Ger's face melted instantly from pleasure to wariness. "Kiss you?"

"Yes, if you please. There can be no objection, now that we are betrothed."

He licked his lips. "Ruth, I do not see... I mean, *why?*"

"Because we are going to be husband and wife," she said quietly. "We are going to be sharing some of the most intimate moments that any man and woman can share, yet we are bound by duty, not love. Our marriage will be one of mutual benefit rather than a deep regard. Nevertheless, there must be *something* between us. When you come to my bed, Ger, you must be able to convince me that you care for me. In public, we may maintain a respectful distance, if that is what you wish. We will have our own paths to follow, and you may be sure I will not hang upon your sleeve or demand your time or attention. But in our most private moments, I must have affection. I do not think I can do this without it. So I should like you to kiss me."

The wariness did not diminish. Yet was she truly asking so much of him? One kiss, that was all. Then she would know what sort of husband he would be, and whether he could make her happy. Or at least not unhappy.

"Ruth, there will be time enough for this... for kissing... when we are married."

"Do you not see? I must know *now*. I have to be sure that it will be enough." She did not mention Miss Chandry, but he must surely understand her fears there, that his mistress would absorb all his love and Ruth would be left with nothing. "Ger, I know you will never love me, any more than I love you, and I accept that. It is a part of our arrangement. Yet I have this terrible fear of ending up as one of those formidable dowagers, a dried up husk, bitter and filled with hatred. I need *some* affection from you, however little it may be."

"Oh, Ruth! I promise you there will be affection. I have always been fond of you, and that can only grow."

"Then prove it to me. Kiss me."

"Now?" he whispered.

She nodded and he moved closer until he stood directly in front of her. And then he froze, arms at his side, his expression pure anxiety. His breathing was ragged, and his eyes were wide with fear. Once he lifted his arms as if to embrace her, then dropped them again.

Tipping her head on one side in puzzlement, she said softly, "Ger?"

He heaved a breath, then another. "I cannot do it." He sounded astonished. "It would seem like such a betrayal. I simply cannot do it."

"Oh." She was breathless suddenly, her insides roiling with some emotion she could not quite identify. But it was not disappointment. It almost felt like... relief? Was that possible? "Then I am very sorry, Ger, but I cannot marry you."

"No. No, of course you cannot." He gave a sudden laugh. "What a fool I am not to realise it before. Ruth, how can I ever say—"

The door burst open and the duchess marched in, attired in a splendid brocade robe and a hastily donned turban to hide her as yet uncoiffed hair. She was almost purple with rage.

"How dare you—?" she began.

Ruth melted into terrified subservience at once. A lifetime of instant obedience could not be overcome so easily. She was firm in her resolve but her mother's inevitable rage would beat at her like a tempest, wearing her down little by little.

With a little whimper, she half hid behind Ger.

He rose magnificently to the occasion, executing a flourishing bow. "Good morning, Duchess. What a very unexpected pleasure. You may be the first to know that your daughter and I have decided that we should not suit. I have realised, very belatedly, what a bad husband I should make. I am very sorry for the disappointment this will cause you, but you may congratulate your daughter on her narrow escape from a truly terrible bargain."

The duchess's mouth flapped open, then closed again soundlessly. Behind her, Pinnock gave a squeak of shock.

Ger laughed. "Do not look so distraught, ma'am. Ruth will find some other duke to marry, I daresay."

"There *are* no others," the duchess said acidly. "Ruth, this has been arranged since you were twelve years old! You cannot, you simply *cannot* walk away now."

"Too late," Ger said crisply. "This betrothal is at an end."

"Your father will cast you off utterly," the duchess said, still addressing Ruth, who was cowering behind Ger. "If you do not marry according to his wishes, you will marry *no one* and be ridiculed and despised and friendless as an old maid. You will end your days as the poor relation to your more obedient sisters, I doubt not. Pinnock, go and fetch His Grace, and perhaps he can instil some sense of what is due to her parents into this miserable specimen of a daughter."

"Ruth will *never* be friendless," Ger said robustly. "Her sweet, gentle nature must always be valued by all who know her, except her own family, seemingly. You need not bother to drag the duke from his bed, for I tell you now, I will *never* marry your daughter, and no amount of browbeating and harassment will change that resolution. How dare you treat her in this infamous fashion, as if she were six instead of a grown woman? She deserves your sympathy, not your anger. You are a dragon, ma'am, and if you were *my* mother, I should buy a castle in the northernmost part of Scotland and banish you there."

The duchess gaped at him momentarily. She could not, however, berate a duke as she berated her daughter, so she gathered her dignity about her, and straightened her back.

"We shall leave as soon as we have packed. Pray have the goodness to order our carriages to be brought round at…" She glanced at the clock. "Shall we say in two hours? Ruth? Pinnock? Follow me."

Imperiously, as if she were not still in her night garments, she marched out into the entrance hall and swept past the butler and row of footmen standing like statues. Pinnock scuttled in her wake.

Ruth exhaled slowly. She was still trembling, but her terror was fading now that her mother had left the room. "Heavens, Ger, how do you dare to say such things to her? She will never forgive you, never."

"What do I care for her good opinion? And what can she do to me anyway? She will never tell anyone that I called her a dragon."

Ruth giggled, but said, "She will tell the world that you jilted me, however."

"Let her. She may set the blame for this debacle at my door, where it belongs. I should have seen the truth much earlier than this. Can you ever forgive me for causing you so much trouble?"

"There is nothing to forgive. We were both misguided, it seems to me."

"What will you do now?"

"I shall go and help with the packing," she said simply.

Pinnock's face appeared outside the open door, watching her. Ruth shivered. There was always someone watching her.

"You need not go," Ger said urgently. "Stay here for a while longer. You could stay with Elizabeth for propriety. Do not leave with people who terrorise you. They will take you to town and try to push you into another marriage as soon as may be, and it might be even less suitable. You should have stuck with Ran. The two of you would suit admirably. Please stay."

Ruth's heart lurched, knowing just how well Ran would suit her. But that was out of the question. She knew now she could never marry a man who did not love her.

"No, I must leave," she said. "You have been very kind, but I have no business staying here without my mother, and she will certainly not stay. I need not marry to oblige them, but I must live under my father's care while I remain unwed."

"He does not care for you at all," Ger cried. "Neither of them cares about *you*, only about the great match you will make. Do not go!"

"There is nothing for me here," she said quietly.

23: Carriages Awaiting

Ran was in his office with Max, wrestling with a particularly tricky letter, when Ger burst in, glowing with excitement.

"Ran, there you are! I have been looking all over for you."

"Where else should I be at this hour?"

"Oh yes, but after yesterday... Never mind, I have found you now, and you must come at once, because it is all off. There is a chance for you, but you must be quick, because she is leaving. You must stop her... tell her how things are. You must get her back, you must!"

"Brother, what the devil are you talking about?"

"*Ruth!* Who else? We have broken it off and—"

Ran cried out, half in disbelief and half in hope. No, not hope. There was no hope.

"—she is leaving within the hour. The carriages are sent for. Make her stay, brother. Do not let her go off with that dragon of a mother of hers."

"Whatever has happened? This was only settled yesterday, yet now she has cried off? Why? What is going on?"

"Oh, we agreed we should not suit. In truth, Ran, I should have made her a terrible husband and she realised it before I did… and in time, luckily. There is still an opportunity for you to speak."

"Is that what you rushed here to tell me? You think that all I have to do is to tell her of my regard and she will fall into my arms? She has already rejected me once, quite decisively. I will not embarrass her by making her do so again. The last thing I need is her pity, Ger. I may have lost her, but please let me keep my dignity."

"But she does not care tuppence about *me!*" Ger cried. "I always thought… I imagine we all thought that she held me in some regard, and therefore it would be cruel to deny her the marriage she hoped for. But she has never loved me, she said so. And that being so—"

"Oh, brother, do you not see? That makes her even *less* likely to accept me. You offered her every temptation to marry me — money, the house, everything — and it was still not enough. She chose you, and if not from love, then she must have been dispassionate in her choice. She must have weighed the two of us, and settled on you as the better option. If she now rejects even you, then where does that place me? Even lower in her estimation."

"She wants affection, Ran. I cannot give it to her but you can."

But Ran could only shake his head in sorrow. "Go and bid them farewell, Ger. You will understand that I cannot."

Ger gave a huff of frustration. "Have it your own way, brother. I just hope you will not come to rue this day's work."

When he had left, Ran sat in morose abstraction, rolling a pen between finger and thumb. "Max, what do you advise? Should I chase after her and try to persuade her back into a betrothal?"

"No."

Ran raised his eyebrows. "Just that? No reasons advanced to convince me?"

"You know the reasons well enough, I imagine, for they are plain to see," Max said, sighing. "Firstly, it is undignified for a man in your level of society to *'chase after'* any woman, especially one who jilted you only yesterday. Secondly, you will not be able to get her away from that mother of hers in all the turmoil of departure. Thirdly, if you follow her more discreetly to London, you will have the humiliation of dangling publicly after the woman who jilted you. Imagine the gossip when the announcement reaches the newspapers that you are not to marry after all, yet there you are, visibly pining for her. Fourthly, and by no means the least, her parents will violently oppose the match. It will not do, Ran. She has had years in which to get to know you and develop an attachment to you. She has had a full year to consider the implications of Ger's presumed death. She accepted you as a suitable alternative, and rejected you the instant he reappeared. Why would you even consider trying again?"

Ran was silent, feeling the force of these arguments. Ger's enthusiasm for the idea derived from his wish to see his brother as happy as he was himself, but that could never be. Ruth did not love him, and there was no getting around that point.

However, he could not tamely sit and dictate letters while the woman he loved was departing from his life, so he left Max working and walked up to the State Apartments. From an upper ante-room he could look down on the carriages gathering on the drive and the luggage being loaded. He saw Ruth's maid emerge, jewel box in her hands, and climb into the second coach. Then the duchess's maid and the duke's valet. The final bags were strapped on, and activity ceased, awaiting the ducal party.

The door behind him opened and closed softly. When he turned, Ginny stood there, a large woollen shawl around her shoulders.

"Why do you not go down?" she said softly.

"You know why, I daresay."

"Are you going to let her simply walk out of your life, without putting up the least fight for her?"

"I must!" he cried. "She does not want me, she has made that perfectly clear."

"Men!" she said, rolling her eyes. "Just because she accepted Ger doesn't mean she wouldn't far rather have had you, but that witch of a mother and tyrant of a father forced her into it. I have seen the way she looks at you, Ran."

"How can you have seen that?"

"This house is full of secret stairs and little galleries looking down on the formal rooms. Ger has shown me many such things. He wanted to know I was close to him, you see, when he had to be the duke and entertain people, so he showed me secret ways and asked me to sit in the galleries, hidden away behind the screens, to watch over him. So of course I watched over you, too, and Lady Ruth, and everyone. That means I've seen how she watches you when you're in the room, but as soon as you look at *her*, she looks away. And I've seen how her parents browbeat her. She's like a little mouse with them. Ger said that she hid behind him when her mother came into the room this morning and found her alone with him. The poor girl was terrified. *Someone* has to protect her from that evil woman, and it ought to be you."

Ran was unsure whether to be amused or angered by her presumption, but he answered her calmly. "You must be mistaken. Ruth has never given me the least indication of any special regard."

"Of course not!" Ginny said, smiling at him. "She's not brash like I am, she is a real *lady*. On the outside she is perfectly cool and composed, but that doesn't mean she has no feelings hidden deep inside. But she will never, ever reveal them to you without some sign from you, Ran. If you want to know what she feels for you, then you have to put it to the test — you have to tell her what *you* feel. There she is now. Go down to her and *tell* her. If you don't even try, then you don't deserve her."

From his perch by the window, he saw the three of them emerge from the main doors almost directly below. The duke first, then the duchess and trailing at the back, turning to look up at the house, was Ruth, so graceful and elegant in her plain travelling pelisse and the bonnet demurely hiding her face. The carriage door was open, awaiting them. The duchess looked back at Ruth, and said something, and still Ruth hesitated, her eyes scanning the windows, as if searching. Then, abruptly, she bowed her head and hurried towards the carriage. In moments she would be gone.

"Go," Ginny said softly.

"I cannot."

"Do you love her?"

"*Yes!* More than anything in the world, but—"

"Then be a man and fight for her, you idiot!"

He turned and fled, racing from the room to the corridor outside. It ended in a door to the small balcony above the front door. He flung open the door and hurled himself forward to lean over the parapet.

"Ruth! *Ruth!*"

She was just stepping into the carriage, the last to enter it, but she turned, looked up, saw him, stepped down again. "Yes?" was all she said, but he thought there was some eagerness in her expression.

"Wait, wait!" he cried. "I am coming down."

He scrambled over the parapet at the side of the balcony, hearing her squeak of fear from below, grasping the solid stems of ivy to lower himself to the ground. Hastily running feet crunched across the gravel, and when he turned to face her, she was standing not a yard away from him, absolute terror on her face.

He was immediately contrite. "I beg your pardon! I had no intention of alarming you."

"You did alarm me! I was sure you would fall and hurt yourself."

"The ivy is very strong. Ger and I have climbed up and down it all our lives."

She laughed in relief. "Never scare me like that again! What was it you wanted to say to me?"

But her smiling face reduced him to incoherence and then silence. He could not find the words. How could he say all that was in his heart? It was so *difficult*, and he was acutely aware of the butler and footmen lining the steps, Ger standing outside the front door, the postilions watching with interest.

"Ran?" she said questioningly.

"I… am sorry you are leaving. Sorry about… about Ger. About everything. Must you go?"

A flicker of uncertainty crossed her face. "How can I stay?"

He stared at her, so lovely, so serene, waiting patiently for him to get his jumbled thoughts in order. Yet there was something not quite calm in her manner. She leaned towards him slightly, as if eagerly, and there was some expression in her eyes… was it hope? Or was that merely his own desperate longing?

"I wish you did not need to go," he blurted. "I wish you could stay. There is so much I want to say to you. I wish—" He stopped, frowning. "No, I could never wish that Ger had not come home, not for a second, but I wish with all my heart that he had done so a month later, for then we would have been safely wed. You would have been mine, as I have wanted for…oh, years."

She stilled, her expression wide-eyed in surprise. Was it possible that she had never guessed the truth of it? Truly she had had no idea. To him, his love for her was so all-consuming that he could not imagine anyone to be unaware of it, but Ruth was. He had tried his level best to conceal it from her and from the world, and he had succeeded better than he had ever suspected.

He waited for her to speak, but she said nothing, and that encouraged him to continue. "For a few weeks, I was the happiest man on earth, because I was about to marry the woman I loved with all my heart and soul."

A little whisper of a sigh escaped her.

"I could hardly believe my luck in being able to share my life with you. And then Ger came back and of course I was happy about that. How could I not be? The only bad part was losing you but... but... What are you doing?"

She had begun tugging at the ribbons fastening her bonnet, but now she tore off her gloves with a cry of annoyance, tossed them to the ground and tried again with her bare fingers. "I am getting rid of this bonnet."

"Oh. It is a very pretty bonnet," he said uncertainly.

She gave a gurgle of laughter. "I daresay, but it is the *wrong* bonnet, you see, and so I have to get rid of it, but I cannot undo this wretched tangle of ribbons."

"May I try? I have a little skill with knots."

"Oh, please do."

Puzzled but willing, he moved nearer to her and began picking apart the ends of ribbon. "I do not quite see why you have to change your bonnet."

"Not change it, remove it. With these stupid, stupid wings, it is entirely wrong, you must see that."

"I... cannot say that I do."

"It has to go, for how else can I kiss you?"

His hands froze on the knotted ribbons, and he almost forgot to breathe. "Do you... do you want to?"

"*Yes!* More than anything!"

"Here and now? On the front drive?"

"This very minute!" she cried. "Let us not waste another moment. Oh, never mind the stupid ribbons!" She tore the bonnet from her head so violently that half her hair fell down and draped itself in the most beguiling fashion on one shoulder. Then she stretched up to wrap her arms around his neck, her nose almost touching his. Her *lips* almost touching his. "There. Is that not better?"

His own arms slid round her back without any conscious thought on his part. In fact, his brain seemed to have disintegrated into an incoherent muddle, he could not catch his breath and his heart was pounding so hard it hurt. He pulled her closer, and she made no protest. He was dreaming, he must be dreaming! This could not be real.

"Ruth..." She looked up at him with such a guileless smile, such warmth in her eyes that he could doubt no longer. "I have nothing to offer you," he murmured. "No title, no fortune, no great house... only myself and my undying love, and a great desire to protect you from every fire-breathing dragon in Christendom. Is that enough?"

"More than enough."

She pulled his head down to hers until their lips touched. The shock was electrifying. This was not the chaste, delicate kiss of the chapel gallery. There was such urgency in her, such *passion*, that he was stunned. And he kissed her back with the same force, his pent-up emotions spilling over with a burning desire that would not be assuaged.

He was dimly aware of voices in the distance, far, far away. Then, a more strident voice closer at hand. And finally, someone screeching in his ear. The dragon duchess.

"Lord Randolph! *Lord Randolph!* Unhand my daughter *this instant!*"

Ran lifted his lips from Ruth's by an inch, gazing into her eyes. She was smiling up at him with a delight that was surely reflected in his own expression.

"Do you wish to be unhanded?"

"Not in the least. I very much wish to be... *handed.*"

That made them both break out in laughter.

"I very much regret, Your Grace, that I am unable to oblige you in this matter," Ran said, when he could speak again.

"Ruth Grenaby, you will not marry a younger son! I absolutely forbid it, do you hear me?"

"I hear you, Mama," Ruth said complacently, without stirring from Ran's embrace.

"You will have nothing, do you understand? No dowry, no title, no money, *nothing.*"

"But I shall have the one thing I want above all else, Mama."

"What is that?"

"To be *loved*. That is a prize greater than any title or riches."

The duchess stamped her foot in frustration. "Your father will have something to say about this, you may be sure. Get back in the carriage at once, young lady."

"Stay," Ran said at once. "Stay here, for we have so much to say to each other."

"She cannot stay without me, and I am leaving," the duchess said smugly.

"Aunt Anne will chaperon her," Ran said. "And Lady Elizabeth."

"Do not be ridiculous! My daughter left to the care of a woman who is asleep half the day, and another whose reputation is already in shreds? I think not."

"Then we will just have to get married at once," Ran said.

"At once?" Ruth said. "How soon is *at once?*"

"As soon as Ponsonby can don his vestments and light a couple of candles in the chapel. Ten minutes? A quarter of an hour?"

"You have a special licence?" she said uncertainly.

"I do. Requested weeks ago, arrived yesterday. Shall we?" he said.

"In my travelling gown? You must give me time to change into something more suitable, and... to pin up my hair again."

"Your hair is charming that way, but very well. An hour then," Ran said, smiling at her. Uncertainty flickered across her face. "Two hours?"

"Will you think me terribly missish if I prefer not to be married instantly? My life has been so topsy-turvy lately that I feel the need to catch my breath. It is only eight days until the date we gave out as our planned wedding day, so may we wait until then? But I do not wish to go back to London. I should very much like to be married in the chapel here. Do you mind waiting?"

"Only if you promise me faithfully not to change your mind again," Ran said with mock severity.

"Wild horses could not induce me to do so."

"Or dragons?"

"No dragon can deter me," she said. "With you standing beside me, I shall never fear dragons again."

The duchess stamped her foot in frustration.

24: Making Friends

Ruth existed in a bubble of delirious joy. *She was loved!* Ran loved her as much as she loved him, however impossible that seemed, and they walked about with dreamy smiles on their faces, hand in hand, in a blissful haze.

Nothing could puncture her happiness, but inside was a little knot of fear. Twenty-one years of filial obedience could not be cast aside overnight. "I shall not be deterred from my present course," she told Ran, "but it would make my joy complete to have Papa's blessing on our marriage. I do not like to be at odds with him. It makes me dreadfully uncomfortable."

"Then I shall do all in my power to persuade him of the disadvantages of a public rift," Ran said. "I should very much prefer him to approve the match, but I fear it is not to be depended upon."

"That is my fear also," Ruth said, "especially as Susan's position is so uncertain regarding Lord Crosby. They are still betrothed, but the quarrel was very fierce and since then she has neither seen nor heard from him. He secludes himself at Crosby Manor, and she has no notion of when they are to be married.

Papa would be more tolerant of our marriage if Susan's future were more secure, but even so, his dislike of younger sons is very fixed. He is not, I trust, so intolerant as to look down on the lesser branches of the Peerage, but a mere courtesy title is not at all what he wants for his daughters."

"Then I shall try to convince your father that this is a respectable and unexceptionable match, if not as illustrious as he had hoped."

"I wish he could be here to give me away," Ruth said wistfully. "It is a father's privilege to give his daughter's hand to her husband at the altar, after all."

"That may be a step too far for him," Ran said ruefully. "I will do my best, however."

Thus it was that just two days after the duke and duchess had left, he followed them to London to plead for their approval, to discuss settlements and to ensure that Ruth's wedding clothes were sent to her.

"Not that I imagine your mama to be quite so vindictive as to withhold them, but it is as well to be sure," he said to Ruth as he left.

Ruth's presence at the home of her betrothed before the wedding was rendered respectable by Lady Anne, but Ruth was most glad of Lady Elizabeth's chaperonage. Each morning she and her friend Mary Bucknell walked across to the main house before breakfast, spending the whole day there, but they were such pleasant company that Ruth was happy to be so chaperoned. Miss Bucknell was a tall lady with somewhat protruding teeth, who was never so happy as when ensconced in a chair with a book in hand and a glass of ratafia nearby, but fortunately Lady

Elizabeth was more sociable. She showed Ruth all the family parts of the house, and some of the secret ways that Ger had shown his mistress.

"The Fourth Duke had all these put in so that he could creep about at night, for he had the most prodigious liking for ladies," Lady Elizabeth said, showing her a row of small windows that overlooked the State Banqueting Room. "Ladies also had the most prodigious liking for him, although I cannot say why for he was not at all handsome. But there, perhaps his portrait does not do him justice."

"Or he may have had a great deal of charm, despite an unprepossessing appearance," Ruth said.

"There is no knowing, to be sure," Lady Elizabeth said. "There must have been some attraction, besides the usual compelling virtues of wealth and a noble rank, for although he had many mistresses who would not have cared if he looked like an elephant so long as he gave them jewels enough, he had also many affairs with women of birth. Now here we are at the Spinsters' Parlour, and you know the way back to the Queen's Room from here."

"So many hidden stairs!" Ruth said. "There is one in my bedroom, too."

"The Lilac Room? I wonder why Mrs Brack put you in there."

"That was Ran's doing," Ruth said. "So that I could escape from my watchdogs if I felt the need, he said."

Lady Elizabeth laughed. "Now with most men, one might suppose the convenience of a secret stair was for the opposite reason — not that the lady might leave her chamber but so that the gentleman might enter it. However, you are quite safe, for Ran is far too gentlemanly to take advantage of such a facility. Have you thought which rooms you would like for your own, once you are married?"

"Ran suggested your old rooms, Lady Elizabeth."

"Oh, an excellent idea! But you must call me Lizzie, and may I call you Ruth? We will be sisters very soon, after all. Come, let us have a look at my apartments. They are in the family wing, of course, and directly above the boys' apartments, which is very convenient. I suppose I should not call them the boys now that they are both grown men, and one of them a duke, after all, but they will always be my baby brothers. I was five when they were born and oh, the excitement! You cannot imagine it! All the church bells were rung, and we had a regiment stationed nearby at the time, who fired all their cannons and loosed off great volleys of musket fire. The celebrations went on for weeks. After four daughters, finally there was not one but two sons to secure the succession. Not that the title was in any danger of extinction for there must be hundreds of cousins of varying degree. No shortage of Litherholms! Still, a son or two in the direct line is very pleasing. But poor Mama was done for. She was never well after that, poor lady. Here we are... my old rooms. This is the sitting room, with a little ante-chamber to the bedroom and a dressing room beyond."

She opened shutters and drew back curtains, and light flooded the room, revealing walls the colour of peaches, pale wood and delicately curved furnishings, a very feminine room. A painted screen divided the room into two halves, for dining and sitting.

"Oh, this is lovely!" Ruth cried. "And all done to your design, as I understand it."

"Yes. I love such work. I refurbished my first room when I was but ten years of age and leaving the nursery for the first time, and have done so three times since. This was my final effort, for I left Valmont soon after."

"Did you dislike it so much here?" Ruth said. "I cannot imagine anyone wanting to leave after having lived here."

"It was not Valmont I disliked but my father," she said. "Do you want to hear the story? Shall we send for some tea, and then we may have a comfortable coze." She pulled the bell, and settled on a handsome brocaded sofa, patting the seat beside her for Ruth. "You know my dreadful history, I suppose?"

"Not at all," Ruth said. "Mama said that your reputation was in shreds, but she said that about Lucy Decker, who liked to show her ankles as she danced rather more than Mama thought proper. So I daresay you have not done anything so terrible."

"You may be the judge, if you please, for I shall tell you the whole of my story, since you do not know it. When I was seventeen, I fell in love with a man who— No, I should name him, for you know him well. Luke Crosby."

"You mean Lord Crosby? The same man who is betrothed to my sister Susan?"

"Indeed, although he was not even within hailing distance of the title in those days. He had no fortune and no prospects of getting one, nothing to recommend him but a good figure, a roguish twinkle in his eye and an irresistible charm. Irresistible to me, in any event. I was seventeen, he was twenty nine and both of us game for anything. So when Papa quite rightly said that a man without a career or expectations was hardly a suitable match for a duke's daughter, we did as thwarted lovers do — we set off for Scotland."

"No!" Ruth cried, awed. "But you seem so... respectable now."

Elizabeth laughed. "Now, perhaps, but... Ah, Thomas. Tea, if you please, and something to nibble upon. Some of Mrs Cromarty's famous ratafia cakes, or those little iced cakes... whatever she has to hand. Or gingerbread! I am so fond of gingerbread."

"She's just making some almond cakes, milady," the footman said.

"Mmm, almond cakes. Mrs Cromarty is a treasure. Thank you, Thomas. Now, where was I? Oh yes, Scotland. Well, we did not get far, of course. We were barely past Basingstoke before something or other broke on the post-chaise, and we had to take shelter at an inn, where Papa caught up with us, and that was the end of that. Aunt Anne told me that if we were patient and could wait until I was of age, that even Papa could not stop us, but we were not patient and Luke, at least, could not wait. He rushed off and married Daphne Swayle within a twelvemonth, only to find that someone had got to her before him and she was already with child."

"Oh!" Ruth gasped, hands to mouth, shocked and riveted in equal measure.

Elizabeth exhaled sharply. "Oh dear! I should not speak of such things to you, should I? You see, that is precisely why your mama warned you against me. My tongue runs on so, and I am sadly shatter-brained, I fear."

"I hope you will never guard your tongue with me," Ruth said. "It is so tiresome to be perpetually kept in the dark and told nothing of interest. I am one and twenty, after all, and soon to be married."

"Very true," Elizabeth said with a sigh of relief. "So I need not protect you from the realities of life. It is not known to this day who the father was, although Lord Bexhill's name was mentioned. Luke wanted nothing to do with the child, and if it should be a boy, he certainly did not want some other man's spawn taking his name and inheriting any money he might have accumulated, so he sent Daphne to Paris. And there she stayed, taking one lover after another, and making an utter fool of Luke, and her brother, too, whose poor wife had to raise Daphne's several children. But there was some good came from it. She brought a good dowry to the marriage — twenty-five thousand, so it was said. Luke sobered up, settled down and learnt to manage his money, and turned that into a sizable fortune. And three years ago, she died, so he was free again, and... and now he is to marry again, so his last venture did not entirely discourage him from matrimony," she ended, in a small voice.

"He would have been much better with someone like you than to dangle after Susan," Ruth said acidly. "I should not say so of my own sister, but she is no fit helpmeet for a man of five and forty."

"Well... I daresay they have their reasons," Elizabeth said, but there was an expression of such hopelessness on her face that Ruth was greatly moved.

Before she could say anything on the matter, the footmen appeared with the tea things and a whole array of cakes, biscuits and pastries, sufficient even for Elizabeth's appetite. For a while, the business of eating and drinking was at the forefront of their thoughts, and when Elizabeth resumed her tale, the subject had shifted.

"When I was two and twenty," she said, "Papa began to despair of making a match for me. All my sisters were settled, but I was increasingly reluctant to brave the choppy waters of the season. I had been out for five years by then, had a fair idea of what I was *not* looking for in a husband, and was increasingly outshone by younger, prettier girls from the schoolroom. So Papa arranged a match for me with Lord Bexhill. I did not especially like him, for he had a certain reputation, but I did not exactly dislike him, either. He had been dangling after me for years, and he was amiable enough, in public. He was someone I considered a friend, of sorts. If he had gone about the business in a sensible way, I might well have taken him. But the fool posted the notice in the Gazette without bothering to ask me my opinion on the matter, and I shall never be hustled into a match. I took the newspaper to Papa and told him I would not have Bexhill. Even then, they might have salvaged the situation, but Papa blustered and told me I had to do it because it had been announced and that made it a binding contract, and Bexhill had not the courage to face me and explain himself. So I jilted him, and, since life at Valmont had become insupportable, I left."

"Oh, how sad!" Ruth cried. "Where did you go to?"

"Only to Andover, where my Uncle Swithin Roswell, Mama's brother, has a house. It was that or Great-aunt Winnie in Blackpool, and since she is stone deaf and has quarrelled with all her neighbours, I should have had a miserable time of it. Uncle Swithin's house at least gave me someone to play whist with of an evening, even if the conversation was not lively. I lived there for eleven years with seven other relations, all of them much older than me, and I was never so glad of anything as when Ran asked me if I wanted to come home. And now I have a house of my own to refurbish exactly as I wish, and a friend with whom to share it, and I live within the walls of Valmont. I want for nothing."

"Except Lord Crosby," Ruth said.

Elizabeth's expression shifted. "True. Is there anyone quite so foolish as a confirmed spinster still dreaming of her first love? I know he is lost to me, but I still *remember,* Ruth. What is he like now? Cheer me up and tell me that he is fat and bald, with a trail of snuff down his waistcoat."

"I am sorry to disappoint you, but I cannot. He has an excellent figure, a full head of hair worn *à la Titus*, and takes no snuff that I have ever seen."

"Ohhh!" Elizabeth wailed. "Wasted on a girl barely out of the schoolroom! She could have her pick of men half his age, I daresay. But does she love him? Or at least have a fondness for him, and he for her? I can bear it well enough if she will make him happy."

Ruth considered her answer carefully. "I cannot say that I have seen enough of them together in public to say, but I have seen enough of *him* to acknowledge him a sensible man who must know where his own happiness lies."

"Ah. A diplomatic answer. However, my correspondents in town say that he stays sequestered on his estate, and has not been near his betrothed since March. His mother had to take her to Surrey to see him, whereupon they promptly quarrelled. Forgive me if I am not sanguine about the prospects for their future happiness. Another almond cake? No? I should not either, but one more will not hurt, I vow. I do love Mrs Cromarty's almond cakes. Shall we go and winkle Mary out of the library? And after that it will not be too long until it is time to dress for dinner. We shall dine here tonight, I believe. There is to be lamb and a lobster ragoût, I am told. So delicious! It makes me so happy to be back at Valmont."

~~~~~

Ruth had seen nothing of Miss Chandry since watching her dance in loving bliss with Ger. She never came down to dinner, even though Ruth was now the only visitor remaining, and no trace of her could be found in any of the public rooms. She was busy setting the Old Manor to rights, for little trains of footmen carrying chairs or housemaids with piles of linen could be observed bustling about, and Pinnock reported that all the estate's carpenters and builders had been brought in, and there was a great pulling down of walls and raising of dust going on there.

It rather suited Ruth not to see Ger's mistress, for she would not feel comfortable meeting her. How did one talk to a mistress? Her previous very brief encounters had not worsened her opinion of Miss Chandry's character, but nor had they imbued her with any desire to improve it. For once, she was in full agreement with her mother. Men might choose to keep a mistress, but such a woman should never, ever be inflicted upon respectable ladies.
~~~~~

Elizabeth, however, had a less rigid moral compass, and very much wished to get to know Miss Chandry better.

"She is important to Ger, and therefore to this family," she said stoutly, as they sat companionably in the Spinsters' Parlour one day.

"But she is his *mistress,*" Ruth protested. "We should not even know of her existence."

Elizabeth laughed. "Indeed we should not, but that is so typical of Ger. He is… well, I need not scruple to speak plainly to you now, since you are no longer betrothed to him, but he is dreadfully volatile, and we do not want him going off into his dark moods again. He is very much in the clouds just now, but I should like to reassure myself that this woman will not precipitate a crisis by suddenly packing up and leaving. He needs a steadying influence, not someone who is as wild as he is. That is why I thought that *you* would be so good for him, for you are always so… so *unruffled.*"

"Yet when he was unhappy, nothing I did had any effect," Ruth said. "I never could reach him. Even Ran could do nothing with him, yet Miss Chandry seems to keep him happy and stable."

"Exactly so, and we must ensure that she continues to do so," Elizabeth said. "I have a great desire to see what is being done to the Old Manor, so I shall go over there to find out, and while I am there, I shall also be finding out a little more of Miss Virginia Chandry of Pendower House in the fine county of Cornwall. Will you come with me? I cannot tear Mary away from the library — I swear she believes she has died and is now in

Paradise — but I should dearly like your company, if you can bear it."

Ruth was very torn. She could not be impervious to such a plea, and she was conscious of her own desire to know more of the woman who held Ger's heart in her keeping, but equally she found herself still assailed by scruples. Such a person had no place in polite society and therefore was not a proper person for Ruth to know.

While she was wrestling with this dilemma, a footman arrived at a run, very out of breath.

"Milady! Milady! Visitors," he puffed.

"Who is it, John?" Elizabeth said. "Not Lady Bamfield! She said she might call but I never supposed—"

"No, no, milady. Not a morning caller. Lord Audlyn. Lady Susan Grenaby. Just arrived this minute."

"*Audlyn?*" Ruth cried. "And Susan? What on earth—?"

Elizabeth rumbled with laughter. "What fun! I like your brother, Ruth, and I shall be most interested to meet your sister. Shall we go and welcome them to Valmont?"

By the time they reached the entrance hall, there was no sign of either visitors or luggage, and whatever conveyance had brought them there had already disappeared. Brent was there, however, and held open the door to the Ante-Chamber. Inside, Audlyn lounged against the mantel, while Susan was simultaneously removing her bonnet and giving instructions to Mrs Newall.

"Susan! Audlyn! What a surprise," Ruth said. "Is anything amiss?"

"Whatever should be amiss?" Susan said. "I notice that you did not say the surprise was a pleasant one. Are you not happy to see us, Ruthie? We have come to provide you with chaperonage, you see, and we shall stay to see you married, and wish you joy. Is that not charming of us?"

"If Mama and Papa think it charming for you to come here, then so do I."

She performed the introductions, the ladies curtsied and Audlyn bowed, but they had not progressed beyond a few polite enquiries as to the state of the roads before the door opened and Ger came in. Susan looked at Ruth expectantly.

"Susan, I should like to present to you His Grace the Duke of Falconbury. Ger, my sister, Lady Susan Grenaby, and my brother, the Marquess of Audlyn."

"I am quite delighted to meet you, Duke," Susan said, flashing him her most flirtatious smile.

Ruth's heart sank. The last thing she needed was Susan practising her feminine wiles on Ger. This visit was going to be difficult.

25: Unexpected Visitors

Susan wanted to be shown all the treasures of Valmont at once, but Ruth determinedly bore her away to the room Mrs Brack was preparing for her. There in the middle of the floor sat a single valise, which a maid was unpacking.

"Where are your boxes?" Ruth said. "Where is Hopwood?"

"Oh, there was no room," Susan said airily, "for Audlyn insisted on bringing his man, and I knew you would not mind me using Pinnock just for a day or two. Hopwood and the boxes are following on the stage."

"No room? You did not travel all this way in Audlyn's curricle?"

"Now you must not poker up like that, Ruthie. I swear you are as bad as Mama, sometimes."

"I should hope so, when it comes to making a spectacle of oneself for all the world to gawk at. Heavens above! And what if it should have come on to rain?"

"Phooey! I care nothing for a drop of rain, for it was the most famous fun, Ruthie. We went so fast, you cannot imagine.

Those bays are such sweet steppers, are they not? Except then Audlyn would not change horses, so we were obliged to rest at a post-house for *hours*, which was abominably tedious, but we had something to eat and I met someone I knew from London, so it was not entirely wasted, but I shall not tell you about it for you will only purse your mouth just the way Mama does. May I borrow your blue muslin? For Hopwood has only packed for the evening and my cambric is sadly crushed and dusty."

"You should not have worn anything so fine to travel in," Ruth said crisply. "Come to my room, and you may choose what you wish to borrow. Mrs Brack, would you send Pinnock to my room, please."

Ruth's room was directly opposite Susan's. While her sister rifled through closets and drawers, Ruth sat on the bed, watching. "Susan, does Mama know you are here?"

"I shall write and tell her in a day or two. Ooh, this is pretty! Is it new? May I have it? We are much of a size, after all."

"Sister, is all well with Lord Crosby? For you left Crosby Manor in such a hurry."

Susan flopped down onto the bed beside Ruth, a gown still clutched in her hands. "It was the most infamous thing, Ruthie! He treated me shamefully, accusing me of who knows what impropriety. Is it my fault that I have a naturally friendly disposition? It is not for Crosby to criticise my behaviour."

"It is precisely for him to do so," Ruth said. "He is your future husband, and has every right to censure you for any perceived transgression. I take it you were flirting with a gentleman other than your betrothed?"

"Not *flirting*. Merely being sociable. He was a cousin of Crosby's and *he* was certainly flirting with *me*, but did Crosby berate him? Not a bit of it! The blame was all set at my door. I did not submit tamely to such treatment, you may be sure, and then he said *such* things to me. I was never more shocked in my life, for he is generally the most courteous of men and quite biddable, you know, but he made me sound like the most wanton person imaginable. And he *shouted* at me, Ruthie. Shouted! Crosby!"

"Goodness! That is very bad, but I suppose he was jealous."

"Oh, I daresay, but that does not make it right, does it? He shouted at me, right there in the Great Hall where I imagine half the household could hear, and said I was not fit to be the wife of a respectable man and I was just a child and should go home until I could learn how to behave in polite society. Have you ever heard the like?"

"No, indeed, that is not at all gentlemanly, but dearest, you must admit that you can be a little over-friendly in company, and a man who loves you very much might well take exception to it. It is not right to chastise you so publicly, but perhaps in the violence of his affection for you, he was not entirely himself."

"Perhaps," Susan said with a shrug. "Mama wished me to write and apologise, and assure him that I will never behave so again, and I told her I would, but I shall not. I have done nothing to apologise for, and if he thinks to prevent me even from talking to other gentlemen, he is very much mistaken. *He* should apologise to *me*."

"Has he not done so?"

"Not a word, but then he has too much pride to admit to any fault. He never has written to me, even when we were apart for weeks on end. I suppose he is not much of a letter writer."

"It does not sound very promising," Ruth said, frowning. "Is your betrothal now at an end?"

"Oh no! At least, I do not think so, not exactly. Neither of us said anything to that effect, so I suppose it is still on."

"Whether it is on or off, please refrain from over-friendliness with anyone here."

Such an admonishment was a waste of breath, for Susan could no more refrain from flirting than a fish could refrain from swimming. While there were only ladies assembled in the Grand Saloon that evening before dinner, Susan sat silent and pensive, responding monosyllabically to Elizabeth's attempts to draw her out and playing idly with the fringe of her shawl. However, as soon as Ger entered the room, she was wreathed in smiles. She was the newest guest, so for politeness' sake he went to her first, and there he stayed, trapped by her smiling chatter. Whenever he began to look around for an escape route, she would rest one dainty hand on his arm and say in an artless manner, "And did you hear about...?" Then he felt obliged to lead her into dinner, and she happened to have Uncle Arthur on her other side, who was not a great conversationalist at the best of times and especially with food before him. Poor Ger had no respite.

When the ladies withdrew, Ruth drew Susan to one side. "If you continue to monopolise the duke in that shameless fashion, sister, I shall have you sent home. Do try for some decorum."

"You have no right to tell me what to do!" Susan hissed.

"As your older sister, I have every right, and as the future Lady Randolph Litherholm, I am at this moment in all essentials the mistress of Valmont. So have a care how you deal with my future relations."

"How high and mighty you are become, Ruthie! You should not be quite so grand in your ways, for whenever the duke marries, you may find your nose put quite out of joint."

Ruth laughed. "That is true enough! It would serve me right if he marries someone quite unbearable, but at the moment he has no thought of it. He has only just escaped a lifetime with me, poor man, and must be feeling the relief extremely."

However she protested at the reproof, Susan was more circumspect in her behaviour for the rest of the evening. Nevertheless, Ruth determined to write to her mother the next day, to be sure that her sister's travels accorded with her wishes.

~~~~~

Ran returned a day later than planned, exhausted but rather pleased with himself for accomplishing everything he had set out to do. He had seen his own lawyers and cautiously advised them of the need for new settlements. He had made a new will in view of both his lower status and his forthcoming marriage. He had bought a wedding gift of emeralds and diamonds for Ruth. He had set Giggs the task of finding a valet for Ger.

He had visited the Duke and Duchess of Orrisdale and secured their permission for the marriage, as well as the ten thousand pound dowry that had been promised before. Since seven thousand was an obligation imposed by the duchess's marriage settlements, it could hardly be said to be a generous offer, but Ran was satisfied. On one point they were determined,
~~~~~

however. No argument that Ran could put forward managed to convince them to attend the wedding, and eventually he gave it up.

He quickly discovered that the wildest of rumours were sweeping across town. Ger's supposed death, much mourned by all who knew him, and his miraculous return from the grave were the wonders of the day, and all Ran's acquaintances were agog to know more about it. He could not visit his club or even walk down the street without a concerned face accosting him and asking questions that he found impossible to answer. His own part in the affair was easy enough to explain, for it was entirely true that he had simply been mistaken in thinking the still, cold, battered body before him was his brother. Easy enough, too, to confess that Ger had engaged an actor to play the part as a joke, for that was entirely consistent with his character.

Ger's actions were harder to explain, for vague mutterings about loss of memory were greeted with outright scepticism, and a whole array of ingenious explanations were proposed — that he had stayed behind in America, and was only just returned, that he had been living as a farmer in Ireland, or that he had suffered some dreadful illness, although opinions differed as to the precise symptoms. The favourite theory was that Ger had, in fact, died and the person now said to be Ger was an impostor. That was an easy one to scotch, for no one could imagine a plausible reason for it, but Ran took the precaution of appearing at the Marchioness of Carrbridge's ball where almost everyone of consequence might be found, and circulating for long enough to show that he was amused rather than worried by such stories.

He was relieved to find that no hint had reached town of the few hours when Ruth had been betrothed to Ger. It had been widely expected that he would lose her to his brother, and now it gave him the greatest pleasure to lay to rest any such talk.

"And how is the Lady Ruth?" his friends asked him warily, watching him carefully for any sign of discomfort.

"Very well," he answered with a smile. "She is at Valmont, preparing for our wedding there in a few days."

"Ah!" they said knowingly, and wished him joy.

Their wedding! Even now, he could scarcely believe it, that she loved him and had chosen him, younger son or not, because for her he was not second best at all. He was counting the days, but on the day he had hoped to leave London, he received a summons from the Duke of Orrisdale.

"I have been considering all the points you made, Litherholm," he said, marching up and down his book room, hands clasped behind his back. "You make the case powerfully. It would look odd indeed for Ruthie to be married and the duchess and I not there. It would appear as if there had been a breach, and that would lead to a great deal of unpleasant talk. One would not wish Ruthie to be the subject of unpleasant talk. That would reflect badly on both our families, and there are the three younger girls to be thought of. So we will come to Valmont, but we cannot drop everything and go haring across to Hampshire in a moment, you know. We have a small dinner tonight, which cannot be put off, and then there is the packing and arrangements... you know how it is. But Ruthie will not mind delaying for a few days, I am certain of it."

"She will not mind at all if it means that some of her family will be there."

"Oh... as to that, Audlyn and Susan are there already, as it happens. Wanted to see their sister wed, and what could be more natural, eh?"

Ran made polite noises and expressed his pleasure at the additional visitors, but he was surprised, all the same. Audlyn, he recalled, had been rusticated from school for some mischief, and was probably bored enough to make the visit a welcome distraction, but Susan had been sent home in disgrace after quarrelling with her betrothed. Instead of either trying to patch things up with Crosby, or returning to town to try to catch another fish, she was gadding about the countryside, with her parents' approval. But she was very young, so perhaps they thought it better to take her mind off matrimony for a while.

Ran travelled back to Valmont with the valets, and also Mr Willerton-Forbes, who wished to talk to Ger to help resolve one remaining puzzle about the passengers of the *Brig Minerva*. Ran was doubtful that Ger had any new information to provide, having genuinely lost his memory of the disaster, but it seemed worth asking.

They arrived too late for any such discussion that day, however. Leaving the valets to Brent, and Mr Willerton-Forbes to Mrs Brack, he went in search of Ruth. Even in a house the size of Valmont, Brent always knew where everyone was, and so Ran turned his steps to the Spinsters' Parlour. He opened the door, his eyes sought and found her, she looked up and saw him... She jumped to her feet, such joy in her face that his heart turned somersaults of delight. He opened his arms and she ran across the room to bury herself in his embrace. How had he ever thought she had no sensibility? She was all warmth, all joyful affection, all quivering happiness at his return.

"How touching!" said a female voice. "Yet how you have the nerve to chastise *me* for unladylike behaviour I cannot guess."

Ruth shook in his arms with laughter. Lifting her head from his shoulder, she said, "Quite right, sister. I have become shockingly forward, have I not? Ran, you will remember my sister Susan."

"Of course," he said, shifting his hold on her so that she could turn round, but not releasing her. "I am happy to see you again, even though I must protest at any criticism of my betrothed, whose enthusiasm for my arrival is quite delightful. One is permitted a little forwardness when one is about to be married, I believe. Oh, good day to you, Lizzie. I did not see you there."

"No, and how should you, when you have eyes for only one person. Come, Susan, shall we take a turn about the garden? It is such a fine day, is it not?"

Giggling, Susan followed Elizabeth out of the room, and the door closed with a click.

For a long, long time, there was silence as the lovers caught up with several days' worth of kisses. When they parted with a deep sigh of satisfaction, Ruth whispered, "I have missed you quite abominably. You must not go away and leave me behind again."

"I shall not, you may take my word on that. Dearest love, it terrifies me how close we came to losing each other for ever. How could I have been so entirely unaware of your regard for me?"

"For the same reason that I was unaware of your affection. We are both of us very good at hiding our feelings from the world. Society frowns on those who display too much sensibility and we have both been very obedient to its dictates. Even when you told me to follow my heart and do what would make me happy, yet I could not do so until I knew that it would make *you* happy too."

"I dared not say too much in case you felt under an obligation," he said.

"It was the same for me. How foolish we were," she said, leaning her head against him with a sigh of pleasure. "Do you know, my love, your shoulder is the perfect height for me to rest upon. How comfortable this is!"

"And convenient for me to kiss your forehead, thus," he said. "Did you receive my latest letter? About your parents coming here? It means we shall have to delay the wedding for a few days."

"I have waited seven years for you, so what is a few more days."

He lifted his head to look at her fully. "Seven years? We only met six years and ten months ago."

"Precisely."

"Was it so for you too? You were fourteen and acknowledged as Ger's intended. I was away in Yorkshire visiting Great-uncle Marcus, but he suffered an apoplectic fit and I was dispatched home early. I heard music coming from the Grand Saloon and walked in and there you were. You looked up at me, still laughing at some jest of Ger's, and you were so lovely I could barely breathe. You wore a white gown with little blue flowers on it, and a blue ribbon in your hair."

That made her laugh, but she said, "And you wore a coat the colour of wine, and such a simple but elegant way of tying your neckcloth. You still carried a very stylish beaver hat and gloves as if you had just that minute stepped from your carriage, and I thought I had never seen such a gentlemanly figure. When Ger introduced you as his brother, I wondered how it was that I had never met you before."

"Do you know, it seems to me now that I was deliberately got out of the way when you visited, as if Father was afraid I would interfere in some way. He should have trusted me more, because look how restrained we were when we did meet."

"Probably he was afraid we would fall in love, and if so, he was right about that," she said.

"True, but we did nothing about it until Ginny goaded me into speaking."

"Ginny Chandry?" she said in astonished tones. "She made you speak that day when you climbed down from the balcony?"

"She did. I would not go down, for it would have been too humiliating to be rejected yet again, and in so public a spot, but she told me that if I did not fight for you, then I did not deserve you. It was almost too late, that was why I ran to the balcony."

"I must express my gratitude to her," Ruth said. "I confess I have tended to think ill of her, but she has a good heart, I believe, and she has certainly done me a good turn in this instance, even if it did cause me to ruin a perfectly good bonnet by hurling it to the ground."

"It was a small price to pay," he said, laughing, "I promise to buy you as many new bonnets as your heart desires. Which reminds me, did your wedding clothes arrive safely?"

"Indeed they did. Susan and I have been bestowing them in my new dressing room."

He frowned at the mention of Susan. "Why is she here? The rumour in town — no, stronger than a rumour, for I had it from Crosby's cousin, who ought to know — is that after she left Crosby Manor under a cloud, she was ordered to stay at Mallowfleet for at least a month, to reflect upon her behaviour. Yet your parents seem quite unconcerned about her leaving there. Either they feel very secure in Crosby, or they do not care if she loses him."

"Susan does not seem to care herself. Indeed, she flirted quite outrageously with Ger the first day she was here, giving me more than sufficient cause to reprimand her. She has been better behaved since then, but as to Lord Crosby, I cannot even find out whether she is still betrothed to him, for it all seems to be dreadfully vague."

"Unless one or other of them has explicitly cried off, then they are still betrothed, and I cannot imagine Crosby doing so. He had a wild youth, but he has never been less than a gentleman."

He leaned forward to kiss her again, but she reached up with a smile to set one finger against his lips. "Delightful as this is, you will want to change out of your travelling clothes and you must have matters to attend to with Ger, or with Mr Lorrimer."

With a sigh, he acknowledged it and they parted, he to the ministrations of Giggs, and she to see if Lady Anne was awake and in need of company. It was some time before he was free again, finding Ruth with Lizzie and her friend Mary Bucknell, who were just on the point of leaving for their own house.

"Ah, there you are, Ran. How could you abandon Ruth for boring paperwork? Valmont will continue to operate without you for a little while. You should enjoy your courting time, for it will be over all too soon."

"Ah, but then I would have missed the very important news of the pig escape at Bursham St Matthew and the beam engine breakage at Cragforth Mill. I am very glad now that I did not buy it when it was offered. Are you joining us for dinner, Lizzie?"

"Not tonight, Ran. My cook is attempting green apricot tarts and a blancmange. I am not optimistic, but she must learn somehow. Good bye, Aunt Anne, and thank you for the receipt for salmagundi. I will let you know if Mrs Brine produces anything edible from it. And now we must go."

Ran and Ruth accompanied the ladies to the front door, and waited while they donned bonnets and gloves, and collected parasols. So it was that they were in the entrance hall when the sounds of a carriage driven at speed were heard. It halted with a spray of gravel and the whinnies of horses pulled up quickly. Booted feet thundered up the steps and practically fell through the door just as Thomas opened it.

"Where is she?" yelled a deep voice. "Where is she hiding? I want to see her *this very minute*, you hear me? Fetch Lady Susan Grenaby to me *at once!*"

Lord Crosby had arrived, and he was very, very angry.

26: Guardian Angel

Valiantly trying to hide his astonishment, and seeing from Brent's bewildered face that he had no idea who this irate man was, Ran stepped forward.

"Lord Crosby, this is an unexpected pleasure."

Crosby rounded on him. "And where is your brother, Litherholm, answer me that? *Where are they?*"

It was a good question. Ran had seen no sign of Ger since his arrival, and Susan only briefly. "Brent, where are His Grace and Lady Susan?"

"One moment, my lord." He conferred with the three footman attending, then said, "His Grace was in the Grand Saloon at the instrument there until three o'clock. Her ladyship went to her room for a rest at about the same time."

"An assignation! I knew it!" Lord Crosby cried. "This is a disaster!"

"If Lady Susan is with my brother, then she is perfectly safe," Ran said coldly.

Crosby looked as if he would speak, then thought better of it.

Ruth said tentatively, "At breakfast, Susan expressed a wish to see the mausoleum."

"Ah, then perhaps they have slipped out of the side door unseen," Ran said. "Allow me to show you the way, Crosby."

"Yes, but quickly, Litherholm. We must make all haste."

Ran increased his pace, but Crosby was at his heels, practically pushing him along. As soon as they emerged from the side door and the mausoleum was visible, Crosby broke into a run, and Ran was forced to do the same to keep up with him. He hoped with all his heart that the girl was there, and that some good would come of her lover's ardour, but he was filled with foreboding.

The door was open... that was a good sign, wasn't it? It meant she was most probably inside, and if Ger was with her there would be two of them to restrain Crosby's wrath. Should he have brought some footmen with him? But that would ensure the entire world knew of the meeting. Besides, Crosby was a gentleman, and would never raise his hand to a woman... would he?

Crosby passed the open door just as Ran tore up the steps behind him, but Crosby's roar of rage would have been heard halfway back to the house. More unintelligible roars and then a very terrified female scream, as Ran burst through the doors.

He wasn't touching her, and that was a profound relief. He stood, hands clenched into fists at his sides, yelling mightily about jades and hussies and untrustworthy minxes, but he had not touched her. Ger held his hands up appeasingly in front of Susan, who was cowering behind him.

"There, Crosby!" Ran said bracingly. "She is safe, you see. Perfectly safe."

He took no notice. "I will not have it, Susan," Crosby said, but his tone was a little lower. "All this running round after other men, instead of staying quietly at home, as I instructed you. Wilful disobedience is unacceptable in a wife."

"I am not your wife yet!" she cried. "I may do as I please."

"Not for long," he growled. "You will learn obedience once we are married or—"

"Or what?" she said, lifting her chin defiantly.

"I shall beat you every day until you stop defying me. And if that does not work you will be locked in your room."

"You would not dare!"

"And if *that* does not work, there is an asylum not too far away where—"

"I hate you!" she shrieked. "You are horrid and I would not marry you if you were the last man on earth! You are only a baron after all, and you are old and bad-tempered and hateful. I shall find a much better husband and then you will be sorry!"

He went perfectly still. The fists unclenched and he answered with surprising calmness, "I shall try to bear the loss with fortitude."

"Ohhh, you are abominable!"

So saying, she picked up her skirts and ran out of the mausoleum. Crosby collapsed onto the nearest sarcophagus, as if his legs would not hold him up any longer. "Oh, thank God!" he said in a low voice. "I swear — and you two are my witnesses — I am never going near a woman again, never!"

A soft giggle came from a dark corner. "I had better leave at once then."

"Ginny!" Ger's face broke into a wide smile. "I was sure you were here somewhere, but I never saw you."

"Quiet as a mouse, that's me."

Crosby's face reflected the same astonishment that Ran felt. "You mean you have been here all the time?" Ran said. "So Lord Crosby need not have worried about any damage to Lady Susan's reputation?"

Crosby chuckled. "It was not Susan whose reputation was at risk, Litherholm. How do you think I ended up betrothed to a chit half my age? She got me into a secluded corner and kissed me. Then she went to her father. In my innocence, I had thought my age protected me from such manoeuvres, but she was determined to get herself a title. When I received word that she had come here, I knew at once that she had set her sights on becoming a duchess."

"So *that* was why you were in such a lather?" Ran said wonderingly. "Why you asked specifically for Ger? You were trying to rescue him from a similar trap?"

"That was one motive, yes, but fortunately this young lady was ahead of me. Will you not introduce me, Falconbury?"

"Of course. Ginny, you will have guessed that this is Lord Crosby, Lady Susan's betrothed — I mean his former betrothed. Crosby, this is Miss Chandry, my... my particular friend from Cornwall. Ginny pulled me from the sea and nursed me back to health after the *Minerva* sank."

"Then I am doubly in her debt," Crosby said, rising to bow to her. "The return of the Duke of Falconbury, alive and well, a year after he was presumed dead is one of the great wonders of our age."

She curtsied demurely. "Since you have sufficient protection now, Ger, I shall return to the house."

"Yes, I am safe now. Thank you, Ginny. Off you go," Ger said, his voice filled with affection.

Crosby watched her go with obvious interest, but he was too gentlemanly to comment on the particular friendship between a duke and a woman not of the first rank, who addressed each other by Christian name.

"We had better return, too," Ran said. "The whole house will be rife with speculation. Crosby, you will stay with us tonight, I take it?"

"I had not a thought of it. Once my horses are rested—"

"Nonsense," Ger said robustly. "You may be *only a baron*, but we will not turn you out of doors so late in the day."

He chuckled, and said, "That is very kind, and most welcome, but I will not inflict myself on the company. A tray in my room will suit me very well."

Ger was about to acquiesce, but Ran said, "That would cause exactly the kind of talk we would all prefer to avoid. Much better if you show yourself publicly now that you have stopped pretending to be a wrathful future husband. Because clearly your other motive, I deduce, was to free yourself from a betrothal to a chit half your age."

"True enough." They stepped outside the mausoleum and Crosby took a deep breath, exhaling slowly. "It feels very good to be free again. I have endured one desperately unhappy marriage, and have no desire for a second. At least Daphne was in Paris and out of my sight. But once I was caught in Susan's web, I could not honourably withdraw, and she clung to me like a limpet. At first, I was too stunned to know what to do, and for a while I foolishly imagined she was actually in love with me. It did not take long to disabuse myself of *that* notion. The child is an incorrigible flirt and as a married woman likely to be something worse. So I set out to shake myself free of her. I whipped up a quarrel at Crosby Manor within three days of her arrival, but although she fought back with words, she never gave me any hint of wishing to cry off. So then I insisted she stay at Mallowfleet for a full month, for I knew that would chafe her, to miss the season. It seemed certain that she would run up to town, and I planned to go after her and play the jealous suitor until she was sick and tired of me. But when I heard she had set off for Valmont, I knew exactly what she was about, and came here to warn you. When I found you both gone, I feared the worst, I assure you. I was very much afraid I was too late, but happily Miss Chandry was keeping watch over you."

They were within sight of the house now, so Ran and Ger handed Crosby over to Mrs Brack to be shown to a room. Ruth was loitering in the entrance hall when they returned. They withdrew into the empty Grand Saloon, and Ran related the whole to her.

"She has no shame!" Ruth said, pacing back and forth. "She is quite unrepentant. I am ashamed to call her sister. I asked if she wanted to leave but she said no, it was for Lord Crosby to leave if he wishes but she will stay to see me married."

"Will she come down to dinner?" Ran said, horrified.

"Certainly she will, and you will not notice anything amiss in her behaviour. She is very skilled in persuading the world that she is a mild-mannered, biddable girl who would not harm a flea." She paused, then smiled at Ger. "And once again, we are all gratitude towards Miss Chandry. What a remarkable lady she is."

Ger's face was alight in moments. "Indeed she is! But Ruth, do you truly think your sister would have trapped me into marrying her, even though she was betrothed already? What in heaven's name am I to do to be safe?"

"Ger, you are a duke," Ruth said gently. "You are under thirty years of age, and apart from a slight limp you are in perfect health. You are one of the wealthiest men in England, and you are unmarried. You will *never* be safe from scheming young ladies and matchmaking mamas."

"Then I must go and live in a cave and never come out," he said, grinning.

"They will find a way to your cave and try to entice you out," she said, laughing.

"I shall place a boulder across the entrance and *never* come out," he said, lifting his chin defiantly, and Ran was only half convinced that he was joking.

~~~~~

Ruth descended early to the Grand Saloon before dinner, but she was not the first there. Elizabeth and her friend were seated on a sofa, quietly reading.

"Lizzie! And Miss Bucknell, too. I had no idea we were to have the pleasure of your company this evening. Did Mrs Brine burn the mutton again?"

Elizabeth laughed, but reached into her reticule and pulled out a slip of paper. "I had this *cri de coeur* from Ran."

'Lizzie, If you have any care for your poor benighted brothers, please abandon your blancmange to dine with us tonight, for we have the most nightmarish company imaginable. Crosby and Susan have broken things off and will both be at dinner. Help! R.'

Ruth could only laugh. "He sounds as if he imagines they will be hurling lamb cutlets at each other! Everyone will be perfectly civilised, I am sure, but we will certainly be glad of more ladies, for we have nine gentlemen at table and there will be no keeping them from talking interminably about horses otherwise."

"I shall be very happy to play my part in preventing such dullness. Is it true that it is broken off? Irrevocably? For he seemed very much the jealous and besotted lover, to me."

Ruth shook her head, smiling. "He was very convincing, but he wished to rid himself of an unwanted engagement. He was trapped into it, you see." Elizabeth was thoughtful, considering this. Ruth went on, "And was I not right about him? He is neither fat nor bald, and not a trace of snuff about him."
~~~~~

"Oh yes! You were quite right," Elizabeth said softly, her eyes glowing.

The room began to fill up so they could have no more private talk, but Ruth watched carefully for Lord Crosby to arrive. He was one of the last to appear, and Ran had also been watching for him, it appeared, for he stepped forward to greet him, and began to introduce him around the room. He began with some of the gentlemen, who were clustered around the door and could not be got past otherwise, but once he had got clear of them and was steering Crosby towards Lady Anne, there was suddenly no obstacle hiding Elizabeth.

Crosby saw her. He stopped, uncertain at first. Then he tipped his head on one side with a little smile. "Lizzie? Is it you?"

"As you see, Luke," she answered composedly, although her cheeks were a little flushed.

He strode towards her, the rest of the room forgotten, and lifted her proffered hand to his lips. "How are you?"

"Well... very well. And you?"

"Oh... yes. Good Lord, Lizzie, it must be sixteen years since I last saw you, but you have not changed a bit. Still outshining every other lady in the room."

She coloured up like a girl. "Still laying on the flattery an inch thick, Luke."

"It is not flattery if it is true," he said promptly. There was a space on the sofa beside her, but he did not sit. "And... and how is Bexhill?"

"*Bexhill?* Lord Bexhill? I have not the slightest idea, not having seen him for above ten years."

"But…?"

From her position behind him, Ruth could not see his face, but she could imagine the bewilderment on it.

"I saw the betrothal notice in the Gazette. Are you not married to him?"

She smiled. "No. He posted the notice without bothering to enquire as to my opinion on the matter."

"Oh. Then if not Bexhill, who did you marry?"

"No one. I have never married, Luke."

"Oh," he said again. And then the words dried up completely and he could only stare at her.

"Sit," she said, patting the sofa beside her. "We have a great deal of catching up to do, it seems."

Obediently he sat and now Ruth could see his stunned face. People came and went, one or two even tried to speak to him, but he could not take his eyes from Elizabeth's face. Even when Susan arrived, late enough to make a dramatic entrance, he never lifted his gaze. When they went into dinner, he escorted Elizabeth into the Buttery and sat beside her.

"Your little strategy worked very well," Ruth whispered into Ran's ear as he helped her into her seat at the table. "Foolish man! Why did he not take the trouble to find out her situation when his wife died? They could have been happy these three years past."

"More than that if he had not run off and instantly married someone else," Ran said. "Why did he do that?"

"He seems to be vulnerable to determined women," she whispered back

They could say no more, for the rest of the company were all around them, and Ran was busy trying to arrange that Susan was as far away from Crosby as could be contrived, and that she had congenial company. In this latter quest he was aided by Captain Edgerton, who could spot a young lady in need of an amusing dinner companion at a distance of half a mile, and had immediately taken charge of her.

Dinner passed off without difficulty, and Ruth followed Lady Anne through to the Grand Saloon rather pleased. No one had fallen out, no lamb cutlets had been hurled and Elizabeth was in such a glow of happiness that Ruth could not resist saying, "I trust you feel suitably recompensed for missing Mrs Brine's blancmange?"

She laughed merrily. "I am excessively disappointed, naturally, although I have been too polite to mention it. Mary, dear, why do you keep looking up at the ceiling? You must be familiar with the scene upon it by now."

Miss Bucknell smiled, her protuberant teeth on full display. "Not the ceiling, Lizzie. You see all these pilasters around the room, with all that filigree work at the top? Some of them hide secret galleries where we may be watched."

"In the pilasters?" Elizabeth said. "Who told you that?"

"His Grace your brother. I saw him looking up there once, quite intently as if he was watching, and he told me that all the principal rooms have something of the sort, and that he hoped Miss Chandry was there watching over him. He said she is his guardian angel, which is rather sweet, is it not? It is such a pity that she cannot join us, for I am sure she would enjoy being part of the company instead of stuck inside a pillar like that."

"Well, I never knew that!" Elizabeth cried. "I know Ger used to be fascinated by the plans of the house when he was a boy, but I never guessed there were so many secrets to be uncovered. Ah, here are the gentlemen at last!"

It was only one gentleman, but it was the one she was waiting for. Lord Crosby made straight for her, and they settled contentedly at the backgammon table.

Ruth, meanwhile, was left to herself, for Lady Anne was dozing, Susan was at the instrument and Mary Bucknell had picked up a book. With no other occupation to fill her hands or her mind, she listened to Susan's performance, trying not to wince at the frequent missed notes, and surreptitiously watched the pilasters for signs of movement behind them. But it was not until the rest of the gentlemen reappeared, and she watched where Ger's eyes turned as he entered, that she finally caught the flash of some lightness — a face, perhaps — behind the filigree.

What must it be like to be a mistress? However much one was loved, could it ever compensate for the perpetual need to keep out of sight, while the man walked about in society as if one did not exist at all? For the first time, she sincerely pitied Miss Chandry and wished that she could emerge from behind the screen and take her place at Ger's side, as he so clearly wanted. Sometimes the world was very harsh.

27: Revisiting The Past

Ran was up early the next morning to attend to the correspondence that had accumulated while he was away, so he called for a tray to be brought to the sitting room he shared with Ger and Ginny. She came in while he was eating, already dressed. He poured coffee for her, wondering with a warm glow inside him what it would be like to share such moments with Ruth. He had not long to wait to find out.

"You won't have to put up with me for much longer," Ginny said, cradling her coffee cup. "There will be enough of the Old Manor habitable for us to move in next week."

"It will be strange not to have Ger in the next room," he said. "We shared a bed before we were breeched, and then a bedroom, and these rooms since we were ten."

"You will have the Lady Ruth," she said with a throaty chuckle. "You will not miss Ger much. Besides, he will not be far away, and I hope you will come and go as you please. The last thing he wants is to create any division between you."

He did not state the obvious, that it was Ginny herself who was the divisive factor. As his mistress, she was not part of his normal life and so she drew Ger away from it, too. He would no doubt spend more time in the Old Manor than in Valmont. But that closeness, closer even than with Ran, gave her an indispensable advantage. She more than anyone knew the workings of Ger's tempestuous nature.

"How is he coping with all this?" Ran said. "So many changes, yet after that first day he has done very well — in public. Is he truly as settled as he appears?"

"He has his restless moments, as always," she said, setting the coffee cup down on the table and reaching absently for a bun. "He was wakeful last night, but I let him talk and it seemed to calm him."

"He used to talk to me, but it never calmed him."

She chuckled again. "A brother is very different from a lover. You will find out soon enough that there is something magical about lying in bed together at the end of the day, all wrapped up in each other's arms. You can talk or kiss or just fall asleep tangled up together, and whatever was preying on your mind never seems so bad, somehow. Everyone needs someone like that."

"Everyone needs to be loved," Ran said, remembering Ruth's words.

"Exactly!" Ginny said. "And not brotherly love, as generous and unquestioning as that is. Something more than that. Ger says that it is like an echo of God's love, something profound enough to sustain one through all of life's uncertainties."

"And he has that with you, and I have it with Ruth," he said wonderingly. "We are very blessed."

And she smiled and nodded and reached for another bun.

Ran had not been at his desk for very long, when Brent came to find him.

"Begging your pardon, my lord, but I thought you would wish to know that Lord Crosby is preparing to depart, and he is to take the Lady Elizabeth with him."

"Is he so?" Ran said, laughing. "He is a swift worker, I will grant him that."

There was a single box already in the entrance hall when Ran reached it, but no sign of Crosby, only Ger, looking rather rumpled as if he had dressed in haste.

"Did you hear?" Ger said as soon as Ran appeared, whisking him into the Ante-Chamber. "Yesterday he was betrothed to Susan Grenaby and today he is set to marry Lizzie! They are going straight to town to get a special licence. Do you think we ought to do something about it? What is Lizzie about, to be agreeing to this? What hold does he have over her?"

"The usual one," Ran said, laughing. "She is in love with him."

"That was *years* ago! But I suppose... did she stay single all this time because of him? Poor Lizzie! I never suspected it."

"Oh, I should not suppose her heart was broken beyond repair, but she told Ruth that she has always had a *tendre* for him, and seemingly it is the same for him. There is no need for them to wait, given their advanced years."

Ger laughed. "She is only five years older than us, brother, hardly in her dotage. Well, if that is so, then I wish them very happy, and no one deserves a bit of happiness more than Lizzie. She should not be the only Litherholm still unmarried."

"No, for that will be you," Ran said.

"So it will!" He grinned and cuffed Ran on the shoulder.

The carriage arrived, Crosby and his valet rushed down the stairs with a couple of portmanteaux, and Ran and Ger got into the carriage with them to be driven the short distance to Elizabeth's lodge to collect her. They found Mary Bucknell dressed for travel, too.

"But of course she is coming with us!" Elizabeth said in surprised tones when Ran asked. "I can hardly leave her behind, and I will not send her back to the Bucknells. They mean well, and they do not mistreat her, but it is all *'Oh, Mary could you just run upstairs and fetch my other parasol'* and *'Mary will not mind staying behind to look after the children while we go out and enjoy ourselves'* and such like. It was positive slavery."

"You exaggerate, Lizzie," Mary said, smiling at her. "I never minded helping, and I *doted* on the dear children, but I confess it is more pleasant to live with you. Although I shall miss the Valmont library. Do you have a library, Lord Crosby?"

"A small book room only—" Her face fell. "—in town, but at the Manor there is a good library, and Lackington's sends me all the new works as soon as they are published. I believe you will not be disappointed."

"Oh, how splendid!"

While the two ladies' boxes were strapped onto the carriage, Ger said quietly to Elizabeth, "Sister, are you quite sure about this? It seems... very sudden."

She chuckled. "Do you think so? I suppose sixteen years is a tad hasty…" But then she said, her face suddenly afire with joy, "Dear Ger, can you not understand how it is? All these years I have thought of him, although I tried very hard not to, and one day there he is and he feels the same way and we are both free. Would you not grasp the opportunity with both hands before it can slip away again? Last night… oh, I felt seventeen again, with all the old turmoil of hopes and fears and desires. I did not sleep a wink, as you might imagine. And then, shortly after dawn, I heard a flute playing and there he was, sitting on the bench in my garden, playing for me… calling me… I walked barefoot across the dewy lawn and straight into his arms, and I will not be parted from him again, in this life or the next."

"Then I wish you all the joy in the world, my dear sister," Ger whispered.

Ger and Ran bade their sister farewell and waved the carriage off before walking back through the park. Ger's enthusiasm about Elizabeth's good fortune soon drifted into silence. Ran knew him well enough not to probe, and after a while, Ger said hesitantly, "What is it that Willerton-Forbes wants to see me about, do you know? For I have told him everything I can remember about the *Minerva*."

"He is a very meticulous man," Ran said with a sigh. "There is some detail or other that he wants to clear up."

"But why is he asking *me?* I hate these interviews! It is like being on trial."

"We will find out soon enough what it is about, but I shall be there with you."

"And Ginny too?" Ger said optimistically. "Everything is better when Ginny is there."

They met Willerton-Forbes and Edgerton in the Royal Withdrawing Room.

"No Mr Neate today?" Ran said, as he ushered the gentlemen in.

"He is at the Pig and Whistle," Edgerton said. "We feel it better to... erm, keep an eye on Mr Michael Chandry."

"What is he up to now?" Ginny said, with a smile.

"Setting the women sighing, mostly," Edgerton said. "But also taking as much money as he can from passing travellers foolish enough to accept his challenge at the card table. He is a formidable player, but... how shall I put this? Neate suspects that there is some manipulation of the cards involved."

She laughed. "He always said it's not cheating if cards just happen to get bent in a certain way, but Mr Neate need not be concerned. Michael never does so to his own advantage. If he seems to be winning quickly, he cheats a little to prolong the game. He never cheats with Ger, or anyone else who plays well."

"I shall put this view of the matter to Neate," Edgerton said gravely. "I must say, Miss Chandry, your brother is a fascinating character, sharp as a needle and full of pluck."

"Oh, yes, he's always up for a fight!" Ginny said.

"Game for anything," Edgerton said. "In fact, I propose to invite him to join in a little venture that I have in mind. Mr Willerton-Forbes, Mr Neate and I have had some small success in the solving of crimes requiring discretion, and it is an enterprise which we greatly enjoy. We are considering creating a business for the purpose. Now, Willerton-Forbes is the son of an earl and therefore far too grand to lend his name officially, and Neate prefers to remain anonymous, but the name *Edgerton, Chandry and Associates* sounds rather good, do you not think? A discreet establishment with a brass plate beside the door, the best quality Madeira to serve to clients… But we would not wish to do anything which might embarrass you or your family, Miss Chandry, given your friendship with His Grace."

"There's some would say that Michael's been embarrassing his family since the day he was born," she said with a smile. "If you think you can keep him out of mischief long enough to do some good, then I shall not stand in your way, Captain Edgerton. Michael is free to do as he pleases."

He bowed to her respectfully. The four gentlemen settled themselves around a circular table, while Ginny found a chair against the wall, somewhat aside from the group. Ran watched Ger anxiously, but although his hands twisted together from time to time, he looked otherwise quite his usual self.

Willerton-Forbes smiled benignly. "Your Grace is most generous in agreeing to see us again, but we do have just a few minor matters to discuss, matters which we did not wish to raise in the immediate aftermath of your return. We wished to do nothing to disturb the celebrations. I trust this is an appropriate moment." He produced a sheet of paper. "Our function as instructed by the Benefactor was to give the sum of one thousand pounds to every survivor or next of kin of the deceased, in whatever form was desired, and to offer such help as might be needed. Nothing else. When the *Minerva* sailed, there was a complete list of all those aboard kept at the Dublin shipping office, and that was our starting point to trace the next of kin of all those drowned, as instructed by the Benefactor. With the captain and his crew there was no difficulty, for we had two surviving crewmen and the ship's owner, who came from Southampton to assist. When the mortal remains of these unfortunates were recovered from the wreckage, therefore, each was readily identified, and the next of kin easily found. All those have received the thousand pounds from the Benefactor.

"Then we came to the paying passengers, seven in cabins, and three travelling steerage. The first name, of course, was that of the Most Noble Gervase Septimus Litherholm, Seventh Duke of Falconbury, returning from three years in America after the death of the Sixth Duke. Mr Herbert Huntly, Esquire, of Willow Place, Hampshire, was returning from a visit to his mother, who lives near Dublin. Mr Abraham Wishaw, a hop merchant of Bursham St Matthew, Hampshire, was returning from visit of business. Mr Philip Kearney, an architect from Liverpool, had been discussing plans for improving Lord Kilrannan's property. Mr Lethbridge Barantine, a jewel merchant of London, and his partner, Mr David Newbold, were leaving Dublin after selling some pieces of jewellery and buying a quantity of diamonds. There was a Mr Louis Fields of unknown origin and trade. And three travelling steerage — James Crick and Robert Palfreyman, valets to Mr Barantine and Mr Newbold, and one Jonathan Ellsworthy, a clerk seeking employment in Southampton, the only passenger to survive."

Willerton-Forbes leaned back in his chair, hands folded over his rounded stomach, smiling benignly. "Most of these presented no difficulties at all. They carried card cases or rings or marked clothing, and were identified by relations. The duke himself was identified by the crests on his clothing, by his jewellery and by

Lord Randolph." He smiled at Ger sympathetically. "Or misidentified, I should perhaps say, for which no blame can attach to any person, for the case was most convincing, even to the tattoo on the back of the head. I have no doubt that Your Grace had reasons for such a deception, but you have no need to explain yourself to us. We are satisfied with the truth, that is all."

"I have no objection to explaining it," Ger said, although his hands twisted again. "Like Mr Neate, I prefer to be anonymous when I can. When I met Joe Meadows, who looked a little like me and acted the duke a great deal better, it seemed an agreeable solution for both of us. I planned to surprise my brother with the trick at Southampton."

"An ingenious jest," Willerton-Forbes said, eyes twinkling. "But at the time, it seemed that the duke was identified, as were most of the other names on our list, and there remained but two mysteries. One was Mr Louis Fields, whom the coroner discovered to be a young woman aged about five and twenty, he estimated. We have been unable to find out anything about her."

"When I heard there was a woman on board, I wondered if she might be Ger's wife," Ran said. "It kept me searching for evidence of a marriage in America for a long time, even when common sense told me it was impossible."

"It was a reasonable theory," Willerton-Forbes said. "The poor quality of her clothes suggested otherwise, however. She remains a mystery, poor lady. The other mystery amongst the passengers was Mr Jonathan Ellsworthy, who was identified by the Second Mate, but appeared to be a man with no history. Although he told several people investigating the sinking that he had been raised in an orphanage in Carlisle, the good captain's rather thorough searches revealed no trace of such a person, nor any record of his birth."

Ger laughed. "Did you truly go all the way to Carlisle to find out if I was telling the truth?"

"We are nothing if not thorough, Your Grace."

"But you never mentioned it to me. We met three times, I think, at various times, but you said nothing about it."

"It is not our place to pry into a man's secrets," Willerton-Forbes said. "We had no right to unmask a man who had clearly changed his name at some point. There is nothing illegal in that. You were a survivor of the *Minerva*, and therefore entitled to your thousand pounds. Beyond that we did not venture. But at that point we were at a standstill. We had everyone on the ship identified and in receipt of one thousand pounds with the single exception of Mr Louis Fields, our mystery lady, and all our enquiries there had proved fruitless. But that is not the only mystery outstanding."

"You love mysteries, don't you, Mr Willerton-Forbes?" Ginny said from her perch across the room. "I can see the gleam in your eye even from here."

"Indeed I do, or rather, a mystery is an irritant, like a splinter in the flesh, that must be worked and pushed and pulled until it reveals itself. Many people wrote to us once word got out that we were handing out a thousand pounds apiece to anyone with a valid claim. A great many people tried to convince us that they had such a claim. Only one interested us. We had a letter from a Mrs Pike, a housekeeper for two ladies in London. She has a brother, Nigel Pike, who grew up with her in an orphanage in

Carlisle. Last year, she received a letter from him, written in Dublin."

He passed across a single sheet of paper, the words scratched in a barely-literate scrawl.

'Dear lil coming home soon you will not beleev it I am a rich man so much to tell you I bring you a big surpris and I met a real duk yes me mixing with the nobs I am in irland waiting for a special ship brig minerva expect me in to weeks nigel'

"But he was not on the *Minerva*," Ginny said. "You read out the names and there was no Pike."

"Well now, that is the mystery," Willerton-Forbes said. "When we first saw this, we concluded, as you do, that Nigel Pike was indeed in Dublin, but did not board the *Minerva*. We could find no trace of Pike in Ireland, but, to our delight, there was a record of him growing up in Carlisle. So now we had Jonathan Ellsworthy, a man with no history, and Nigel Pike, a man with a long history who had vanished. It was not hard to conclude that Jonathan Ellsworthy was Nigel Pike, but naturally we did not suggest such a thing to Mrs Pike. We told her that to the very best of our knowledge he was still alive."

Ger burst out laughing. "You thought *I* was this Pike fellow? But I have never heard of him."

"Yet you franked his letter," Ran said quietly.

Ger snatched it from his hands. "So I did. Good God! Then he was *there*, but... I do not understand. The only letters I franked were... oh... it was Joe Meadows. So he changed his name?"

"That is the conclusion we came to as well," Willerton-Forbes said. "And if Jonathan Ellsworthy was the Duke of

Falconbury, then the man wearing his clothes must have been Nigel Pike. She gave us a likeness of her brother to show you, Your Grace. She told us that it was drawn some years ago but it is a good likeness."

He drew the paper from the pile in front of him and passed it to Ger, who burst out laughing. "That is Joe to the life! Much younger, of course, but I would know him anywhere. So his name was Nigel? Well I never! And he had a sister. He never mentioned her."

"It will grieve her to know that her brother is indeed dead," Willerton-Forbes said softly. "Do you have any idea what surprise he had in mind, Duke?"

"I have no idea. He said nothing of it to me."

"She told us that he had hinted once or twice in his letters that there was a special lady."

Ger smiled at him. "He *did* have a lady when I first met him. She was part of the acting group he belonged to but when they all separated she went to her sister in New York. Her name was Louisa Fogg and—"

"Louisa?" Edgerton said. "Louis Fields… Louisa Fogg… It could be."

"Meadows!" Ginny cried. "Joe Meadows… Louis Fields was Louisa *Meadows.* She was his *wife!*"

Willerton-Forbes leaned back in his chair with an expression of satisfaction on his face. "Ah! Splendid. Thank you, Miss Chandry. There now remain only two mysteries to be resolved. One is why a sound ship travelling in good conditions with an experienced captain and crew should be driven onto the rocks of Cornwall. And the other—"

"The other?" Ran said.

"The Benefactor. I have been faithfully carrying out the Benefactor's instructions for more than a year now, yet I am no nearer to knowing who that reclusive person may be." He sighed. "I do not suppose we shall ever know, now. How extremely *irritating.*"

28: The Eve Of The Wedding

There were letters to be written, arrangements to be made, matters to be set right, as far as that was possible, but the first requirement was to set enquiries in motion to determine the truth about Nigel Pike. Had he really married Louisa Fogg, and were there any children resulting?

"This is last year all over again," Ran said to Max, as he sealed a letter to the agent in Boston. "Marriage records, birth records… everything we have already been through."

"It is not quite so grievous when it is not your own brother."

"True. Max, what are we to do with the body in the mausoleum? Should we send it off to London, for Mrs Pike to rebury?"

"Oh, you want my advice now, do you?" Max said, amused. "You never listen to it."

"You wound me greatly! I always listen most carefully to your advice. I may not always follow it, however."

Max laughed. "You *never* follow it, and just as well, in some cases. If you had listened to me and not spoken to Lady Ruth, you would still be unhappy today, instead of looking forward to your wedding day. That is one instance where I am not ashamed to admit that I was utterly wrong, and I am very glad that you disregarded my misguided recommendations. When is your wedding day to be? There is no difficulty, is there?"

"What a worrier you are! Do you imagine Ruth will change her mind again? We await the arrival of her parents, that is all. Then it will be done. There is no rush."

"The great rush would be to get your bride's sister away from your brother," Max said sourly. "She is a dreadful flirt, that one, and now that Crosby has very wisely defected—"

"Susan is harmless, I think. Ger is too sensible to fall for her wiles."

"I hope you are right, for she would be a disaster as the Duchess of Falconbury, even worse than—" He had the grace to look embarrassed.

"Even worse than Ginny Chandry? A great deal worse," Ran said evenly. "Ginny has many good qualities, Max. She is very good with Ger, and he would cope better in company if she was with him, I think. I should not object to their marriage at all."

Max grunted, eyebrows raised in disbelief, but he said nothing more. He had no need to, for Ran knew all the arguments perfectly well. She was barely gentry, let alone nobility, and the jump from the lowest rung of the ladder to almost the highest was a massive one. She had no education to speak of, and no familiarity with the world of the nobility. She might be able to mingle at an evening party with Ger's family, who were disposed to be kind, but it was hard to see her coping with the high sticklers of the *beau monde.* She would never be accepted, and then Ger would retreat from society too. He needed a wife accustomed to that life.

And yet... Ran could not deny that Ger was calmer, more amenable when she was with him. He had experienced none of the violent mood swings that had so characterised his younger days. His spirits were still uneven, but instead of veering from high good humour to the depths of despair, now he never descended lower than bored placidity. If he grew restless, as he often did in company, he would take himself off to the instrument and get rid of his fidgets that way, and if that failed he would disappear and find Ginny. She kept him sane, and Ran would do a great deal to ensure that she stayed with Ger, even if it meant accepting her as duchess. It would be a small price to pay to prevent any repeat of those stomach-churning moments of the past, where Ran had had to coax Ger out of a black mood and convince him that life was worth living. He still occasionally woke sweating and terrified, dreaming he was up on the roof again and trying desperately to talk Ger out of jumping to his death. He never, ever wanted to go back to those days.

~~~~~

Ruth received a brief note from her mother to say that they were delayed by some important political matter in Parliament which the duke could not miss. It was difficult to quibble over it when she was very grateful that they were to come at all, but she wished it could all be over. She had moved into her new apartments, her wedding clothes filled the wardrobes in the dressing room and the wedding breakfast was planned, together with a celebratory dinner that evening. Ger and Ginny had moved into the Old Manor. Everything now awaited the arrival of the duke and duchess.
~~~~~

The delay caused another difficulty, too. Ran had carefully refrained from informing anyone of their plans, to avoid the unwanted appearance of hordes of relations. Elizabeth, however, had had no such scruples, industriously writing to every uncle, aunt, sister and cousin to suggest they hurry to Valmont to help celebrate the wedding. A great number of them had decided to do just that. It was not precisely a horde, but enough to terrify Ger into hiding away in the evenings.

Ruth's own relations were behaving well, for once. Audlyn was happy as a flea, having made the acquaintance of Michael Chandry and Captain Edgerton, the three finding much of mutual interest to absorb their energies. They rode together in the mornings, and as often as not spent the evenings at the Pig and Whistle, where the entertainment was less refined than at Valmont, but of a nature to appeal to gentlemen.

As for Susan, she was suspiciously well-behaved, and Elizabeth's departure meant she was less well chaperoned. The arrival of Ran's other sisters and a number of aunts alleviated the problem somewhat, for there were now always ladies about in the Queen's Room or the Spinsters' Parlour. However, when Ruth went there, she often found that Susan was missing and then she felt obliged to track her down. Sometimes she was harmlessly in her room, or walking in the grounds with her maid, but sometimes she was in the Grand Saloon at the instrument with Ger, quite alone, and that made Ruth uneasy. She had fretted at the close chaperonage she herself had suffered and wished for a little less confinement, but Susan had altogether too much freedom. Neither Aunt Maria nor Cousin Patience had been sent to watch over her, Ruth had other activities to absorb her time and the other ladies could not be relied upon. The sooner Mama arrived the better.

Finally, that day arrived, and the little train of carriages and outriders drew up outside the front door. Ger could not be found, but Ran, Ruth, Audlyn and Susan stood on the top step to greet the arrivals. The duchess was all cordiality, kissing Ruth, patting Susan's cheek, and smiling benevolently at the two men. They proceeded to the Ante-Chamber, where an array of Litherholms had assembled to greet the ducal party with appropriate ceremony, and to make sure the honour of the host family was upheld by the superiority of their elegance and civility. The duke and duchess, however, had been the most recently in town, and therefore had the triumph of being able to impart the very latest gossip.

Ruth and Ran stood a little apart, watching them. "Tomorrow," he murmured. "Tomorrow we shall be married."

His words warmed her from head to toe. "Yes," she said shyly. "At last."

At that moment, Brent came softly into the room, and even with her small experience of the household, she could see that there was something very wrong. The imperturbable retainer was ashen, and although he approached Ran, he seemed uncertain what to say.

"Whatever is it?" Ran said, his voice sharp with unease.

Brent leaned forward and whispered in his ear. He murmured, "Oh my God," and without a word the two hurried out of the room.

Ruth could not hear all that was said, but the words *'His Grace'* were unmissable. She rushed out after them. Ran had already disappeared, and Brent was in huddled conference with the footmen.

"Brent! What has happened?"

"My lady, I—" He gestured uncertainly with his hands.

"Brent, by this time tomorrow, I shall in effect be the mistress of this house, so *tell me* what has happened to His Grace?"

"His Grace was observed entering the old schoolroom, my lady."

Ruth went cold. She knew the implications of that all too well. She picked up her skirts and ran up the stairs, along the corridor to the family wing then more stairs, up and up... the nursery suite, long disused now, lay on the top floor, just below the attics. The night nursery, the day nursery and then the old schoolroom. The door stood open and she crept in.

Only one shutter was open, and at first she could not see anything but the outline of a neat row of desks, the lectern for tutor or governess, the large working table. Then, as her eyes adjusted, an assortment of large toys — a rocking horse, a baby house, a model of a castle for battles with tin soldiers. But in the furthest corner, almost invisible in the gloom, two huddled figures. Ger was sitting on the floor, knees drawn up to his chest, his face buried. Ran knelt beside him, close but not touching him, murmuring soothingly.

"Is he all right?" she said, weaving through the furniture to reach them. Such a stupid thing to say. "Oh, Ger! Do not despair!"

There was no response.

"I thought he was past all this," Ran said helplessly. "He will not even talk to me!"

"May I try?" He nodded, and she knelt on the dusty floor, and reached out cautiously to stroke Ger's arm.

He threw both hands in the air, brushing her off, and raised an angry face. "Do not *touch* me! Go away! Both of you... leave me alone. "

"We only want to help," she whispered. "Is there nothing we can do for you? Tell us what troubles you, Ger."

"I wish I were *dead. I should* have died. When the *Minerva* sank, it should have taken me with it. Leave me to do what I must."

Ran cried out, "No, Ger, no! You have so much to live for!"

But he had lowered his face to his knees again, unresponsive.

"Ginny," she said distractedly. "She can reach him if anyone can."

"Of course," Ran said, relief in his tone. "She will be in the Old Manor."

"I shall find a footman to—"

"No, it will be quicker to go yourself."

"Yes, yes! Where?" She jumped up, bursting to be off.

"Straight down the Stable Stair to the lowest level, through the tunnel, then up again."

Her feet flew. She crashed open the door to the stair in her haste, then down, down, down, her slippers pattering on the stone steps, endlessly down. Past the door to her apartments, past the floor with Ran's rooms, on downwards past the door she used coming in from the stables, and down, down again. The stairs decanted her into an ante-room with doors on three sides, and the fourth... There was no door, just a dark, empty opening. The tunnel... but it was night-black, not a glimmer of a light anywhere. Frantically, she looked about her for a candlestick, found one on a high shelf, then she fumbled to light it from the smoky tallow candle in the nearest sconce.

The tunnel was not as bare and forbidding as most cellars, for the walls were plastered, the sconces set out on the floor at intervals ready to be affixed. Here and there, a ladder had been left, or a box of tools, but she raced on, the candlelight flickering wildly. Abruptly, the candle blew out and she was plunged into darkness. She stopped, gasping for breath.

A light ahead of her! Dim and wavering, but enough to set her running again, although she kept one hand on the wall of the tunnel to guide her. Once she tripped and almost fell, but she righted herself at once and ploughed on. She must find Ginny! There was no time to lose...

Another ante-chamber, this one carpeted, with polished wood consoles and a single lamp burning. There were no doors here, only stairs leading upwards, where daylight filtered down, encouraging her.

Up and up again, to another ante-chamber, a twin to the one below. Her lungs protested the unaccustomed exercise. A single door — she hurled it open and rushed through. She was in a large entrance hall, panelled and high-ceilinged, with an arched wooden roof to proclaim its medieval origins. It was empty.

"Help!" she shrieked, as loud as her tortured lungs could contrive. "Ginny! *Someone!* Where is... everyone?"

For several agonising moments, there was no sound but her own laboured breathing as she struggled for breath. Then, with a loud creak, a door half opened.

"Yes?" said a suspicious male voice.

"Where is she? Ginny... Miss Chandry? It is imperative—"

"Kitchen."

He pointed to a door, and off she raced again, and as she drew nearer the inevitable sounds and smells of the kitchen led her on without the need for further guidance. She burst in upon a scene of such peaceful domesticity that she would have smiled had the case been less urgent. The cook, the kitchen maid and Ginny herself were floured to the elbows at the kitchen table, while Molly sat with her sewing at the other end, well away from the encroaching flour. All four were enjoying a joke, laughing together like old friends. As Ruth burst in, they turned to her as one, surprise writ large on their faces.

"Lady Ruth!" Ginny cried. "Whatever is the matter?"

"Ger... schoolroom... needs you..."

Ginny, bless her, required no other information. Wiping her hands hastily on a cloth, she ran straight out of the room.

Ruth could not follow. She could not even breathe. It was Molly who pushed her into a chair, lifted a fallen lock of hair from her face, soothed her and reassured her.

"Poor Jon! I mean His Grace. But don't you worry, milady. Ginny will sort him out."

"Will she?"

"Course she will! He's clay in her hands, so he is."

"But he wants… to kill himself!" Ruth cried. "Did he… feel so… in Cornwall?"

Molly pulled a chair nearer to Ruth, and gestured to the cook and kitchen maid to carry on working. "No, I can't never say he was that desperate in Pendower. I only once saw him bad, milady, a little while after that London lawyer came to talk to him."

"Mr Willerton-Forbes?"

"Aye, that were him. He came to give him some money from that Benefactor person, and you'd think that would be good news, wouldn't you? But Mr Ellsworthy — His Grace, I mean — he got terrible quiet, and one day he went and sat out by the old fountain all by himself, his arms all wrapped around himself and his head down, really sad-looking. But Miss Ginny went out to him, and talked him out of it, and he never did such a thing again. Very happy he was, after that."

"Molly, with all my heart and soul I pray that she will be able to do so again, because he is as bad now as I have ever seen him."

~~~~~
~~~~~

Ran sat cross-legged in the half-light of the schoolroom beside his brother. He could not touch him and nothing he said seemed to reach him, but he could not sit impotently in silence, so he maintained a patter of soothing nothings. He talked about Ginny and the coming child, he talked about the home they shared and the prospect of many years of happiness ahead of them. None of it raised the least reaction from Ger, and that was more disheartening than anything else. If even the thought of his beloved Ginny could not rouse him, what hope was there? But as long as Ger sat passively in the schoolroom there was *some* hope. He had not yet taken the next step, of going up to the roof. So Ran talked and prayed and hoped.

And then Ginny was there. She still wore an apron, and smelt of flour and stewed gooseberries, but she was *there* and at the sound of her voice, Ger lifted his head.

"Jon."

That was all she said, but it was enough. He looked up at her with such grief in his face as wrung Ran's heart. She flew across the room, sat down on the other side of him and took him in her arms, and he wept piteously on her shoulder.

"Jon, Jon. Hush now. It isn't so bad."

"It *is*, it is."

"Nonsense. You mustn't get yourself into such a state. There's nothing to be so upset about."

"There *is*. I am the lowest worm in the world, Ginny. I am nothing but a piece of pond scum."

"*No!* You are a good man, Jonathan Ellsworthy. Have I not told you so a hundred times? You are a *good* man."

"You do not know what I have done, Ginny. I have done a wicked, wicked thing. I should have died that night when the *Minerva* sank. Then Ran would have been the duke, as he should have been, and you would never have been burdened with a useless man like me."

She pulled away from him, cupping his face in her hands so that he was forced to look her directly in the eye. "Don't you *dare* to talk like that. Do you know how insulting it is to be told that the man I love — the father of my child — thinks he's useless? You are a *good man* and you've done nothing wrong."

"But I have," he said in a low voice. "It was all my fault. I killed them, all those people on the *Minerva*. They died because of me. It was my fault. I am a *murderer*, Ginny."

29: The Schoolroom

Ran could barely breathe. How was it that Ger could have caused a ship to founder? For one wild moment, he considered whether Captain Edgerton had been in the right after all when he wondered if Ger had deliberately sunk the ship in an attempt to end his own life. Yet even now, he could not believe it of his brother. So he listened as Ginny coaxed the story out of him.

"I was so miserable, coming home," he said, his face streaked with tears. "I was the duke, the last person I wanted to be. I had been in America for three years, and for two and a half years I had been able to live in the shadows while Joe Meadows dealt with all the sycophancy. It was wonderful, Ginny. I was free to be myself, to lurk in the background and no one took the least notice of me. But then Father died and I had to come home, and it would be all over. I would be trapped in this cage for ever. Dublin was the last of my freedom, the last time I could hide from the world. Or so I thought."

He fell silent, and Ginny settled herself more comfortably beside him, one arm around his shoulders. He rested his head against her with a sigh. In the darkness across the room, Ran caught the shimmer of Ruth's gown as she returned, but she said nothing, drawing a little closer, then waiting, listening.

"Tell me about the *Minerva*," Ginny said softly.

"The *Minerva*... but first I must tell you about Dublin. I had always played cards for money. I paid my way across America with my winnings, earning enough to keep Joe and me in the best hotels, and cover his losses. He was a terrible player. Anyone who knew anything about me would have known that he was not me, for I would never have played so badly. In Dublin, we stayed at the Earl of Kilrannan's house, and two of his sons ran a very genteel gaming room, where Joe lost night after night, and I won. I met Barantine there, the jewel merchant, and Lord, was he a good player! After the regular tables had closed, we played piquet for hours, coins on the table, as I always insist. He lost almost a thousand to me, but I would not take his vowels, so that was that.

"But two nights later, the last night before the *Minerva* sailed, he asked if I would play him again. He had no coins, but he had diamonds, he said, worth around six thousand pounds, and would I accept them instead? Just the two of us, privately, but he said he had never enjoyed playing more and to him it was worth it, even if he lost the whole amount. I accepted. We started at three in the afternoon, and we came to an end at three the next morning. I had won everything, and he smiled and said he would remember that night for his whole life, and hoped we would meet again, and perhaps he would have a chance to win some of his gems back."

When he lapsed into silence again, Ginny said, "So what about the *Minerva?*"

"Barantine told me to sew the diamonds into the seams of my coat, to hide them, so that was what I did. I spent the last hours before boarding the ship sewing. Some went into my boots, as well, and what was left of the coins after Joe had taken some to play with. Then onto the ship. There was no cabin free, so I went steerage with the two valets. That was quite an experience, a hammock down below with the ordinary sailors! So soothing, being gently rocked.

"Not that it helped much. I was still terrified of coming home, of being the duke, so my spirits were low, but then something happened that—" A long pause. The only sound in the room was Ger's ragged breathing. Ginny gently stroked his cheek and he gave her a wan little smile. "Barantine was travelling with his business partner. Newbold, his name was. An unpleasant man. He complained about everything. He cornered me after breakfast, when everyone else had gone about their business, and he laid into me in no uncertain terms. I had ruined his friend, he told me, everything was over for him. It was my fault that he had been sucked into a gambling fever, so that the earl's sons drew him into madness. He had seemingly gambled away the title to his entire business to them, and then *I* had taken everything he had left, the diamonds with which he might have rebuilt. He would have no alternative but to end his existence, and then his daughter, who thought herself a great heiress, would be a penniless orphan and what was to become of her?

"Naturally, I at once offered to return every last diamond to Barantine, but the fellow just laughed. Do you know what he said to me? *'If you were a gentleman and had any concept of honour, you would know that Barantine could not accept.'* I said to him that Barantine had accepted his loss with equanimity, and had never given the least sign of being ruined. He laughed that off. Of course he was cheerful in public, but in private he was devastated, he told me." Ger turned his face towards Ginny. "I could not bear it, not on top of everything else! To be the means of destroying a man utterly, and his daughter, too — it was too much. It is the one thing I have always tried to avoid, never taking vowels or anything but cash on the table. I had to find a way to return the diamonds to him, and the perfect plan came to me in a flash. I would end my own existence, but bequeath him the diamonds. He could not refuse to accept them then!

"I had paper and pencil, so I scratched a note to say that if anything should happen to me, Barantine was to have all my clothes. I left it in my hammock, with my coat and boots. I had got hold of a flask of rum to build up my courage, so I set off up to the deck to drink myself into the state of mind to throw myself overboard. Of course, it was just my luck that Captain Caldicott was still up and about, just descending from the deck. Seeing me with my flask, he said, *'Going above to view the stars? You will need your coat... and your boots. It is freezing up there.'* I had no option but to don coat and boots, thinking that I could remove them again before throwing myself overboard.

"Caldicott was right! It *was* freezing up there, and the stars were magnificent, but I was not there to enjoy the view. I found a quiet corner out of the biting wind, and settled down to become miserably drunk. If fortune favoured me, the world might look rosier through a rum-soaked haze, but if not, I was but three steps from the rail. I had not taken more than two mouthfuls before I was discovered. The deck boy first, and then he must have told the Second Mate, Blackwell. I daresay he saw what I was about, for he sat down beside me and tried his level best to talk me out of it. Well, he just talked, but every time I suggested he need not linger, he chattered on. He had a woman in Dublin, it seemed, and an urge to tell me all about her. It seemed only polite to share the rum with him. How was I to know that he was in sole charge of the vessel? Captain Caldicott had only been making a final check before retiring to his cabin, and Blackwell was supposed to be at the helm. Instead, he was talking to me, keeping me from jumping overboard. We were pretty well foxed, the pair of us, when he leapt up yelling something about a rock — somebody's rock."

"Tomey's Rock," Ran said. "It came up at the inquiry. It was marked on the newer charts as a hazardous rock underwater at high tide, but the locals called it Tomey's Rock. So Blackwell not only knew of it, but knew its name. Interesting."

"Why is it interesting?" Ger said.

Ran's fears began to recede somewhat. Ger was talking, he was asking questions and that was a promising sign. "Because the fellow denied all knowledge of it. Claimed it was not even on the charts. Go on, brother. What happened next?"

"We hit it! Almost at once there was this horrible scraping, splintering sound and the ship shuddered and lurched. I was pitched forward and slid across the deck until I hit something — coiled ropes, I think. I ended up against the rail, then there was icy water and I remember nothing after that until I woke up in Ginny's house, with Molly bending over me. I have no idea why I survived, but I wish to God I had died that night! So many people died because of me... so many children orphaned, so many wives made widows. *I* should have died, not them."

"But God chose otherwise, in His mercy," Ginny said quietly. "Besides, it seems to me that the blame, if blame there must be, lies with Mr Blackwell. He was steering the ship, after all. He came to see you, afterwards. He came several times, but you were not well enough to talk to him at first. Eventually, Mama let him see you, and after that he never came back."

"He asked me if I remembered what had happened, and I told him I recalled nothing after leaving Dublin. He just smiled and said that was good, but that if I remembered anything, it would be best not to mention it to anyone. And I never did until now. But it was not his fault, it was mine, Ginny. I was the one who took the rum on deck, I was the one who offered him the flask, I was the one who let him drink and talk and neglect his work."

"No, it was his choice to do that," Ran said quietly. "You cannot blame yourself for his failings, and he lied to the inquiry, so he knew he was in the wrong. He came to see you to ensure that you would not betray his negligence."

"Do you think so?" Ger said uncertainly. "I assumed... he was trying to protect me from exposure as the cause of the catastrophe."

"Protect himself, more than likely," Ginny said, tartly. "He forgot his duties, and wants to conceal his laxness."

"That... that makes it seem a little better," Ger said, in a small voice. He snuggled a little more into her shoulder, wrapping one arm around her waist. "But I am still a bad person, Ginny. It was my fault that Barantine lost everything."

Ruth's voice emerged from the darkness. "I may be able to relieve your worries on that score, Ger." She came forward and knelt at his feet. "I met Miss Barantine last autumn, quite by chance. It was just after she had discovered that the people who had fêted and admired her as an heiress worth a hundred thousand pounds were very cool towards one with only a thousand from the Benefactor and a few pieces of jewellery to her name. She was distressed by the fickleness of society. I was able to help her a little, I am happy to say, and kept in touch with her. She discovered that her father was not quite the reckless gambler he sounds. It was true that he had lost the business to the sons of the earl, but it had happened before. They would hold the papers for him until he could win them back. It was just a game to them, until he died and had no opportunity to retrieve them."

"But his daughter!" Ger murmured. "Poor girl!"

"The only tragedy to befall her was losing her father," Ruth said. "When she examined all the little gifts of jewellery her father had given her over the years, she found bars of solid gold hidden beneath the silk lining of the boxes. Her hundred thousand was quite safe, she is very rich after all and is perfectly happy. She is very likely to marry one of Lord Kilrannan's sons in time."

"Oh," Ger said, his eyes wide in wonder. "But the business... what became of the business?"

"The earl's sons are running it, to great success, as I understand it. They gave one third of it to the former Miss Barantine as a gift."

"Oh," he said again.

"You see, love?" Ginny said. "Nothing is quite so terrible when brought out into the light of day."

Ran allowed himself to feel cautiously optimistic, enough to ask a question. "What happened to the diamonds? Are they at the bottom of the sea?"

"No, no. They were sewn into my coat, remember, which I was wearing. As soon as I was well enough, I retrieved them all, and the money. Peter took most of it when he came to see me. You knew about that?"

"Yes, he told me of his involvement, but what did he do with it? Hoard it away for Ginny?"

"It was all for the fund. I had not quite enough saved already, so the diamonds were sold and the proceeds and the additional money — all I had won from Barantine — went to top it up. Ginny was to have whatever was left, although I can afford to settle more on her now."

Ran's head spun as he worked it out, and Ruth gasped, jumping to the answer before he did.

"You are the *Benefactor!*" she cried. "It was you!"

"You did not know?" He turned to look at Ran, puzzled. "I thought you said that Peter told you?"

"Only that he had seen you — carried out some financial and legal matters for you. Nothing of *this.*"

"It was my atonement," Ger said quietly. "I could not bring back the dead, but I could help the living. My first thought was to give everything to Miss Barantine. It ought to be hers, after all — the diamonds, and the money I had won. But Peter said that would raise some very awkward questions, and draw attention to me, which was precisely what I wished to avoid. He pointed out that she was not the only one left bereaved by the *Minerva's* loss.

So we created an anonymous Benefactor. It… it seemed like such a good idea, but it has caused trouble, too. Families fought over the money, some was stolen and sometimes rich people became richer while others got nothing." He buried his face in Ginny's shoulder again. "Everything I do turns to dust, Ginny. I am so useless."

"It was a wonderful idea," she said fiercely. "You've done a very good thing, to balance the tragedy of the *Minerva* just a little. Think how many people were helped by it, Jon, people who were struggling and you gave them a helping hand. People who were given an opportunity to make something of their lives, all because of you. You could even keep it going, if you want to. You're so rich now, you could put money aside every year to help people — orphans, or widows, or the families of those drowned at sea. You could do so much *good*, Jon. I won't have you saying you're useless. God tossed you out of the sea at my feet for a purpose, and maybe this is it, to use your money and your power as a duke to improve poor people's lives."

"Yes!" he said wonderingly. "I could! I could even— Shh!" His eyes widened in sudden fear, and he whispered, "Say nothing! She may go away."

Silence fell in the schoolroom, but away in the distance a voice could be heard.

"Susan!" Ruth hissed.

"She follows me everywhere," Ger said, his voice filled with panic. "I cannot escape, and sooner or later she will catch me alone, and then—"

"I will get rid of her," Ruth said softly, rising gracefully to her feet. "Keep very still, and she will not see you here."

She weaved through the desks to the door, just as it opened a little wider, and Susan's head appeared.

"Oh, what is this? The schoolroom. Oh, Ruth… I was just… what are you doing here?"

"Exploring, sister, but it is inches deep in dust. Do not come any further, in case you dirty your dress. The housemaids have not been in here these six months past, I am sure. Where is Mama? I am sure she must be looking for you. Tell her I shall be down as soon as I have changed into something clean."

The voices softened and eventually disappeared, then the door closed again softly.

"They have gone," she said. "Ger, has Susan been bothering you?" He made no reply, so she said, "You may speak freely to me. Nothing you could say of her would surprise me."

"She appears in the oddest places," he said. "She… I am sure she is trying to trick me, as she did Crosby, and Ruth, I like her well enough but I do *not* want to marry her!"

"Then you shall not," Ruth said soothingly, "but you must be aware that you are the most eligible bachelor in the country just now. Wherever you go, you will find ambitious young ladies and mamas even more determined than Susan."

"I cannot bear it!" he cried. "It is bad enough being a duke, knowing that I shall have to attend Parliament, suffer the season, all that dreadful business with people everywhere — so many people! I need to escape sometimes, to be alone or with Ginny, but she cannot always be with me. I feel so… so *helpless*."

"Ger," she said, "there is only one way to put yourself beyond the reach of those aiming to be your duchess, and that is to marry."

"I cannot! Not when I love Ginny so much… it is impossible, you have shown me that."

"Then you will just have to marry Ginny," Ruth said firmly.

There was a long silence. Then Ger smiled and nodded his head. He even laughed. Ran thought it was the best sound he had heard all day.

At the same moment, Ginny said, "No!" in anguished tones.

"Why not?" Ran said.

"You know why not."

"Tell me. Is it the whole nobility idea? You do not want to be part of it?"

"Not so much," she said slowly. "You and Ger have convinced me that even the aristocracy can be useful members of society sometimes."

"Thank you very much," Ran said. "A compliment indeed."

She laughed. "I have nothing against you two, or Ruth, and some of your family are kind, too. It's not that. But all the grand dowagers would look down their noses at me, and that would upset Ger."

"Some high sticklers will, it is true," Ruth said, "but so long as you do nothing outrageous, most will accept you. It takes excessive arrogance to snub a duchess, you know. And even the most disparaging will come round in time, when they see that you make Ger happy. Provide him with an heir or two and most of them will be eating out of your hand, I promise you."

"You make it sound easy, and I do want to protect Ger from all the ambitious Susans who would harass him to death, but what about managing Valmont? And there are other houses too. I can deal with half a dozen servants, but not hundreds of them, and planning meals and holding balls and... and knowing when to call on people and when they call on me. I shall make an utter mess of it."

"You will not, because you will have me to help you out," Ruth said. "Just as Ran and Ger support each other, so you and I will support each other. We will be sisters, after all."

"Sisters!" Ginny said. "Oh, I should like that very much. And Ger's sisters would be mine, too. If they are all like Lizzie, I shall be very blessed. Do you know, Ruth, I thought you were very aloof and superior and cold when I first saw you, but you're not like that at all."

"And I thought you were a bad influence on Ger," Ruth said. "I was completely wrong about that, I admit it."

"Ginny is the best thing that has ever happened to me," Ger said.

"I believe you are right," Ruth said, smiling. "So, shall we all get married at once? That would be fun, do you not agree?"

"It will mean getting another special licence," Ran said ruefully. "That means postponing our own wedding once more."

"That is a small price to pay," she said.

30: Invitation To Dinner

JUNE

Notice posted in the marriages section of the London Gazette:

'Privately at Valmont, Hampshire on the 3rd day of June, the Most Noble Gervase Septimus, Duke of Falconbury, to Miss Virginia Chandry, eldest daughter of the late Patrick Chandry Esq of Pendower House, Cornwall.

'At the same place and on the same date, the Right Honourable Randolph Augustus Litherholm, commonly called Lord Randolph Litherholm, to the Right Honourable Lady Ruth Grenaby, eldest daughter of the Most Noble the Duke of Orrisdale.'

~~~~~

Two footmen sprang to attention to open the doors as they approached.

"Thank you, Thomas, James," Ruth murmured.

They passed through into the tunnel, very different now from the last time she had seen it, racing through in terror with a single sputtering candle. Now the sconces were in place and filled
~~~~~

with the best beeswax candles, while carpet on the floor, a dado rail, and a long line of tapestries and gilt-framed paintings made it seem almost like a stretched-out drawing room rather than a tunnel.

It was just as long a walk, however. "I am glad Lord Arthur and Lady Anne chose to take the carriage," Ruth said. "They could not have walked so far, but they were determined not to miss the occasion."

"The first dinner in the Old Manor for years — this will be so much fun!" Ran said. "Ger will be at his best in such unthreatening society, and the Lorrimers are always good company. I am so glad you will meet the rest of them at last. You will like Alice."

"That is certain, for one hears nothing but good of her. Assuredly the company will be excellent tonight, but I advise you not to raise your hopes too high regarding dinner. Ginny has acquired Mrs Brine from Lizzie, whose reports were not promising."

"I care nothing for elaborate dishes anyway," Ran said. "Good plain food — roasted beef or mutton, and a ragoût or two with some vegetables in butter — how hard can that be, even for Mrs Brine?"

Ruth laughed. "We shall find out tonight just how much Lizzie exaggerated."

There were twelve covers at table, evenly spaced about a round table, and they quickly discovered that Lizzie had not exaggerated at all. Fortunately the kitchen maid had been recruited from Valmont and had a light hand with pastry, and Molly had contrived some of the sweet dishes, so there was enough to satisfy appetites, even if Lord Arthur looked a little disappointed by the scanty fare.

"You have been spoilt by Ger's French man-cook and all those fancy dishes he produces," Ginny said to him, when she saw him picking at a slice of beef.

"I daresay I have, my dear," he said amiably. "Never lived anywhere else, you see, and Ger's father would have everything of the very finest, and hang the expense. But the difficulty is not with my palate, but with my teeth, which are not at all what they used to be. But wine, now — I have no difficulty with wine." He chuckled, raising his glass to her. "To Her Grace the Duchess of Falconbury - your health and happiness, my dear."

She blushed prettily. "I have both in abundance at the moment, Lord Arthur."

No one else had the least difficulty demolishing even Mrs Brine's mangled efforts at fricassée of veal or braised lambs' tails. The conversation was the minutiae of family life — the stiffness in Lady Anne's knees, Lizzie's happiness, and Michael Chandry's dazzling progress through the saloons of London.

"He went to Almack's last week, would you believe, but he said it was sadly flat," Ginny said. "He was far more excited about Lady Craston's card party, where he and Captain Edgerton played whist against two of the Marford brothers, and won a hundred and fifty pounds."

"My correspondents tell me that he is likely to leave a trail of broken hearts behind him," Ruth said. "My very strait-laced and deeply religious aunt said that she rather wished she were twenty years younger."

"The captain will keep him out of mischief," Ginny said serenely. "They will be going out of town soon anyway. There has been a most interesting murder in Hartlepool, seemingly."

"The business is going well, then," Ran said, his voice amused.

Ruth had little to contribute. Her own family was back in town with both Audlyn and Susan in tow, and she could only approve of that. After losing both the Duke of Falconbury and Lord Crosby almost simultaneously, it was absolutely necessary to show smiling faces to convince the world of the family's indifference. Audlyn, young as he was, would be a welcome distraction, and perhaps Mama had a possible future match in mind. Mama always had a match in mind.

For herself, Ruth could only be glad to be free of her mother's control. Free... it was a strange thing, but even though she had been transferred body and soul from her father's care to Ran's, yet she felt free for the first time in her life. She no longer had chaperons at her heels day and night. She was no longer repressed by her mother's dictates, bound to her iron will. She was subject to Ran's wishes, of course, but that was the most feather-light of constraints and she was barely aware of it. Each morning they sat in bed drinking their morning chocolate together discussing their plans for the day, and he *listened* to her as perhaps no one had ever done in her life before.

She was not free of worries, of course. Ger was a constant seam of anxiety in her mind, and even as she talked equably to Mr Lorrimer on one side of her and Uncle Arthur on the other, she watched Ger covertly. She knew Ran was doing the same, for she saw his eyes drift in that direction very frequently. Tonight Ger was the very picture of contentment. His eyes fell often on

Ginny, and always there was a soft gleam as he gazed at her, and a little smile playing across his lips. He was a man deep in love, and in Ruth's newly free mind, there could be no better foundation for marriage, duke or not.

There was only one awkward moment, when Max Lorrimer said, as if it were the most normal thing in the world, "There was a last-minute acceptance from the Prestons today, so that will be seventy tomorrow, or seventy-one if Ponsonby is recovered from his head cold."

There was a little silence following this pronouncement, before Alice Lorrimer began some tale of a drunken groom, and the moment passed. Ruth shivered, all the same. Seventy guests, and they would be using the Gold Saloon, the State Banqueting Room and then the State Boudoir and Music Room. Ger himself had suggested it, inviting all the local worthies and a few of the family who lived within reach to celebrate his marriage. *I want to see them all bow down to my duchess,'* he had said, and no arguments had deterred him. It would be a severe test, although not of the guests, who would not dare to snub a duchess, even one with such humble origins as Ginny. No, the real test would fall on Ger, and if he could face seventy guests with anything approaching equanimity, there would be hope for the future.

~~~~~

Ginny looked magnificent. Even Pinnock, the most exacting judge, smiled at the sight of her. From the satin slippers of palest blue on her feet, to match the satin slip under silver-embroidered net, to the sapphire-encrusted tiara on her softly curled hair, she was every inch the duchess.
~~~~~

Ruth sent up a silent prayer of thanks to Lizzie, who had rounded up a *modiste* of the first stare, two expert and fast seamstresses, and a carriage laden to the roof with lengths of material, and boxes of hats, stockings, slippers and half-boots, gloves and all manner of exquisitely worked fans and reticules and delicate little folderols. Two of her sisters were still at Valmont, eager to help, which had caused Lizzie to send an impassioned letter to Ruth. *'Let Madame Poulain decide the gown, but Ginny must wear the Litherholm Sapphires. Aunt Anne will know. On no account take any advice from Etta or Alice, they have terrible taste. Lizzie Crosby. Post script - What a joy to write my name thus. Be assured my dear Luke and I are lightheaded with happiness. We will join you at Valmont in August.'*

Ruth had followed her advice to the letter, and the results were better than she had dared to hope.

"Oh, Ginny!" breathed Lady Alice, the most romantic of Ran's sisters. "You look like… like a queen!"

"Heavens, a duchess is plenty high enough for me," Ginny said, laughing. "Is it all right? I won't put Ger to shame?"

Madame Poulain and her helpers tittered at this jest, for jest it must surely be.

"Trust me, he will be delighted," Lady Henrietta said briskly. "Come, ladies, we must go down. The first guests will be arriving at any moment, and we must be there to greet them."

Ruth reached the Gold Saloon a few steps behind Ginny, who had a sister-in-law hovering protectively on either side of her. From her vantage point, Ruth had a clear view of the faces of all those gathered in the saloon — the chaplain, the secretaries and attorneys, the Comptroller, the steward, various members of the family, and Ran and Ger. Around the perimeter, Brent and half a dozen footmen stood like statues, awaiting a call to action. Every man present stood a little straighter as the ladies came into view. Every face registered some degree of admiration, from the slight lift of surprised eyebrows to the open-mouthed awe of one of the footmen. And Ger was speechless, gazing at his wife as if he had never seen her before.

"She is so beautiful!" Ran said in astonished tones, as Ruth reached his side.

"Indeed she is," she said complacently. "She always was, but it took a little town polish to make her truly shine."

It was not long before the first guests arrived, and for half an hour or so there was the business of announcing names, bows and curtsies, introductions and greetings. Ran and Ruth were part of the ceremony, too, since Ruth was unknown to many of the guests. And then Brent announced dinner and there was the dignified procession into the State Banqueting Room. Ruth had wondered whether Ger would want Ginny sitting next to him, but he had said no, she must take the duchess's chair at the other end of the table, that was her right. The only stipulation he made was that there must be no epergne or candelabrum in the centre of the table to obscure his view of his wife.

The meal passed without incident. Ger smiled constantly, and if he ate little and said less, on account of being quite unable to take his eyes off his lovely duchess, no one minded, least of all the Squire's kindly wife and eldest daughter who sat either side of him. Ginny herself was perfectly composed, sitting straight-backed in her over-sized carved chair like a bejewelled doll. When the covers had been cleared and only the desserts, fruit and nuts remained on the table, there was a round of toasts before Ginny rose and led the ladies with great dignity to the State Boudoir, where the formality of the dining table was abandoned in a rising tide of feminine chatter and laughter.

There was only one unsettling moment. When Ger led the gentlemen through to meet the sea of satins and silks, sparkling jewels and nodding feathers on beturbaned heads, for an instant he looked utterly panic-stricken. His eyes even rose briefly to one of the pilasters, as if he had forgotten that Ginny was no longer hiding away. But then the sea parted and Ginny moved forward to meet him.

"There you are at last!" she said to him, with her warm smile. "Now what would please you — cards or music?"

At once his panic melted away, replaced by a smile of relief. He raised her gloved hand to his lips, and then tucked it into his arm. For the rest of the evening he never strayed far from her side.

Eventually the last duet had been sung, the last hand of whist played and the last guest had departed. Ruth went to her room, allowed Pinnock to ready her for bed and then went through to her sitting room to await Ran. Already, after just two weeks of marriage, they had their little rituals. She poured his brandy and her own tea, and settled on the sofa. He arrived a few minutes later with a frown.

"I always have the misfortune to encounter your maid on the stairs, and she gives me the most disapproving glare, as if a husband should not be on his way to his wife's room at this hour. Perhaps my robe offends her sensibilities. I shall need to find a different stair to use."

"Or you could use the adjoining rooms to mine," Ruth said sweetly. "This floor is arranged exactly as for you and Ger downstairs. Behind that panel over there is a door to another bedroom and dressing room. You need never bump into Pinnock on the stairs again."

"What a splendid idea, my wife."

He settled beside her, brandy in hand, one arm comfortably around her shoulders and she nestled into him with a sigh of contentment.

"That went better than I expected," he said. "Ger survived the evening without running away, and Ginny… makes rather a splendid duchess." His tone was surprised.

"I confess, I rather despised her at first," Ruth said, "but now I can see the natural dignity in her. Even the *beau monde* will not disconcert her, I feel sure. Did you notice how well she managed after dinner? She played the room with just as much skill as Ger played the instrument. She moved here and there, talked to everyone, drew out even the vicar's shy daughter, flirted in the most delicate manner imaginable with the Squire and made sure no one was neglected, yet all the while she watched Ger and made sure she was never out of his sight, not for a moment. That was well done of her, and considerably better than I should have done."

"Your social skills are unequalled," he said with a slight frown. "Do not disparage yourself, my love."

"It is honesty, not disparagement. Mingling in company is easy for anyone raised to it, as I was, but she is a natural, and I could never, ever have reassured Ger in that way. I shudder still to think that I almost married him. He would never have coped with evenings like this with me by his side, and I—" She stopped, hesitant even now to voice her thoughts.

As if he could read her mind, Ran said softly, "He would not have made you happy."

"No. Ger is a good, kind man, but he has his own burdens, and he would never have loved me as he loves Ginny. I should have been so dreadfully *alone*, Ran."

"You will never be alone again, darling." His arm tightened around her as he spoke.

"I know. Even when we are apart, I know that you love me. It is glorious to be married to you, my dearest."

He gently kissed her forehead. "It is rather splendid. Marriage is such a wondrous invention."

"Not marriage, precisely, for Ger and Ginny were happy enough without it," she said.

"Having someone to love, then," he said. "Even dukes and their brothers need someone to love."

"Ah, yes. Loving and being loved. That is what brings me such joy, my husband — being loved. I had no understanding of it... no idea how much I needed it... until that night you kissed me. Then I knew that I could not live without it."

"Then I must fill your life with love and kisses, beloved one. My dearest, most adored and delightfully kissable wife. Enough of talking." He set down his brandy glass and reached out to cup her cheek. "We have better things to do."

The Duke: Silver Linings Mysteries Book 6

She laughed and raised her face eagerly for his kiss.

THE END

That is the end of the story of the ill-fated *Brig Minerva* and those who found their lives changed by the tragedy. I hope you enjoyed uncovering the final mysteries and learning how the Duke of Falconbury and his brother found happiness with the ladies of their heart. If you still have questions or comments, feel free to email me at mary@marykingswood.co.uk.

The next series is called *Strangers*, and you can read a sneak preview of chapter 1 of the first book, *Stranger at the Dower House,* after the acknowledgements. You can find out more at http://marykingswood.co.uk..

Thanks for reading!

If you have enjoyed reading this book, please consider writing a short review on Amazon. You can find out the latest news and sign up for the mailing list at my website at http://marykingswood.co.uk.

What's next? This is the final book of the *Silver Linings* series, and therefore the end of the story of the *Brig Minerva*, of those who survived its foundering and the families of those who lost their lives. There will, of course, be another series, filled with more characters whose lives change, for good or ill, and who have secrets to hide and dreams to cherish. There is a famous saying attributed to John Gardner, that there are only two story plots: a stranger comes into town, or a person goes on a journey. My next series, *Strangers,* is based on the first of these ideas — in every book, a stranger will arrive to disrupt the lives of the existing residents. I hope you will enjoy it.

Family trees: Hi-res versions are available on my website at http://marykingswood.co.uk..

A note on historical accuracy: I have endeavoured to stay true to the spirit of Regency times, and have avoided taking too many liberties or imposing modern sensibilities on my characters. The book is not one of historical record, but I've tried to make it reasonably accurate. However, I'm not perfect! If you spot a historical error, I'd very much appreciate knowing about it so that I can correct it and learn from it. Thank you!

About dukes: This is the first book I've ever written featuring a duke as a central character, and my beta readers raised some interesting questions:

1) Isn't it rude to address a duke as 'Duke'? Shouldn't it be 'Your Grace', always?

Answer: No. The lower orders always address a duke or duchess as 'Your Grace' (never 'my lord'!). Their social equals, however, address them as 'Duke' and 'Duchess'. There's some debate about what constitutes the social equal of a duke, but I've taken it to mean the whole of the peerage and their families. So Ran can call the Duke of Orrisdale 'Duke', and so could Mr Willerton-Forbes, who's the son of an earl (but he's not used to his rank, so he usually forgets). Captain Edgerton, being a commoner, would always use 'Your Grace'.

2) If Ran's older brother hated the idea of being a duke, couldn't he just relinquish the title? Or his father could have made Ran his heir instead?

Answer: No. It's just one of those quirks of the peerage that the eldest legitimate son inherits the title and that's the end of it. There are very, very few exceptions to that rule. The King or Queen can abdicate, but a duke can't. He doesn't have to take his seat in the House of Lords (Parliament) or even use the title if he doesn't want to, but legally he is still the duke.

The Duke: Silver Linings Mysteries Book 6

Isn't that what's-his-name? Regular readers will know that characters from previous books occasionally pop up. Lawyer Mr Willerton-Forbes, his flamboyant sidekick Captain Edgerton and the discreet Mr Neate have been helping my characters solve murders and other puzzles ever since *Lord Augustus*. The Duke of Camberley's heir, the Marquess of Ramsey, made a fleeting appearance in *The Earl of Deveron,* and became an improbable suitor in *The Betrothed*. The relations of Lord Randolph Litherholm, previously seen in *The Lacemaker,* include his uncle, Lord Arthur, his aunt, Lady Anne, and his sisters Lady Henrietta Redpath, Lady Alice Winne, Lady Elizabeth Litherholm, Lady Narfield (Georgiana). Lady Charlotte Litherholm and her timorous companion, Camilla, of Durran House, were last seen in *The Apothecary.* Mr Jonathan Ellsworthy, survivor of the *Brig Minerva*, and his particular friend, Miss Ginny Chandry, were previously seen in *The Clerk* and *The Orphan*. Ginny's brother, Mr Michael Chandry of Pendower, appeared in *The Clerk*. Lady Ruth Grenaby made a fleeting appearance in *The Orphan*, helping the distressed Violet Barantine.

About the Silver Linings Mysteries series*:* John Milton coined the phrase *'silver lining'* in *Comus: A Mask Presented at Ludlow Castle,* 1634

> *Was I deceived, or did a sable cloud*
> *Turn forth her silver lining on the night?*
> *I did not err; there does a sable cloud*
> *Turn forth her silver lining on the night,*
> *And casts a gleam over this tufted grove.*

Ever since then, the term *'silver lining'* has become synonymous with the unexpected benefits arising from disaster. The sinking of the *Brig Minerva* results in many deaths, but for others, the future is suddenly brighter. But it's not always easy to leave the past behind...

Book 0: The Clerk: the sinking of the *Minerva* offers a young man a new life *(a novella, free to mailing list subscribers)*.

Book 1: The Widow: the wife of the *Minerva's* captain is free from his cruelty, but can she learn to trust again?

Book 2: The Lacemaker: three sisters inherit a country cottage, but the locals are surprisingly interested in them.

Book 3: The Apothecary: a long-forgotten suitor returns, now a rich man, but is he all he seems?

Book 4: The Painter: two children are left to the care of a reclusive man.

Book 5: The Orphan: a wilful heiress is determined to choose a notorious rake as her guardian.

Book 6: The Duke: the heir to the dukedom is reluctant to step into his dead brother's shoes and accept his arranged marriage.

Any questions about the series? You can email me at mary@marykingswood.co.uk- I'd love to hear from you!

About the author

I write traditional Regency romances under the pen name Mary Kingswood, and epic fantasy as Pauline M Ross. I live in the beautiful Highlands of Scotland with my husband. I like chocolate, whisky, my Kindle, massed pipe bands, long leisurely lunches, chocolate, going places in my campervan, eating pizza in Italy, summer nights that never get dark, wood fires in winter, chocolate, the view from the study window looking out over the Moray Firth and the Black Isle to the mountains beyond. And chocolate. I dislike driving on motorways, cooking, shopping, hospitals.

Acknowledgements

Thanks go to:

All those fine people in Albany, Australia who restored the *Brig Amity* and gave me the germ of an idea.

Allison Lane, whose course on English Architecture inspired me.

Shayne Rutherford of Darkmoon Graphics for the cover design.

My beta readers: Charles Crouter, Quilting Danielle, Barbara Daniels Dena, Amy DeWitt, Megan Jacobson, Rosemary Paton, Melanie Savage, and the readers of Rachel Daven Skinner's Romance Refined

Last, but definitely not least, my first reader: Amy Ross.

Sneak preview of Stranger at the Dower House: Chapter 1: The Dower House

MARCH

The post-chaise made a violent turn, throwing the ladies within against the squabs. Louisa gritted her teeth once more, and for about the hundredth time that day wished with all her heart for her own carriage and her faithful, and very gentle, coachman. The chaise made a final lurch before stopping so abruptly that Marie was thrown almost from the seat.

Peering through grimy, rain-spattered windows, Louisa said, "We appear to have arrived."

"*Dieu merci!*" Marie muttered, through the lavender-scented handkerchief held to her mouth.

"Courage, Marie. No more journeys for a very long time."

Unseen hands turned the outer handle of the chaise door, then rattled it and finally, as if in desperation, heaved it open with a crash. An unknown footman peered in. Hers, Louisa supposed, hired three days before from the agency in Shrewsbury. Well, he looked respectable enough, and he had an umbrella open, so he was not unintelligent.

She stepped down onto a weedy gravel drive, and looked at her new home. "Oh... Palladian. Not bad at all." The classical lines and symmetry, the pedimented door with its fanlight and the arched windows suggested it was no more than fifty years old. "Not the old ruin I was expecting."

"*C'est très petit,*" Marie said under her breath.

"Well, yes, it is small, but it is *mine*, Marie. Only mine. Not to be shared with anyone else." It would do, she thought. It would suit her purposes.

The house looked well-kept, with not a shutter askew or a tile missing, and nothing else amiss that a dab of paint would not fix. The gardens were another matter. Long, desiccated grass stems had been flattened by winter rain, so that the lawns looked like an abandoned hayfield, and beyond it were an orchard on one side and a collection of overgrown shrubs on the other, dank and dripping in the drizzle.

Several figures stood awaiting her at the top of the steps. A maid in a neat cap and apron, also from the agency. A man in an atrociously unfashionable coat and knee breeches — the attorney, she supposed. Crossley. He had said he would meet her here. And two ladies in black. No idea who they were.

She ascended the steps unhurriedly, so that the footman and his umbrella could keep pace with her.

"Welcome to Great Maeswood, Mrs Middlehope," said the older of the two ladies in black, with a neat little curtsy. "I am Miss Saxby, and this is my sister, Miss Agnes Saxby. We bear greetings from our mother, Lady Saxby, who is indisposed today, but hopes to invite you to dine with us very soon. You know Mr Crossley, I think?"

Louisa reassessed the two ladies. She had not taken much notice of whose dower house she was to inhabit, but clearly these two were from the local big house. The elder was above twenty-five, at a guess, with undistinguished features and a dowdy appearance. The younger, about twenty, was dressed with more opulence but less taste, and was perhaps the plainest girl she had ever seen, poor child.

Nodding politely to the attorney, she said, "Thank you for your diligence, Mr Crossley. Good day to you all, and thank you for your welcome. I would invite you in, but I fear I have nothing in the house to offer you."

"Oh, but there is," said the younger Miss Saxby brightly. "We brought some supplies for you — tea, coffee, sugar, bread, that sort of thing. Oh, and a cherry cake and a lemon cake."

"How very kind of you," Louisa said. "Then I shall be able to offer you tea and cake, but for myself, I think I need brandy after the way the chaise careered through the gates. I brought a bottle with me, and a few other odds and ends, but forgot most of the staples." And wine, she realised. How was she to manage without wine?

"Yes, but do come in," Miss Saxby said. "Mr Crossley has all the keys for you, and then may we show you around? Or would you prefer to be left alone? Travelling is so upsetting to the system, is it not? Mama is always quite overset by it, so we will quite understand if you wish to rest and not be bothered by company."

"Company is never a bother to me," Louisa said firmly, "especially when it comes bearing cake."

The entrance hall was small, and with herself and Marie, Mr Crossley and the two Saxby sisters, not to mention the servants and the boxes now being unloaded from the chaise, it felt uncomfortably crowded. It was the work of a few moments to dispatch Marie upstairs to unpack, the maid downstairs to make tea and Mr Crossley off the premises altogether, his work done once he had surrendered both sets of keys.

"Now, Miss Saxby, Miss Agnes, do give me a tour of the house. It should not take long, I think."

She was quite right. Downstairs there was a parlour, a dining room, a drawing room and a study. Upstairs revealed a large bedroom with a dressing room attached, and two smaller bedrooms. She declined the offer of inspecting either the attics or the basement level, so they returned to the drawing room. Like the rest of the house, it displayed a classical elegance that was very pleasing, and the furnishings, although old-fashioned and a little faded, were of excellent quality. There was a good fire burning, with plenty of the best candles in the sconces, and everything was clean and polished.

While they waited for the manservant to lay out the tea things and the cherry cake, Louisa said, "This is a very pleasant room. I shall call it the saloon, I think. Every house should have a saloon. And a bottle of brandy," she added, spying it already set out on the sideboard, with glasses at the ready. "That will do me more good than tea, I fancy. I had no idea a hired post-chaise could be so uncomfortable."

"Will your own carriage be arriving soon?" Miss Saxby said, sipping her tea daintily, as Louisa poured herself a generous measure of brandy.

Her own carriage! How she would miss it, but she answered gaily, "I shall not need a carriage here, I fancy. I might buy a gig, perhaps. That will do very well."

Miss Saxby said at once, "We have a gig and pony for sale. No longer required."

"Cass—" her sister said, with an anxious glance.

"No longer required," Miss Saxby said firmly.

"That would be most convenient, if we can agree a price," Louisa said cautiously. "There is no hurry, however. It will be pleasant to drive about in the summer, but it will not be much needed at this time of year. My greatest need is for some more servants — a woman to help with the heavy work and laundry, and a man for the gardens. Have you any suggestions?"

"Mrs Preece's sister will come for the indoor work. You will find her at the smithy on Glebe Lane," Miss Saxby said crisply. "She is a good worker, and reliable. She will do plain needlework, as well — sheets, curtains, nightshirts, that sort of thing. The gardener is more difficult. The experienced ones are snapped up as soon as they become available. You would need to advertise in the Chronicle and see if you can attract an under-gardener looking to move up, unless you are prepared to train one up yourself."

"I should not mind that," Louisa said. "I enjoy nothing better than grubbing about in the earth, so I shall do a great deal of the work myself, but I shall need a man to do the serious digging and scything."

"Oh, in that case, the Timpson twins can help out. Mr Timpson from the shop has a vast brood of youngsters for hire. The twins are only thirteen… no, fourteen, but you pay only one and tuppence a day for the two, and excellent value it is, I assure you. If you want another maid, their sister Tilly is about ready to go into service."

"You are a fount of useful information, Miss Saxby. Just one more question, if you please. Is there an inn nearby where I might obtain a proper meal? For my cook will not be here until next week, and I fear I cannot live on the scraps of food I brought with me and your cherry cake, excellent though it is."

"Oh, you must not eat at the inn!" Miss Saxby cried. "Beth Brownsmith is the world's worst cook." Miss Agnes nodded her head in agreement. "It will do for your servants, but you must dine with us at the Hall. The carriage will collect you at half past five."

~~~~~

Louisa agonised over the choice of gown. Most of her things would come by the carrier whenever her ladyship condescended to organise it. Well, her own fault, of course, for leaving in such a rush, but as soon as she had received Esther's letter telling her of the Dower House, she had been wild to be gone, to be alone at last, to be free. Now she found herself in a quandary, invited to dine at the house of Lady Saxby, who could be a marchioness, for all she knew, yet the daughters were in black. Difficult.
~~~~~

She discarded one of her favourite gowns, a deep peach velvet, which seemed too bright a colour for a house of mourning, and the pale green silk was altogether too grand for what she supposed would be a family dinner. Sighing, she allowed Marie to ease her into the dark blue muslin she had worn every evening for a week now.

"Are your quarters satisfactory, Marie?" Louisa said, as the maid laboriously buttoned the back of the gown.

"Pft," was all the response she got.

Louisa laughed, for Marie complained about everything. "Too small, eh?"

"Je ne peux pas respirer, madame."

"You will survive. We both will."

"Oui, madame." But she sounded unconvinced.

The carriage was prompt, and deposited her on the doorstep of Maeswood Hall at twenty minutes to six precisely. It was too dark to see much of the exterior, but inside she could see at once that it had been designed by the same sure hand responsible for the Dower House, albeit on a grander scale. From the marble-floored entrance hall, she was led through an inner hall with an elegant double staircase and thence to the saloon, a splendid room worthy of the name. She immediately revised her own saloon to a mere drawing room.

A woman of middle years rose to greet Louisa as the butler announced her, and despite her age, the remains of great beauty were discernible. She wore her widow's weeds in a fashionably flimsy style, her hair all drooping loose curls, and a fine muslin scarf dangling from her elbows, as if to emphasise her air of delicate fragility.

"Mrs Middlehope," she said unsmilingly. "I am Lady Saxby. Welcome."

"Thank you so much for such unlooked for hospitality," Louisa said, as she made her curtsy. "But I am so glad to be here. This is a lovely house!"

Lady Saxby's face at once lit up. "It is beautiful, is it not? This is the finest room, but the library is much admired, too. Do meet my family, Mrs Middlehope. Cass and Agnes you know already, but this is Flora, and here is my youngest, Honora."

Flora, at least, had benefited from her mother's looks, for she was the beauty of the family, and just as dainty. Louisa felt like a lumbering giant beside her. Honora was not so handsome, but would have been accounted a pretty girl in other company. How unfortunate to have an outstanding diamond in the family, constantly casting her sisters into the shade.

"These are my sons, Jeffrey Rycroft and Timothy Rycroft," Lady Saxby continued.

Two young men, a little younger than Louisa herself, who looked gentlemanlike enough, and nothing more. The products of Lady Saxby's first marriage, presumably, although she could not quite work it out, since the eldest Miss Saxby looked older than the younger Mr Rycroft. She really should have made more enquiries about the local society before coming here, then she would not be floundering quite so badly. It would be helpful to know who, precisely, was being mourned — Lord Saxby, perhaps? Yet it would be indelicate to ask. She would have to be careful what she said, for it would never do to rampage over the feelings of the recently bereaved.

The meal was excellent, and bespoke a cook almost as accomplished as Louisa's own… no, not her own, *Pamela's* own. Her sister-in-law had inherited the long-fought-for man-cook, just as she had inherited the carriage, the coachman, all the footmen, the well-trained gardeners, her excellent butler and the noble rank that should have been Louisa's. Not that she cared for the title, but she would have loved to keep just a few of the servants. Ah well, repining was pointless.

Not surprisingly, Louisa found herself the main topic of conversation. The questions were diplomatically phrased, but she understood what they wanted to know.

"My husband died just over a year ago. He was the eldest son, but we were never blessed with children, so when my father-in-law died last spring, the younger son inherited. They offered me a permanent home at Roseacre, but once my year of mourning was over, I thought it best to move away from Durham."

"Ah yes," Lady Saxby sighed. "That is much for the best. The new mistress will have her own way of doing things, no doubt, and it would be trying for you to see the changes."

That was not the trying part, but Louisa said nothing of that, merely smiling and praising the sauce with which the woodcocks were served, and regretting, for the hundredth time, the loss of her man-cook.

After dinner, the ladies retreated to the saloon again. Lady Saxby and Honora retired to a matching pair of chaises longues, *'to rest a little'*, Lady Saxby said, closing her eyes and settling down more comfortably to snooze. Agnes commandeered the pianoforte, leaving Louisa to Flora, flicking idly through the pages of a journal to find the fashion plates, and Cass, the eldest, who politely enquired after her home and family. She was so tempted to say, *'I have no family'*, but that would be too impolite for words. Besides, she was here to forget her losses, after all. So she talked of Roseacre and its multitude of dilapidated and rambling wings, but she could not suppress the sigh of envy as she gazed around the elegantly beautiful saloon.

"Roseacre sounds charming," Cass said. "There is so much history in an older house. I hope you will not miss it too greatly. Are you pleased with the Dower House?"

"Oh yes! Such a cosy little house. I shall be very content there, I am sure. I do love these modern designs. Such lightness and classical simplicity! Such order and regularity, and no danger of going astray and finding oneself in a previously unsuspected wing of the house. Delightful."

Cass chuckled. "Some would say the Hall is too austere, but it has its charms too. Would you like to see the library?"

She would. They left Flora to her journal, and Cass took a candelabrum and led the way back to the hall and then through a richly appointed room decorated in a deep crimson, to a short corridor.

Here she paused. "I will let you enter first, Mrs Middlehope. You will see why." Then she threw open one of the doors to the library and stood aside for Louisa to enter.

The room was flooded with light. There were deep windows on three sides, and the moon must be full, for it filled the room with a ghostly luminance. And there above the far wall—

Louisa cried out in amazement, for the lunette was filled with colour, a Biblical scene in painted glass that was lit up by the moonlight. "That is astonishing!" she said, as Cass followed her into the room. "How lucky you are to live in a house with such wonders."

Cass grimaced. "Not for much longer, unfortunately. We live from day to day, as we wait for the lawyers to find the new Lord Saxby, who will promptly turn us out of our home."

"So it is your father whom you mourn," Louisa said.

"And my brother, Miles," she said quietly. "A curricle accident, not two months ago. Papa was killed instantly, and Miles... poor Miles lingered for a fortnight."

"My dear, how awful for you all. Your poor mama! And the heir... you do not know who it is?"

"Not the slightest idea. Not a near relation, anyway, for all the uncles and cousins we know of are dead now. The lawyers are going back to the third earl, or even earlier, to find a living male descendant. Mama is certain he will be a disgrace to the family name — a coal miner, or a pie seller, or some such. I think myself he is more likely to be an attorney or a clergyman."

"Yes, very likely," Louisa said. "But what a shock for him! There he will be, stuck in some rural wasteland far from civilisation, struggling to maintain a wife and seven children on a hundred pounds a year, and one day a man in a black suit and a wig will arrive on his doorstep and inform him that he is Lord Saxby, and a rich man, and insist that he must leave his hovel and move into your lovely house. Poor fellow."

"You pity *him?*" Cass said, although she smiled. "We are in worse case, I should have thought."

"No, because you will know how to go on. You will always have a respectable place in society, not just because of your family name, but because you know how to behave. You will be received everywhere, whereas he will be treated with contempt wherever he goes. If he tries to act the great lord, he will be scorned, and if he takes the meat before the soup or prefers ale to claret, he will be mocked. His own servants will bow and *'Yes, my lord'* him, and laugh at him behind his back. Poor fellow, indeed."

"I had not thought of it like that," Cass said slowly. "Yes, he is much to be pitied, whoever he is. Let us hope he may be found quickly so that he can begin to grow accustomed to his new life, and we can begin to grow accustomed to ours. Is it hard, the change from a house like this with a full complement of servants to something much simpler?"

"I cannot tell you," Louisa said with a smile. "I left Roseacre not two weeks ago, stayed a few nights with my friend in Shrewsbury and then — here I am! My first day of something simpler."

"But why here?" Cass said, smiling back in a friendly way. "Great Maeswood is so out of the way, and such a long way from Durham that I cannot imagine what made you choose to settle here."

"No one knows me," Louisa said at once. "I am, if you like, a slate wiped clean, and, perhaps more pertinently, I am free at last of other people's expectations. Consider, Miss Saxby. I spent seventeen years under my father's very careful control. I was married practically from the schoolroom, and spent twelve years bowing to the wishes of my husband and his father, who avoided company. Then there was a year of mourning. I was not at all discontented with my lot, for my path was laid down for me and I knew no other. But now… I am set free, and with only my own wishes to consider, I intend to go out into the world at last and be sociable and *enjoy* life."

"Well," Cass said, eyebrows raised. "Prepare to be gay to dissipation, Mrs Middlehope. On Tuesdays, Miss Gage holds a card party for select friends, with a small glass of sherry on arrival at eight o'clock, whist until eleven, then a cold supper, with a glass of claret. On Thursdays, Miss Beasley returns the compliment, except that we get ratafia to drink and a hot supper with Tokay. Once a month, one or other of the carriage families holds a dinner. And twice a year — do try not to allow your anticipation to overwhelm you — there is an assembly at the Boar's Head, where as many as fourteen or fifteen couples of dairymaids and farm labourers tread on each other's toes. Can you bear the excitement, do you suppose?"

Louisa laughed. "It sounds perfect!"

END OF SAMPLE CHAPTER of *Stranger at the Dower House.* For more information, or to buy, go to http://marykingswood.co.uk..

Made in United States
North Haven, CT
10 August 2022

22526873R00243